P9-DVH-680

SNAPDRAGON

McKenzie Co. Public Library
112 2nd Ave. NE
Watford City, ND 58854
701-444-3785
librarian@co.mckenzie.nd.us

SNAPDRAGON

KAT LEYH

First Second
NEW YORK

PART 1: THE WITCH

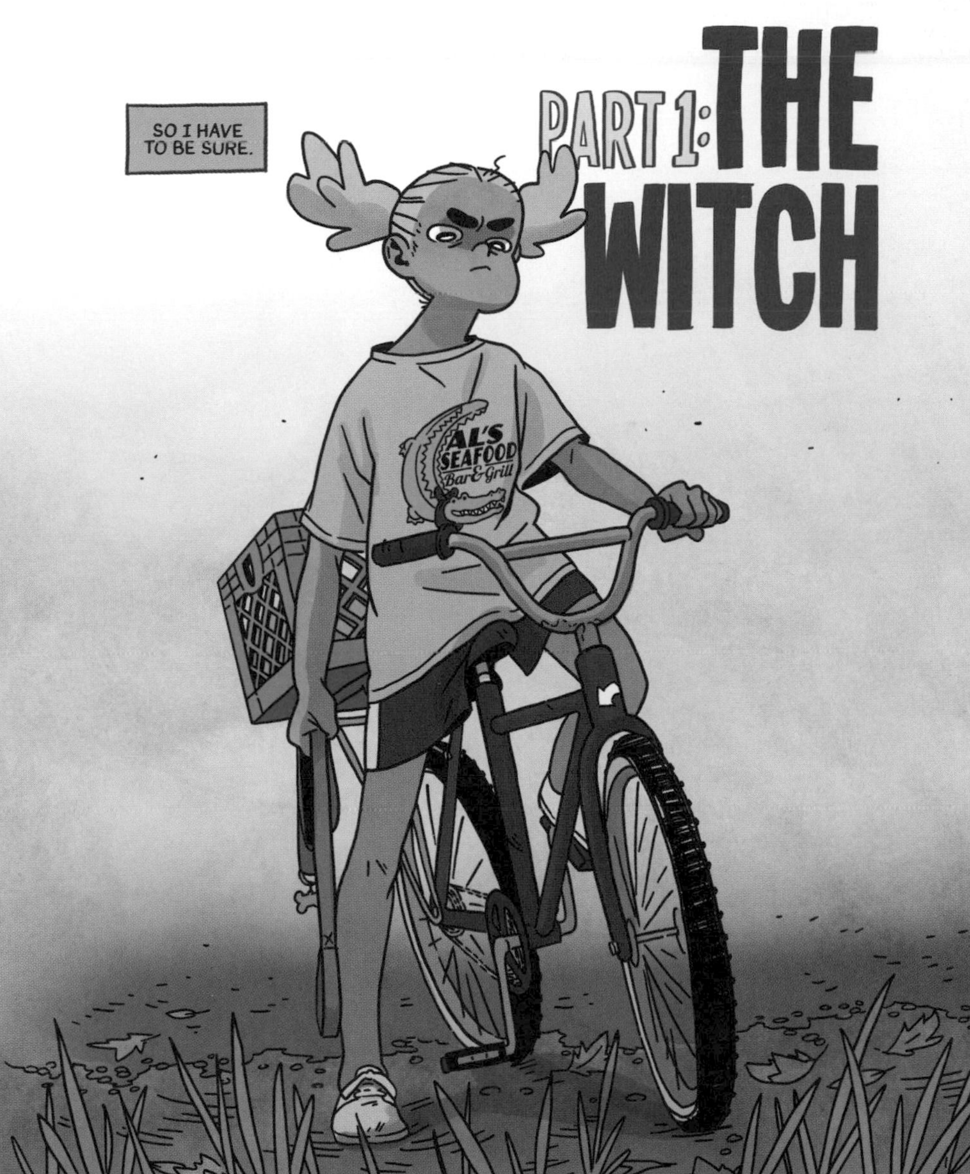
SO I HAVE TO BE SURE.
AL'S SEAFOOD Bar & Grill

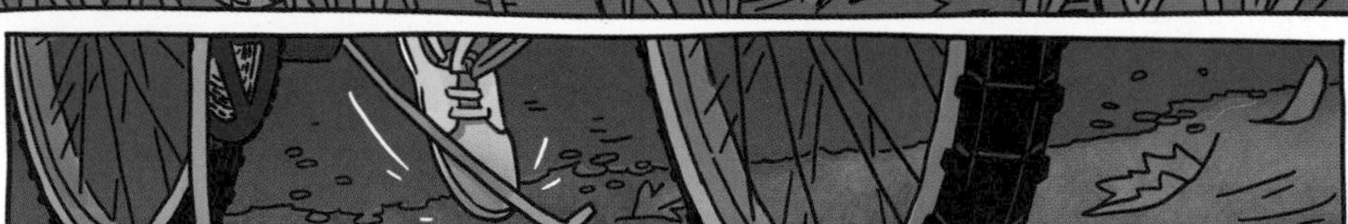
KICK

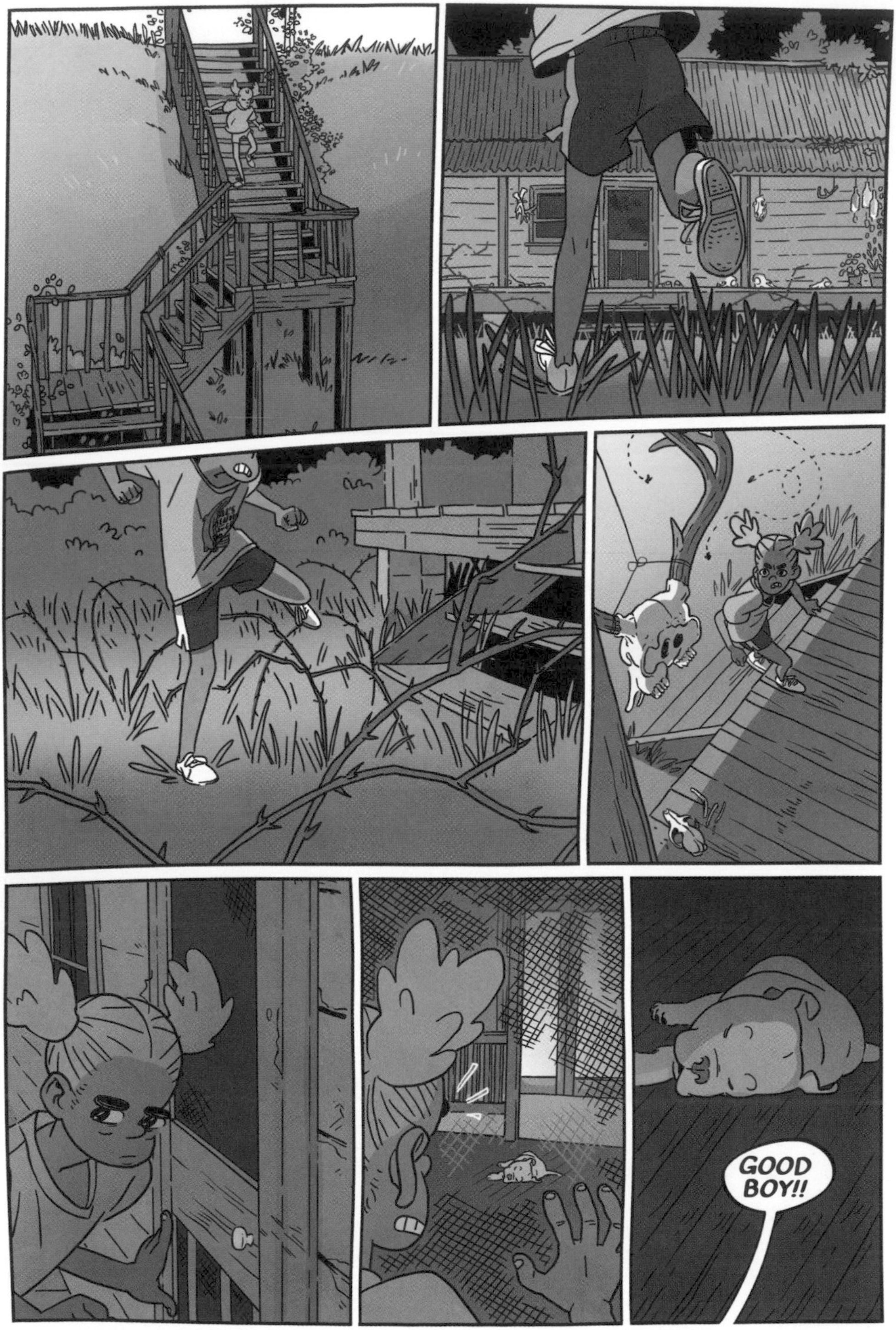
GOOD BOY!!

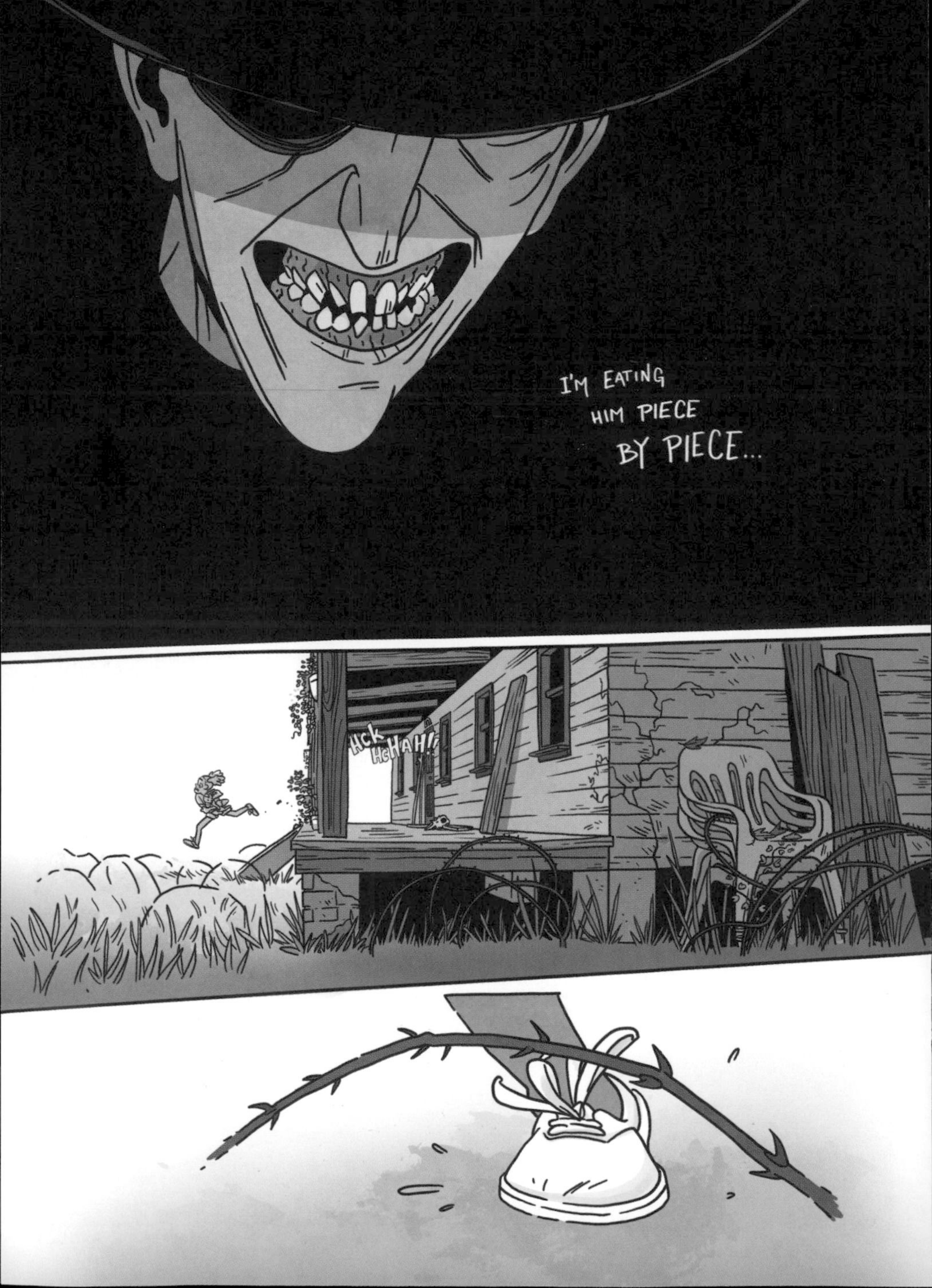
I'M EATING HIM PIECE BY PIECE...
HCK HcHAH!!

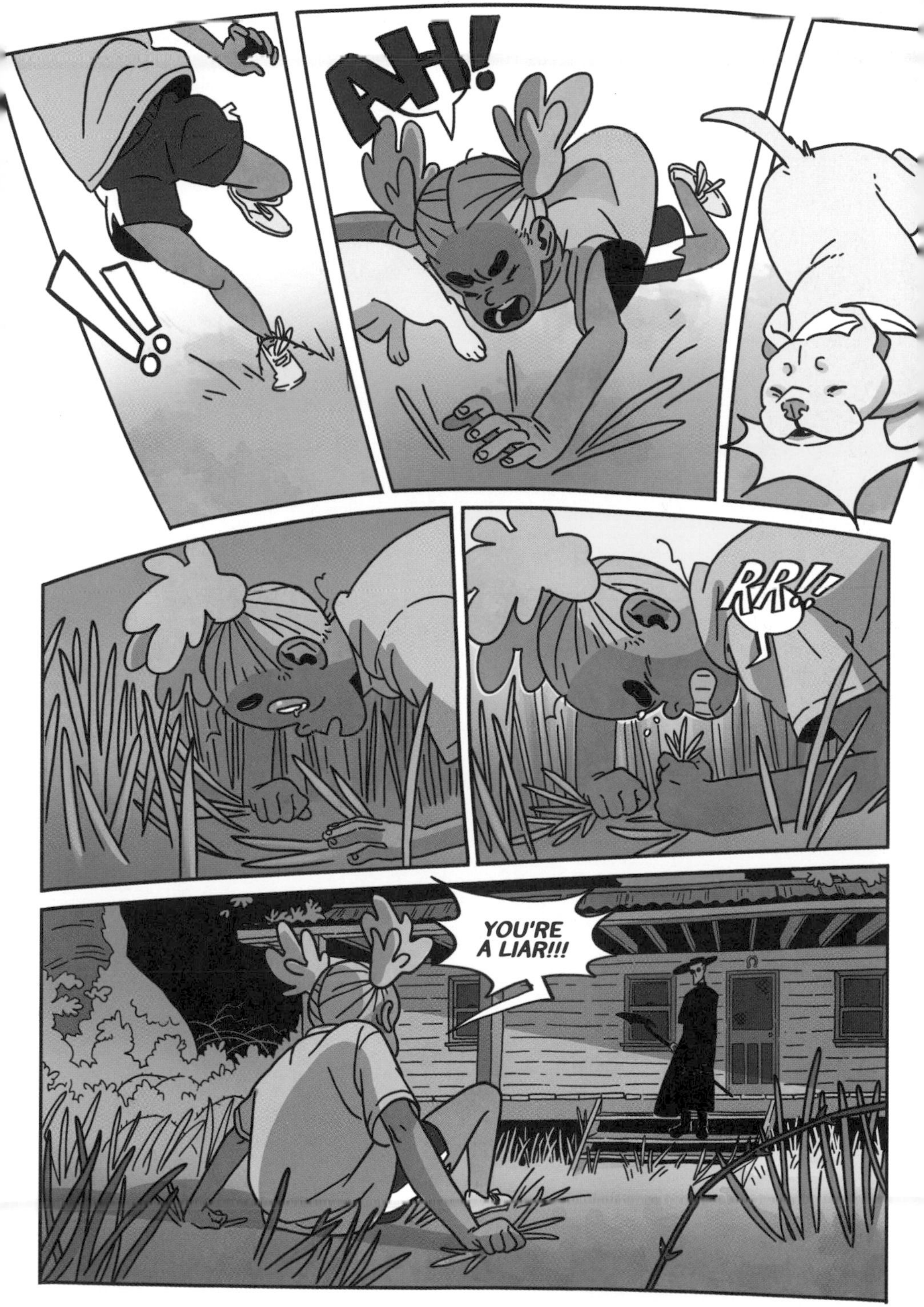
!!
AH!
RR!!
YOU'RE A LIAR!!!

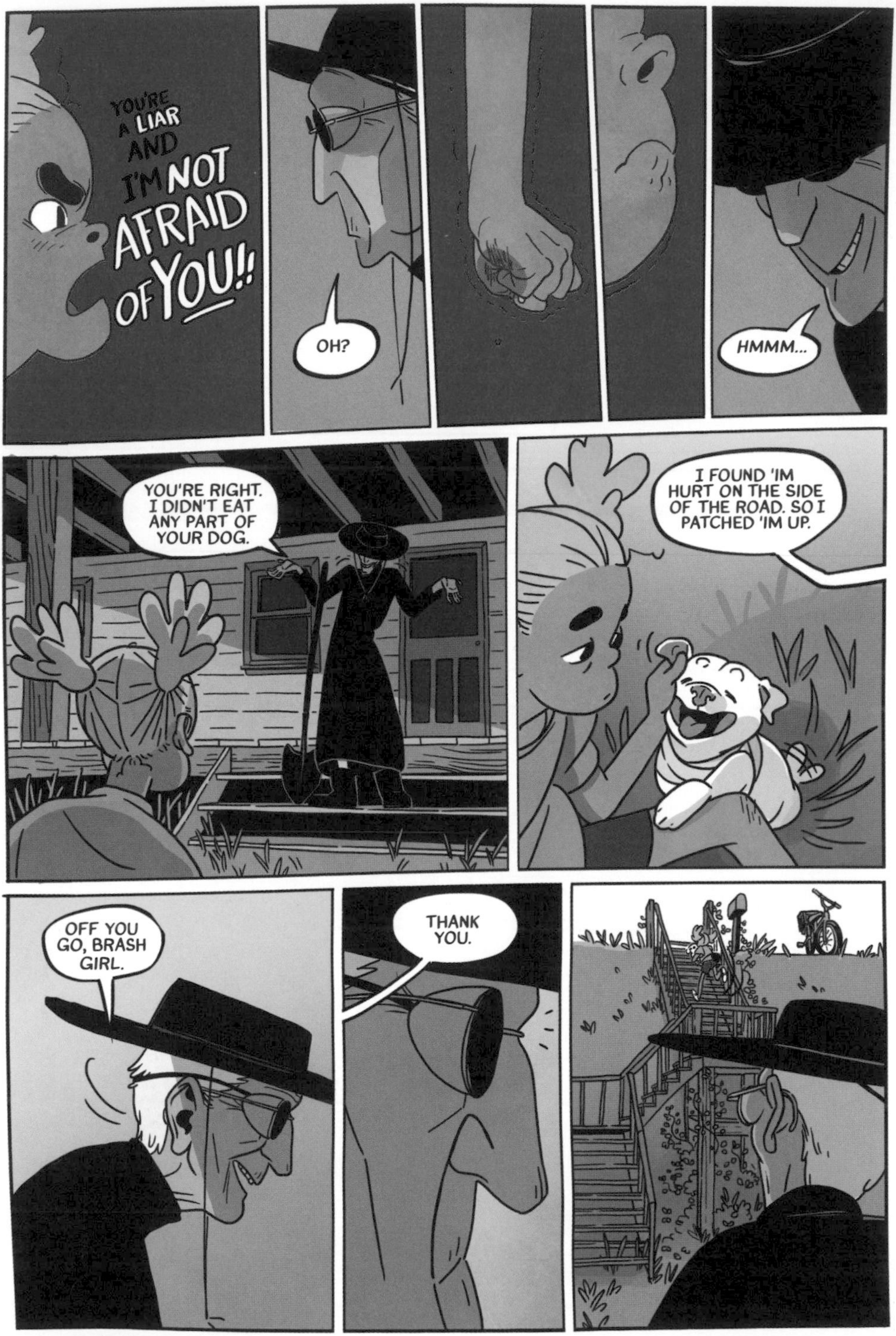
YOU'RE A LIAR AND I'M NOT AFRAID OF YOU!!
OH?
HMMM...
YOU'RE RIGHT. I DIDN'T EAT ANY PART OF YOUR DOG.
I FOUND 'IM HURT ON THE SIDE OF THE ROAD. SO I PATCHED 'IM UP.
OFF YOU GO, BRASH GIRL.
THANK YOU.

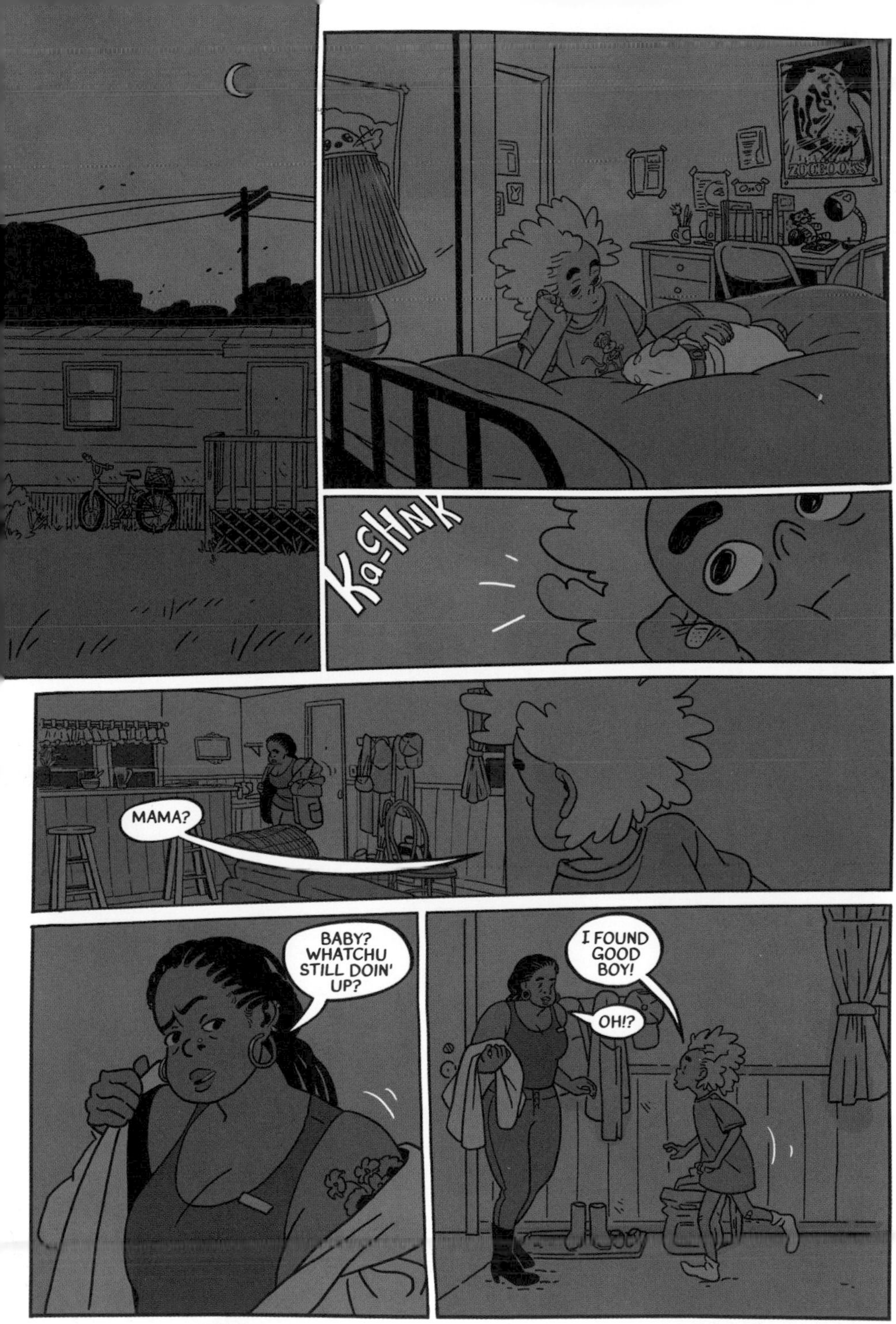
ZOOBOOKS
Ka-CHNK
MAMA?
BABY? WHATCHU STILL DOIN' UP?
I FOUND GOOD BOY!
OH!?

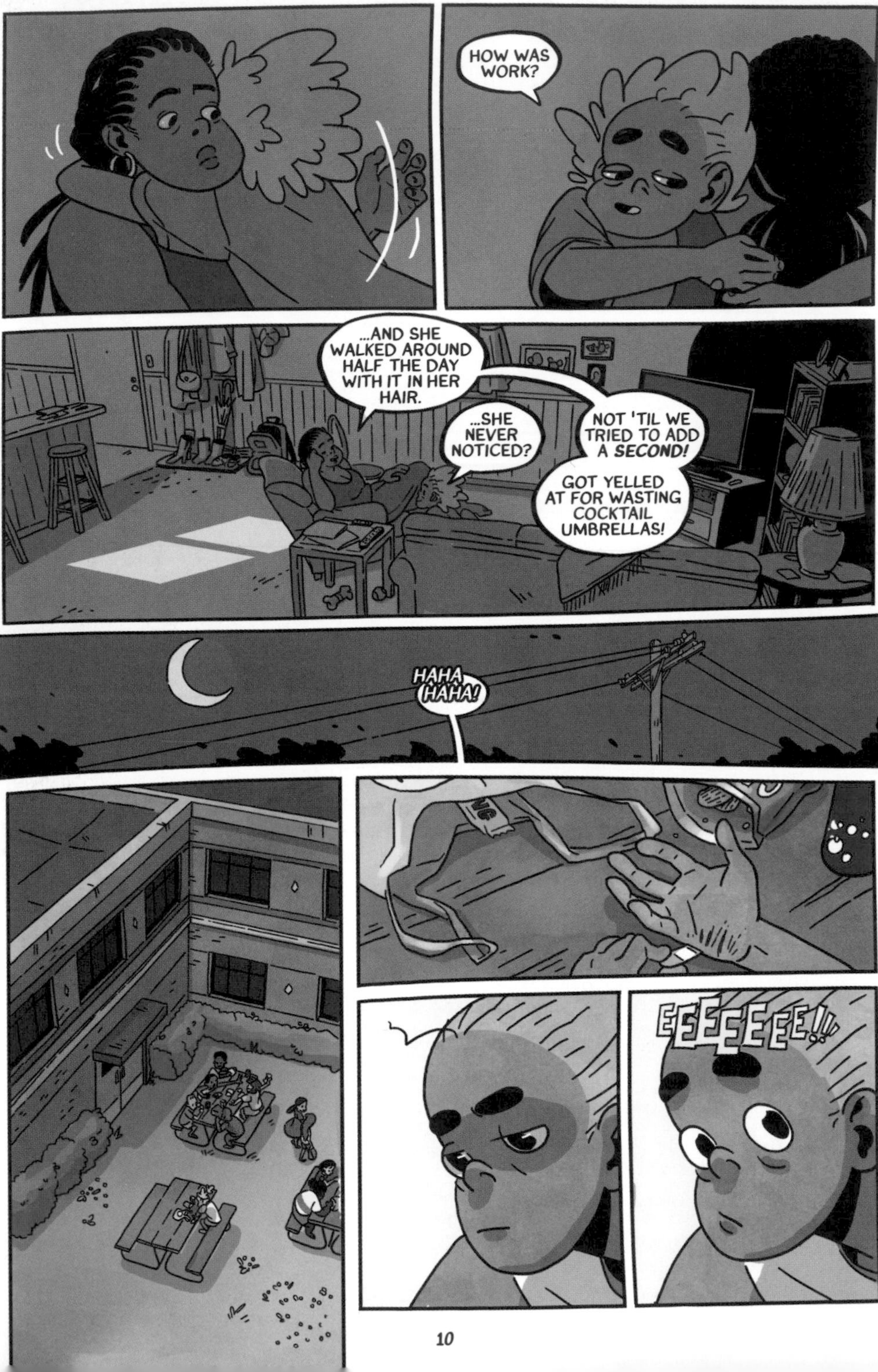

HOW WAS WORK?
...AND SHE WALKED AROUND HALF THE DAY WITH IT IN HER HAIR.
...SHE NEVER NOTICED?
NOT 'TIL WE TRIED TO ADD A *SECOND!*
GOT YELLED AT FOR WASTING COCKTAIL UMBRELLAS!
HAHA HAHA!
EEEEEEE!!!

11

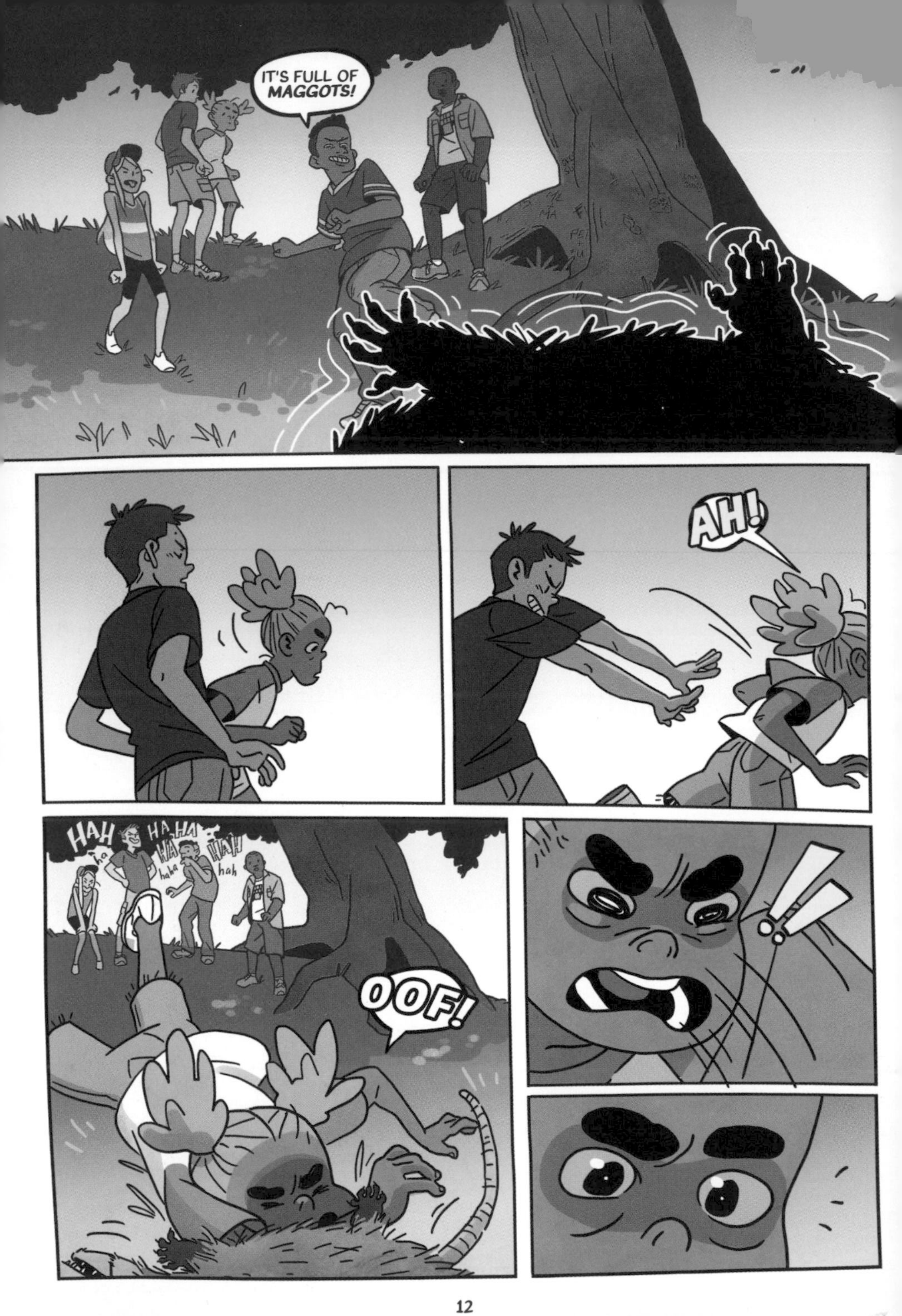
IT'S FULL OF MAGGOTS!
AH!
HAH
ha
HA HA
HA
haha
HAH
hah
OOF!

13

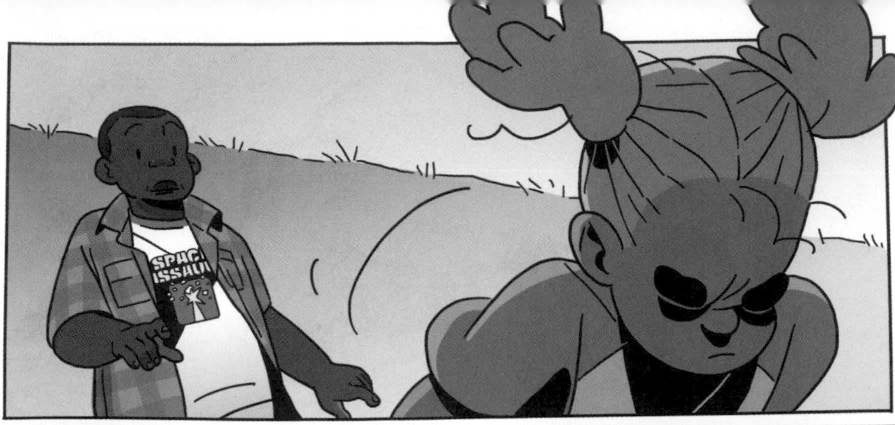

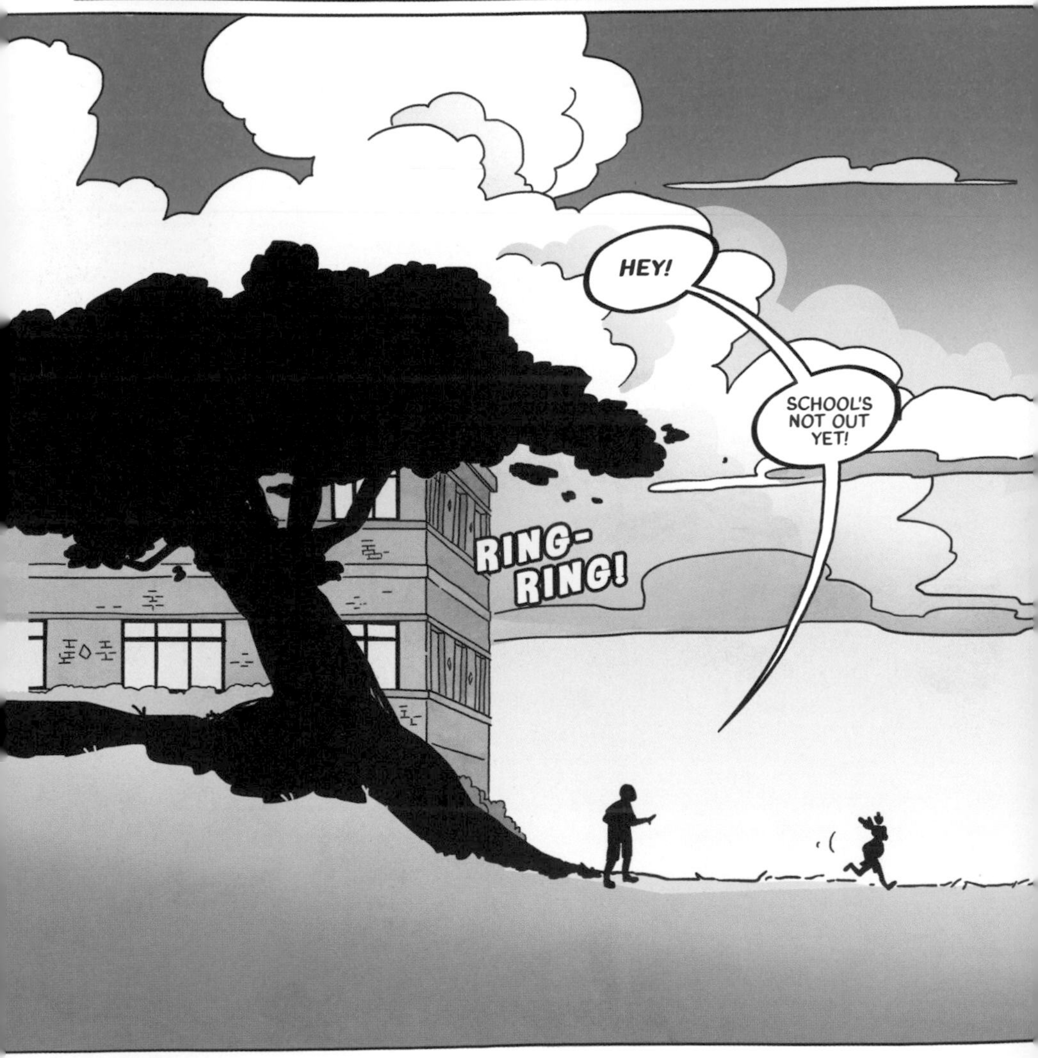
HEY!
SCHOOL'S NOT OUT YET!
RING-RING!

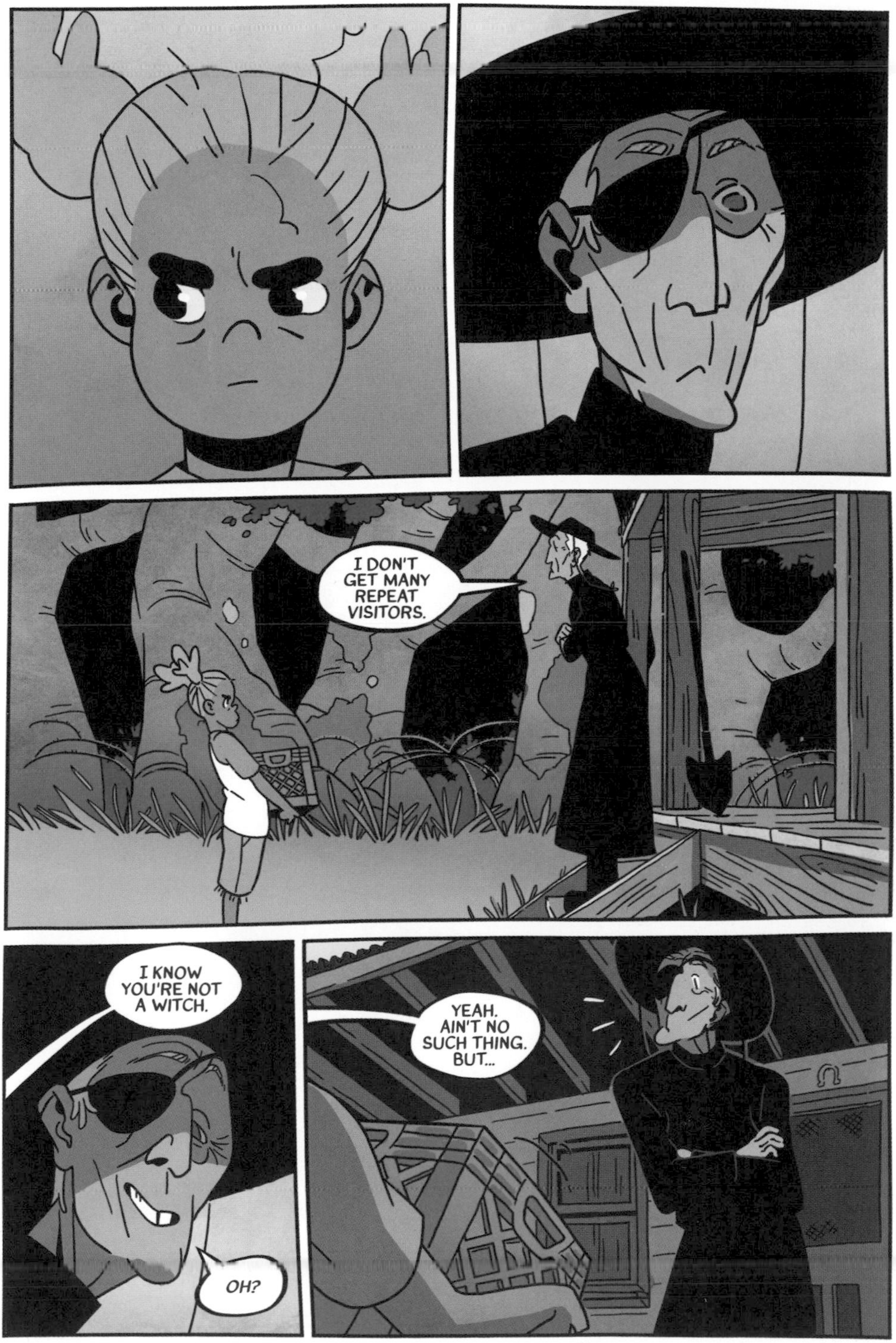
I DON'T GET MANY REPEAT VISITORS.
I KNOW YOU'RE NOT A WITCH.
OH?
YEAH. AIN'T NO SUCH THING. BUT...

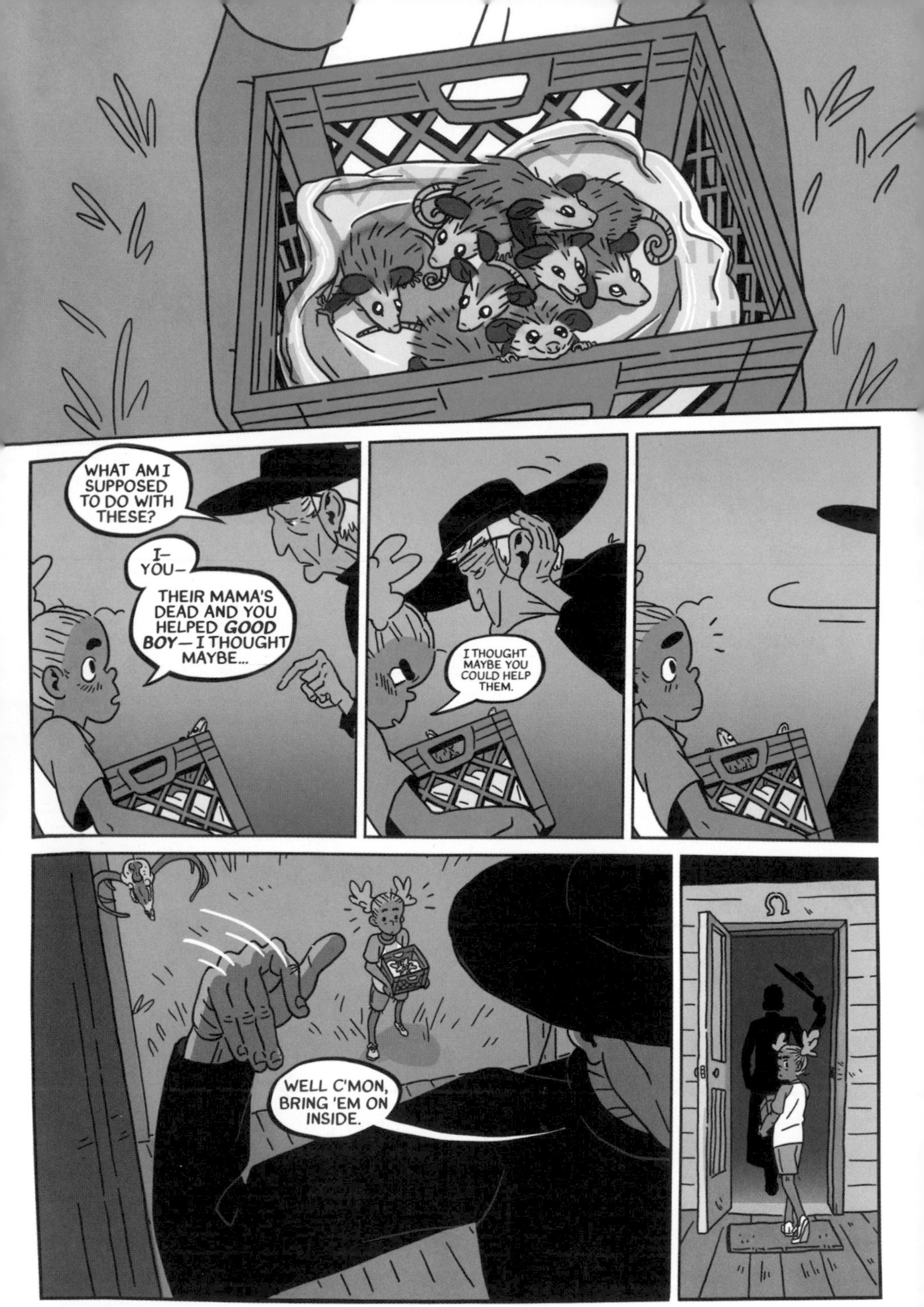
WHAT AM I SUPPOSED TO DO WITH THESE?
I— YOU—
THEIR MAMA'S DEAD AND YOU HELPED GOOD BOY—I THOUGHT MAYBE...
I THOUGHT MAYBE YOU COULD HELP THEM.
WELL C'MON, BRING 'EM ON INSIDE.

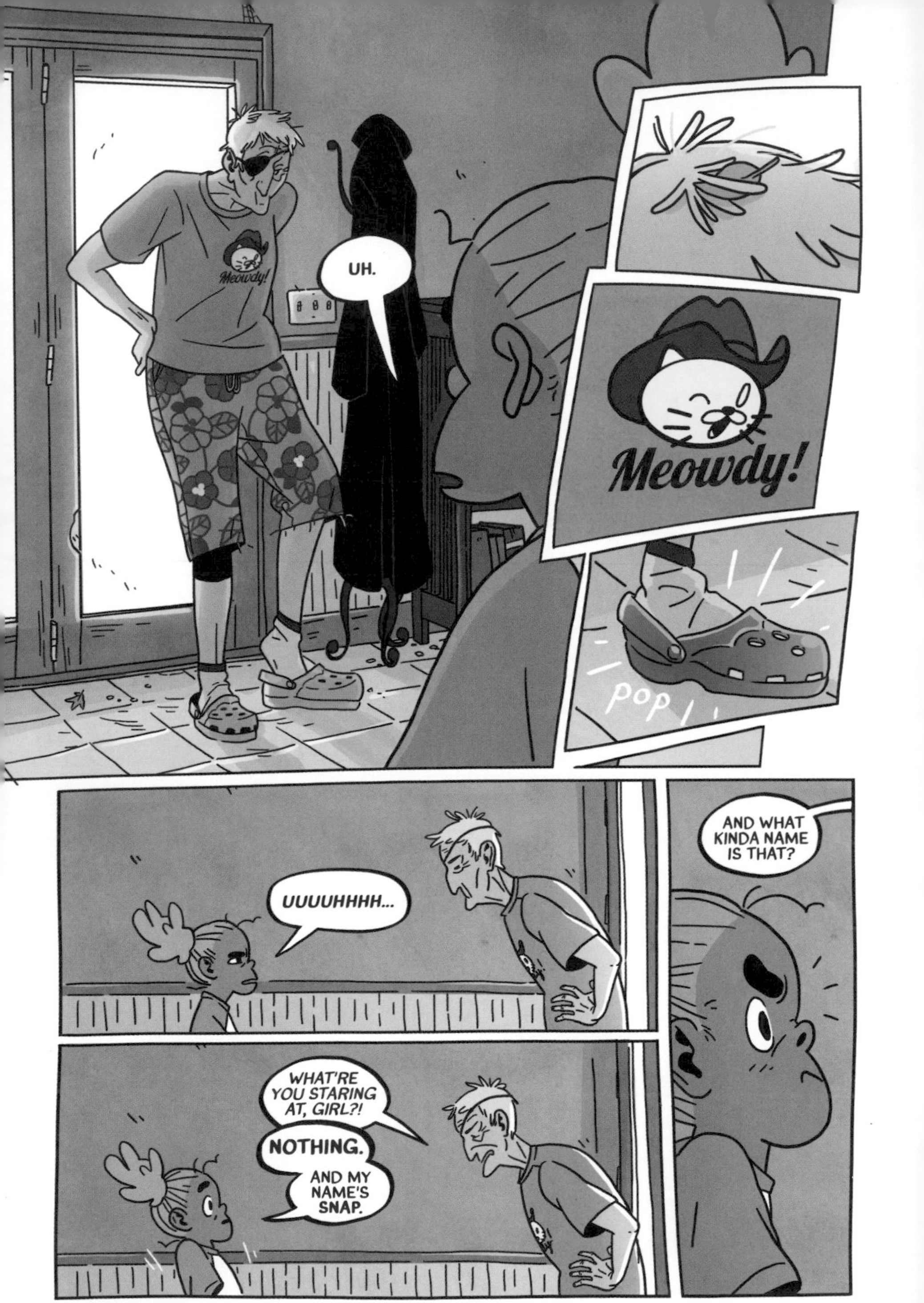

Meowdy!
UH.
Meowdy!
POP
UUUUHHHH...
AND WHAT KINDA NAME IS THAT?
WHAT'RE YOU STARING AT, GIRL?!
NOTHING.
AND MY NAME'S SNAP.

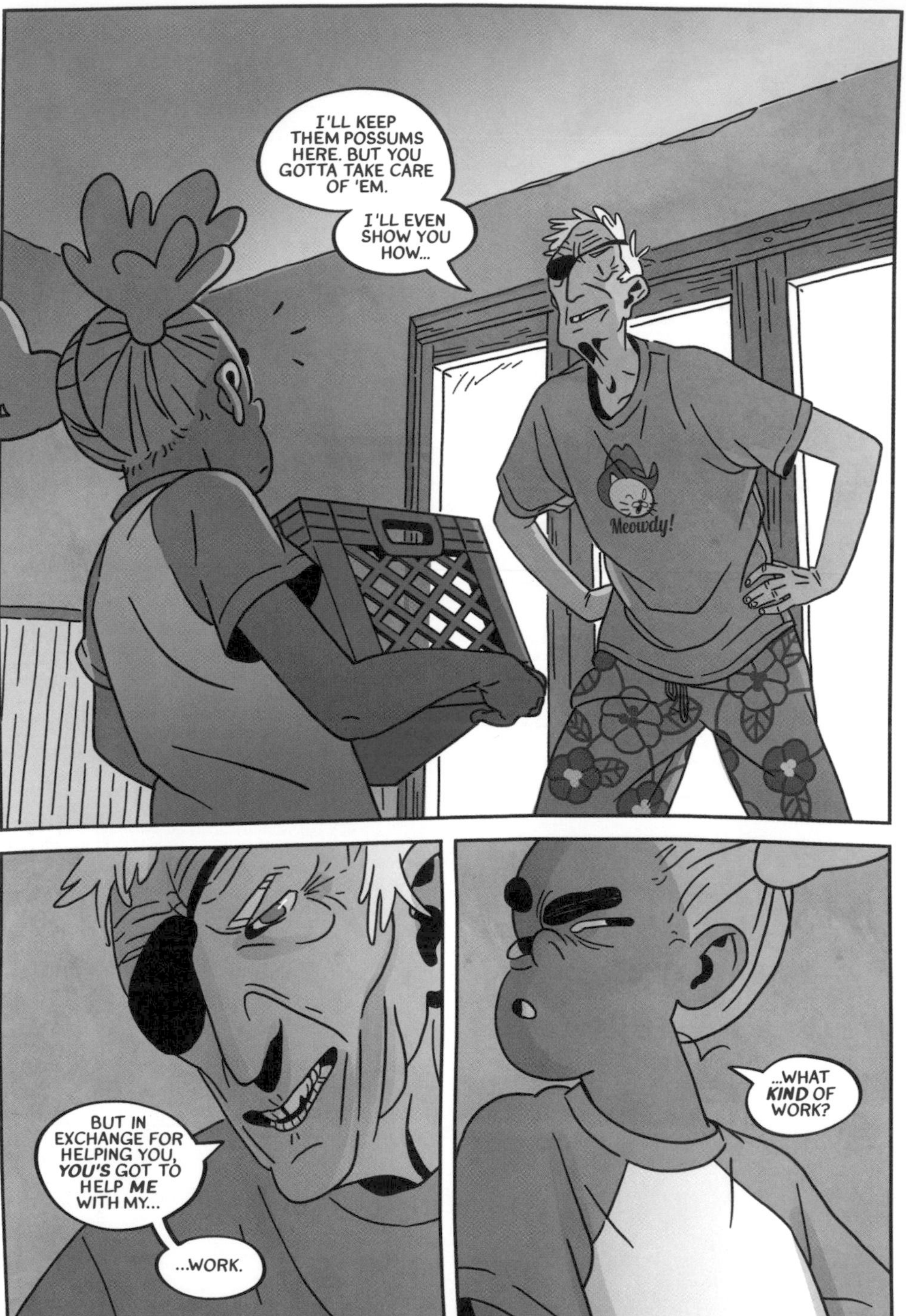
I'LL KEEP THEM POSSUMS HERE. BUT YOU GOTTA TAKE CARE OF 'EM.
I'LL EVEN SHOW YOU HOW...
Meowdy!
BUT IN EXCHANGE FOR HELPING YOU, YOU'S GOT TO HELP ME WITH MY...
...WORK.
...WHAT KIND OF WORK?

22

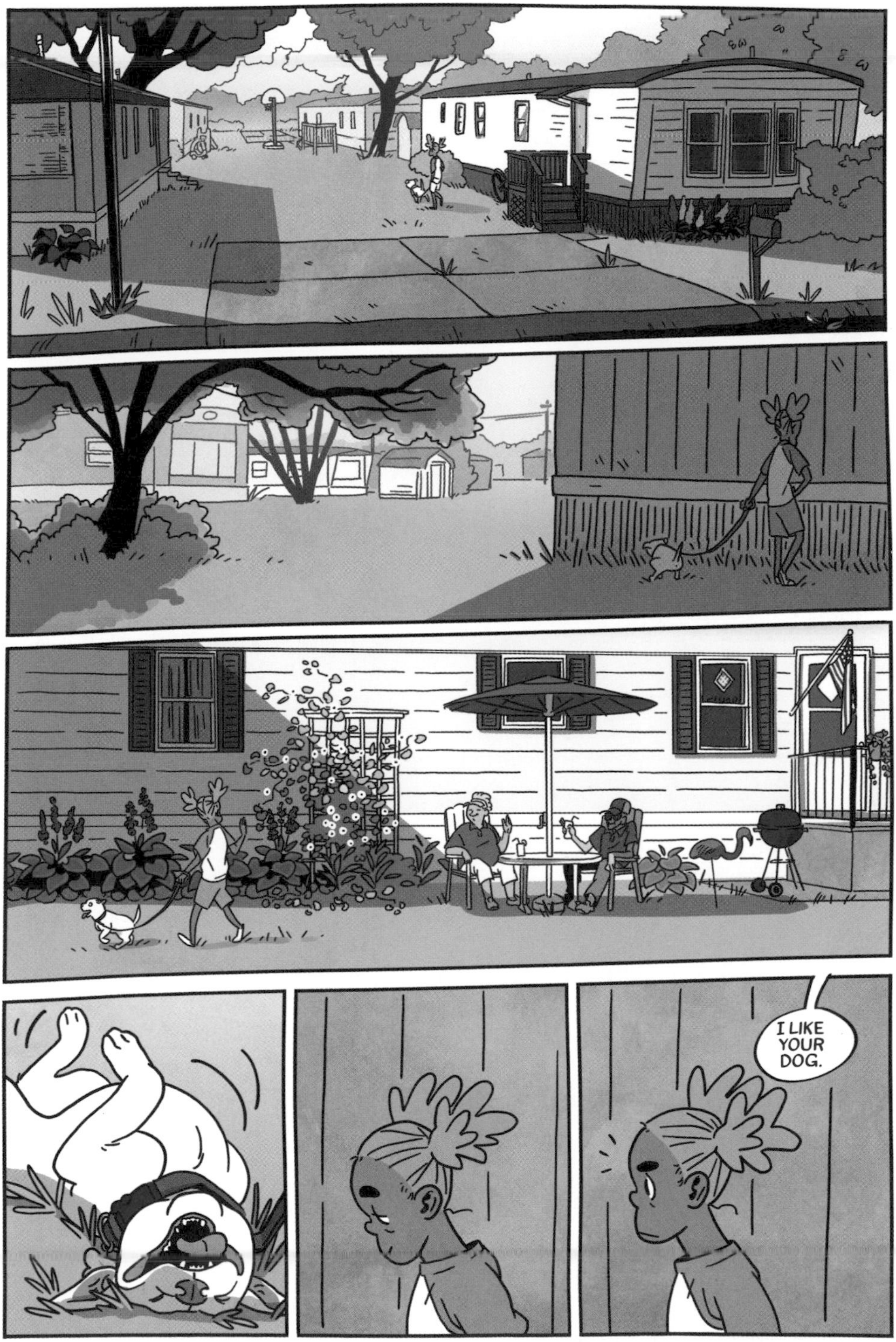
I LIKE YOUR DOG.

24

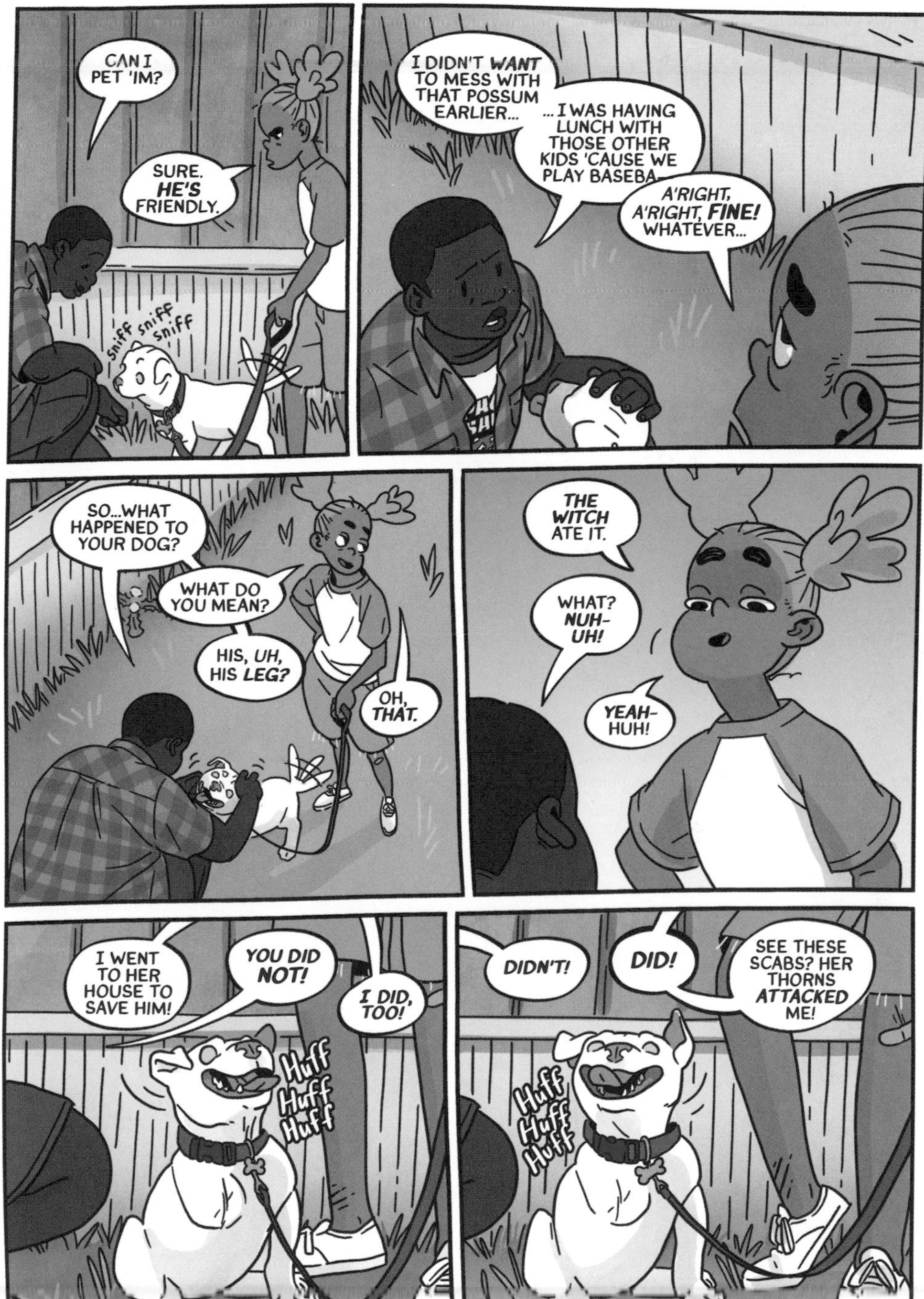
CAN I PET 'IM?
SURE. HE'S FRIENDLY.
sniff sniff sniff
I DIDN'T WANT TO MESS WITH THAT POSSUM EARLIER...
...I WAS HAVING LUNCH WITH THOSE OTHER KIDS 'CAUSE WE PLAY BASEBA-
A'RIGHT, A'RIGHT, FINE! WHATEVER...
SO...WHAT HAPPENED TO YOUR DOG?
WHAT DO YOU MEAN?
HIS, UH, HIS LEG?
OH, THAT.
THE WITCH ATE IT.
WHAT? NUH-UH!
YEAH-HUH!
I WENT TO HER HOUSE TO SAVE HIM!
YOU DID NOT!
I DID, TOO!
Huff Huff Huff
DIDN'T!
DID!
SEE THESE SCABS? HER THORNS ATTACKED ME!
Huff Huff Huff

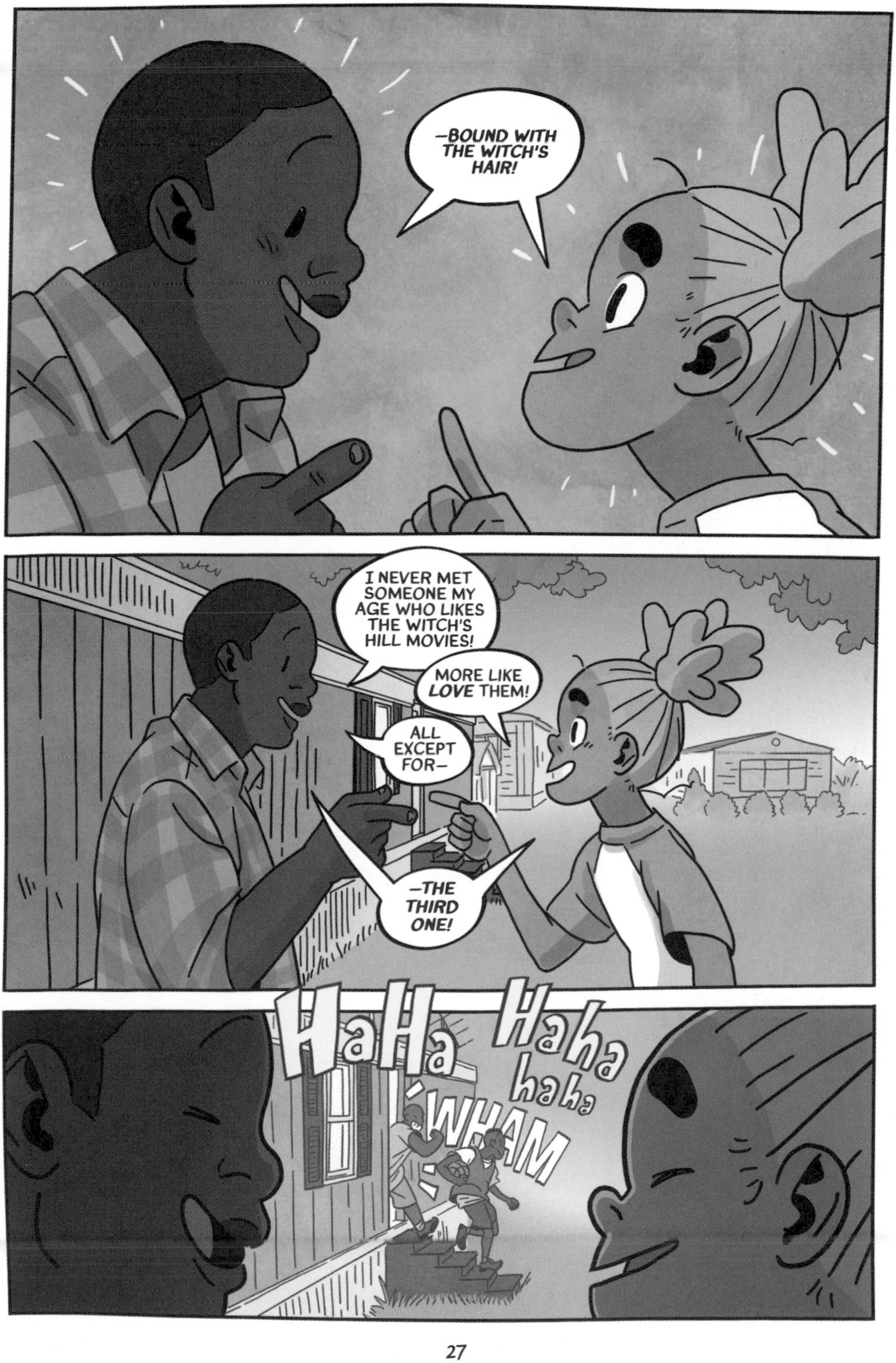
—BOUND WITH THE WITCH'S HAIR!
I NEVER MET SOMEONE MY AGE WHO LIKES THE WITCH'S HILL MOVIES!
MORE LIKE *LOVE* THEM!
ALL EXCEPT FOR—
—THE THIRD ONE!
HaHa
Haha haha
WHAM

HEY, LOUIS! WHO'S YOUR LITTLE *GIRLFRIEND?*

Oof!

YOU LIKE *WEIRD ONES,* HUH, BRO?

SHUT IT, GEORGE!

GET OFF, JAIME!

SHOVE

IGNORE THEM, SNAP, THEY'RE IDIOTS.

HAHAHA haha

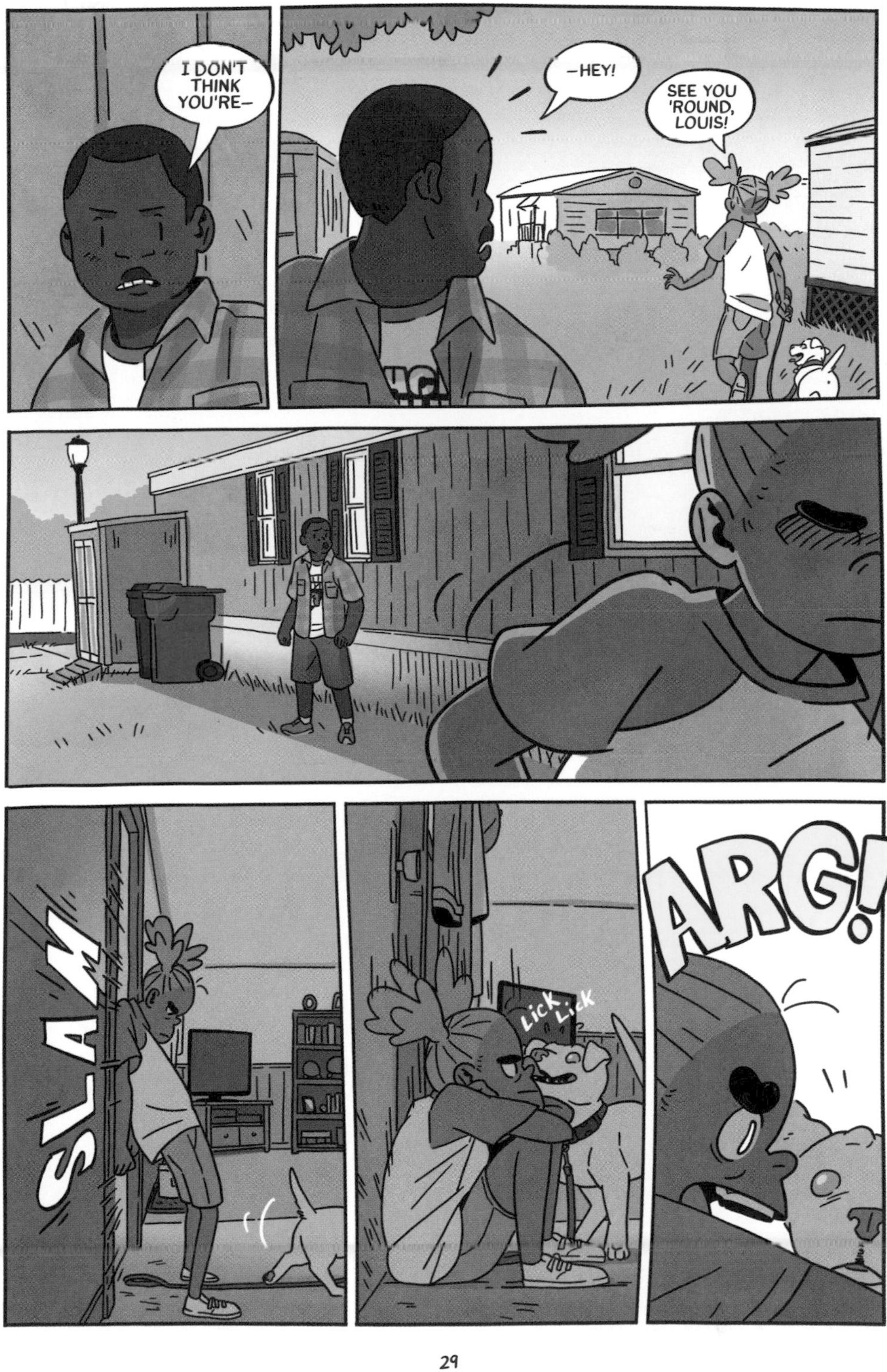
I DON'T THINK YOU'RE—
—HEY!
SEE YOU 'ROUND, LOUIS!
SLAM
LICK LICK
ARG!

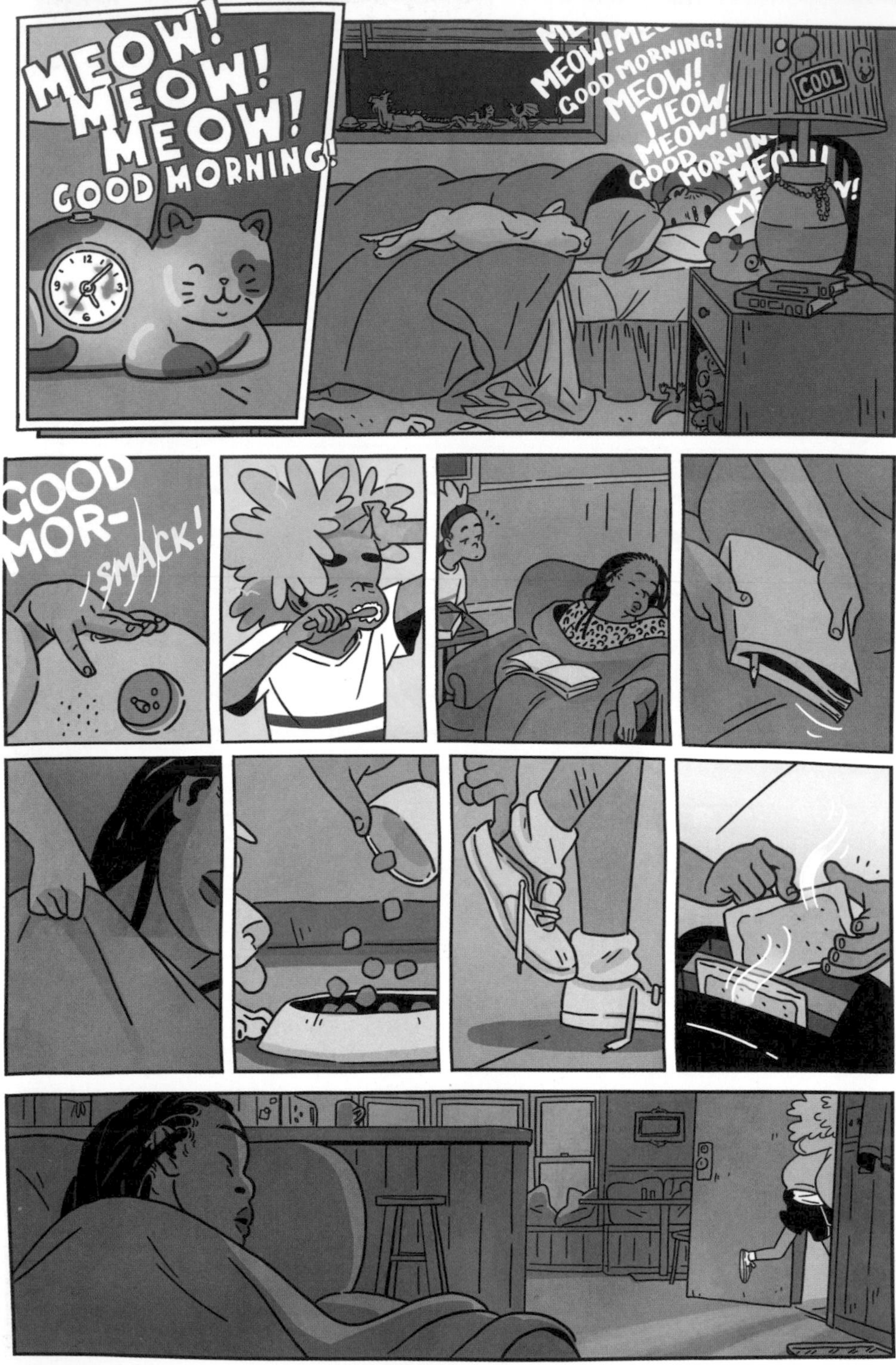
MEOW! MEOW! MEOW! GOOD MORNING!
COOL
GOOD MOR-
SMACK!

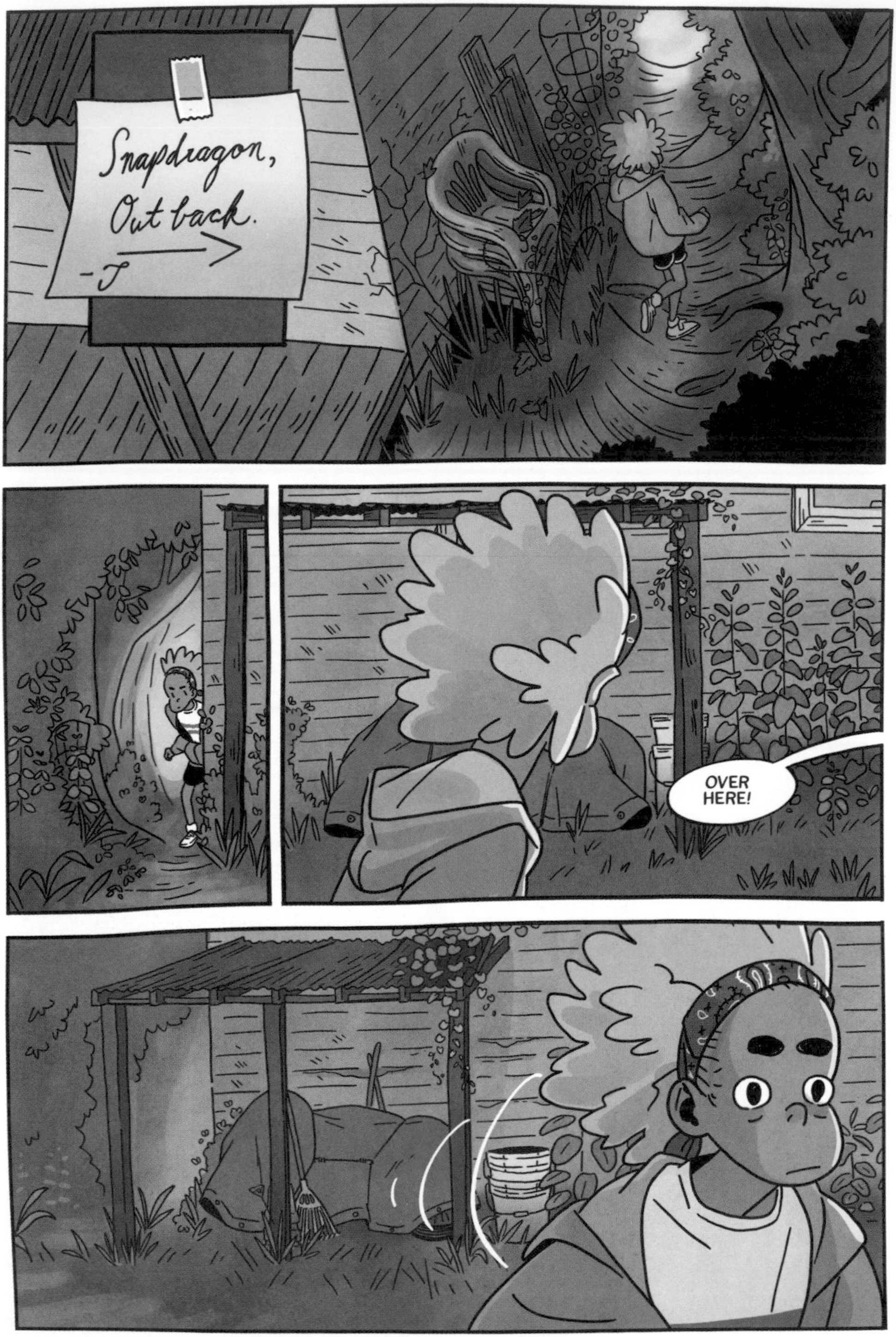
Snapdragon,
Out back.
-J
OVER HERE!

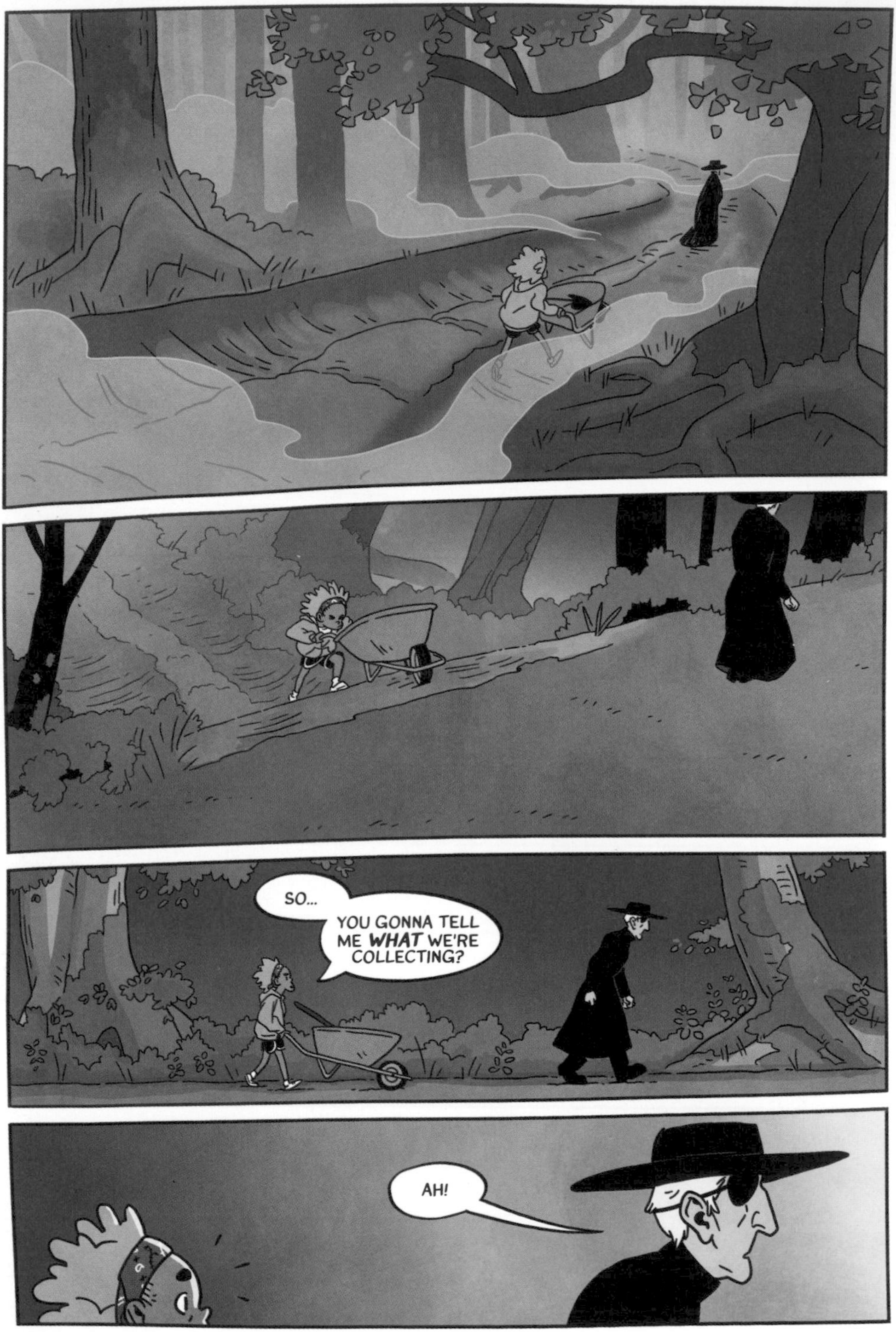
SO...
YOU GONNA TELL ME WHAT WE'RE COLLECTING?
AH!

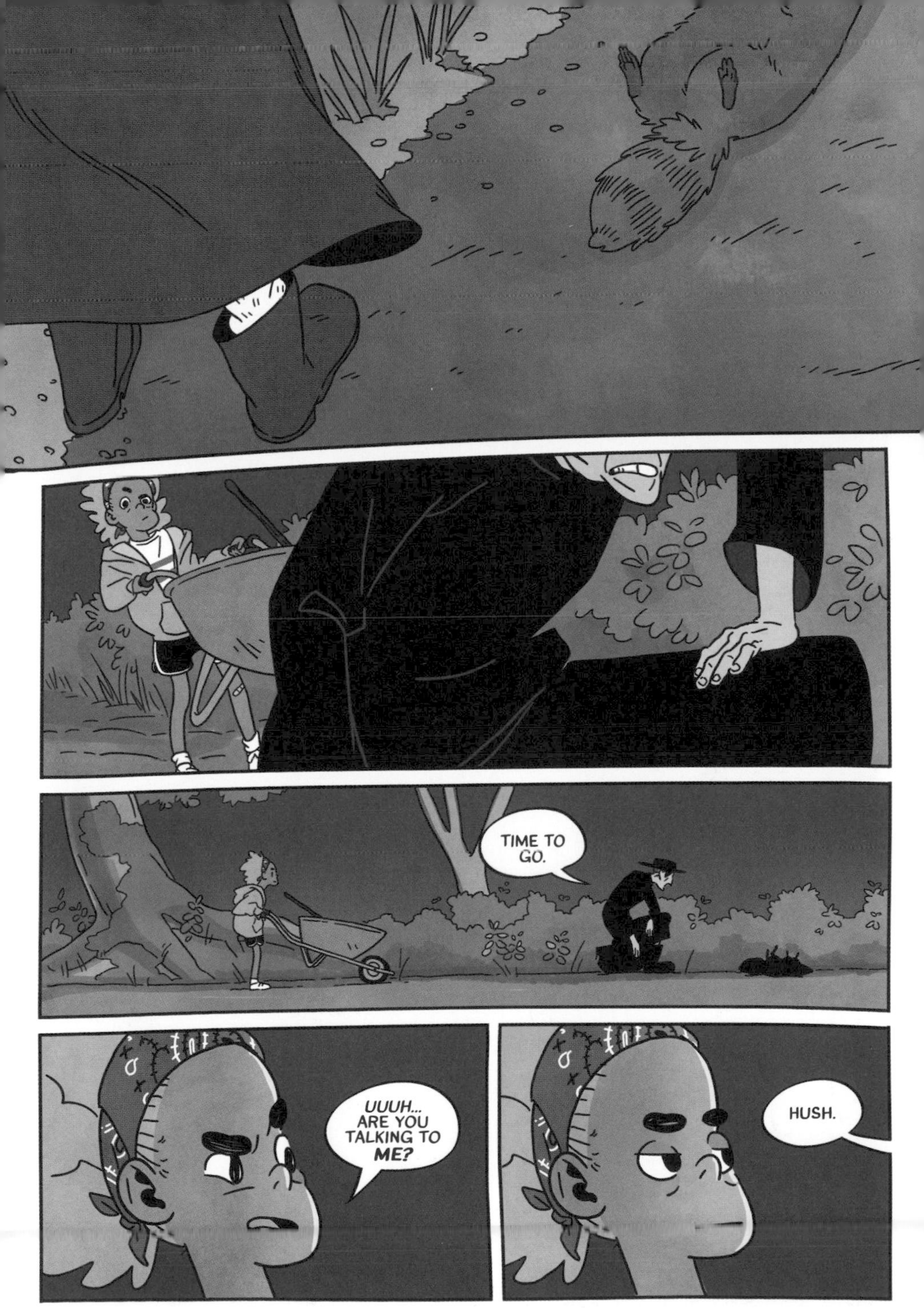
TIME TO GO.
UUUH... ARE YOU TALKING TO ME?
HUSH.

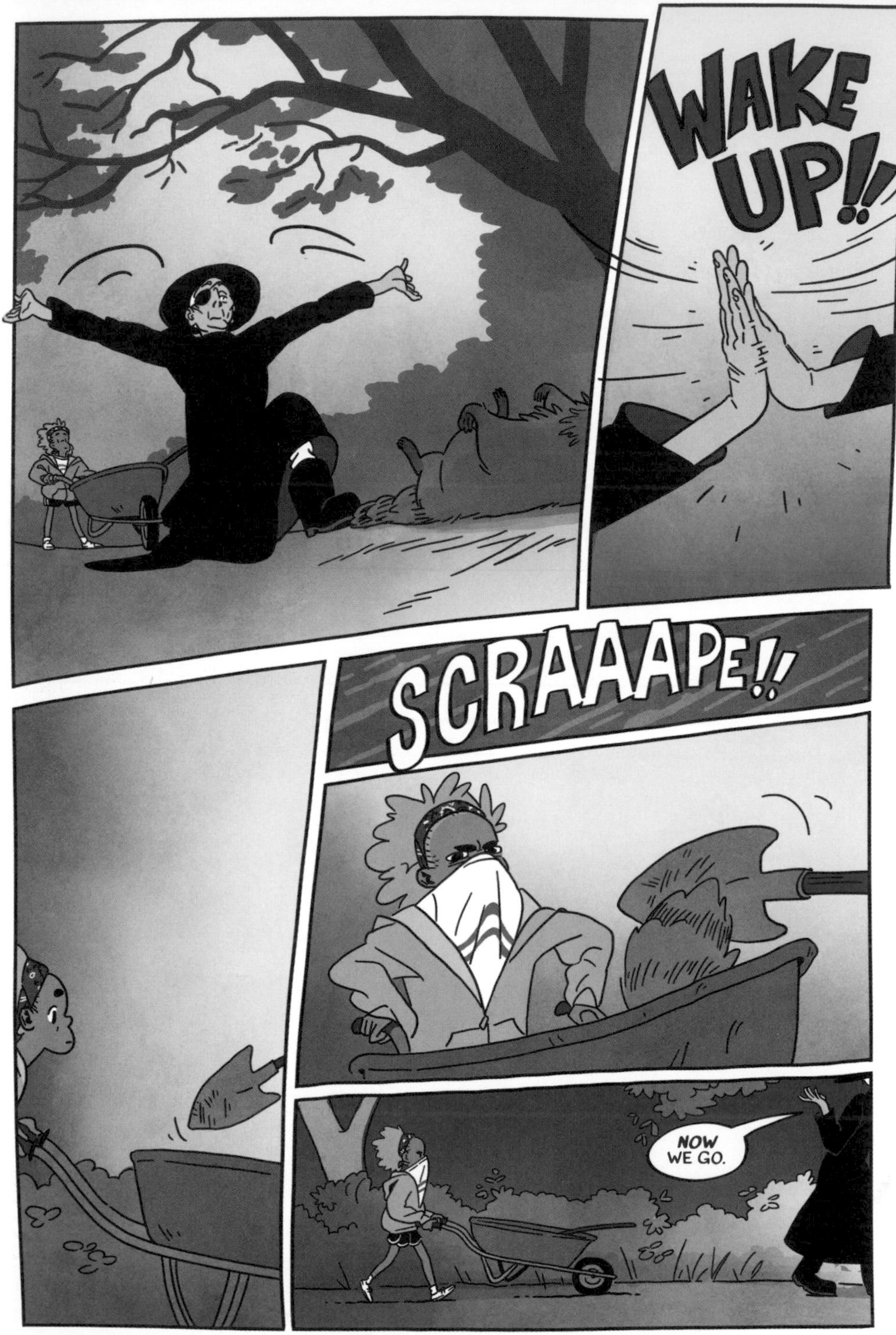
WAKE UP!!
SCRAAAPE!!
NOW WE GO.

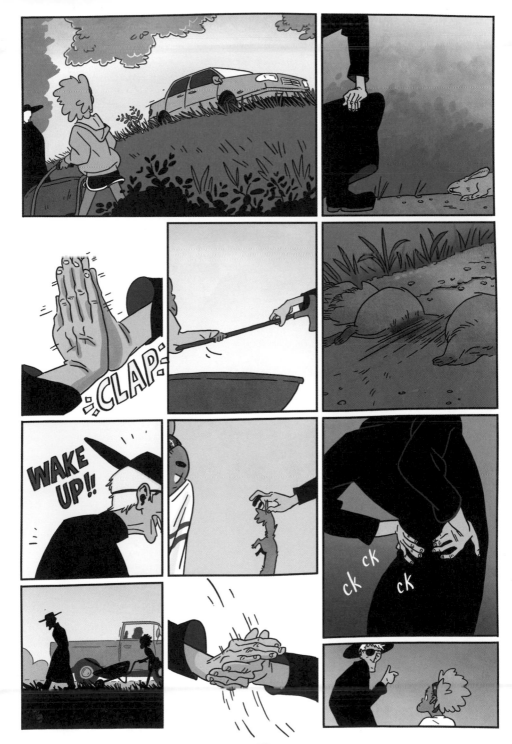

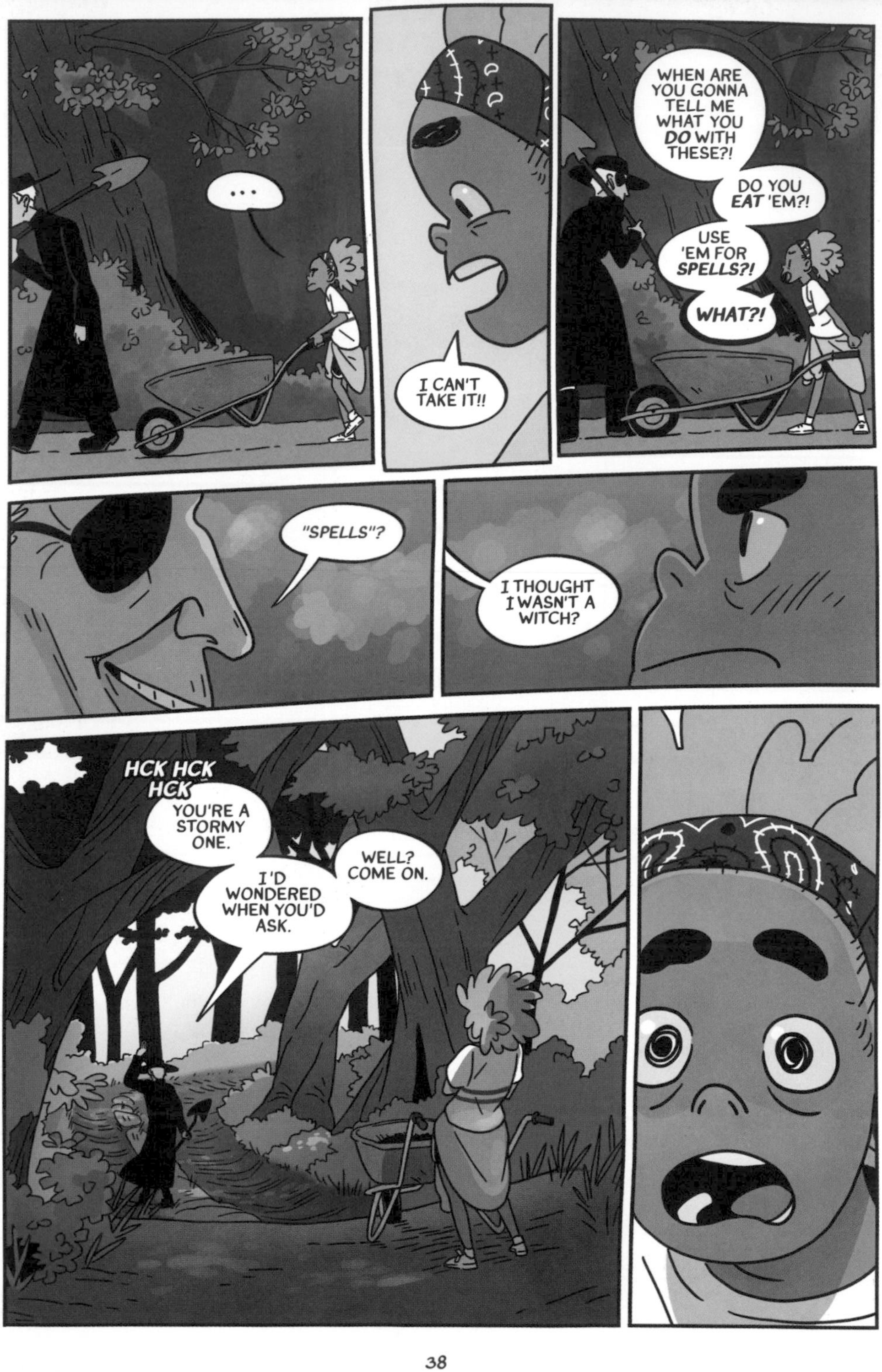
...
I CAN'T TAKE IT!!
WHEN ARE YOU GONNA TELL ME WHAT YOU DO WITH THESE?!
DO YOU EAT 'EM?!
USE 'EM FOR SPELLS?!
WHAT?!
"SPELLS"?
I THOUGHT I WASN'T A WITCH?
HCK HCK HCK
YOU'RE A STORMY ONE.
I'D WONDERED WHEN YOU'D ASK.
WELL? COME ON.

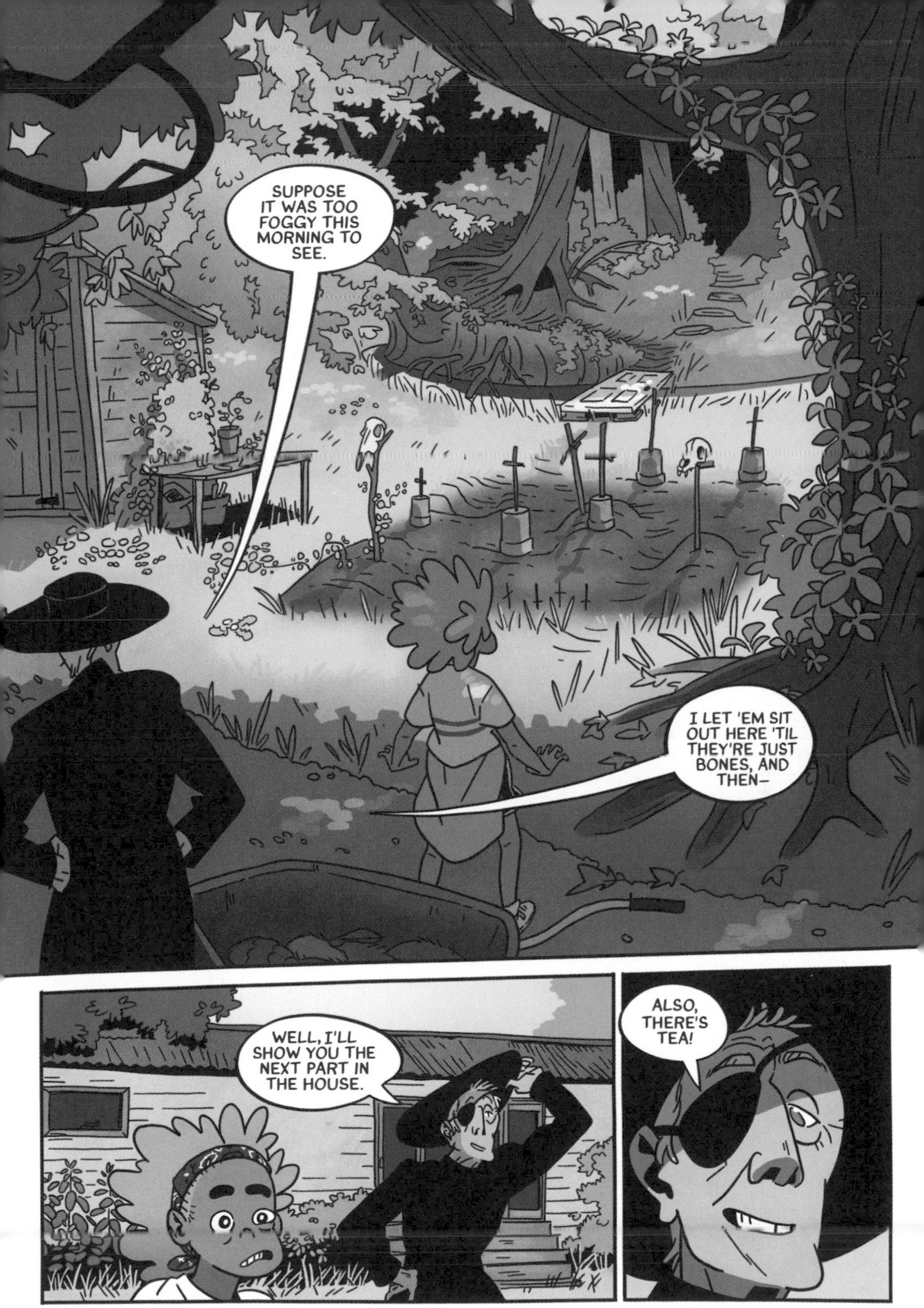
SUPPOSE IT WAS TOO FOGGY THIS MORNING TO SEE.
I LET 'EM SIT OUT HERE 'TIL THEY'RE JUST BONES, AND THEN–
WELL, I'LL SHOW YOU THE NEXT PART IN THE HOUSE.
ALSO, THERE'S TEA!

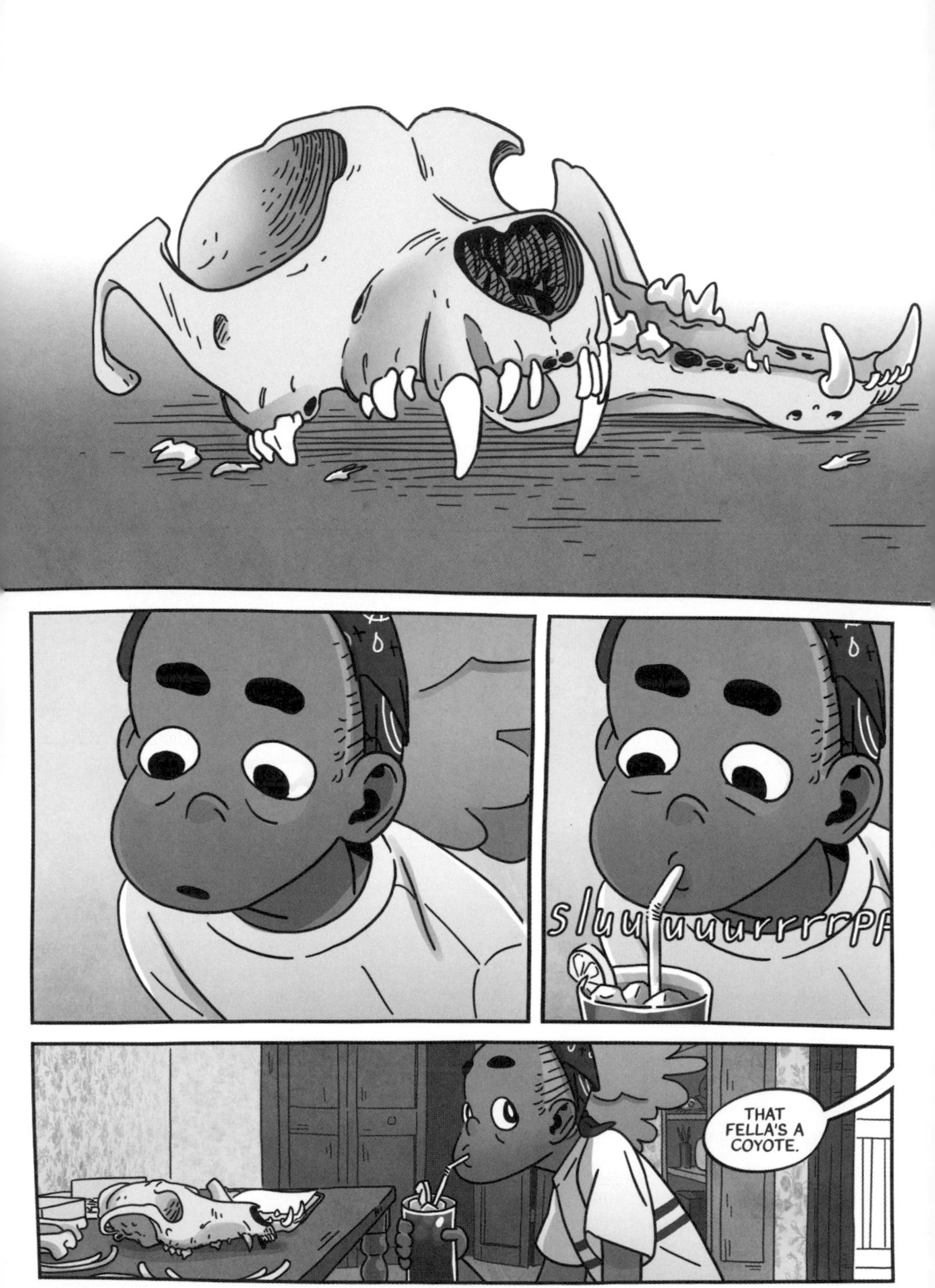
sluuuuuurrrrpp
THAT FELLA'S A COYOTE.

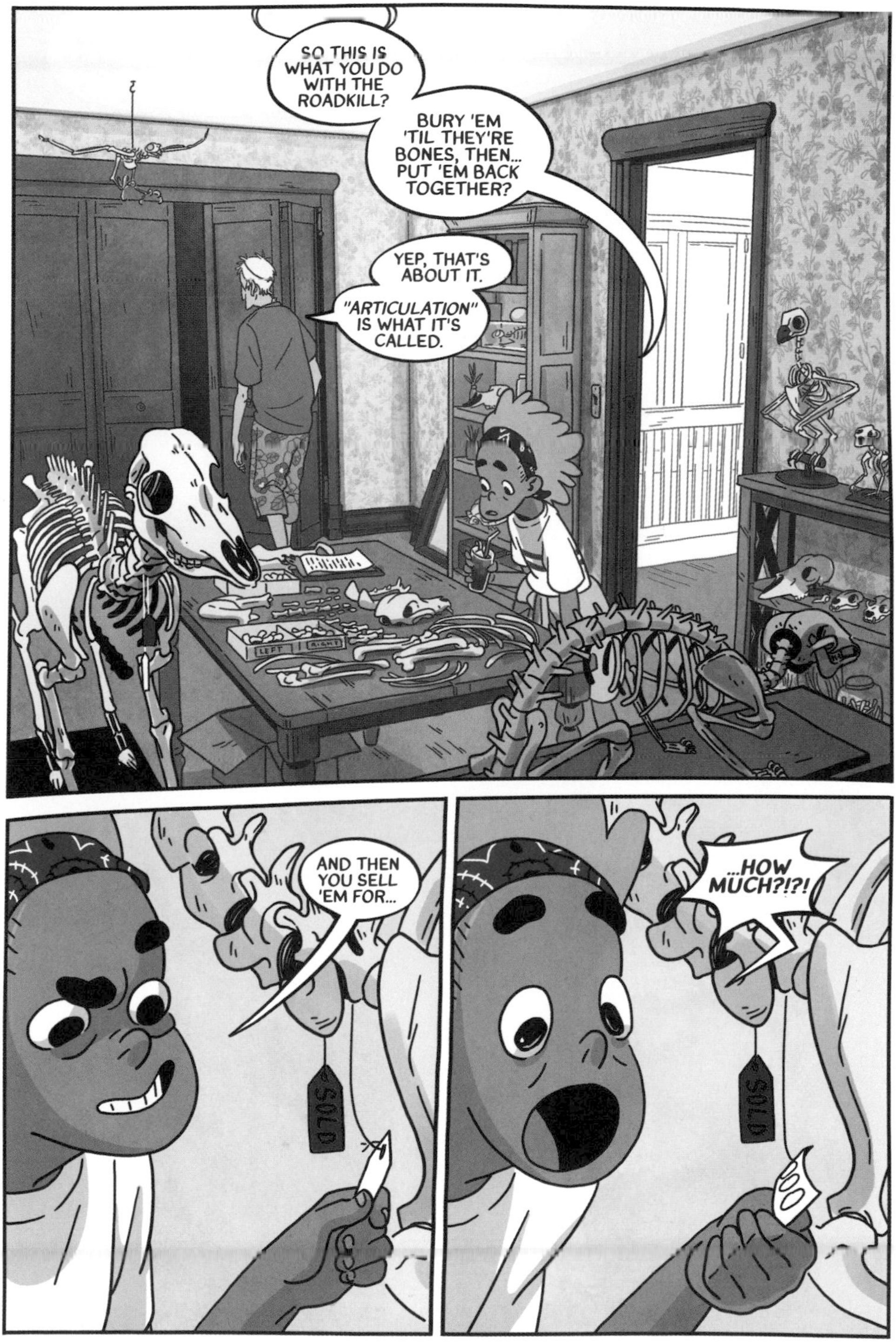
SO THIS IS WHAT YOU DO WITH THE ROADKILL?
BURY 'EM 'TIL THEY'RE BONES, THEN... PUT 'EM BACK TOGETHER?
YEP, THAT'S ABOUT IT.
"ARTICULATION" IS WHAT IT'S CALLED.
AND THEN YOU SELL 'EM FOR...
...HOW MUCH?!?!

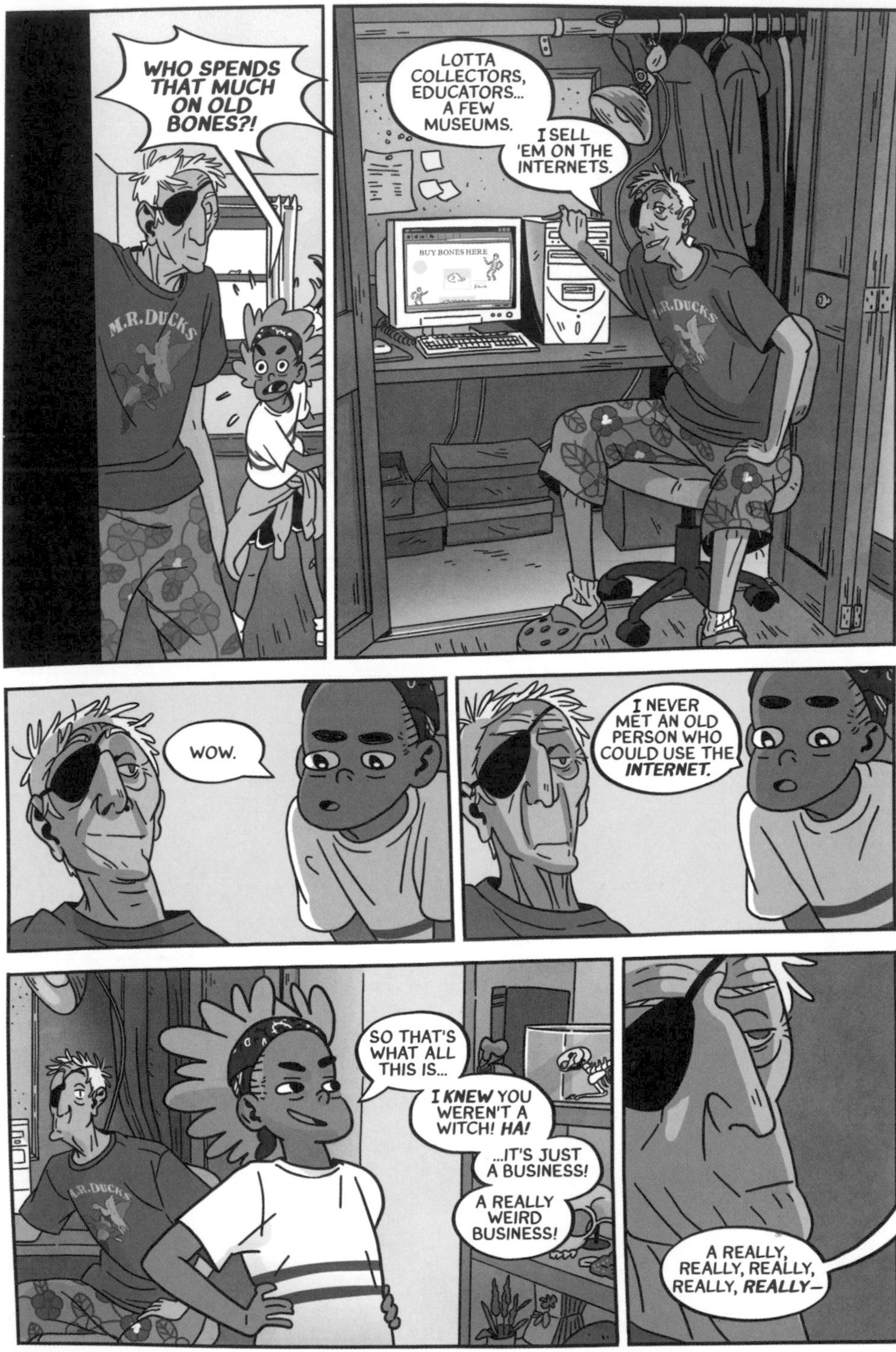
WHO SPENDS THAT MUCH ON OLD BONES?!
LOTTA COLLECTORS, EDUCATORS... A FEW MUSEUMS.
I SELL 'EM ON THE INTERNETS.
BUY BONES HERE
WOW.
I NEVER MET AN OLD PERSON WHO COULD USE THE INTERNET.
SO THAT'S WHAT ALL THIS IS...
I KNEW YOU WEREN'T A WITCH! HA!
...IT'S JUST A BUSINESS!
A REALLY WEIRD BUSINESS!
A REALLY, REALLY, REALLY, REALLY, REALLY—

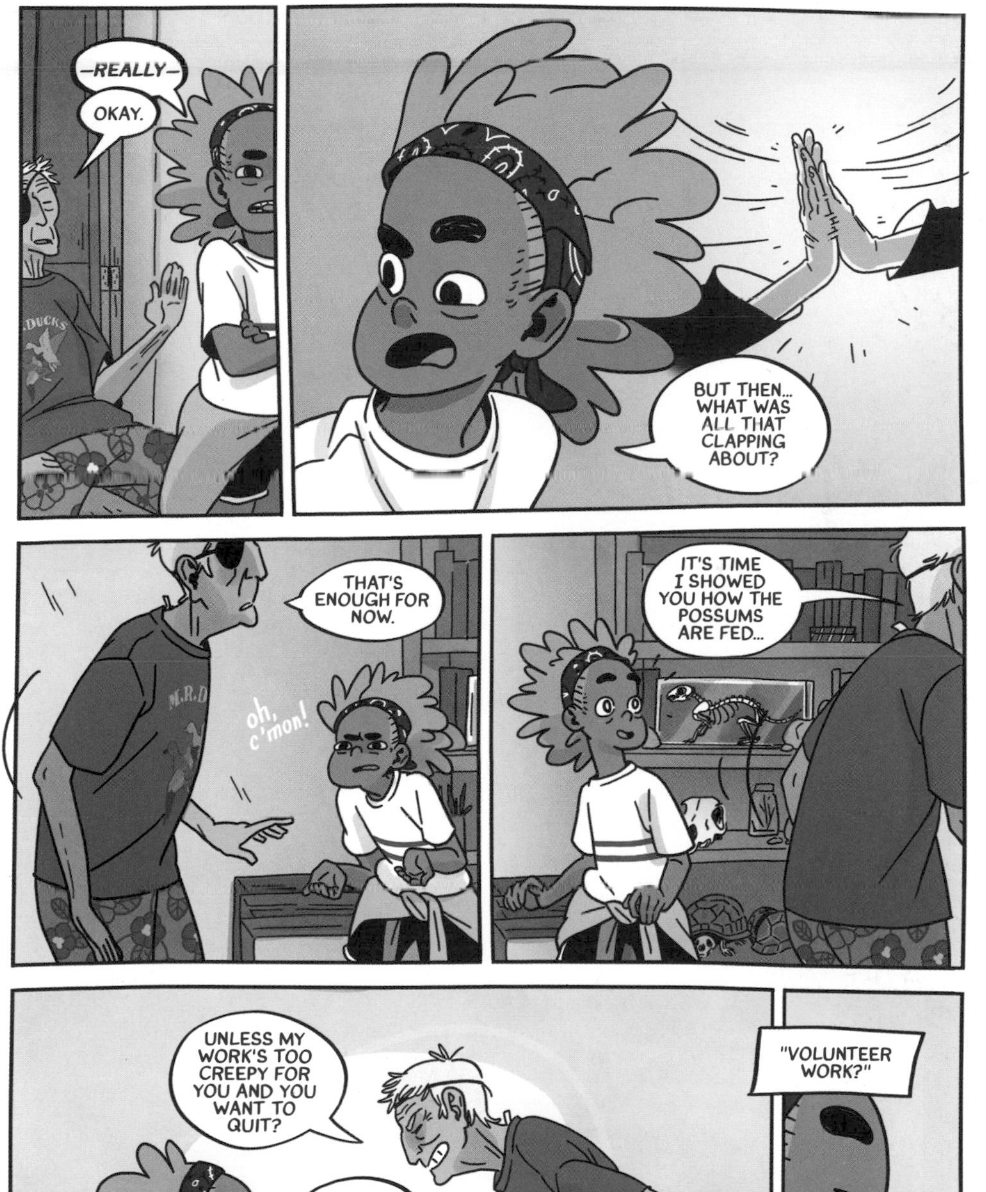
—REALLY—
OKAY.
BUT THEN... WHAT WAS ALL THAT CLAPPING ABOUT?
THAT'S ENOUGH FOR NOW.
oh, c'mon!
IT'S TIME I SHOWED YOU HOW THE POSSUMS ARE FED...
UNLESS MY WORK'S TOO CREEPY FOR YOU AND YOU WANT TO QUIT?
HELL NO, MA'AM!
"VOLUNTEER WORK?"

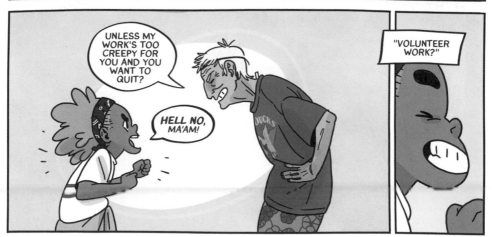

YEAH. HELPIN' AN OLD LADY WITH CHORES AND STUFF.

THAT'S REAL NICE, BABY!

MM–HM.

ARE YOU DONE YET, MAMA?

NOT YET.

BUT I'M *HUNGRYYY!*

WE'LL GET FOOD WHEN I'M DONE.

GO LOOK AROUND.

UUUURRGH.

SALE

YOU FIND EVERYTHING OKAY?

YEAH, THANKS. I'LL TAKE THESE. WITH THE STUDENT DISCOUNT.

AND THIS ONE!

OH, HONEY... THIS ISN'T A NICE BOOK FOR LITTLE GIRLS.

WE HAVE A LOT OF CUTE BOOKS ABOUT ANIMALS!

COMPARATIVE ANATOMY of VERTEBRATES

ACTUALLY, SHE'LL TAKE THIS ONE.

THANK YOU.

WHICH DO YOU THINK HAS MORE BONES: A HUMAN OR A MOUSE?

45

HMM... HUMAN?

MICE! THEY GOT A BUNCH MORE VERTEBRAE THAN WE DO 'CAUSE OF THEIR TAILS!

AH.

DID YOU KNOW WHALES HAVE THE SAME ARM BONES PEOPLE HAVE? IN THEIR FLIPPERS?

REALLY?

RUH RUH RUH RUH RUH RU

YEAH, AND SO DO *BATS!* THEIR WINGS ARE LIKE GIANT HANDS WITH *REEALLY* LONG FINGERS!

THAT'S CREEPY.

I THINK IT'S *COOL!*

A'RIGHT, A'RIGHT, *DOCTOR BLOOM*—

BOOK DOWN. TIME FOR DINNER.

WHICH PIECE YOU WANT?

CHICK CHICK

FEMUR, PLEASE!

THAT'S THE—

LEG BONE. YEAH, YOUR MAMA KNOWS SOME STUFF, TOO.

SO WHAT'S ALL THIS FOR? SCHOOL PROJECT?

I JUST THINK IT'S INTERESTING.

chew chew chew

YOU BEEN MAKIN' ANY NEW FRIENDS AT SCHOOL?

NAH. I'M OKAY ON MY OWN.

OH?

EVERYONE THINKS I'M WEIRD.

YOU SURE THAT'S WHAT *EVERYONE* THINKS...

47

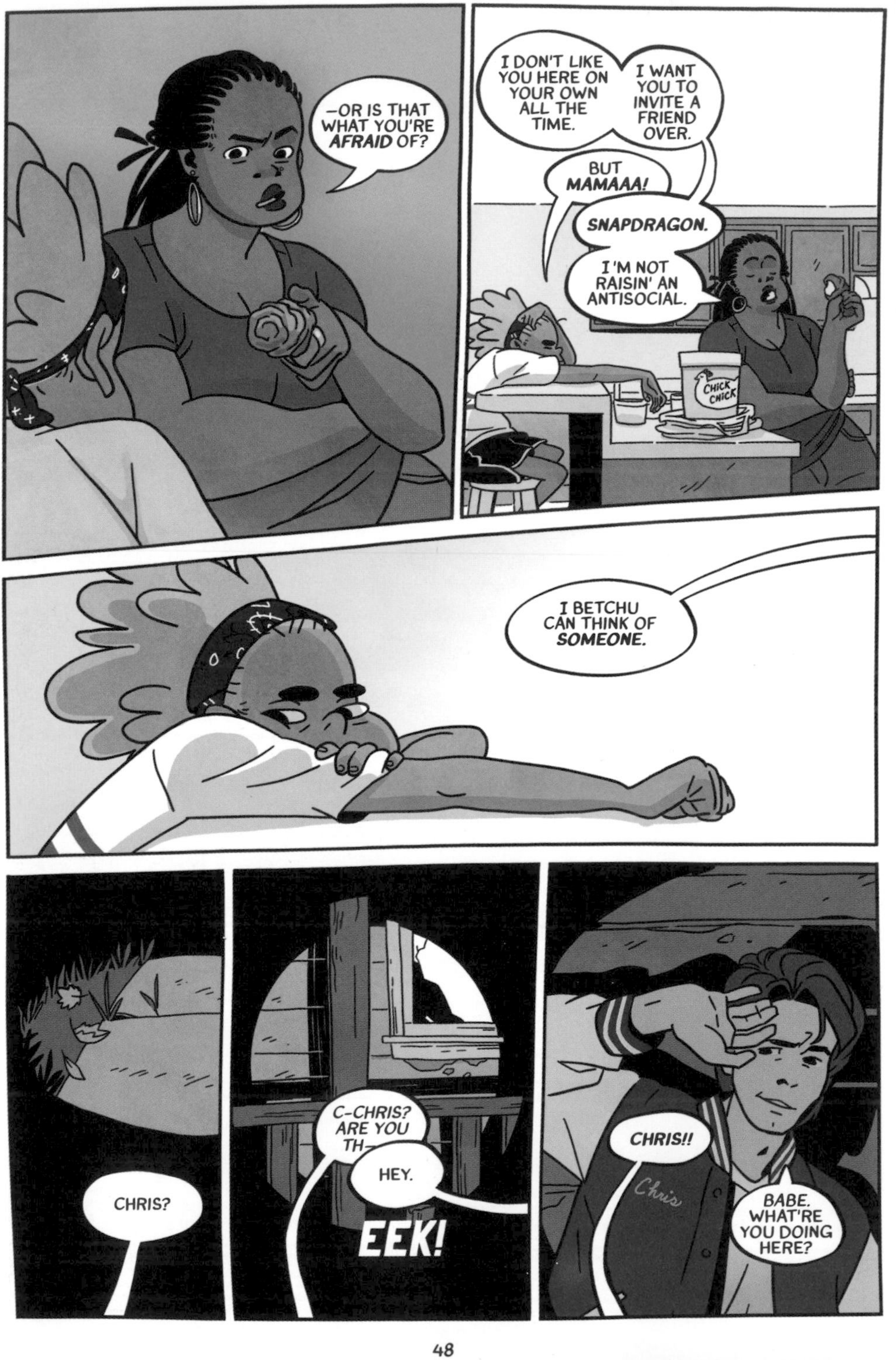
—OR IS THAT WHAT YOU'RE *AFRAID* OF?
I DON'T LIKE YOU HERE ON YOUR OWN ALL THE TIME.
I WANT YOU TO INVITE A FRIEND OVER.
BUT *MAMAAA!*
SNAPDRAGON.
I'M NOT RAISIN' AN ANTISOCIAL.
CHICK CHICK
I BETCHU CAN THINK OF *SOMEONE.*
CHRIS?
C-CHRIS? ARE YOU TH—
HEY.
EEK!
CHRIS!!
Chris
BABE. WHAT'RE YOU DOING HERE?

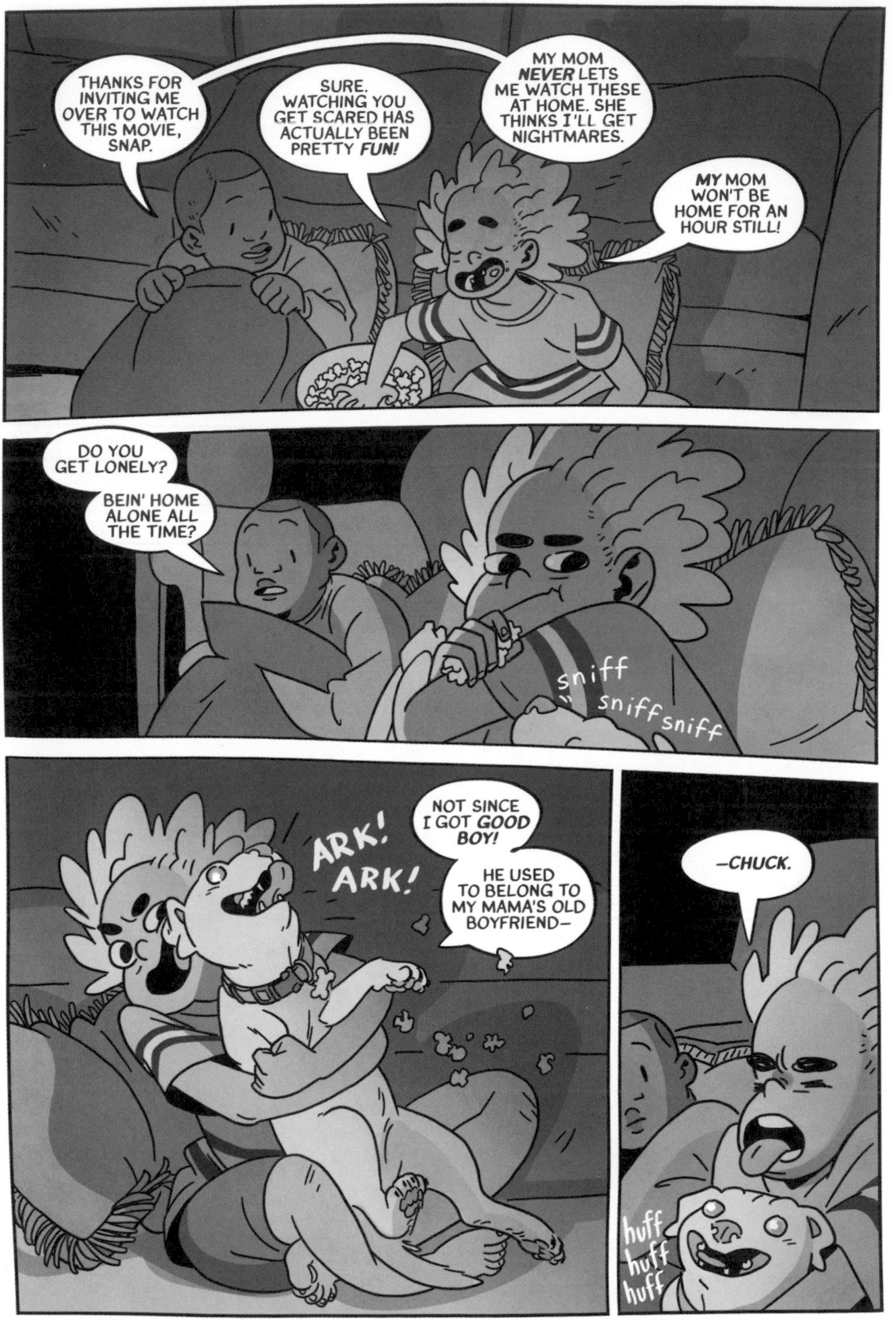
THANKS FOR INVITING ME OVER TO WATCH THIS MOVIE, SNAP.
SURE. WATCHING YOU GET SCARED HAS ACTUALLY BEEN PRETTY *FUN!*
MY MOM ***NEVER*** LETS ME WATCH THESE AT HOME. SHE THINKS I'LL GET NIGHTMARES.
MY MOM WON'T BE HOME FOR AN HOUR STILL!
DO YOU GET LONELY?
BEIN' HOME ALONE ALL THE TIME?
sniff
sniffsniff
ARK! ARK!
NOT SINCE I GOT ***GOOD BOY!***
HE USED TO BELONG TO MY MAMA'S OLD BOYFRIEND—
—CHUCK.
huff huff huff

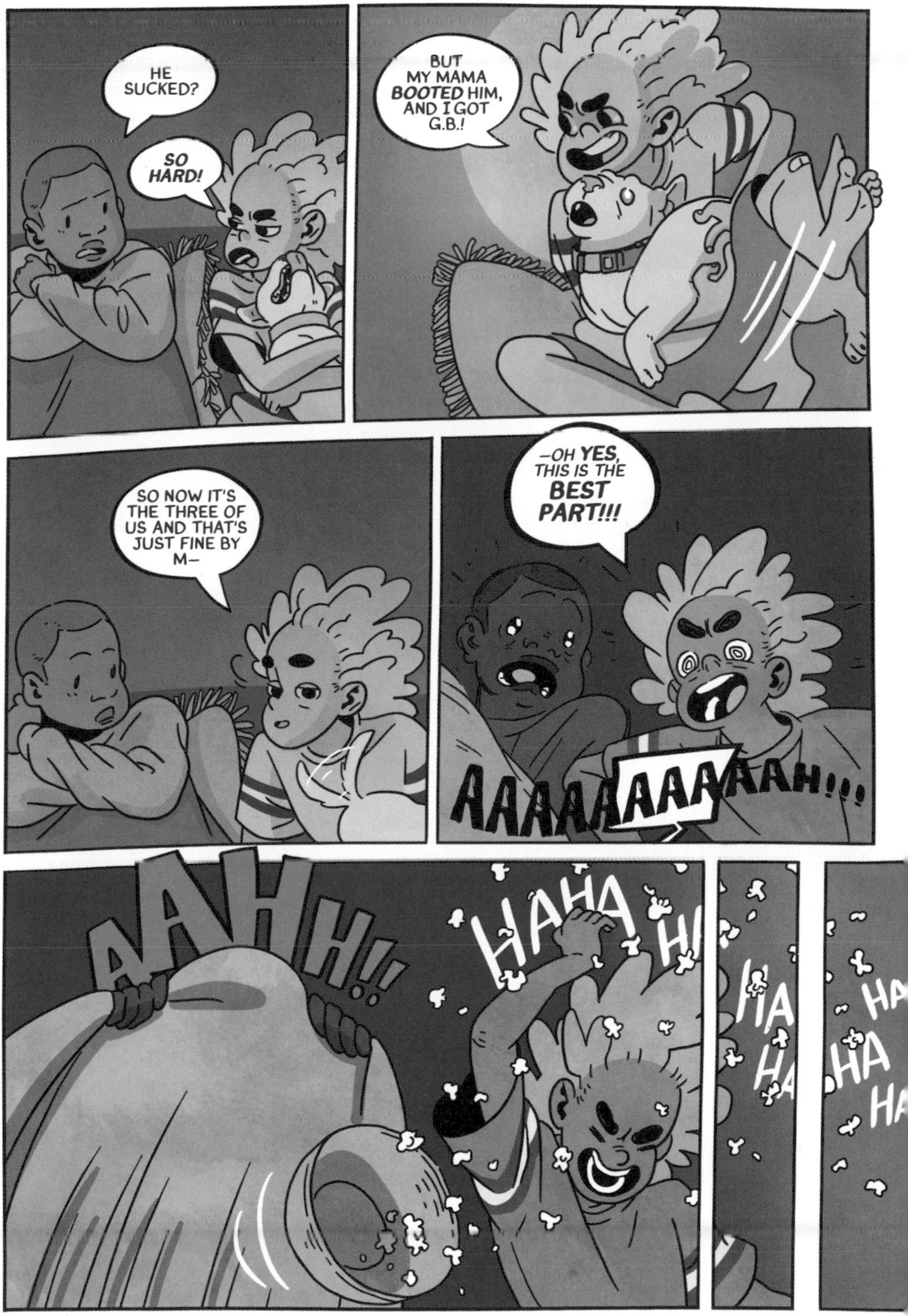
HE SUCKED?
SO HARD!
BUT MY MAMA BOOTED HIM, AND I GOT G.B.!
SO NOW IT'S THE THREE OF US AND THAT'S JUST FINE BY M—
—OH YES, THIS IS THE BEST PART!!!
AAAAAAAAAAAH!!!
AAHH!!
HAHA
HA
HA
HA
HA
HA
HA

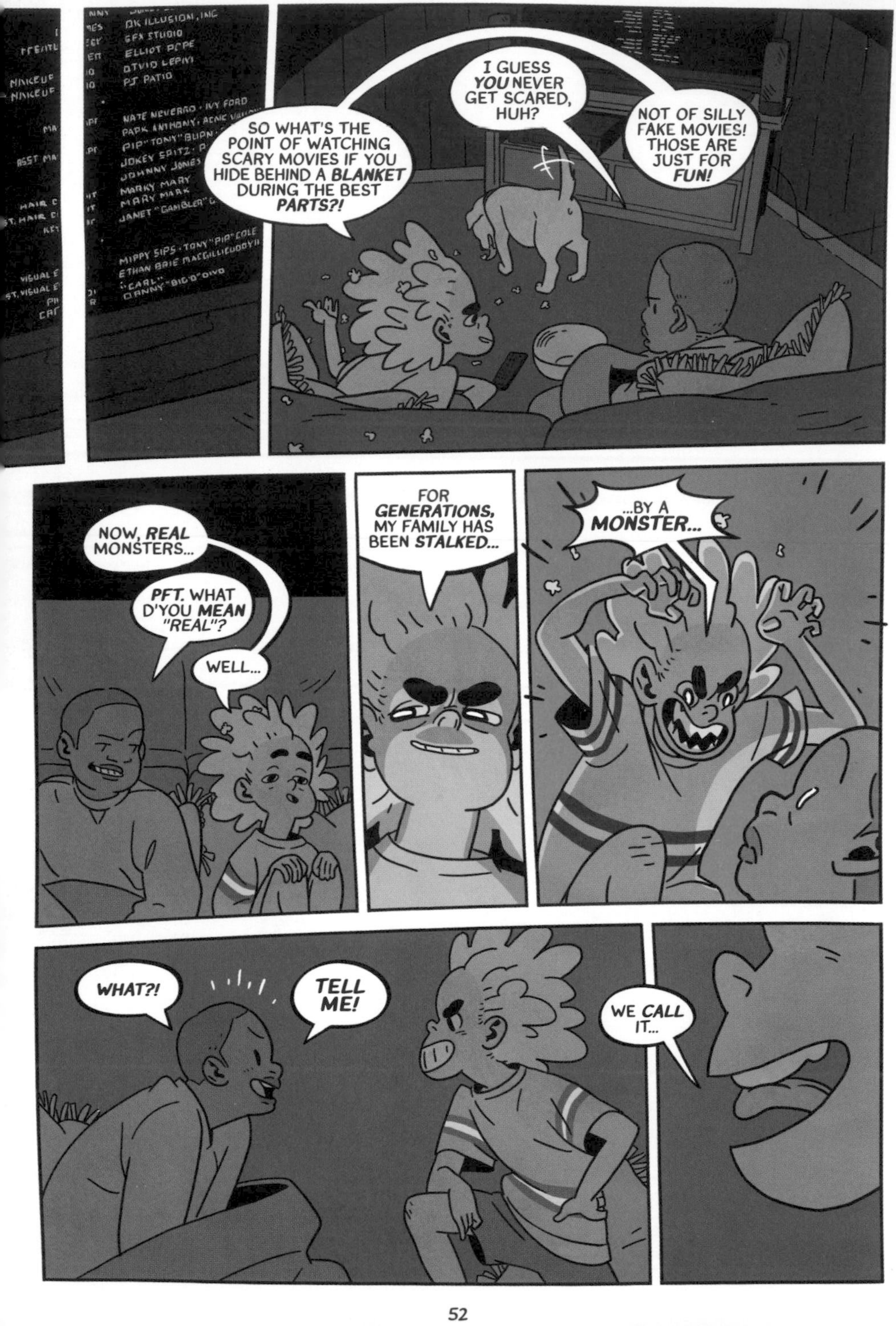
SO WHAT'S THE POINT OF WATCHING SCARY MOVIES IF YOU HIDE BEHIND A BLANKET DURING THE BEST PARTS?!
I GUESS YOU NEVER GET SCARED, HUH?
NOT OF SILLY FAKE MOVIES! THOSE ARE JUST FOR FUN!
NOW, REAL MONSTERS...
PFT. WHAT D'YOU MEAN "REAL"?
WELL...
FOR GENERATIONS, MY FAMILY HAS BEEN STALKED...
...BY A MONSTER...
WHAT?!
TELL ME!
WE CALL IT...

ONE-EYED TOM

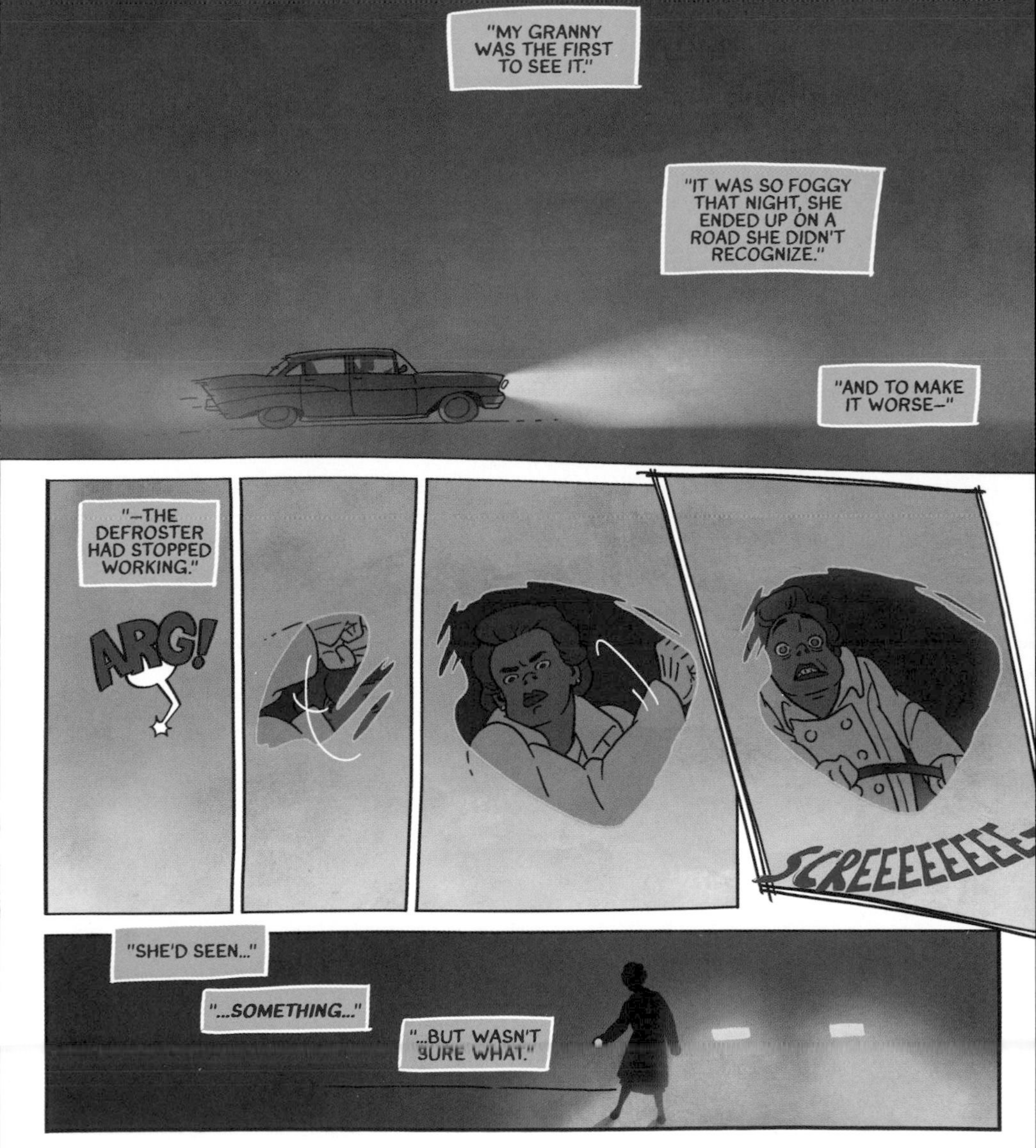
"MY GRANNY WAS THE FIRST TO SEE IT."
"IT WAS SO FOGGY THAT NIGHT, SHE ENDED UP ON A ROAD SHE DIDN'T RECOGNIZE."
"AND TO MAKE IT WORSE–"
"–THE DEFROSTER HAD STOPPED WORKING."
ARG!
SCREEEEEEEE–
"SHE'D SEEN..."
"...SOMETHING..."
"...BUT WASN'T SURE WHAT."

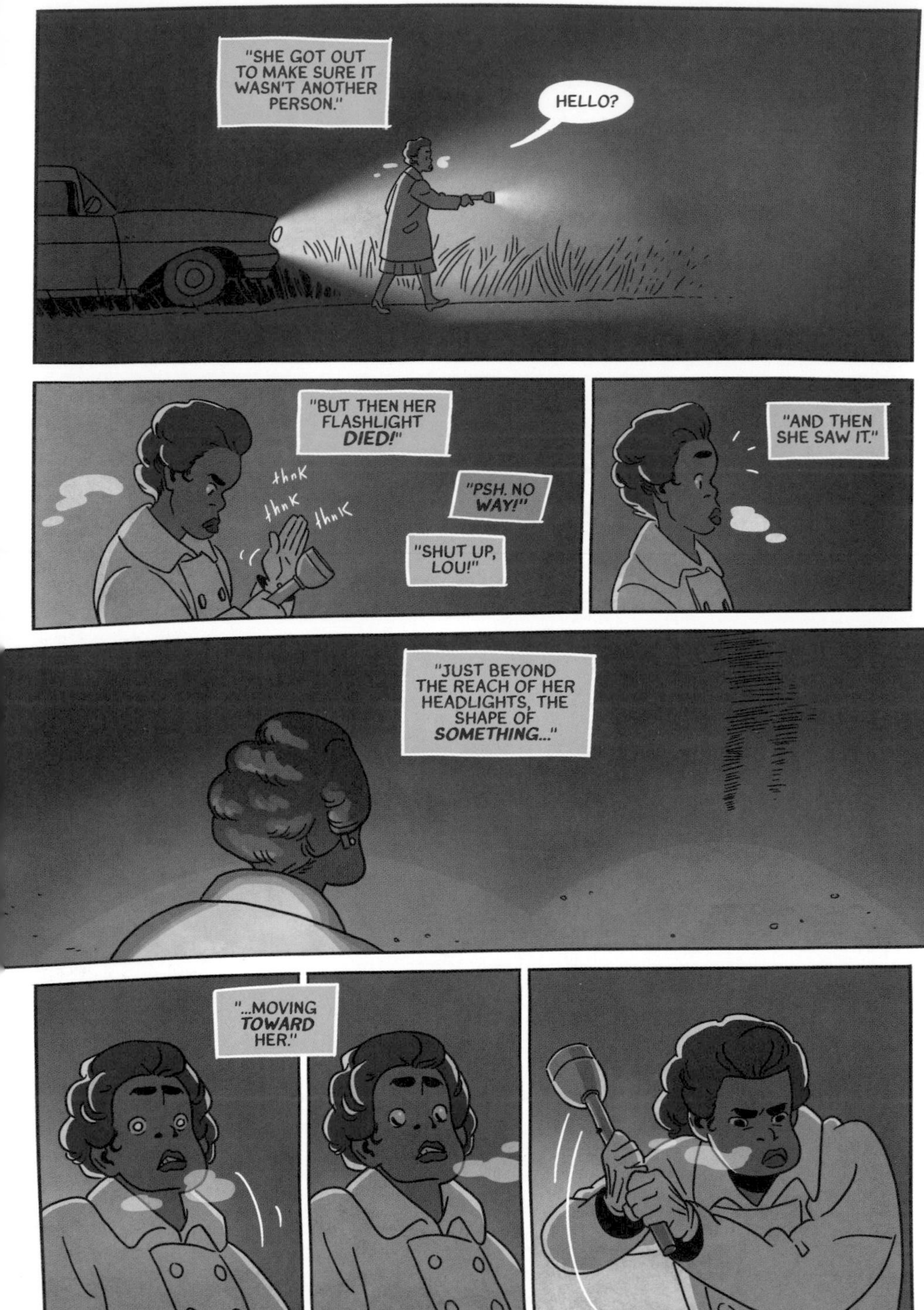
"SHE GOT OUT TO MAKE SURE IT WASN'T ANOTHER PERSON."
HELLO?
"BUT THEN HER FLASHLIGHT DIED!"
thnk
thnk
thnk
"PSH. NO WAY!"
"SHUT UP, LOU!"
"AND THEN SHE SAW IT."
"JUST BEYOND THE REACH OF HER HEADLIGHTS, THE SHAPE OF SOMETHING..."
"...MOVING TOWARD HER."

OH MY *GOD,* LOUIS!!

IT'S JUST ALLEY CATS! SAME AS EVERY NIGHT!

THEN WHAT HAPPENED?!

KEEP GOING!

ONE-EYED TOM GOT *THIIIS* CLOSE TO GRAN...

...THEN SHE HOOFED IT!

RAN TO HER CAR, TURNED AROUND, AND FOUND MAIN STREET!

DIDN'T LOOK BACK.

WH—

AND THAT'S THE FIRST TIME ANYONE SAW HIM! GET HOME SAFE, LOU!

WHOA! WHAT ABOUT THE OTHER TIMES?

IT'S LATE.

I'LL HAVE TO TELL 'EM TO YOU ANOTHER TIME!

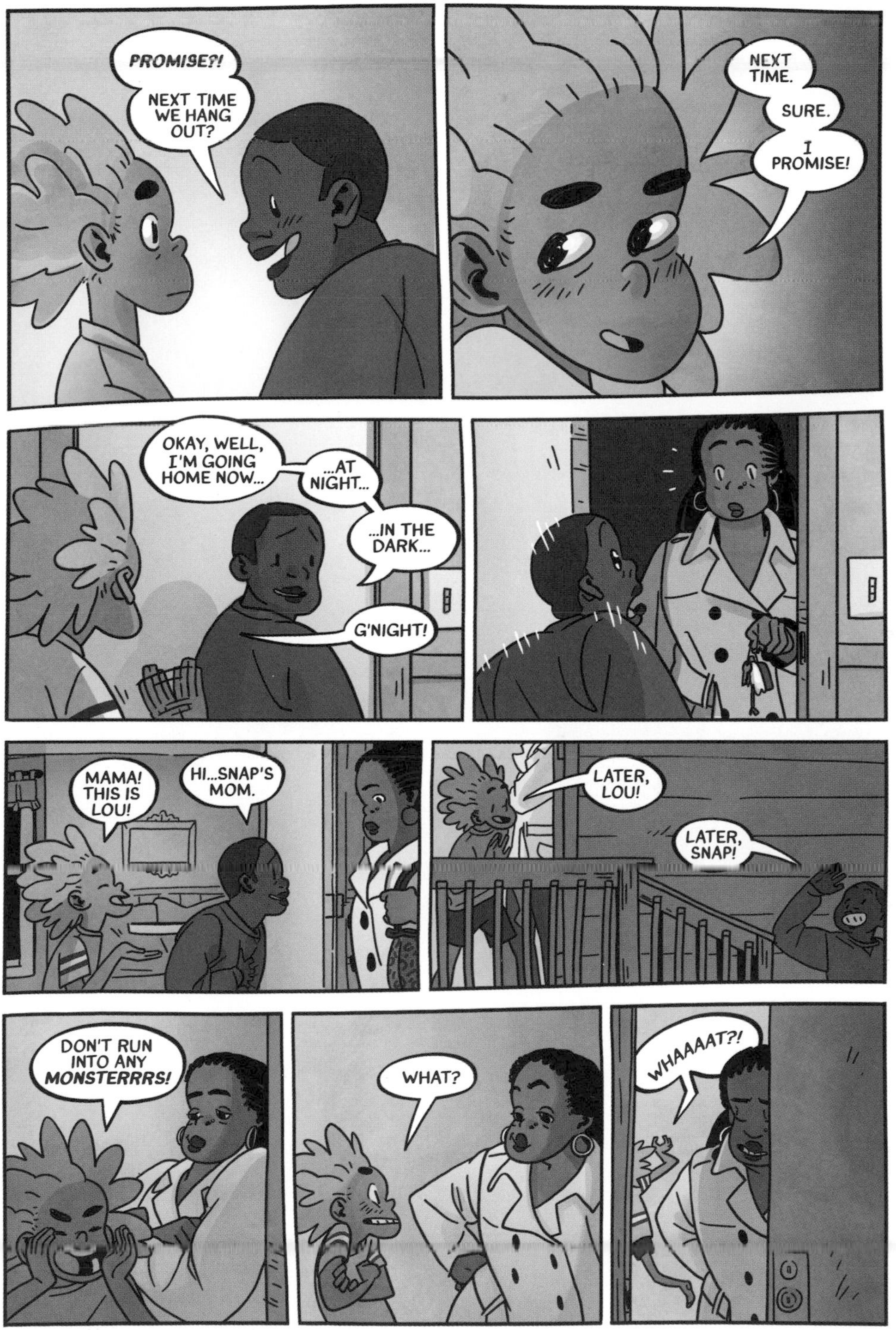
PROMISE?!
NEXT TIME WE HANG OUT?
NEXT TIME.
SURE.
I PROMISE!
OKAY, WELL, I'M GOING HOME NOW...
...AT NIGHT...
...IN THE DARK...
G'NIGHT!
MAMA! THIS IS LOU!
HI...SNAP'S MOM.
LATER, LOU!
LATER, SNAP!
DON'T RUN INTO ANY MONSTERRRS!
WHAT?
WHAAAAT?!

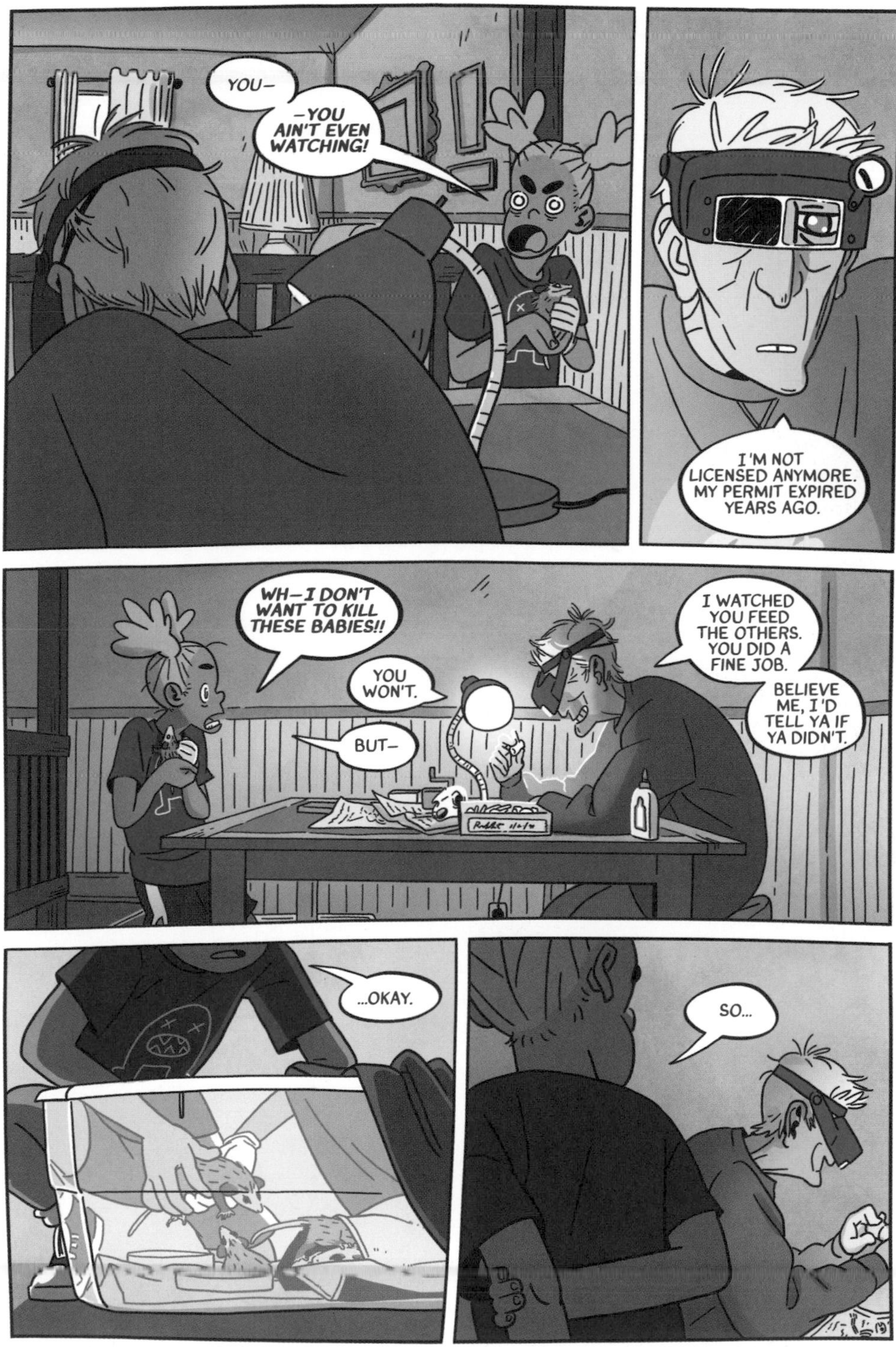
YOU–
–YOU AIN'T EVEN WATCHING!
I'M NOT LICENSED ANYMORE. MY PERMIT EXPIRED YEARS AGO.
WH–I DON'T WANT TO KILL THESE BABIES!!
YOU WON'T.
BUT–
I WATCHED YOU FEED THE OTHERS. YOU DID A FINE JOB.
BELIEVE ME, I'D TELL YA IF YA DIDN'T.
...OKAY.
SO...

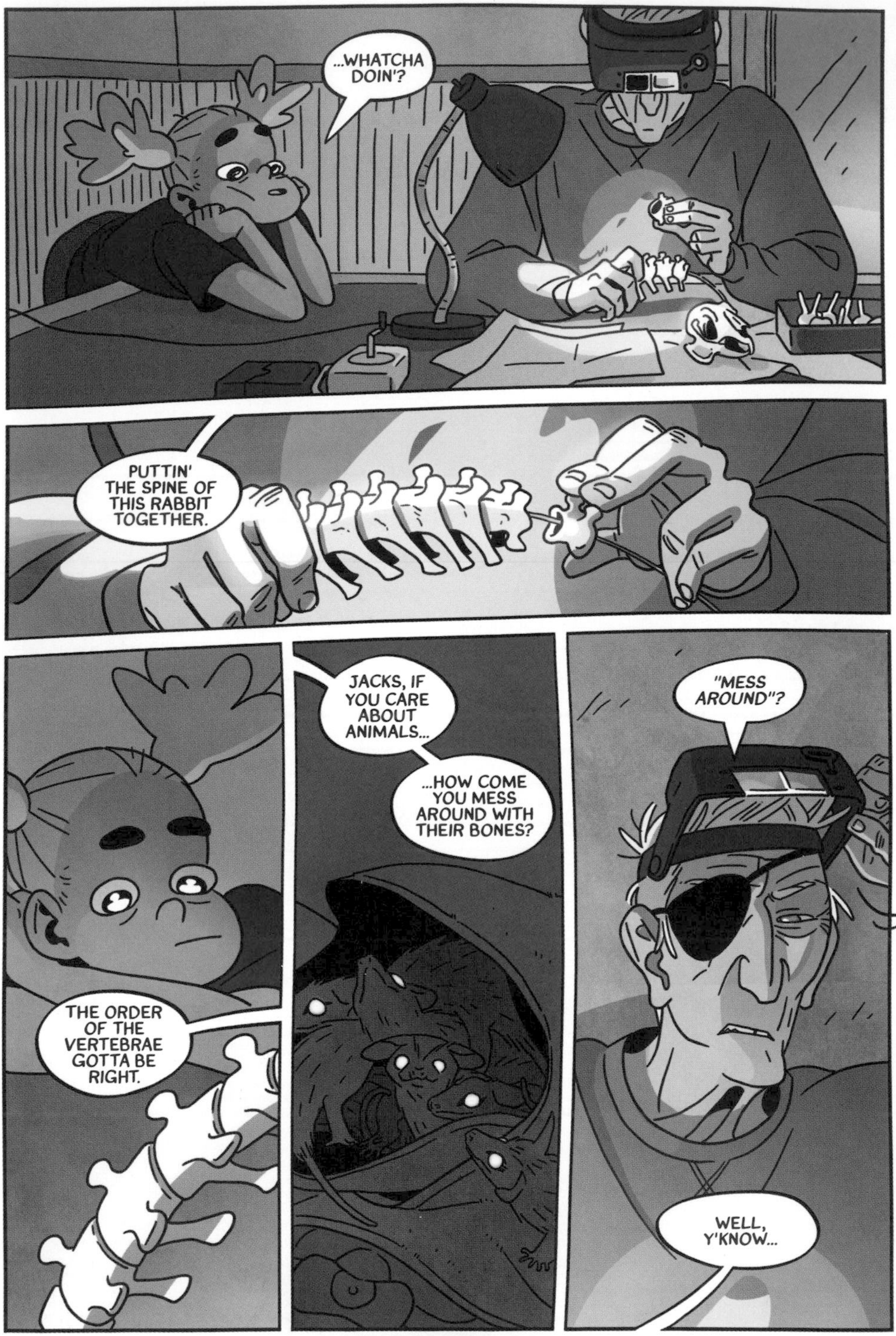
...WHATCHA DOIN'?
PUTTIN' THE SPINE OF THIS RABBIT TOGETHER.
THE ORDER OF THE VERTEBRAE GOTTA BE RIGHT.
JACKS, IF YOU CARE ABOUT ANIMALS...
...HOW COME YOU MESS AROUND WITH THEIR BONES?
"MESS AROUND"?
WELL, Y'KNOW...

61

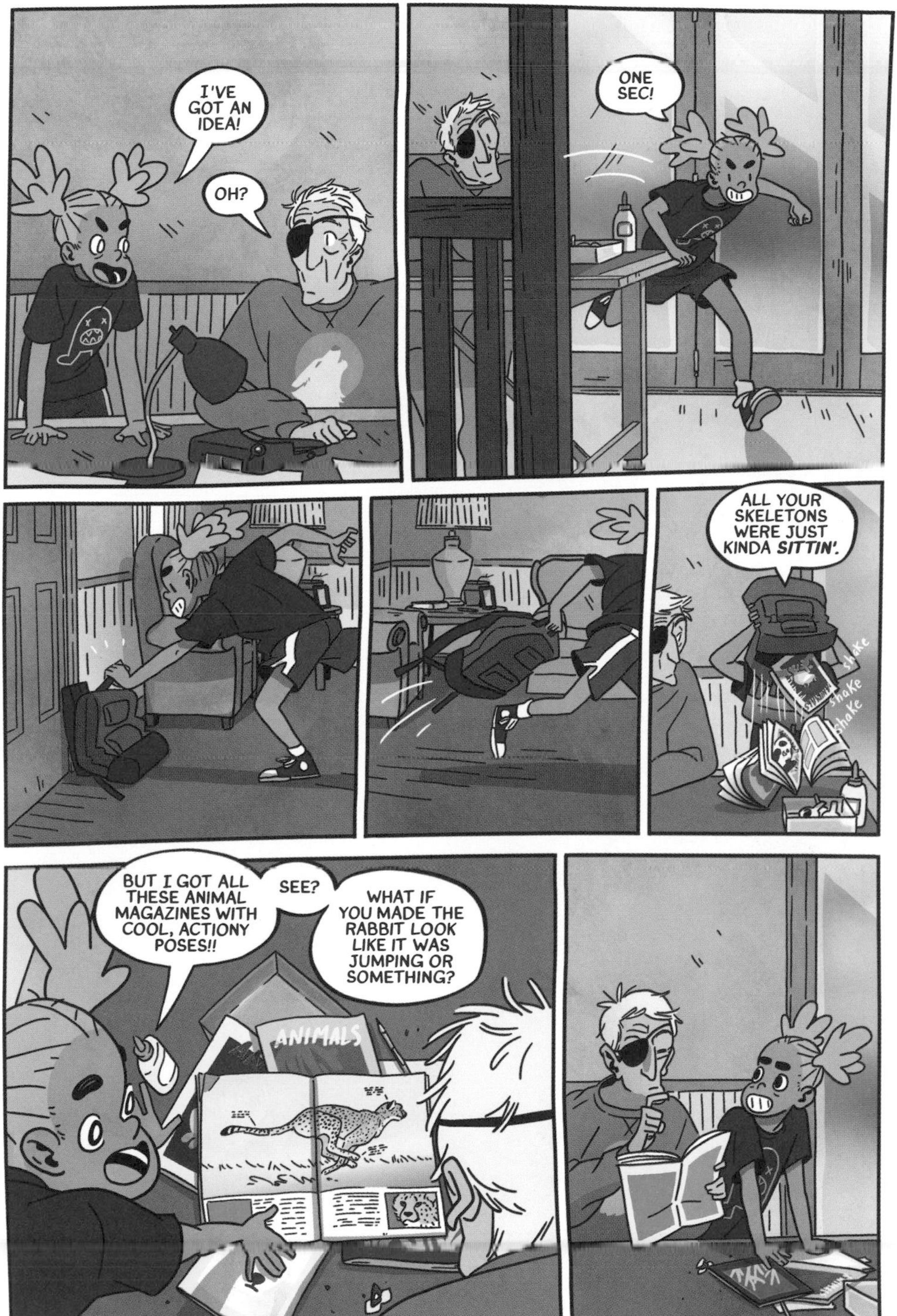

I'VE GOT AN IDEA!
OH?
ONE SEC!
ALL YOUR SKELETONS WERE JUST KINDA *SITTIN'*.
shake
shake
shake
BUT I GOT ALL THESE ANIMAL MAGAZINES WITH COOL, ACTIONY POSES!!
SEE?
WHAT IF YOU MADE THE RABBIT LOOK LIKE IT WAS JUMPING OR SOMETHING?
ANIMALS

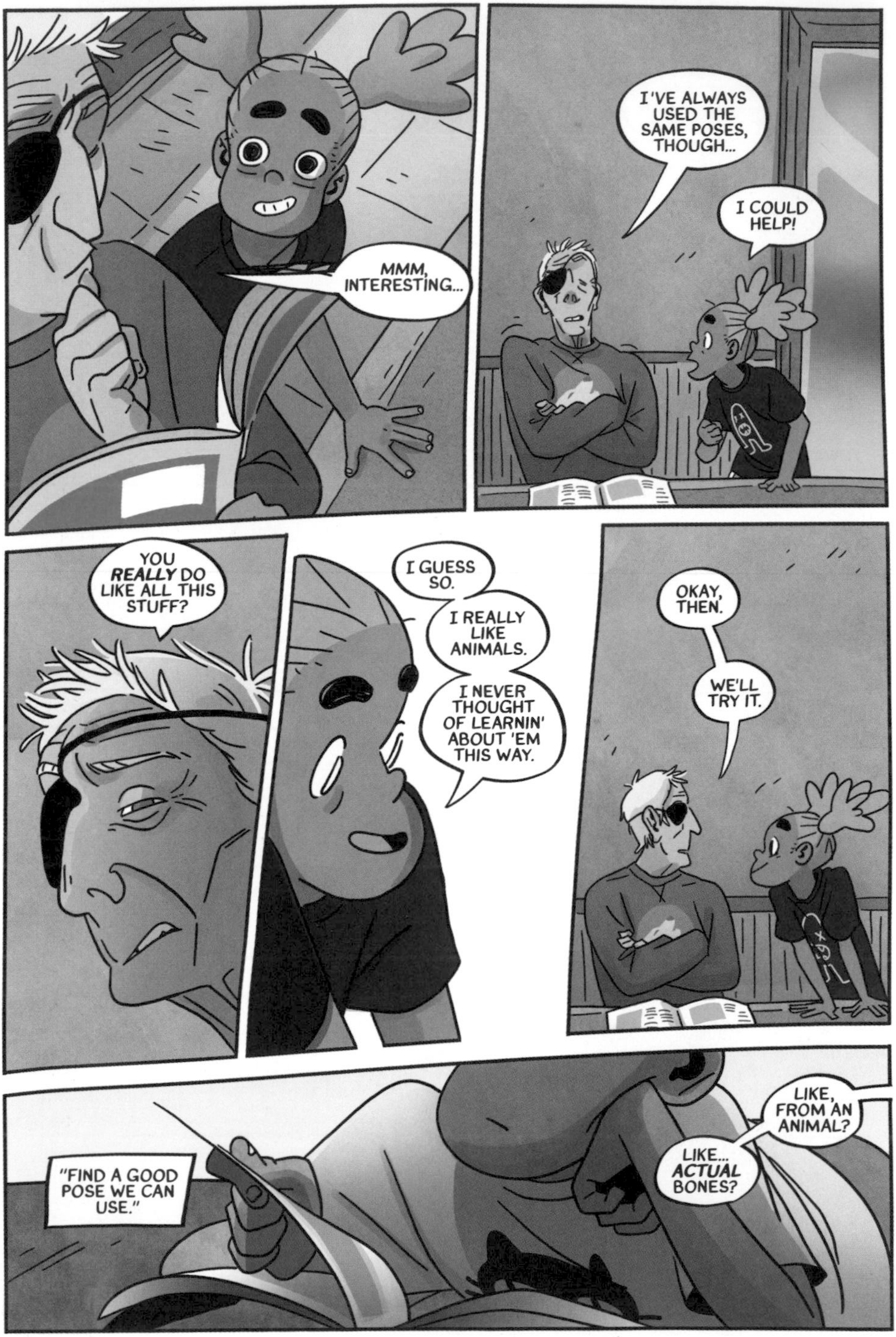
MMM, INTERESTING...
I'VE ALWAYS USED THE SAME POSES, THOUGH...
I COULD HELP!
YOU **REALLY** DO LIKE ALL THIS STUFF?
I GUESS SO.
I REALLY LIKE ANIMALS.
I NEVER THOUGHT OF LEARNIN' ABOUT 'EM THIS WAY.
OKAY, THEN.
WE'LL TRY IT.
"FIND A GOOD POSE WE CAN USE."
LIKE, FROM AN ANIMAL?
LIKE... **ACTUAL** BONES?

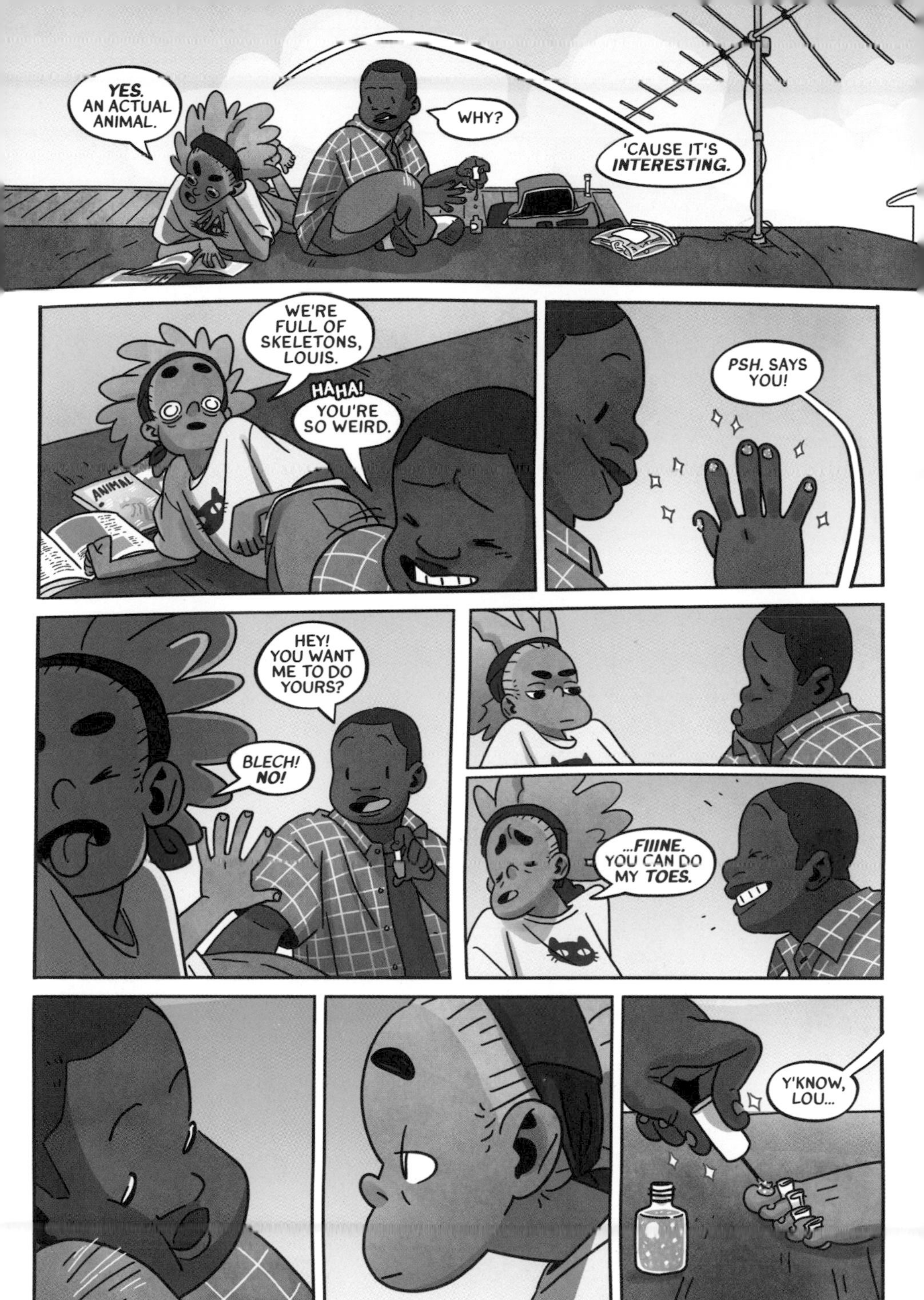
YES. AN ACTUAL ANIMAL.
WHY?
'CAUSE IT'S INTERESTING.
WE'RE FULL OF SKELETONS, LOUIS.
HAHA!
YOU'RE SO WEIRD.
PSH. SAYS YOU!
HEY! YOU WANT ME TO DO YOURS?
BLECH! NO!
...FIIINE. YOU CAN DO MY TOES.
Y'KNOW, LOU...

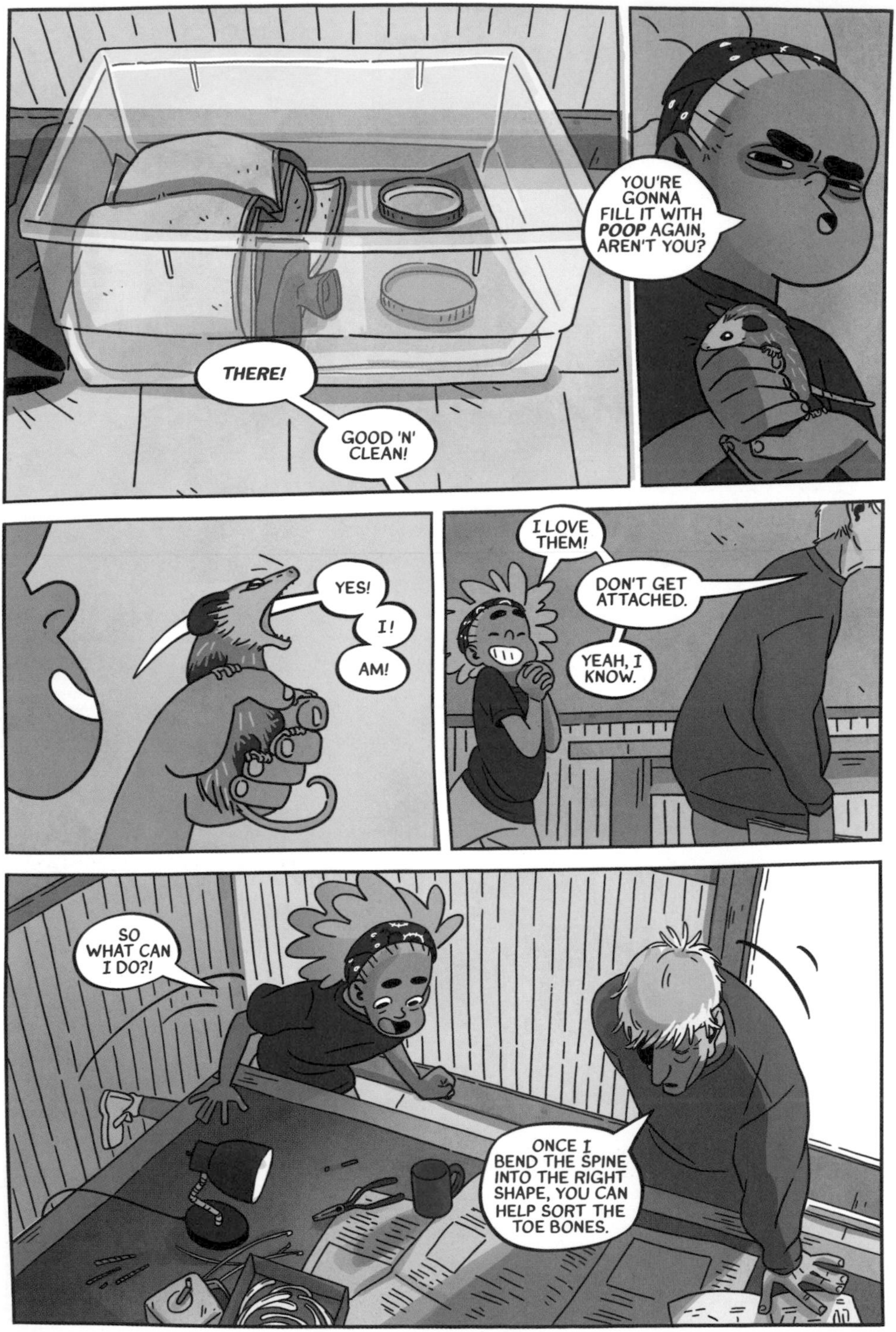
THERE!
GOOD 'N' CLEAN!
YOU'RE GONNA FILL IT WITH POOP AGAIN, AREN'T YOU?
YES!
I!
AM!
I LOVE THEM!
DON'T GET ATTACHED.
YEAH, I KNOW.
SO WHAT CAN I DO?!
ONCE I BEND THE SPINE INTO THE RIGHT SHAPE, YOU CAN HELP SORT THE TOE BONES.

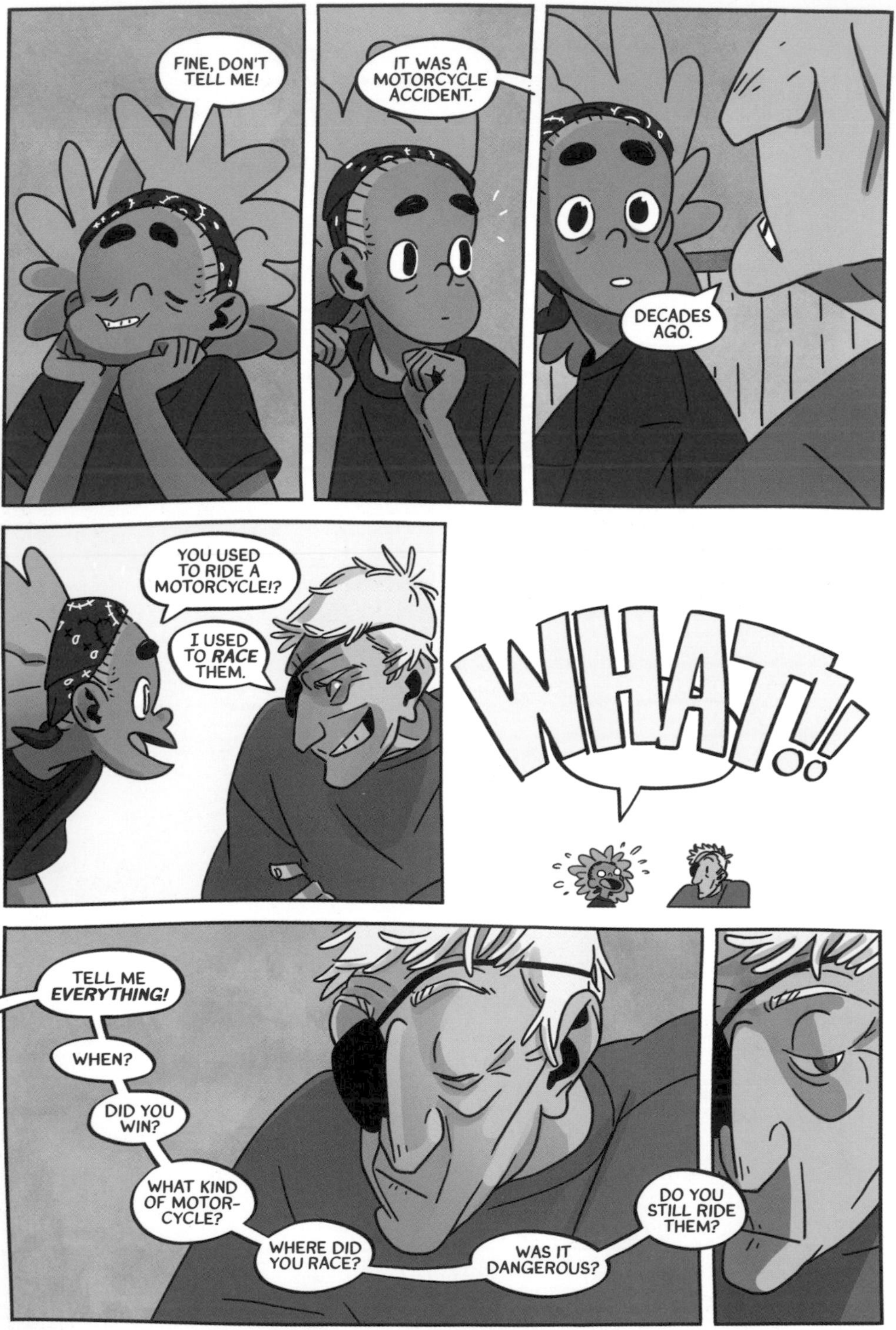

FINE, DON'T TELL ME!
IT WAS A MOTORCYCLE ACCIDENT.
DECADES AGO.
YOU USED TO RIDE A MOTORCYCLE!?
I USED TO *RACE* THEM.
WHAT!!
TELL ME *EVERYTHING!*
WHEN?
DID YOU WIN?
WHAT KIND OF MOTOR-CYCLE?
WHERE DID YOU RACE?
WAS IT DANGEROUS?
DO YOU STILL RIDE THEM?

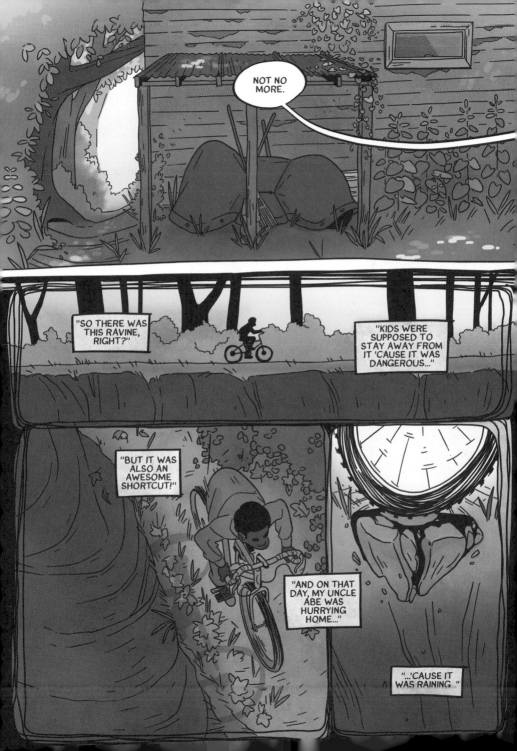

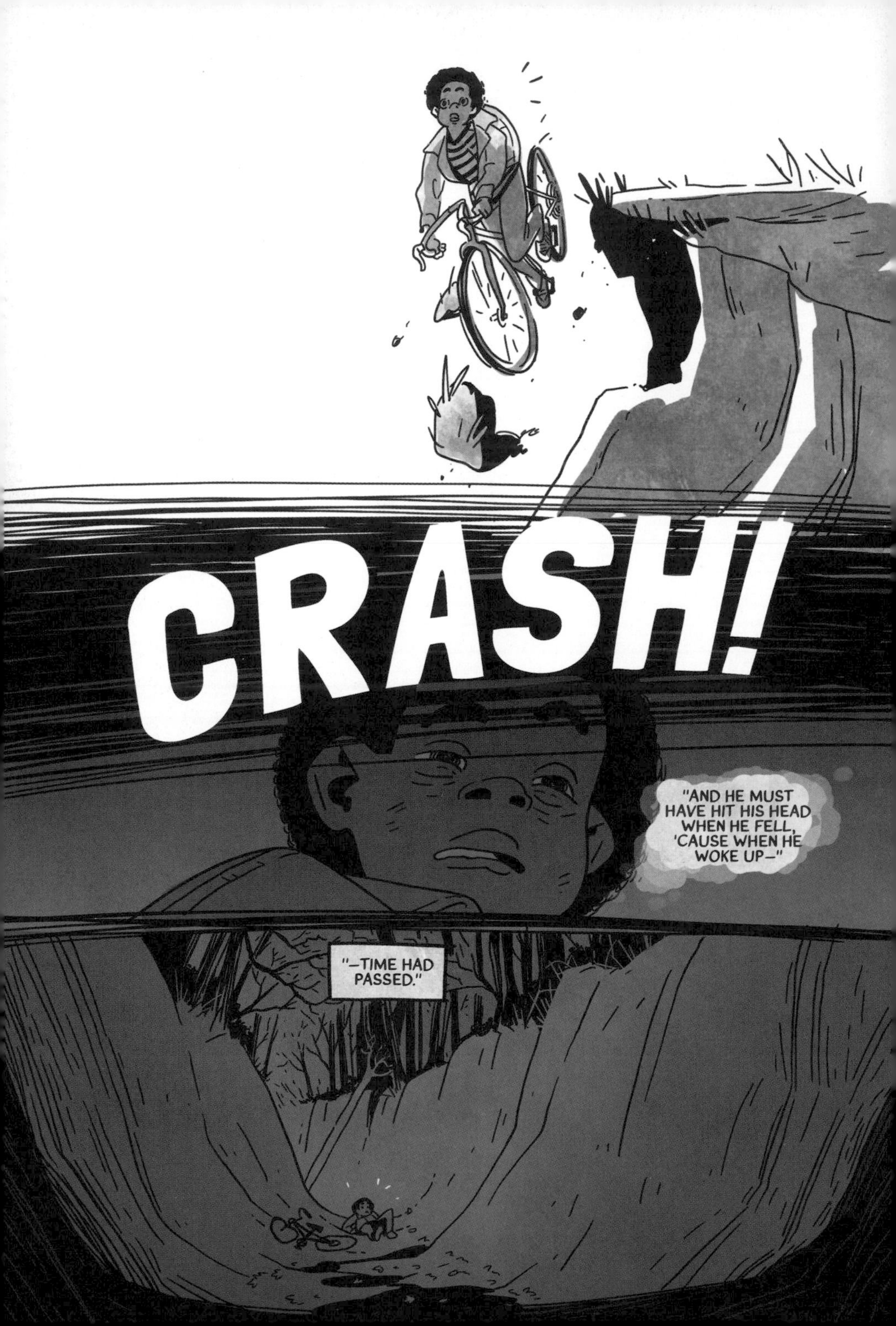
CRASH!
"AND HE MUST HAVE HIT HIS HEAD WHEN HE FELL, 'CAUSE WHEN HE WOKE UP—"
"—TIME HAD PASSED."

McKenzie County
Public Library

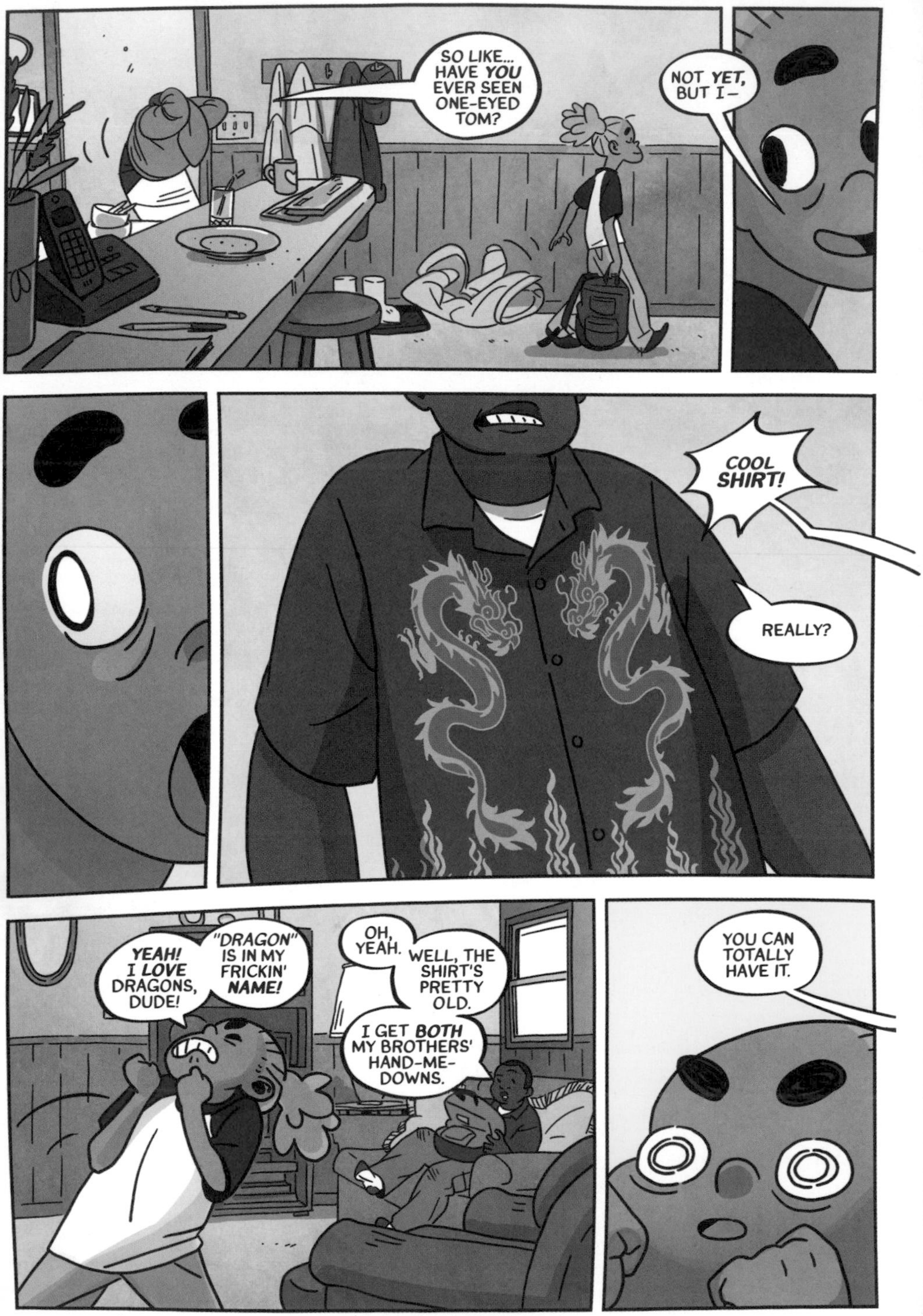
SO LIKE... HAVE *YOU* EVER SEEN ONE-EYED TOM?
NOT *YET,* BUT I—
COOL SHIRT!
REALLY?
YEAH! I *LOVE* DRAGONS, DUDE!
"*DRAGON*" IS IN MY FRICKIN' *NAME!*
OH, YEAH.
WELL, THE SHIRT'S PRETTY OLD.
I GET *BOTH* MY BROTHERS' HAND-ME-DOWNS.
YOU CAN TOTALLY HAVE IT.

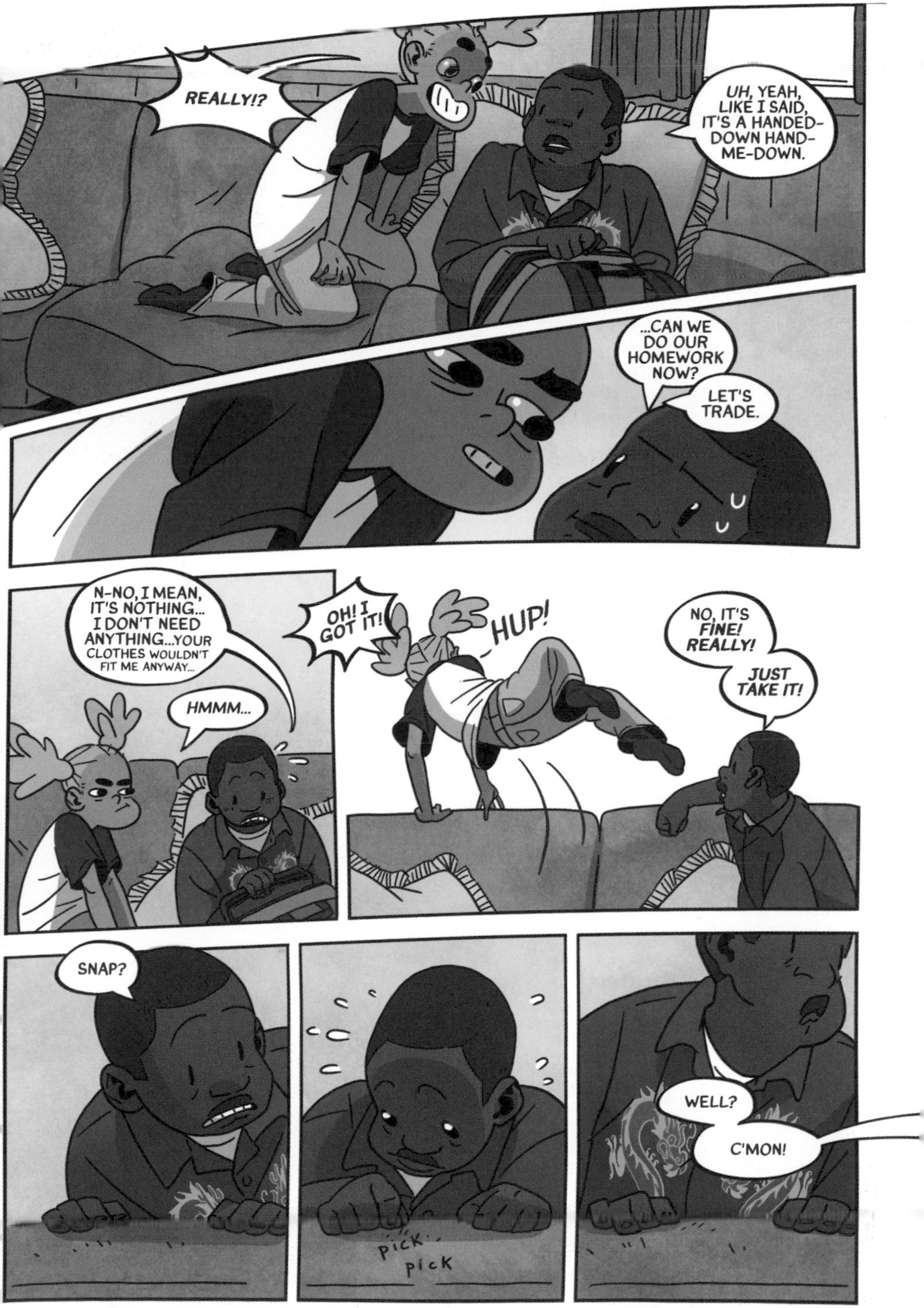
REALLY!?
UH, YEAH, LIKE I SAID, IT'S A HANDED-DOWN HAND-ME-DOWN.
...CAN WE DO OUR HOMEWORK NOW?
LET'S TRADE.
N-NO, I MEAN, IT'S NOTHING... I DON'T NEED ANYTHING...YOUR CLOTHES WOULDN'T FIT ME ANYWAY...
HMMM...
OH! I GOT IT!
HUP!
NO, IT'S FINE! REALLY!
JUST TAKE IT!
SNAP?
PICK PICK
WELL?
C'MON!

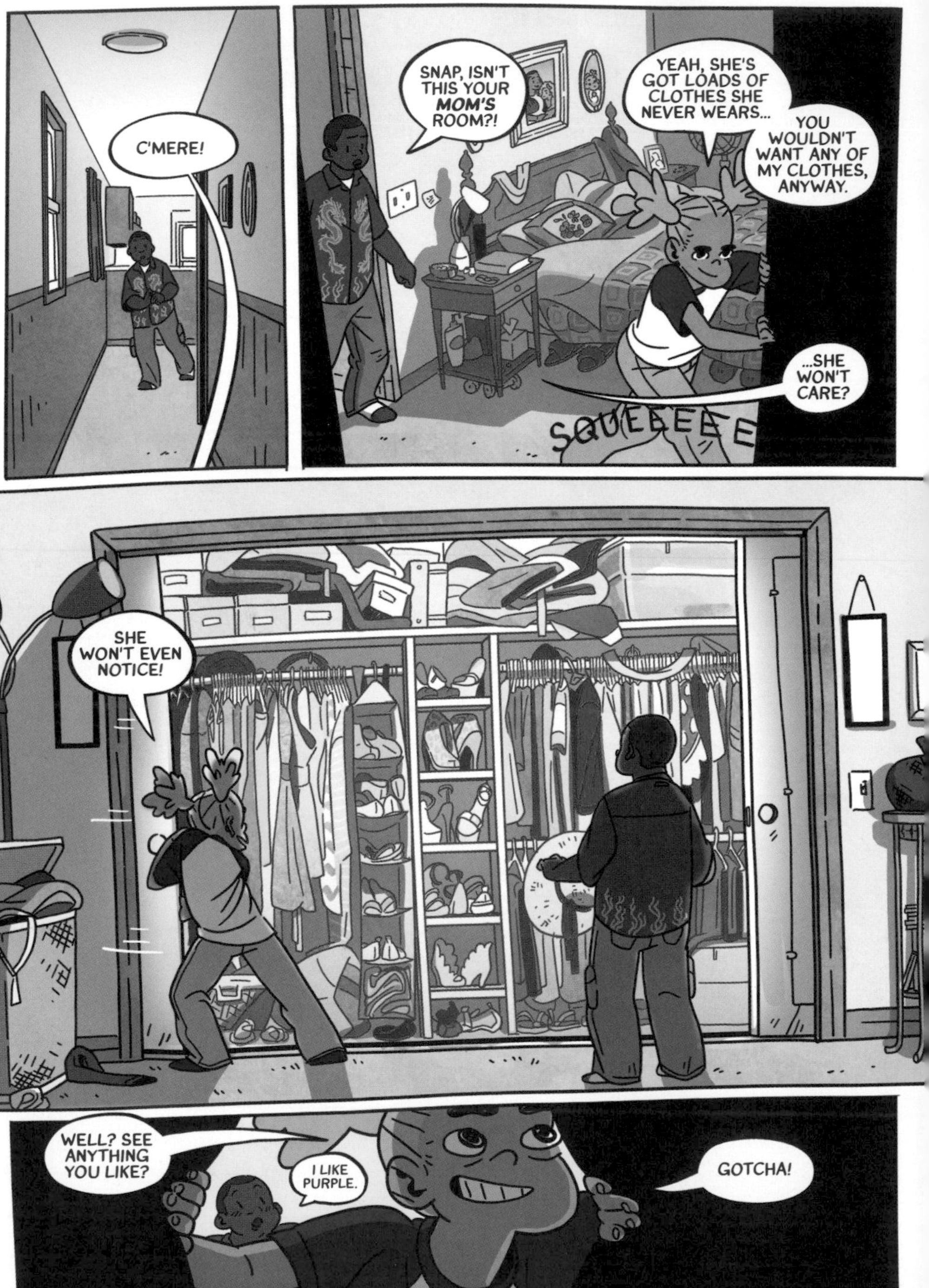
C'MERE!
SNAP, ISN'T THIS YOUR **MOM'S** ROOM?!
YEAH, SHE'S GOT LOADS OF CLOTHES SHE NEVER WEARS...
YOU WOULDN'T WANT ANY OF MY CLOTHES, ANYWAY.
...SHE WON'T CARE?
SQUEEEEE
SHE WON'T EVEN NOTICE!
WELL? SEE ANYTHING YOU LIKE?
I LIKE PURPLE.
GOTCHA!

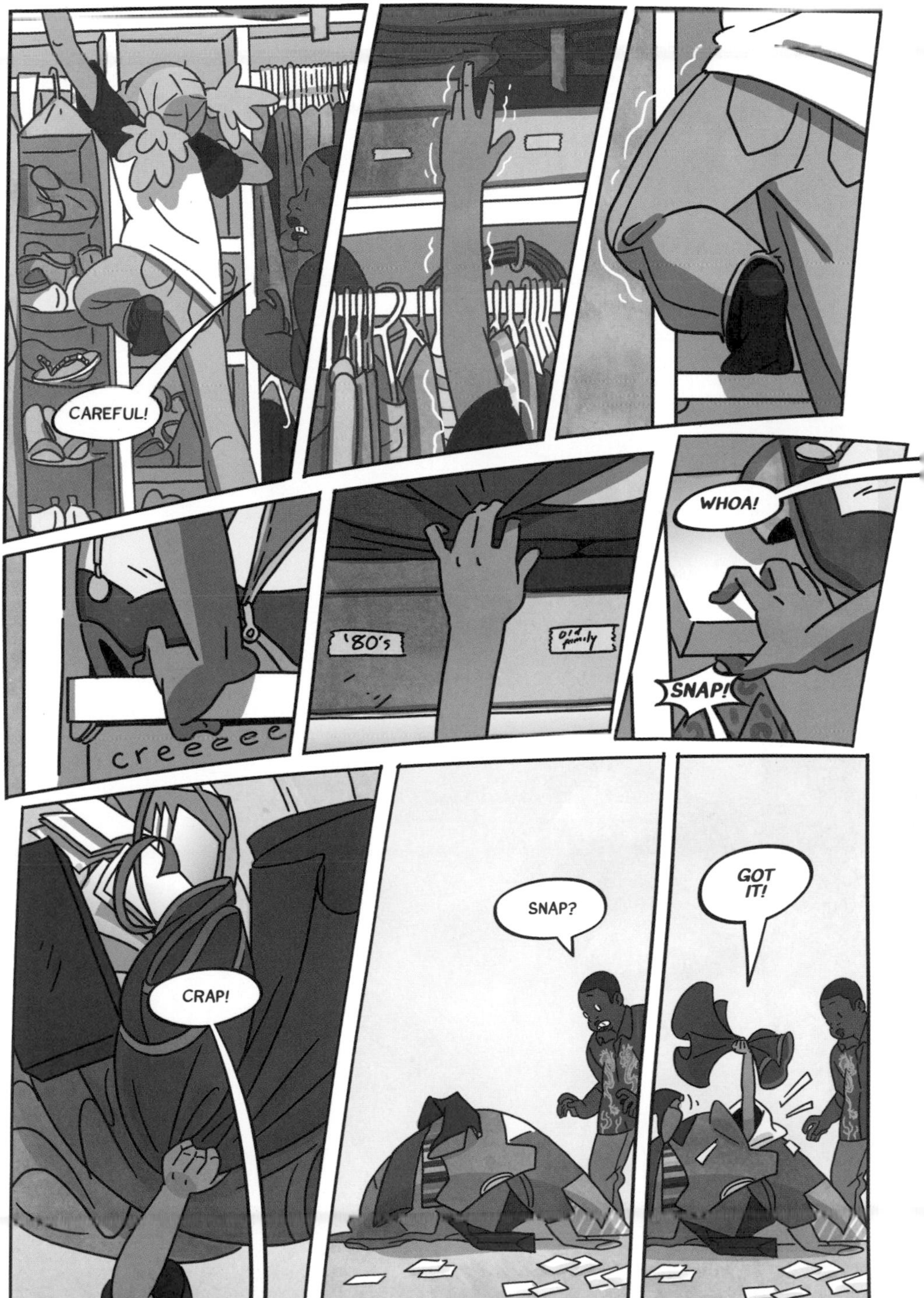
CAREFUL!
'80's
old family
creeeeee
WHOA!
SNAP!
CRAP!
SNAP?
GOT IT!

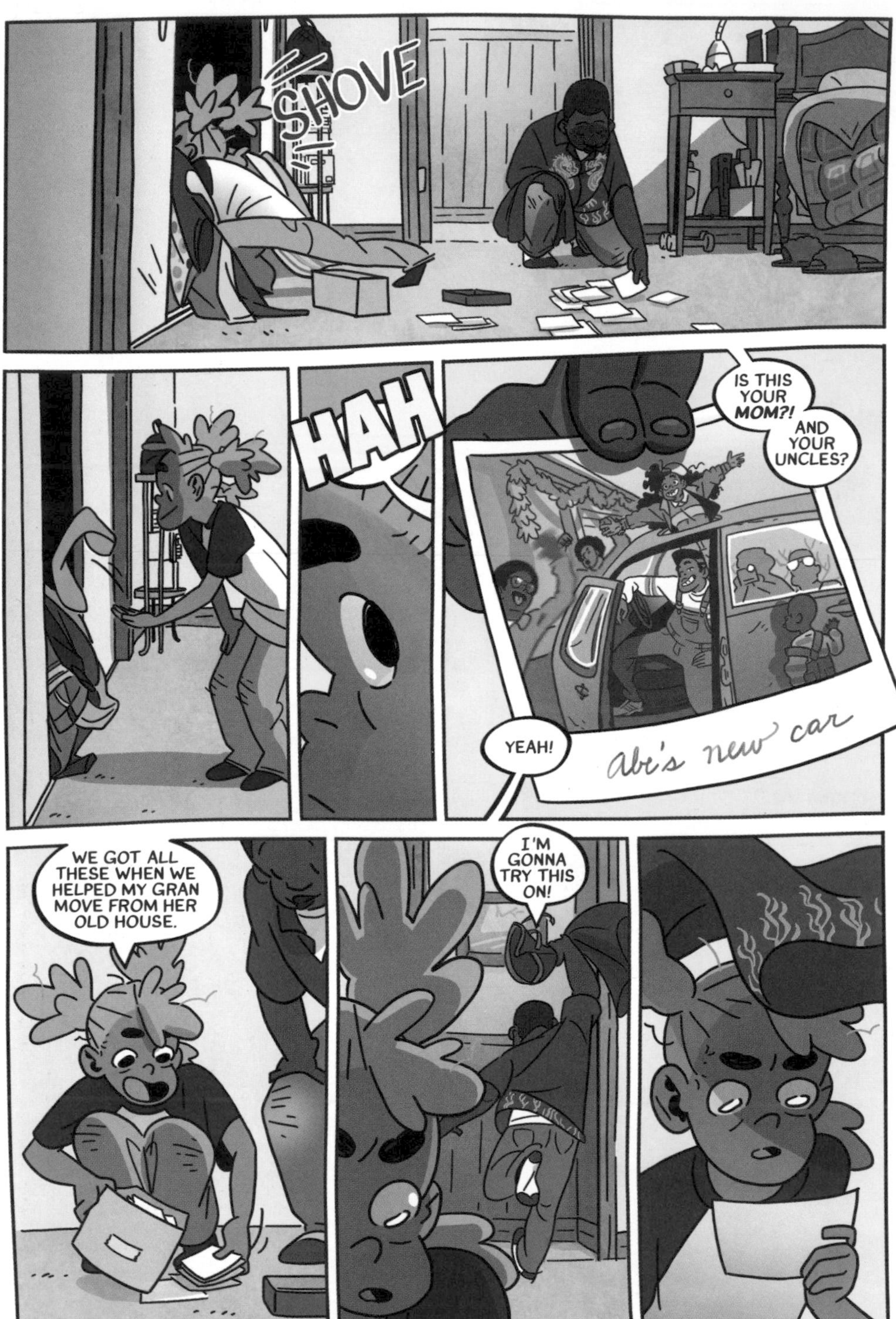

SHOVE
HAH
IS THIS YOUR *MOM?!*
AND YOUR UNCLES?
YEAH!
abi's new car
WE GOT ALL THESE WHEN WE HELPED MY GRAN MOVE FROM HER OLD HOUSE.
I'M GONNA TRY THIS ON!

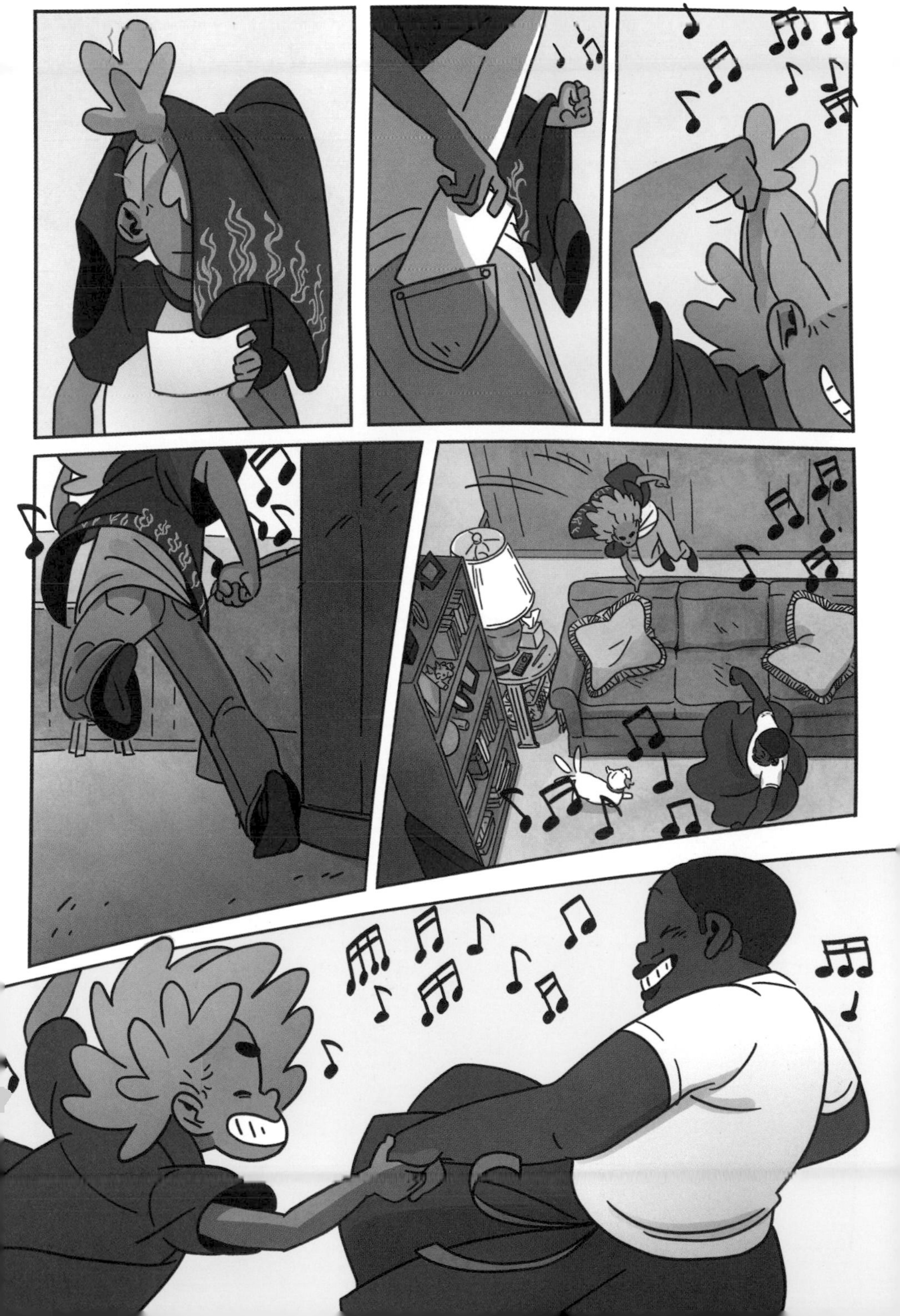

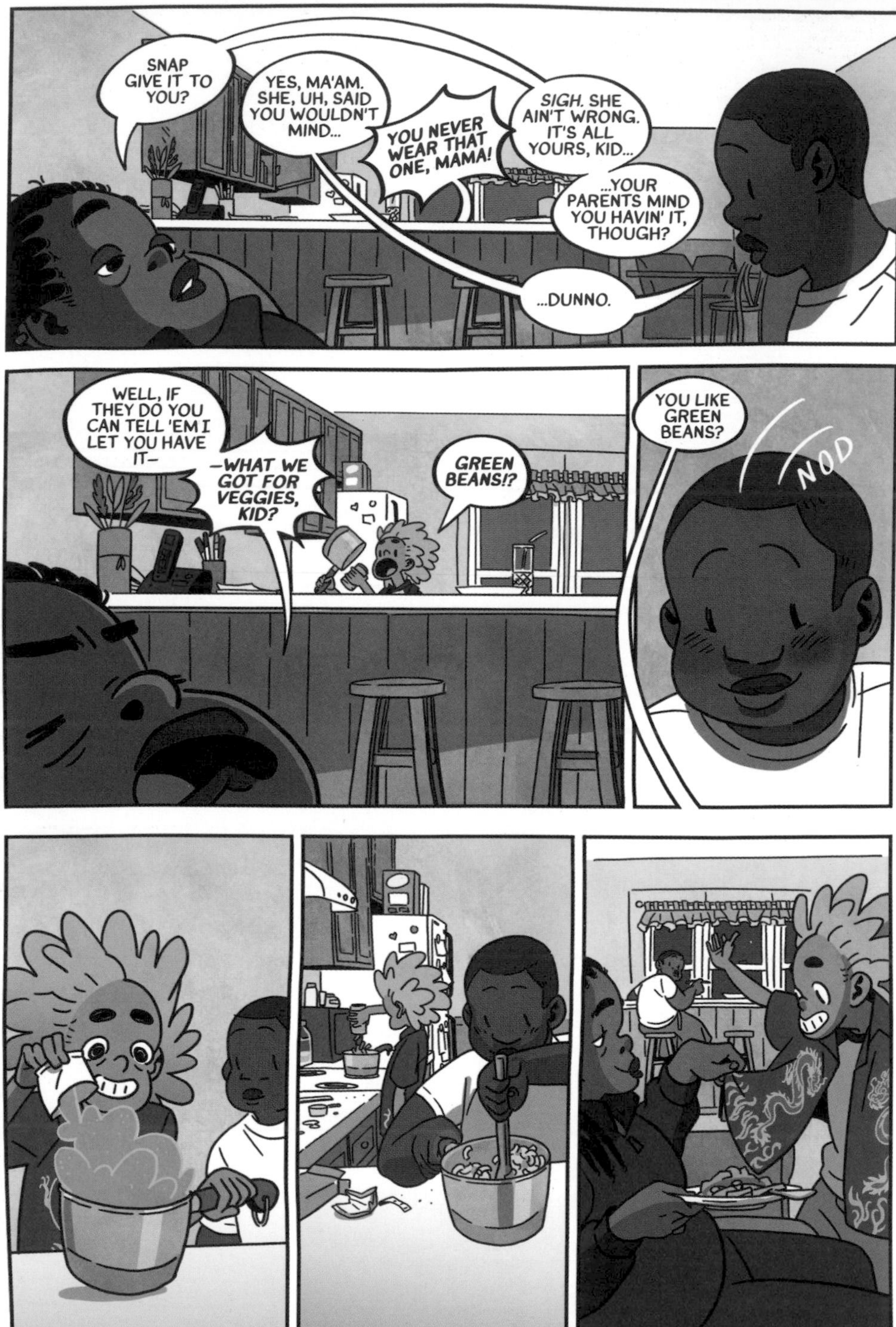
SNAP GIVE IT TO YOU?
YES, MA'AM. SHE, UH, SAID YOU WOULDN'T MIND...
YOU NEVER WEAR THAT ONE, MAMA!
SIGH. SHE AIN'T WRONG. IT'S ALL YOURS, KID...
...YOUR PARENTS MIND YOU HAVIN' IT, THOUGH?
...DUNNO.
WELL, IF THEY DO YOU CAN TELL 'EM I LET YOU HAVE IT—
—WHAT WE GOT FOR VEGGIES, KID?
GREEN BEANS!?
YOU LIKE GREEN BEANS?
NOD

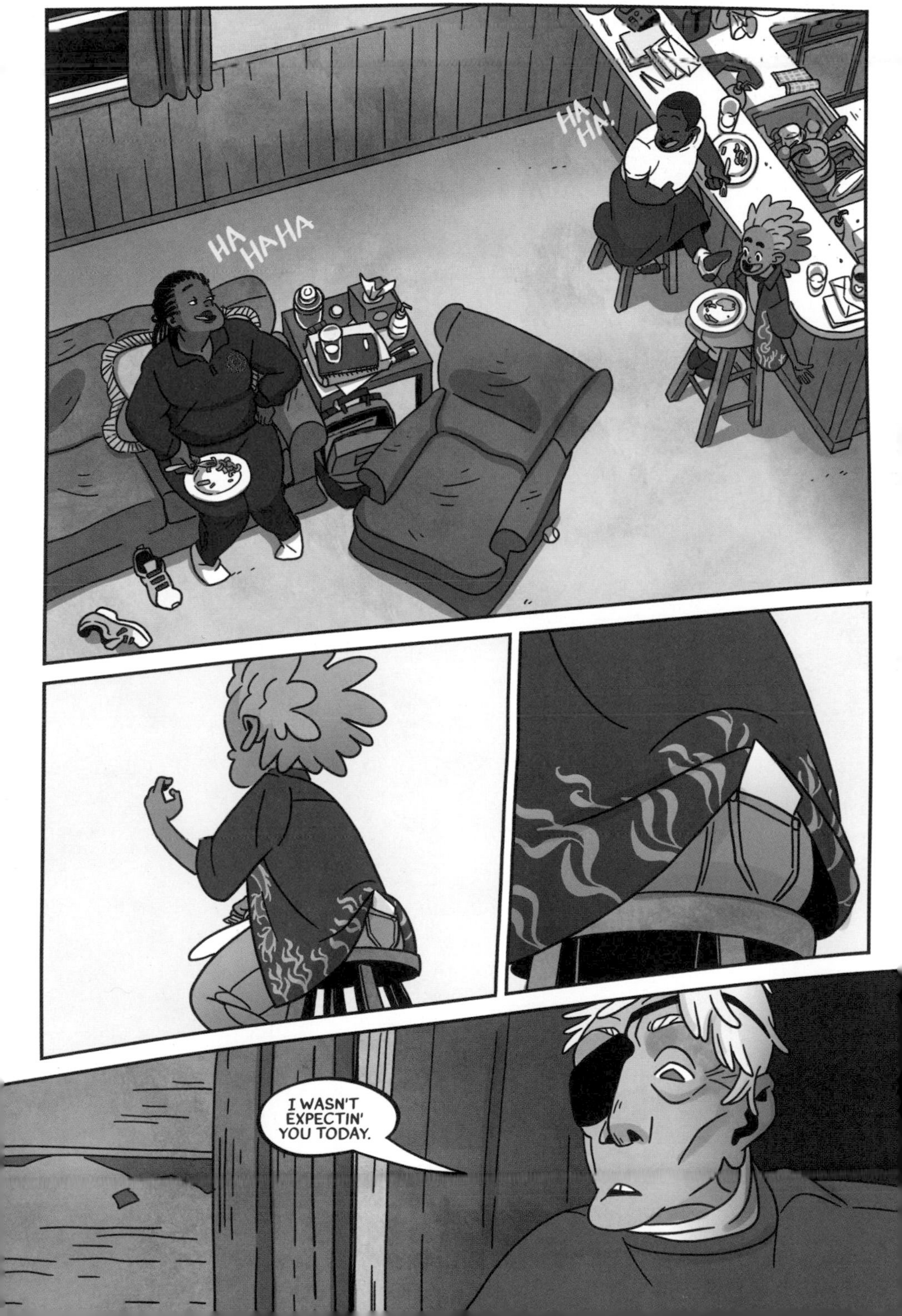
HA HA!
HA HAHA
I WASN'T EXPECTIN' YOU TODAY.

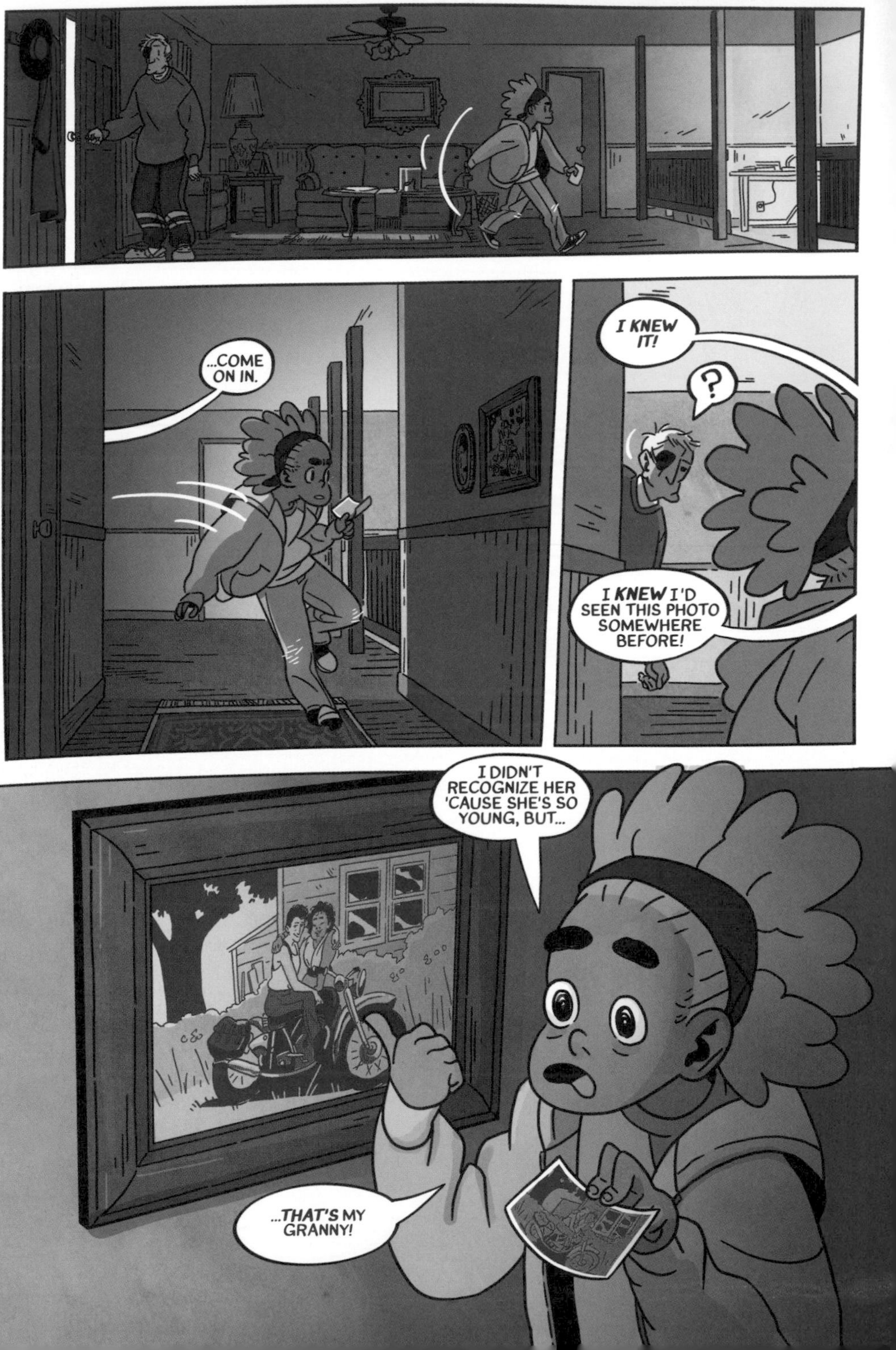
...COME ON IN.
I KNEW IT!
?
I KNEW I'D SEEN THIS PHOTO SOMEWHERE BEFORE!
I DIDN'T RECOGNIZE HER 'CAUSE SHE'S SO YOUNG, BUT...
...THAT'S MY GRANNY!

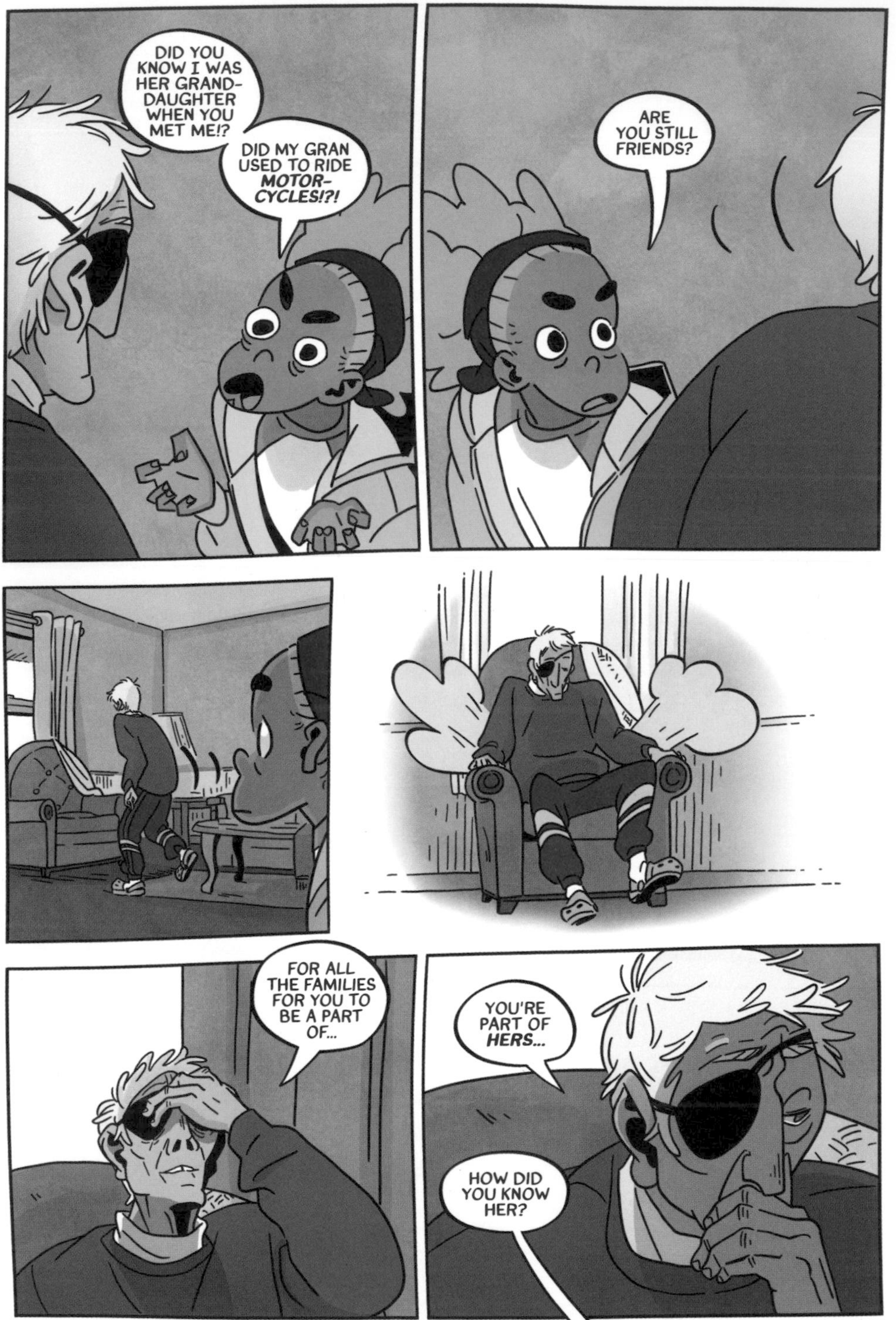

DID YOU KNOW I WAS HER GRAND-DAUGHTER WHEN YOU MET ME!?
DID MY GRAN USED TO RIDE *MOTOR-CYCLES!?!*
ARE YOU STILL FRIENDS?
FOR ALL THE FAMILIES FOR YOU TO BE A PART OF...
YOU'RE PART OF *HERS...*
HOW DID YOU KNOW HER?

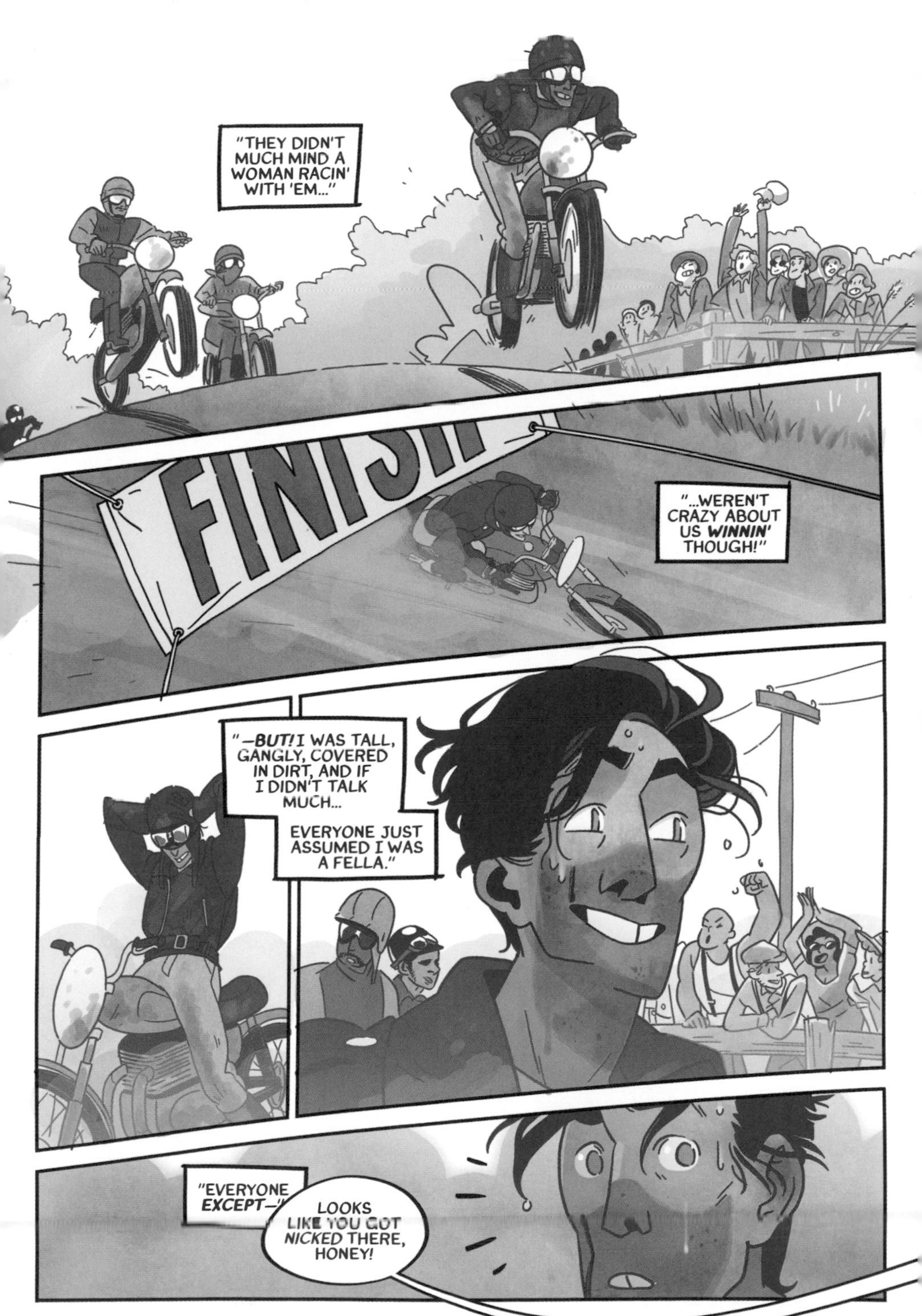
"THEY DIDN'T MUCH MIND A WOMAN RACIN' WITH 'EM..."
FINISH
"...WEREN'T CRAZY ABOUT US *WINNIN'* THOUGH!"
"—*BUT!* I WAS TALL, GANGLY, COVERED IN DIRT, AND IF I DIDN'T TALK MUCH...
EVERYONE JUST ASSUMED I WAS A FELLA."
"EVERYONE *EXCEPT*—"
LOOKS LIKE YOU GOT *NICKED* THERE, HONEY!

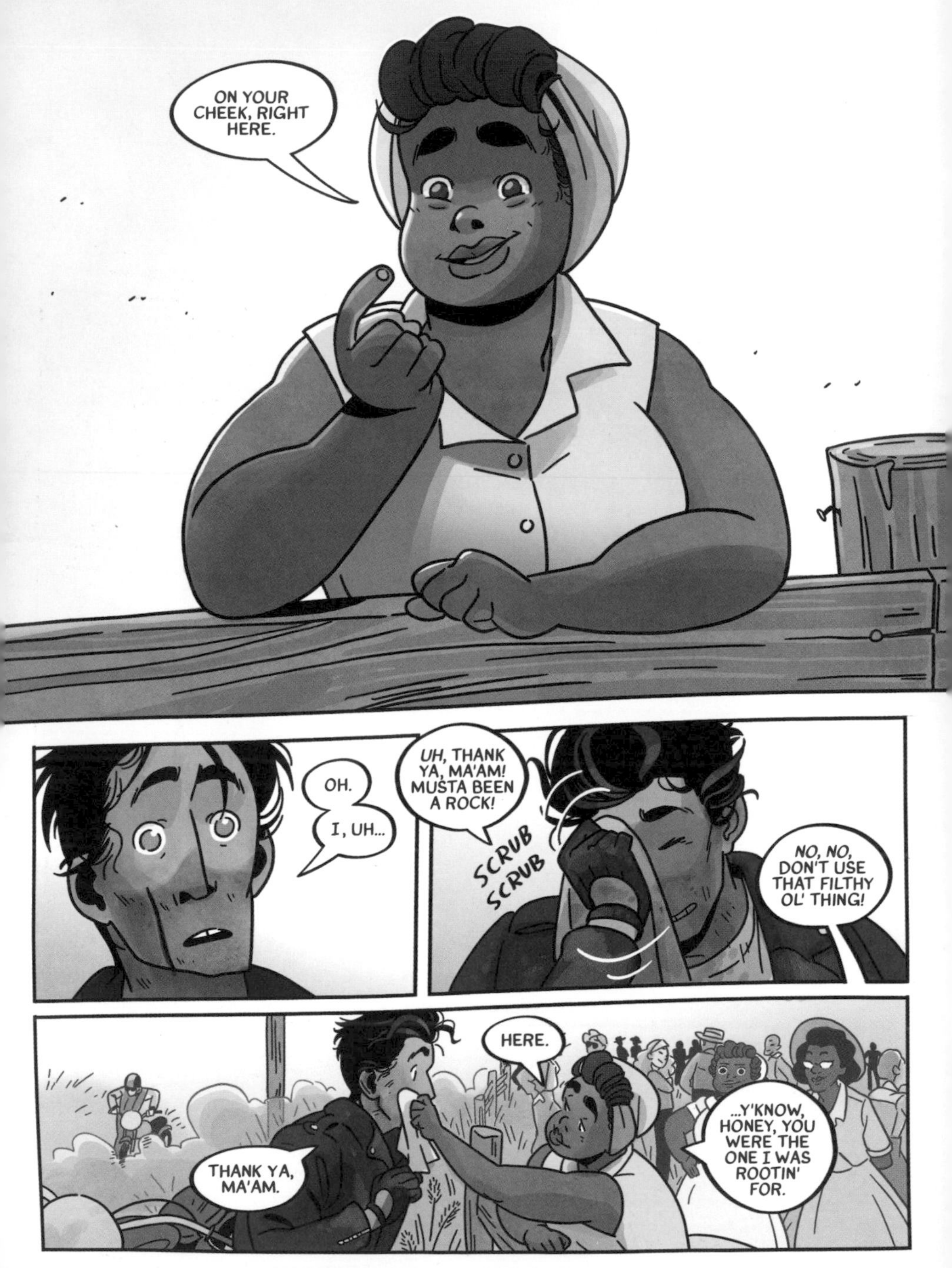
ON YOUR CHEEK, RIGHT HERE.
OH.
I, UH...
UH, THANK YA, MA'AM! MUSTA BEEN A ROCK!
SCRUB SCRUB
NO, NO, DON'T USE THAT FILTHY OL' THING!
HERE.
THANK YA, MA'AM.
...Y'KNOW, HONEY, YOU WERE THE ONE I WAS ROOTIN' FOR.

93

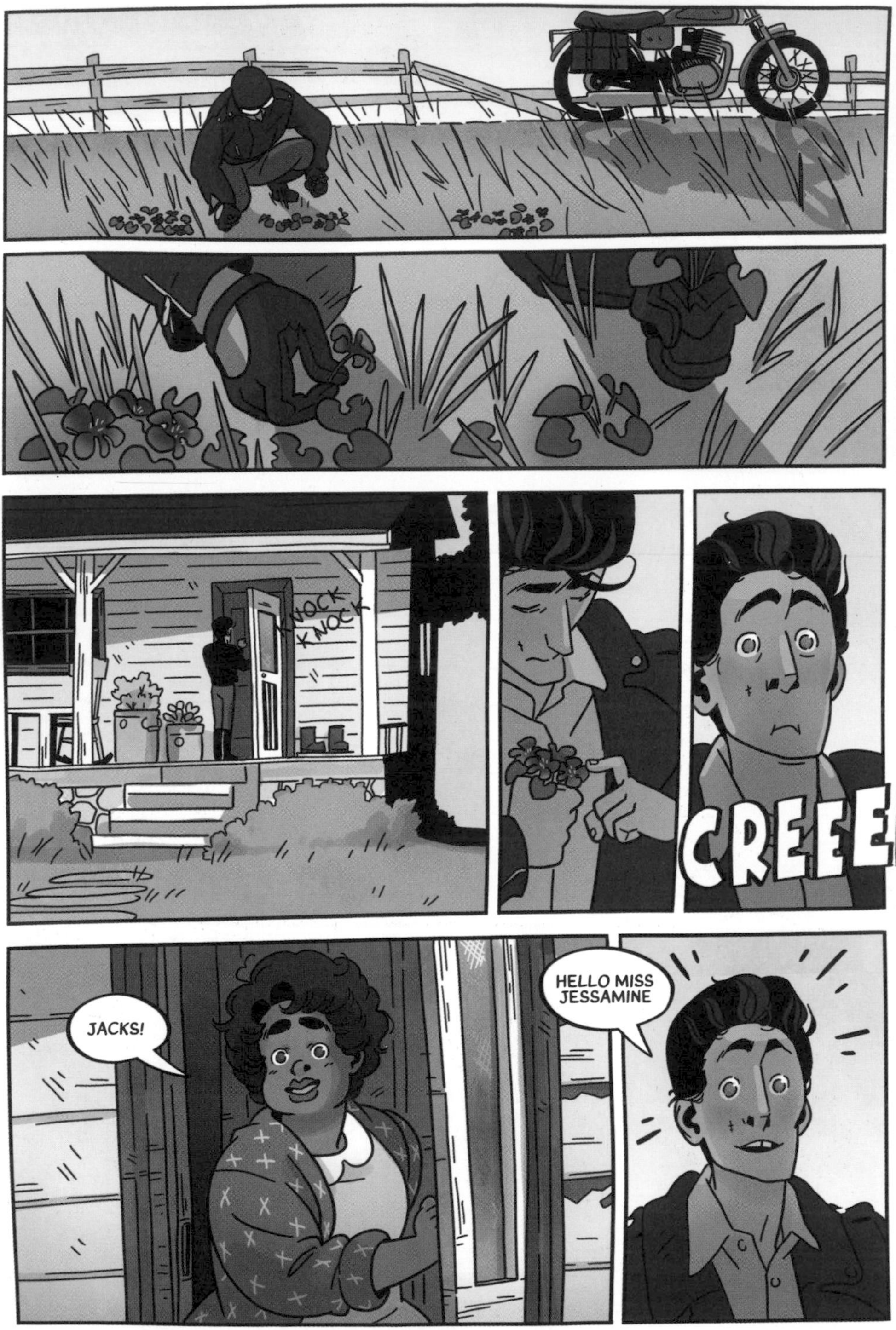
KNOCK KNOCK
CREEE
JACKS!
HELLO MISS JESSAMINE

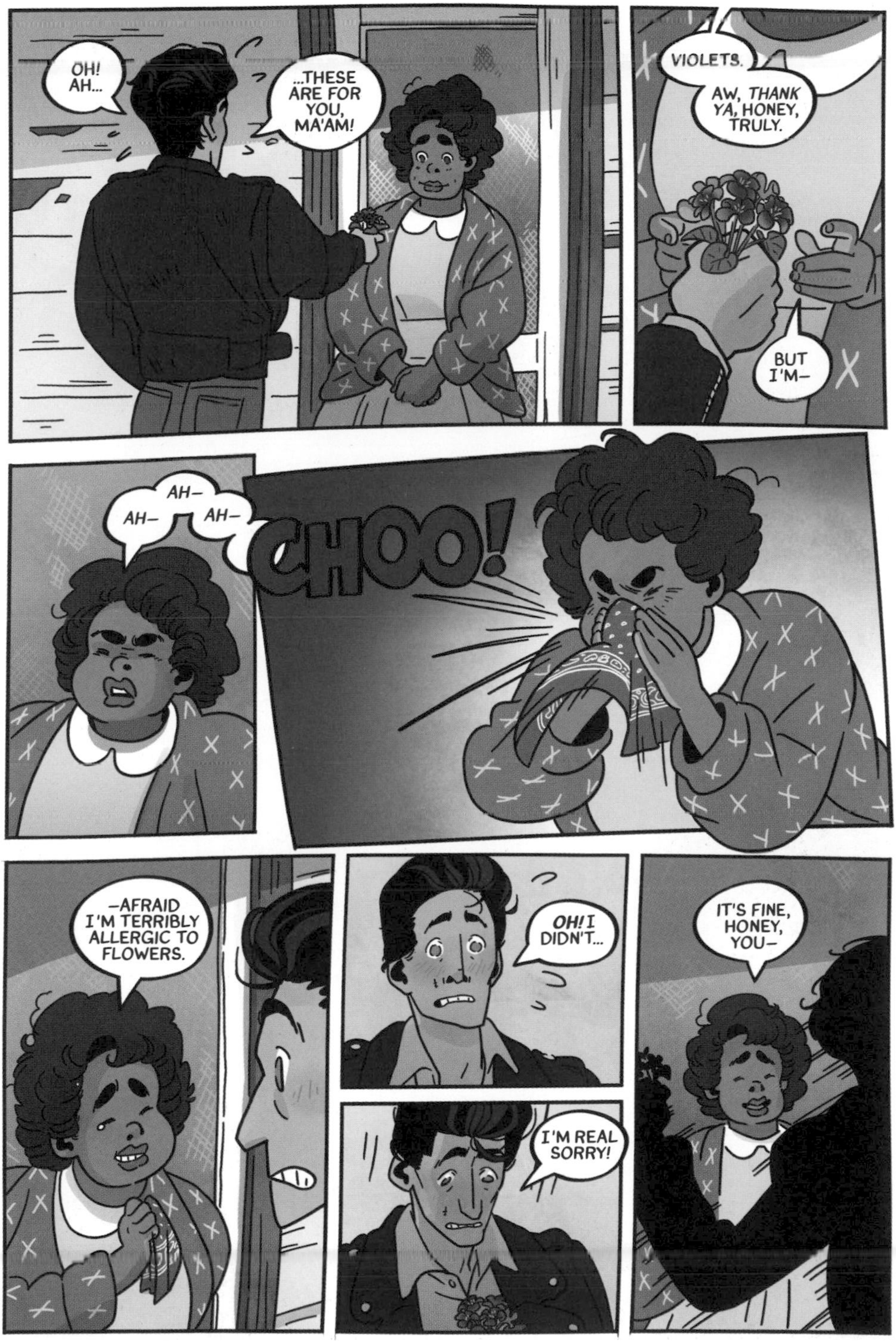
OH! AH...
...THESE ARE FOR YOU, MA'AM!
VIOLETS.
AW, *THANK YA*, HONEY, TRULY.
BUT I'M—
AH— AH— AH—
CHOO!
—AFRAID I'M TERRIBLY ALLERGIC TO FLOWERS.
OH! I DIDN'T...
I'M REAL SORRY!
IT'S FINE, HONEY, YOU—

"LOTTA FOLKS SAW US TWO TOGETHER AS *ALL KINDS* OF WRONG..."

"...SO WE HAD TO MAKE THE MOST OF IT!"

"AND *SOME* GOOD FOLKS STILL SAW US AS NEIGHBORS."

"I COULDA STAYED LIKE THAT, WITH JESSAMINE, FOREVER."

"WE WERE *HAPPY*."

"BUT THERE WAS ONE THING..."

IT JUST AIN'T FAIR!

MY FAMILY GOT *ONE* TRADITION:

NAMIN' OUR BABY GIRLS AFTER OUR *FAVORITE FLOWERS.*

SHOULD BE THE SIMPLEST THING IN THE WORLD, HM?

I AIN'T EVER LIKED A FLOWER MY *WHOLE LIFE!*

SO WHAT AM I SUPPOSED TO DO...

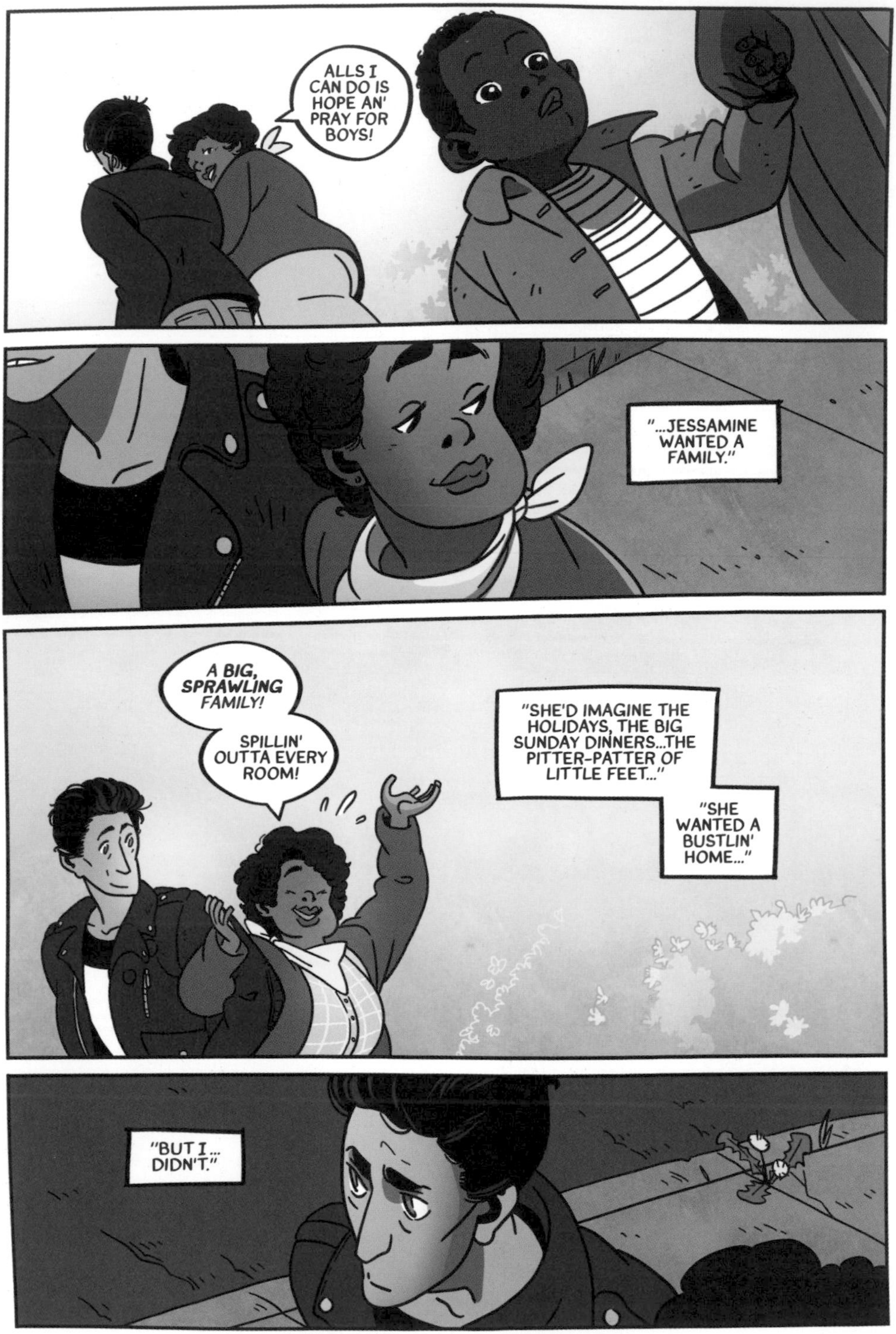

ALLS I CAN DO IS HOPE AN' PRAY FOR BOYS!
"...JESSAMINE WANTED A FAMILY."
A *BIG, SPRAWLING* FAMILY!
SPILLIN' OUTTA EVERY ROOM!
"SHE'D IMAGINE THE HOLIDAYS, THE BIG SUNDAY DINNERS...THE PITTER-PATTER OF LITTLE FEET..."
"SHE WANTED A BUSTLIN' HOME..."
"BUT I... DIDN'T."

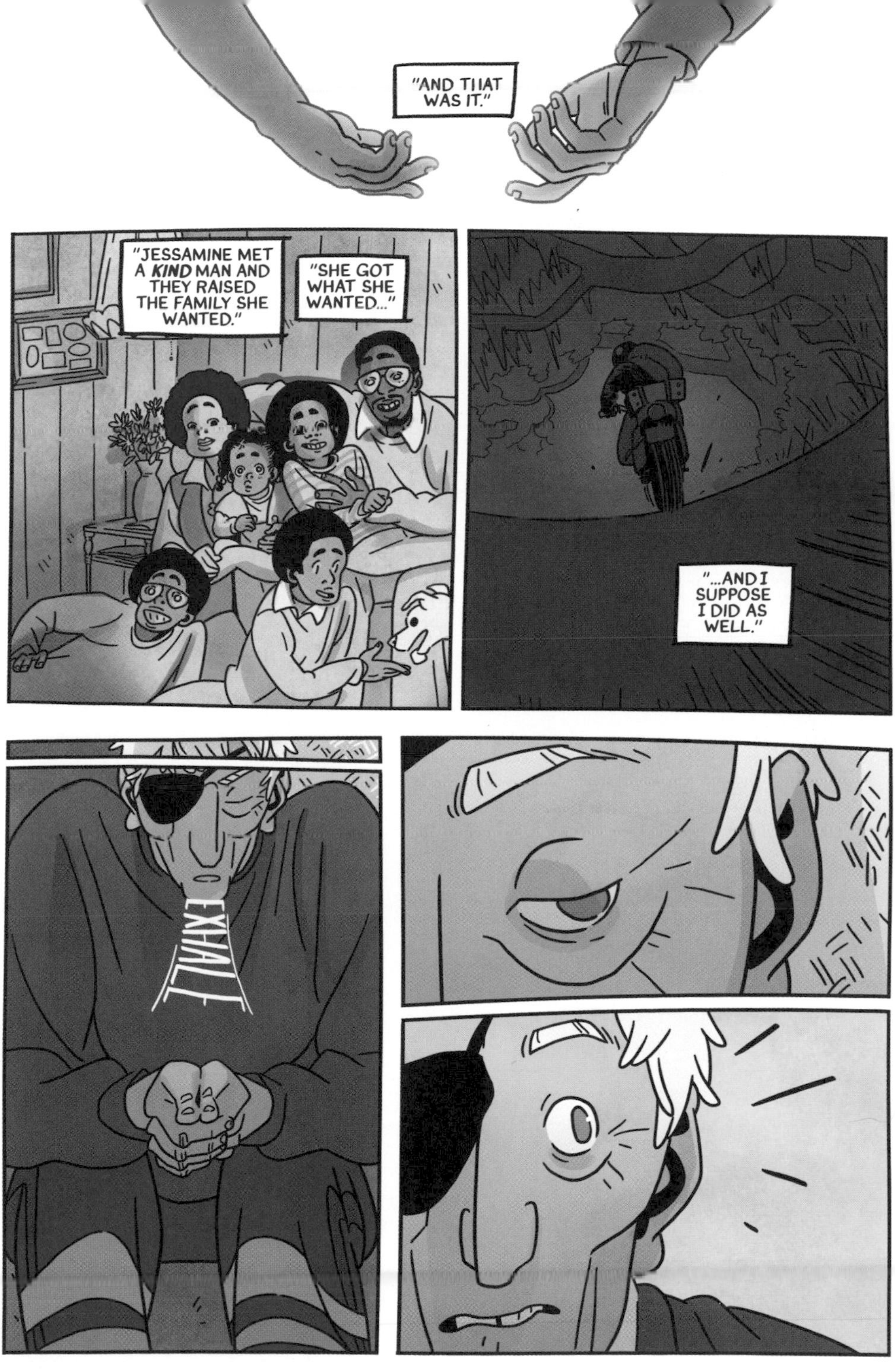
"AND THAT WAS IT."
"JESSAMINE MET A KIND MAN AND THEY RAISED THE FAMILY SHE WANTED."
"SHE GOT WHAT SHE WANTED..."
"...AND I SUPPOSE I DID AS WELL."
EXHALE

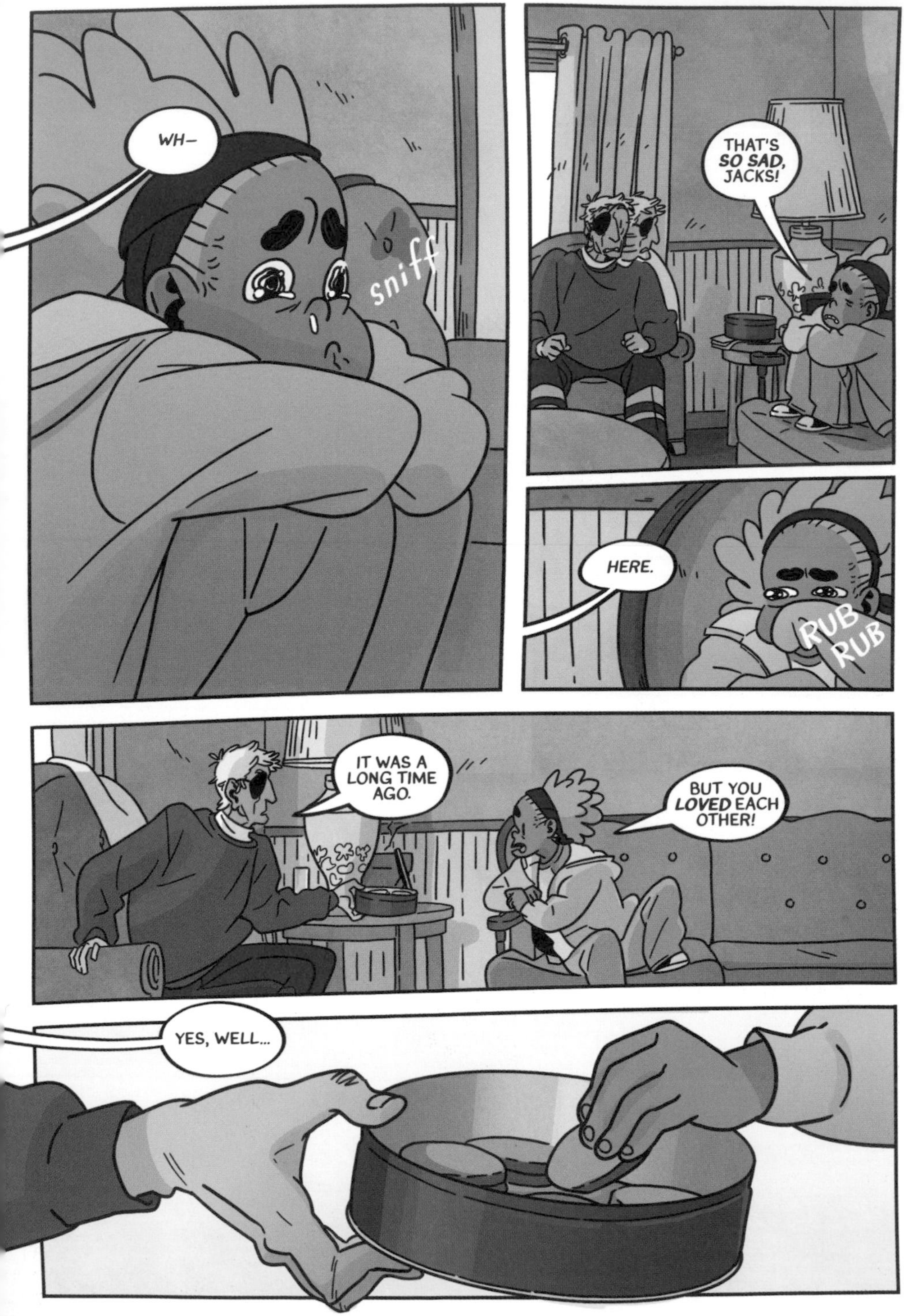
WH–
sniff
THAT'S SO SAD, JACKS!
HERE.
RUB RUB
IT WAS A LONG TIME AGO.
BUT YOU LOVED EACH OTHER!
YES, WELL...

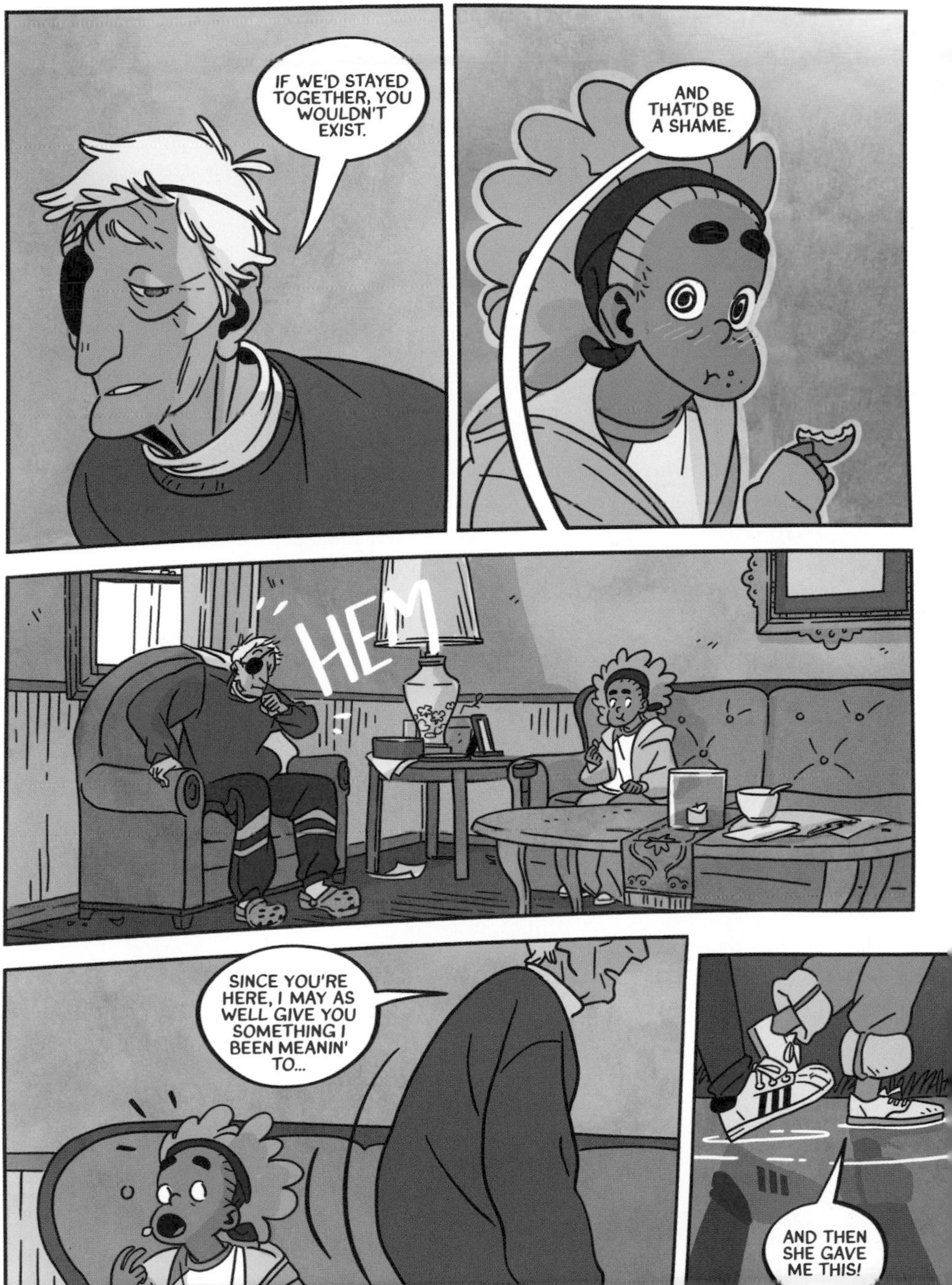

IF WE'D STAYED TOGETHER, YOU WOULDN'T EXIST.
AND THAT'D BE A SHAME.
HEM
SINCE YOU'RE HERE, I MAY AS WELL GIVE YOU SOMETHING I BEEN MEANIN' TO...
wsh wsh wsh
AND THEN SHE GAVE ME THIS!

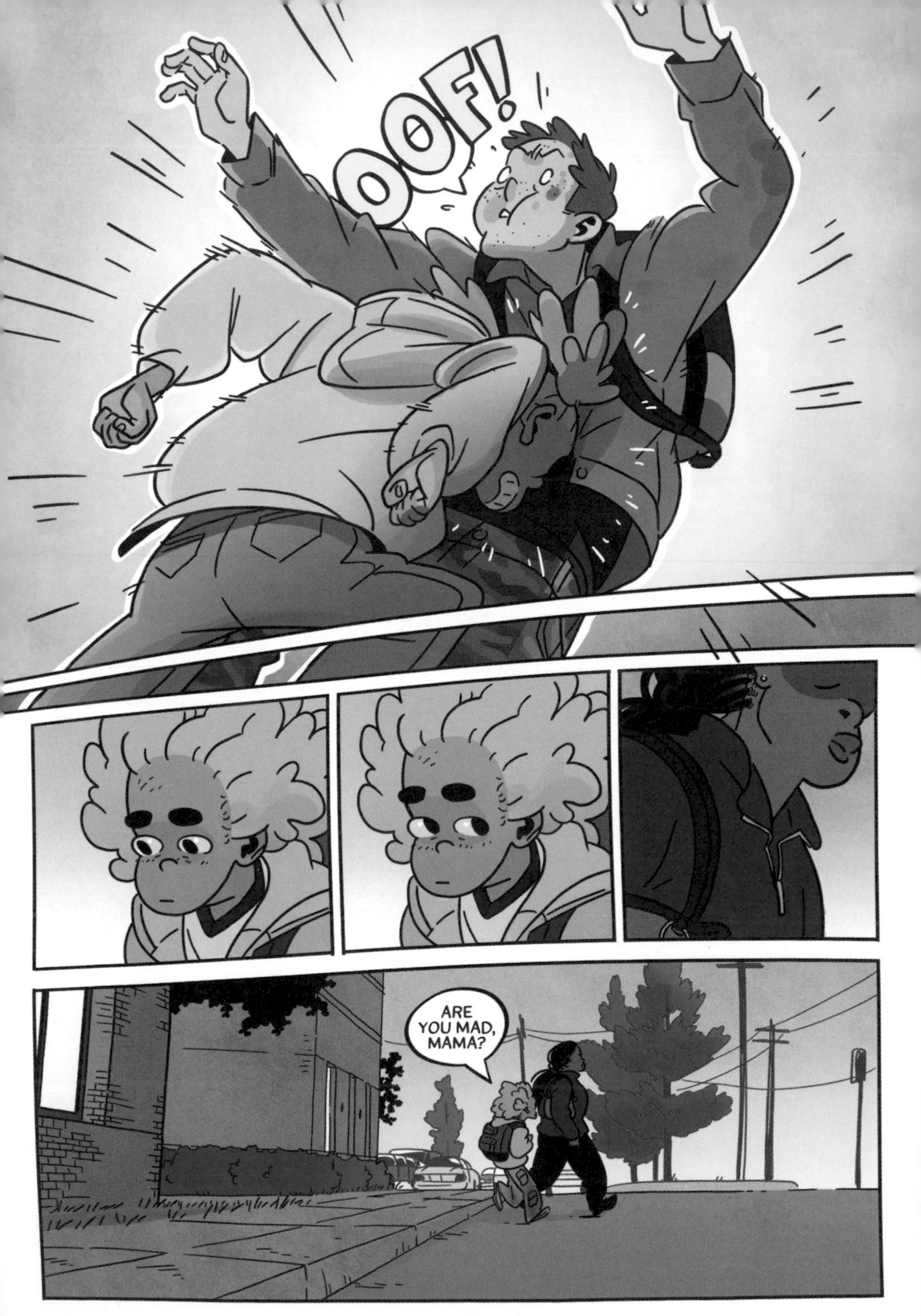
OOOF!
ARE YOU MAD, MAMA?

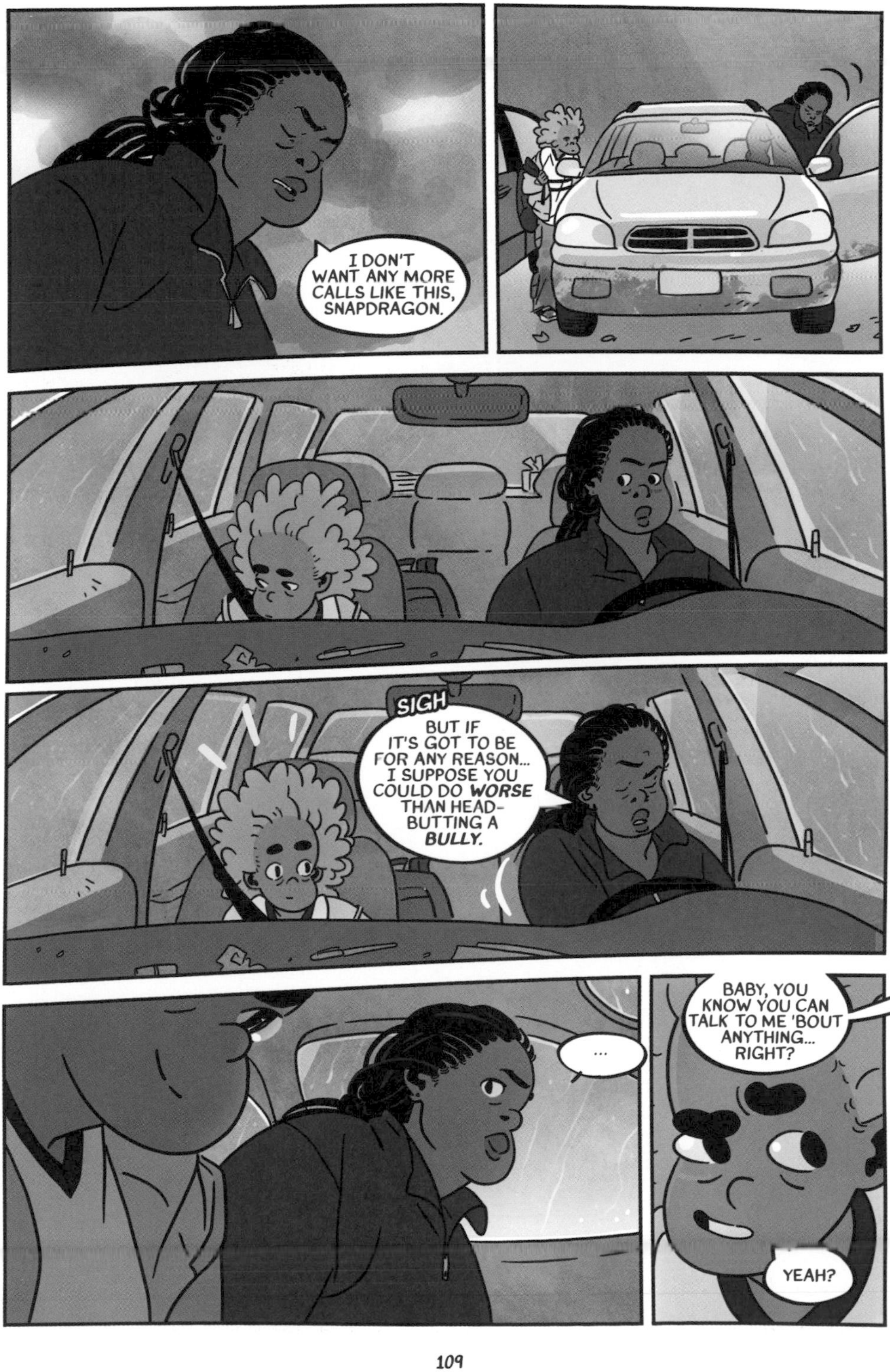
I DON'T WANT ANY MORE CALLS LIKE THIS, SNAPDRAGON.
SIGH
BUT IF IT'S GOT TO BE FOR ANY REASON... I SUPPOSE YOU COULD DO **WORSE** THAN HEAD-BUTTING A ***BULLY.***
...
BABY, YOU KNOW YOU CAN TALK TO ME 'BOUT ANYTHING... RIGHT?
YEAH?

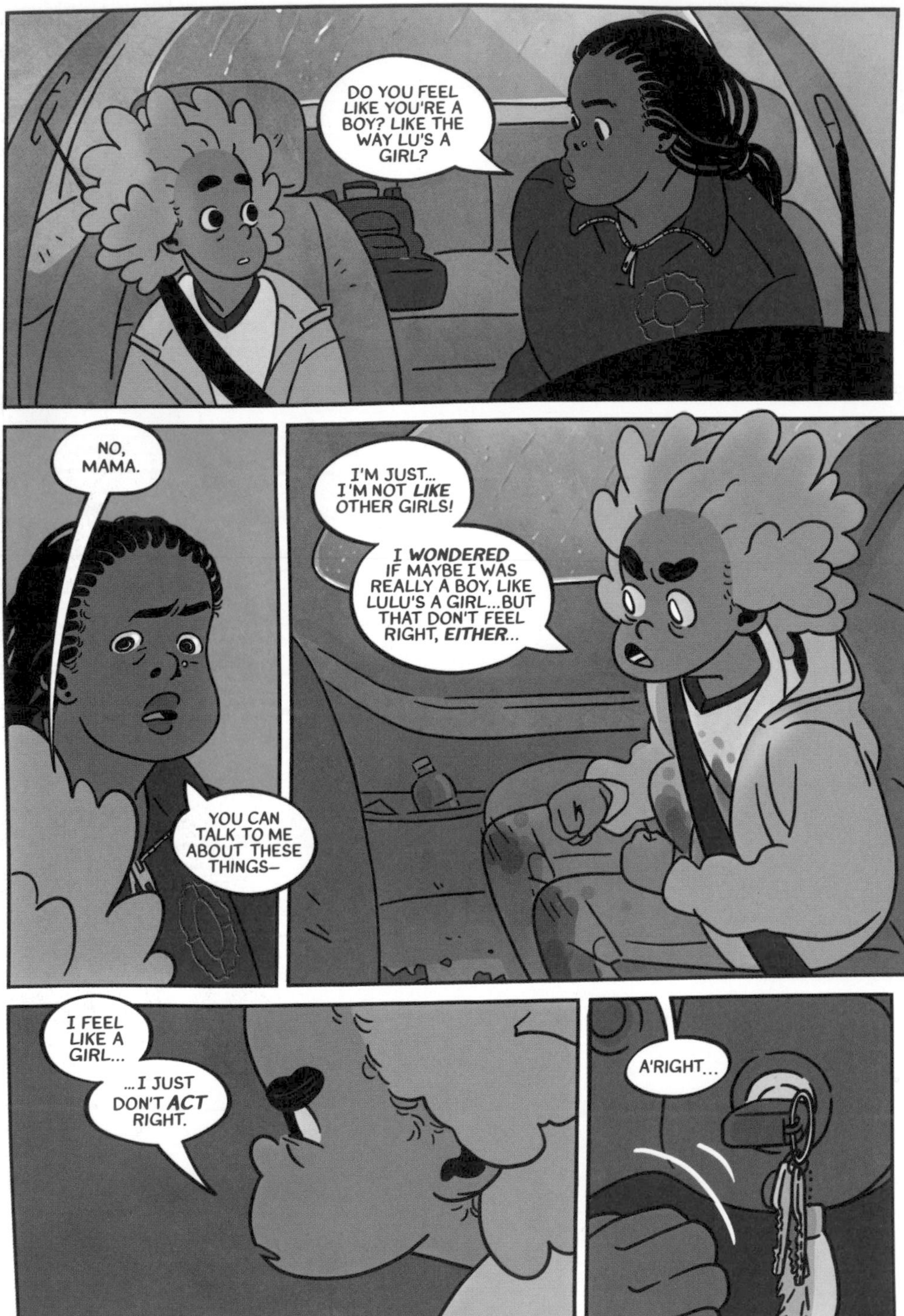
DO YOU FEEL LIKE YOU'RE A BOY? LIKE THE WAY LU'S A GIRL?
NO, MAMA.
I'M JUST... I'M NOT *LIKE* OTHER GIRLS!
I *WONDERED* IF MAYBE I WAS REALLY A BOY, LIKE LULU'S A GIRL...BUT THAT DON'T FEEL RIGHT, *EITHER*...
YOU CAN TALK TO ME ABOUT THESE THINGS–
I FEEL LIKE A GIRL...
...I JUST DON'T *ACT* RIGHT.
A'RIGHT...

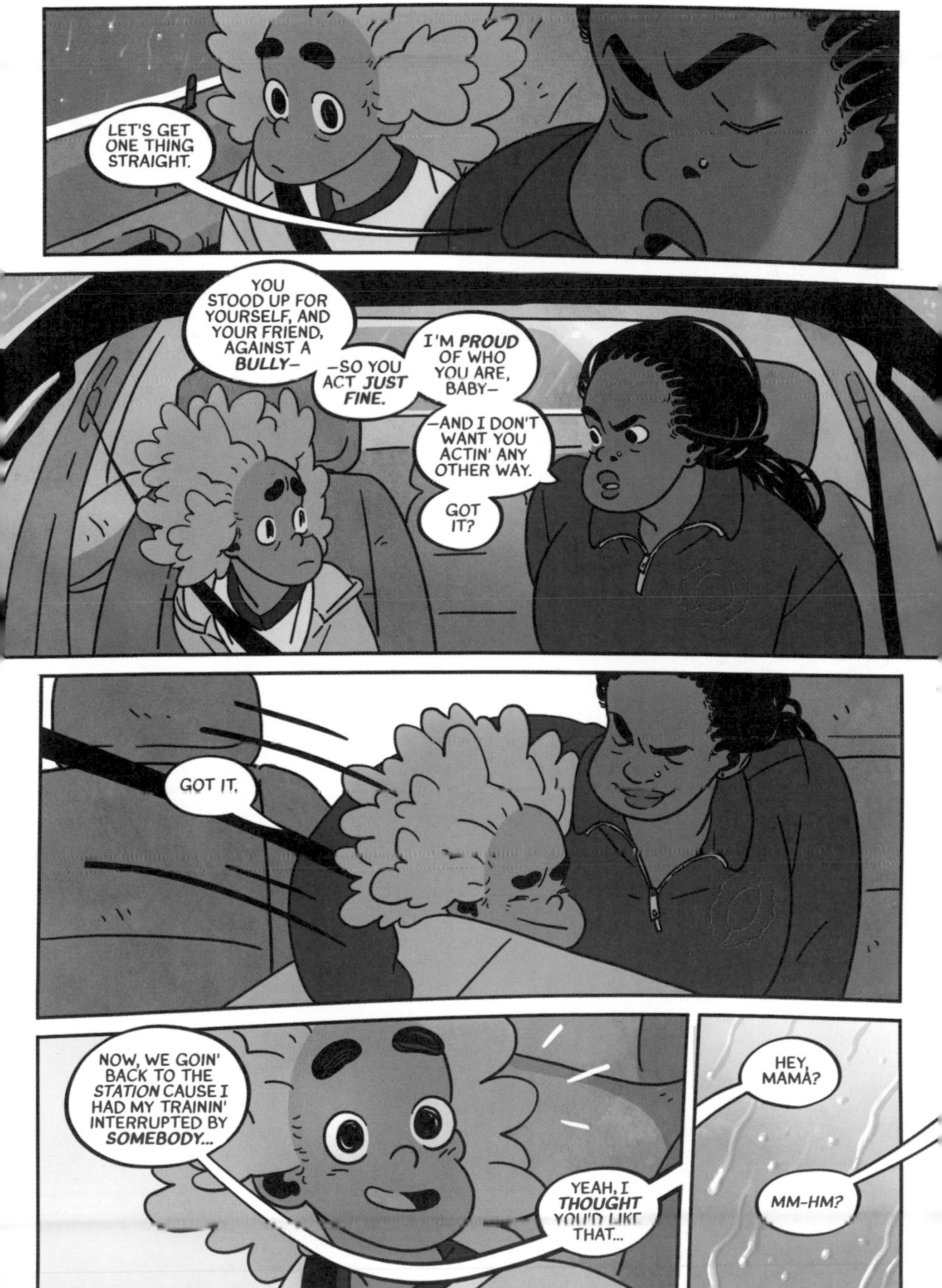

LET'S GET ONE THING STRAIGHT.
YOU STOOD UP FOR YOURSELF, AND YOUR FRIEND, AGAINST A BULLY–
–SO YOU ACT JUST FINE.
I'M PROUD OF WHO YOU ARE, BABY–
–AND I DON'T WANT YOU ACTIN' ANY OTHER WAY.
GOT IT?
GOT IT.
NOW, WE GOIN' BACK TO THE STATION CAUSE I HAD MY TRAININ' INTERRUPTED BY SOMEBODY...
YEAH, I THOUGHT YOU'D LIKE THAT...
HEY, MAMA?
MM-HM?

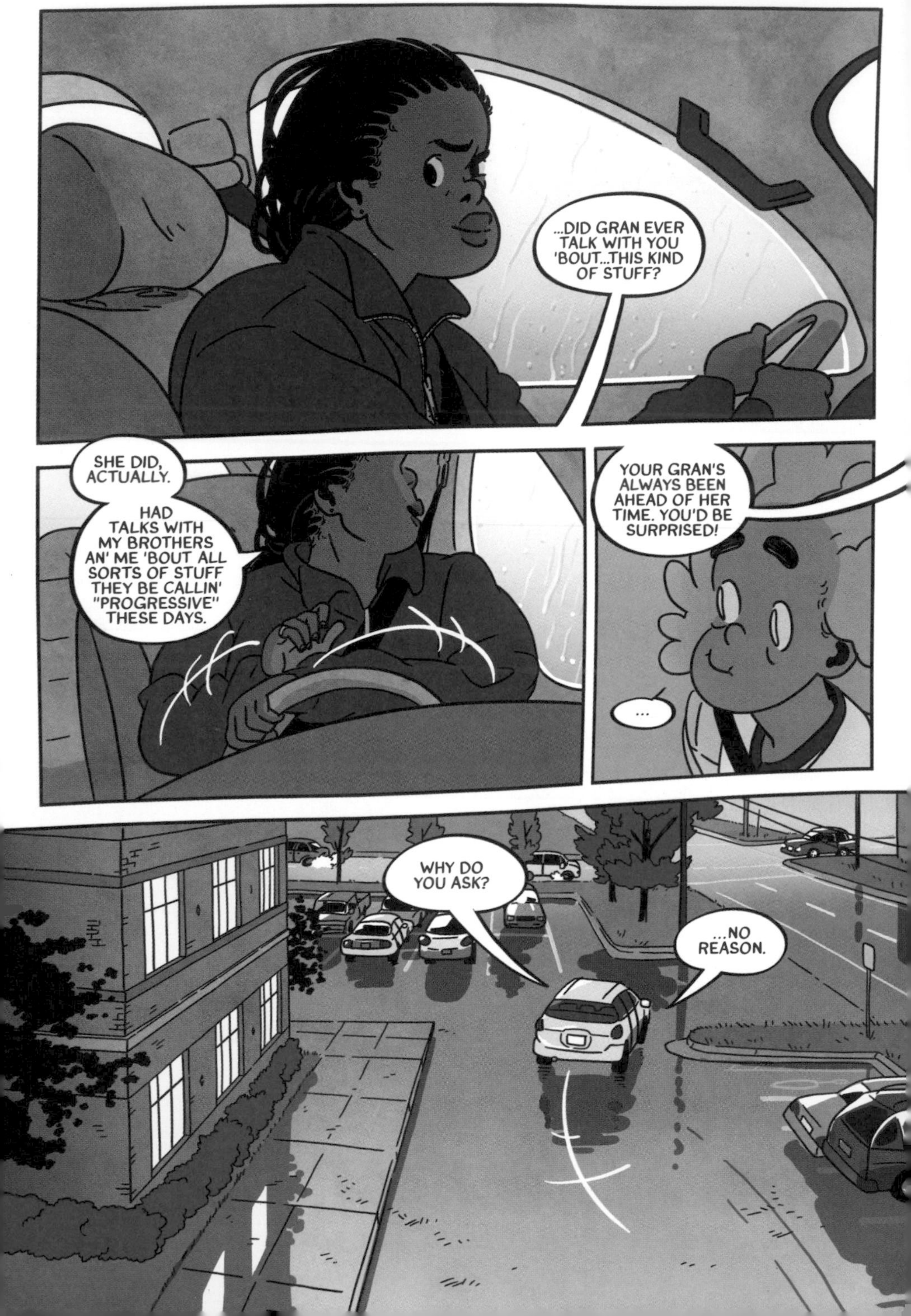
...DID GRAN EVER TALK WITH YOU 'BOUT...THIS KIND OF STUFF?
SHE DID, ACTUALLY.
HAD TALKS WITH MY BROTHERS AN' ME 'BOUT ALL SORTS OF STUFF THEY BE CALLIN' "PROGRESSIVE" THESE DAYS.
YOUR GRAN'S ALWAYS BEEN AHEAD OF HER TIME. YOU'D BE SURPRISED!
...
WHY DO YOU ASK?
...NO REASON.

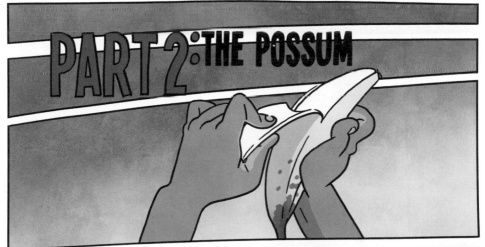

PART 2: THE POSSUM

AAAW, ARE YOU FEELING LEFT OUT, GEEBIES?

HERE YOU GO!

READY?

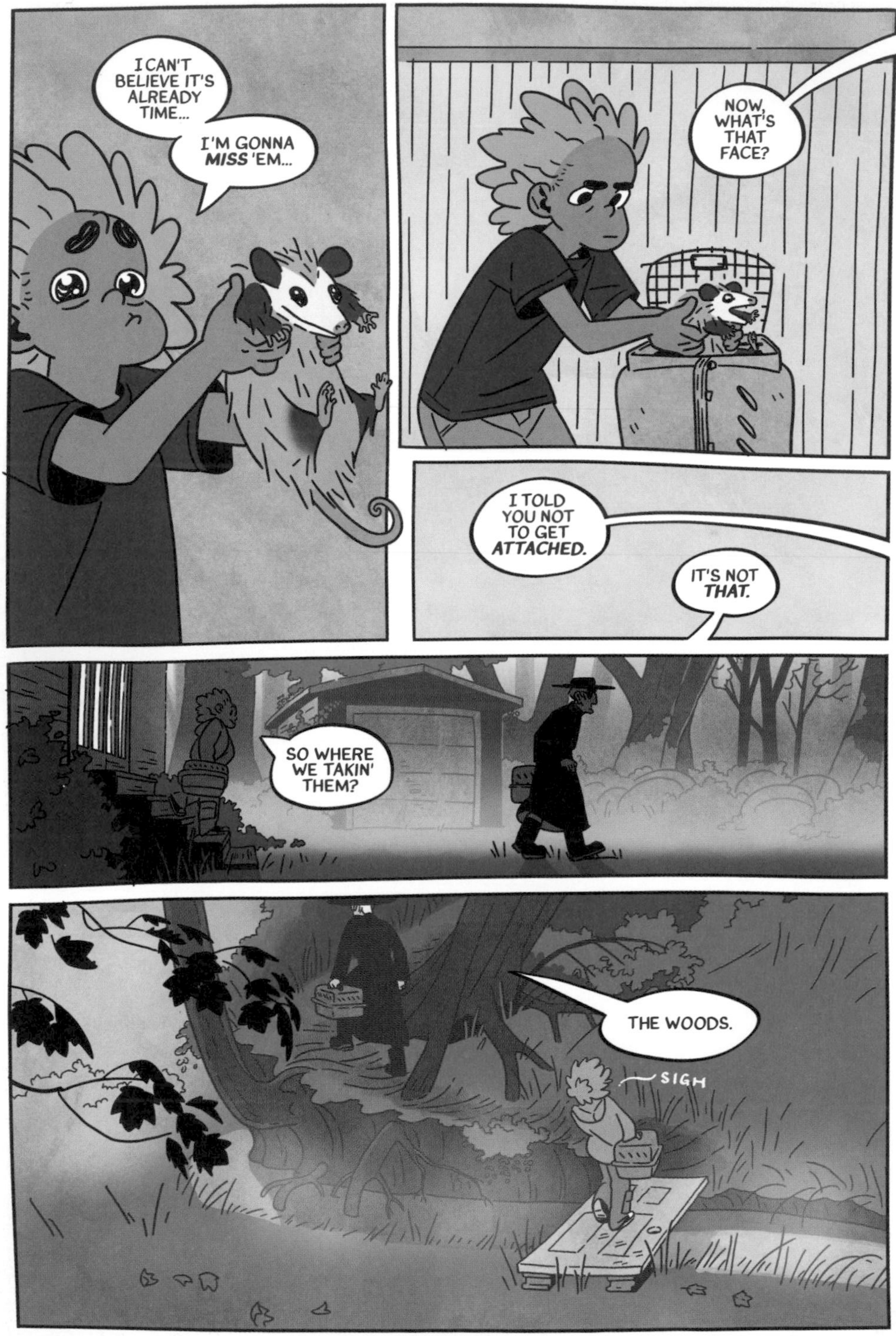

I CAN'T BELIEVE IT'S ALREADY TIME...
I'M GONNA *MISS* 'EM...
NOW, WHAT'S THAT FACE?
I TOLD YOU NOT TO GET *ATTACHED.*
IT'S NOT *THAT.*
SO WHERE WE TAKIN' THEM?
THE WOODS.
SIGH

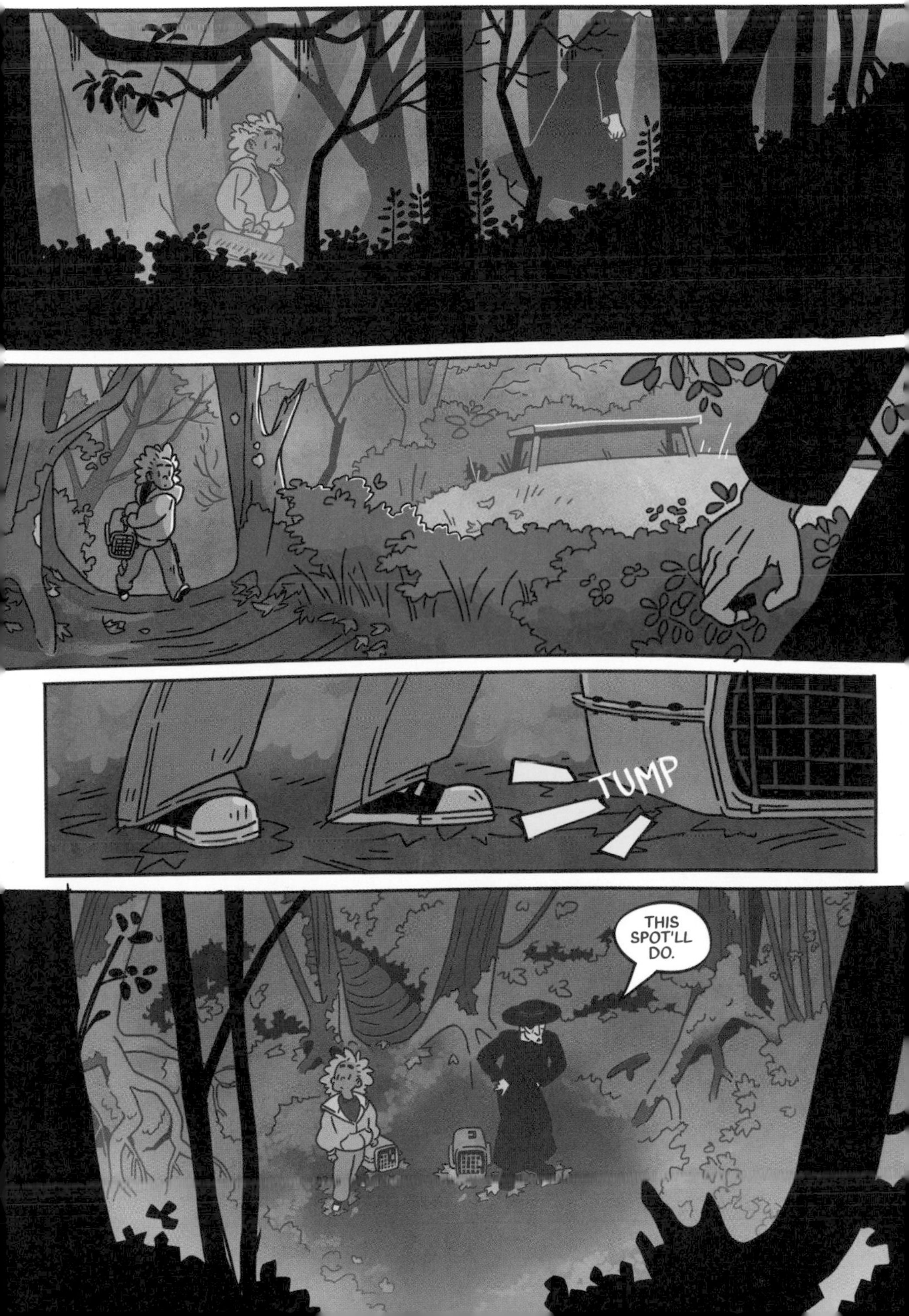
TUMP
THIS SPOT'LL DO.

ALL RIGHT, LITTLE BUDDIES...

...OFF YOU GO!

HEY, JACKS?

NOW THAT THE POSSUMS ARE FREE...

...AND I DON'T NEED YOUR HELP WITH 'EM ANYMORE...

WHAT ABOUT THE OTHER STUFF?

EH?

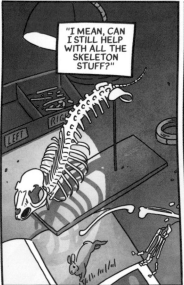

"I MEAN, CAN I STILL HELP WITH ALL THE SKELETON STUFF?"

...IF... Y'KNOW...YOU STILL *WANT* MY HELP...

IF YOU LIKE.

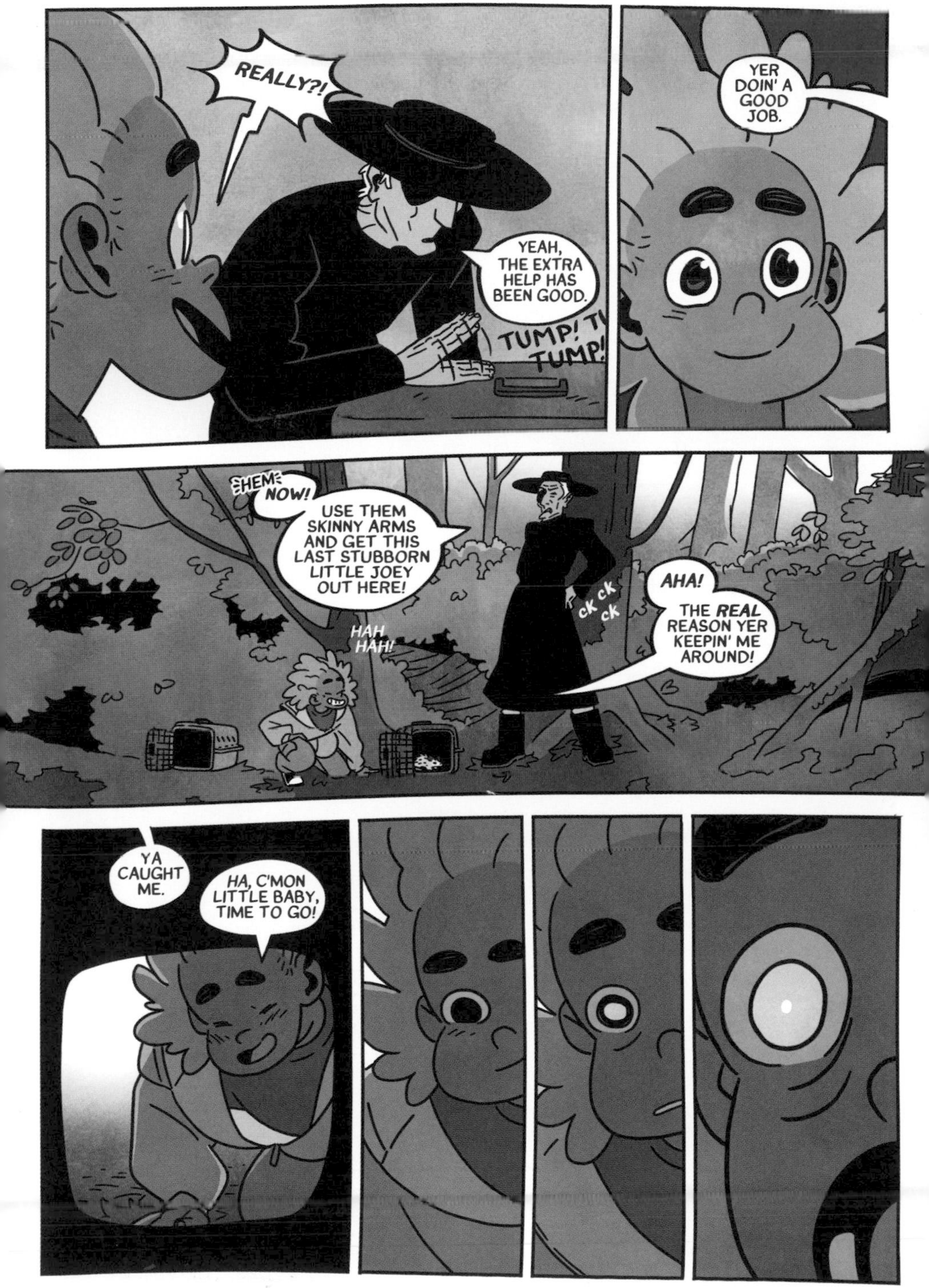
REALLY?!
YEAH, THE EXTRA HELP HAS BEEN GOOD.
TUMP! TUMP!
YER DOIN' A GOOD JOB.
HEM NOW!
USE THEM SKINNY ARMS AND GET THIS LAST STUBBORN LITTLE JOEY OUT HERE!
HAH HAH!
ck ck ck
AHA!
THE REAL REASON YER KEEPIN' ME AROUND!
YA CAUGHT ME.
HA, C'MON LITTLE BABY, TIME TO GO!

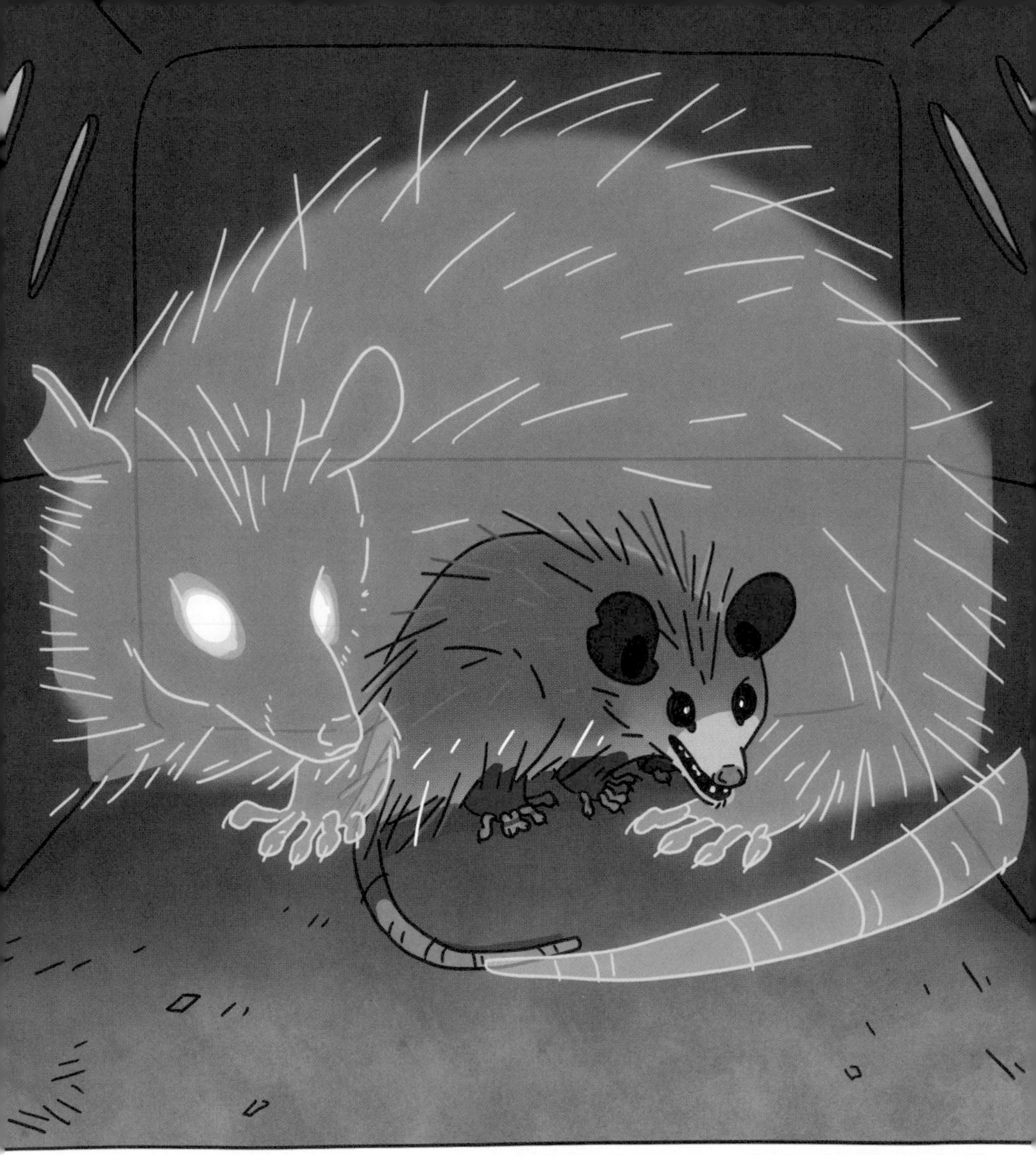

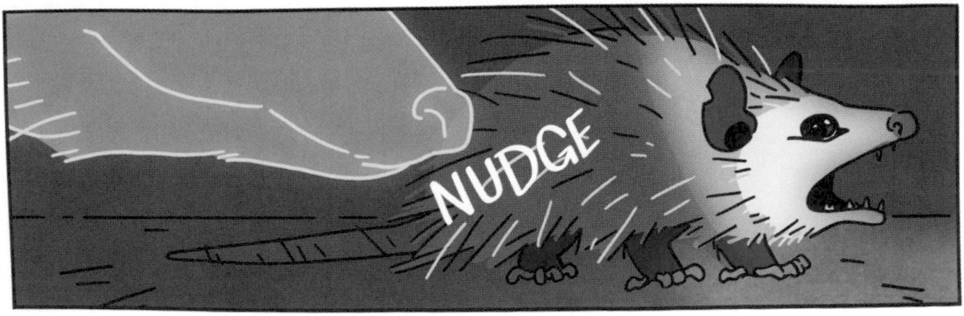
NUDGE

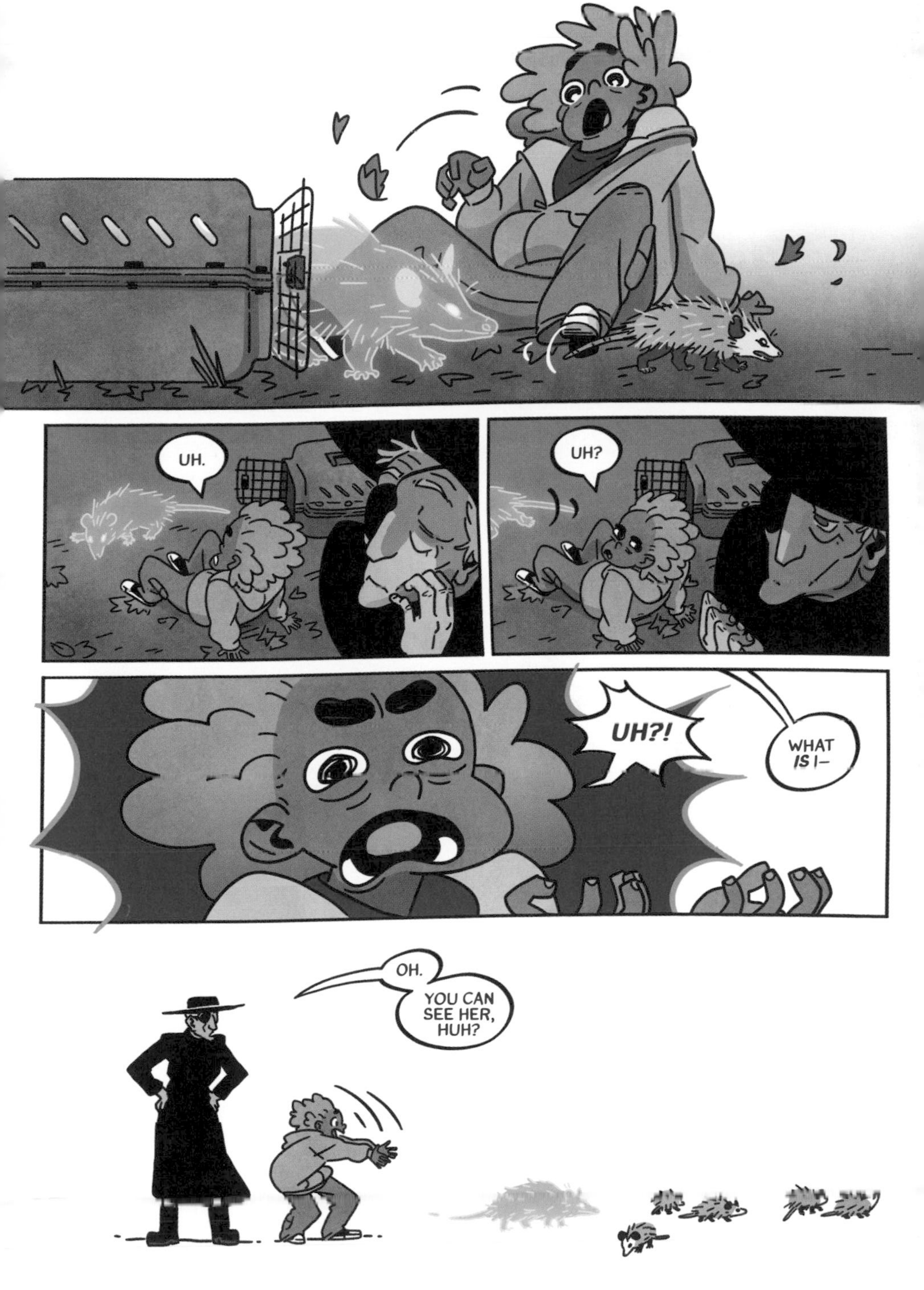
UH.
UH?
UH?!
WHAT IS I—
OH.
YOU CAN SEE HER, HUH?

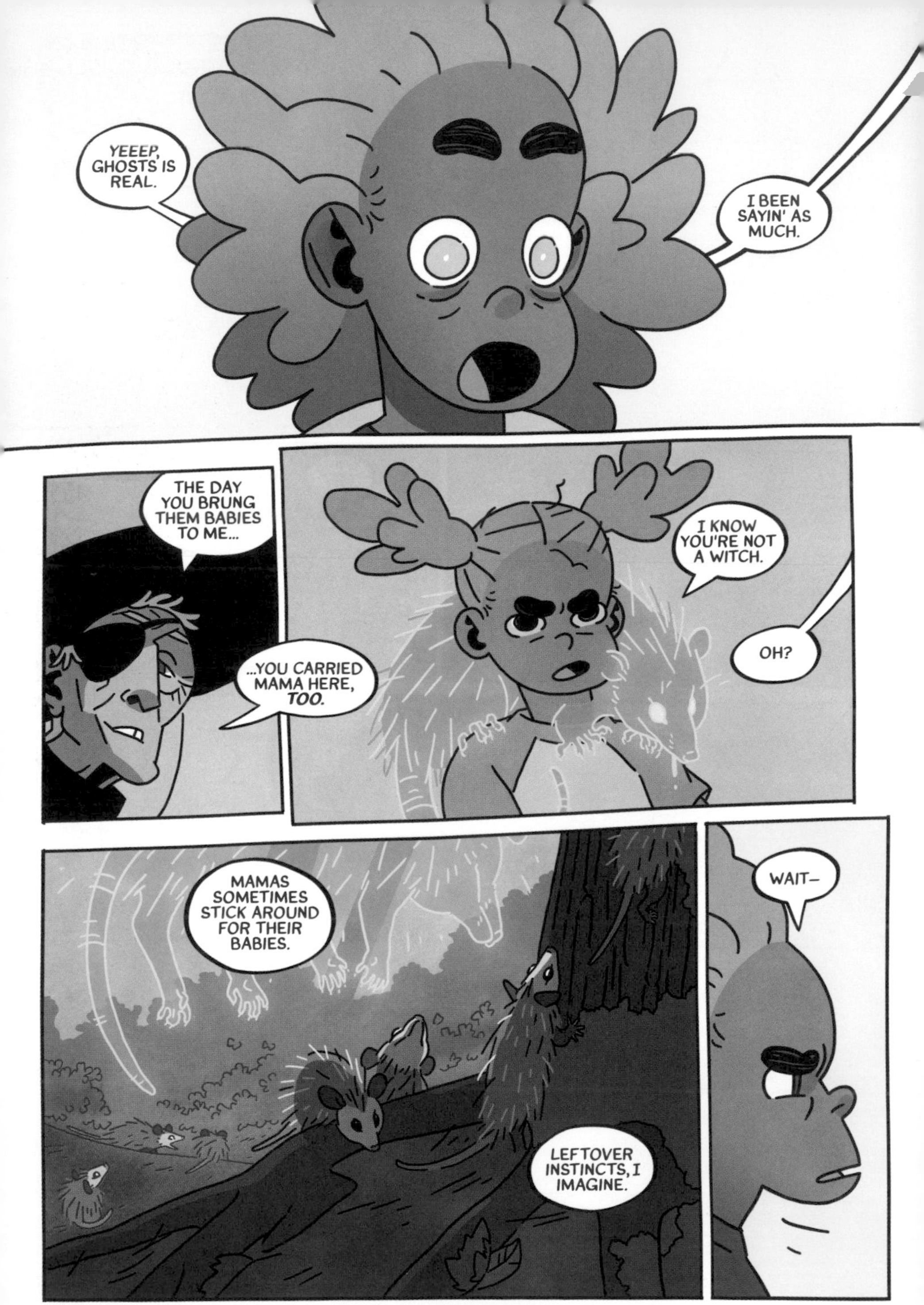
YEEEP, GHOSTS IS REAL.
I BEEN SAYIN' AS MUCH.
THE DAY YOU BRUNG THEM BABIES TO ME...
...YOU CARRIED MAMA HERE, *TOO.*
I KNOW YOU'RE NOT A WITCH.
OH?
MAMAS SOMETIMES STICK AROUND FOR THEIR BABIES.
LEFTOVER INSTINCTS, I IMAGINE.
WAIT–

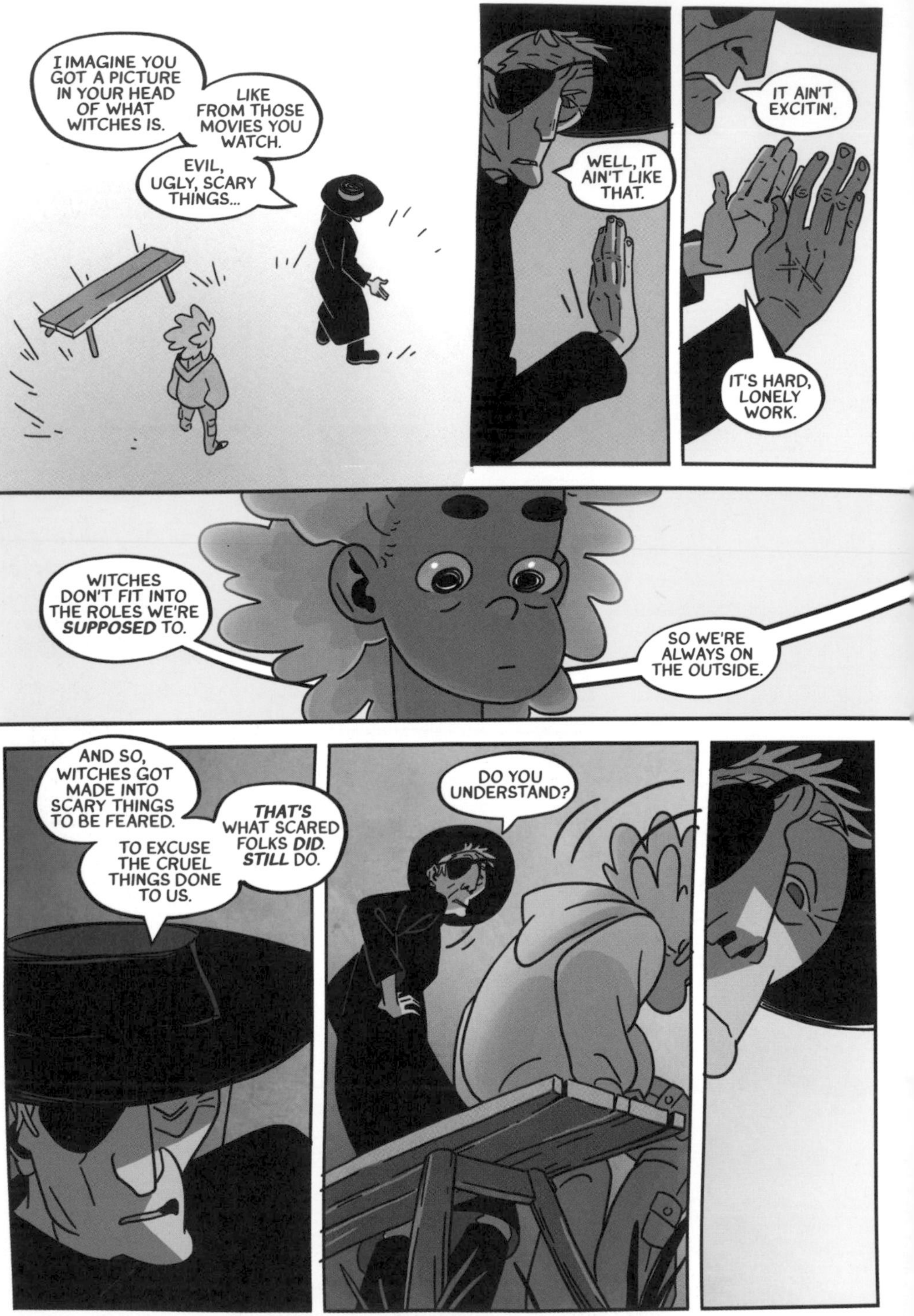
I IMAGINE YOU GOT A PICTURE IN YOUR HEAD OF WHAT WITCHES IS.
LIKE FROM THOSE MOVIES YOU WATCH.
EVIL, UGLY, SCARY THINGS...
WELL, IT AIN'T LIKE THAT.
IT AIN'T EXCITIN'.
IT'S HARD, LONELY WORK.
WITCHES DON'T FIT INTO THE ROLES WE'RE *SUPPOSED* TO.
SO WE'RE ALWAYS ON THE OUTSIDE.
AND SO, WITCHES GOT MADE INTO SCARY THINGS TO BE FEARED.
TO EXCUSE THE CRUEL THINGS DONE TO US.
THAT'S WHAT SCARED FOLKS *DID*. *STILL* DO.
DO YOU UNDERSTAND?

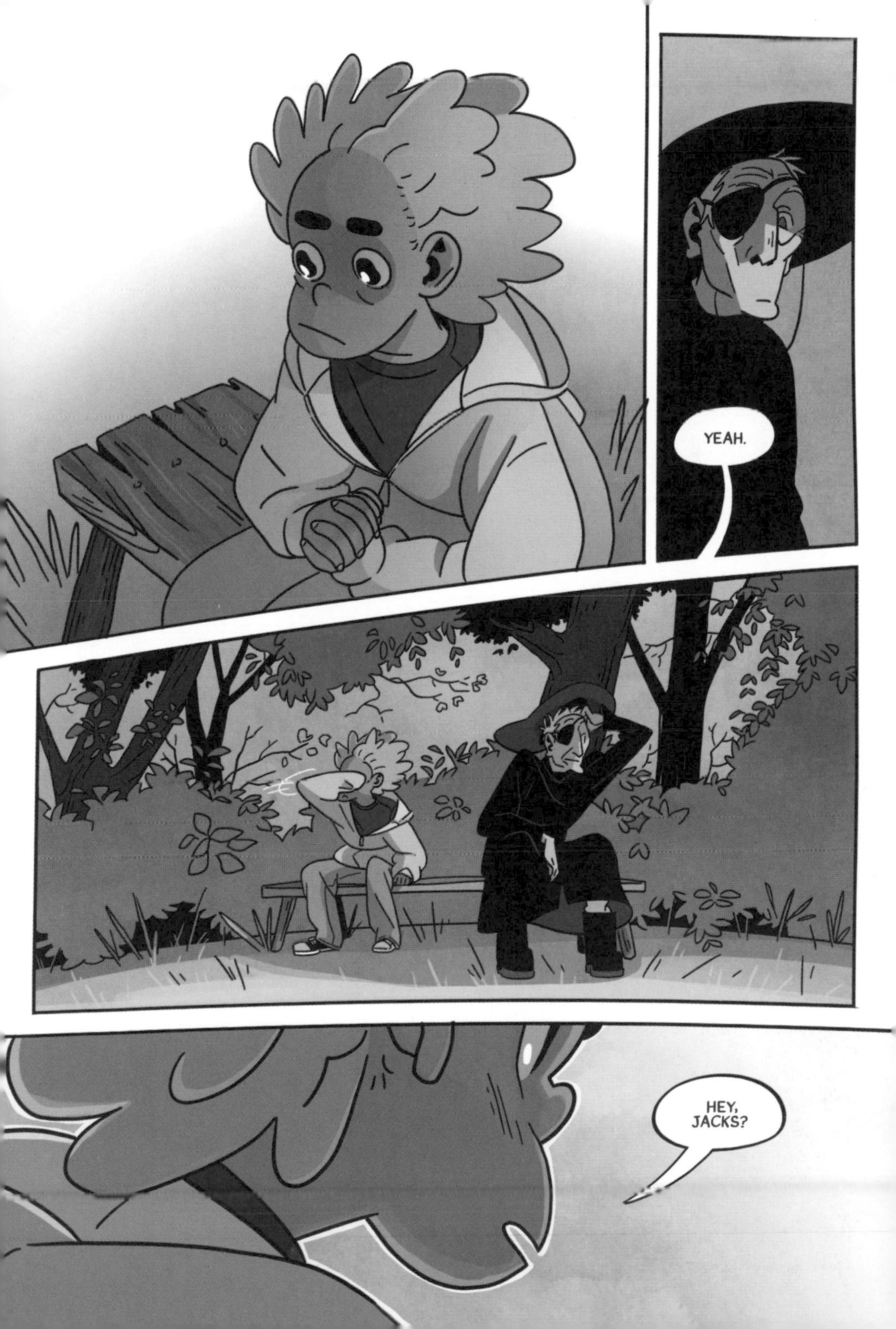
YEAH.
HEY, JACKS?

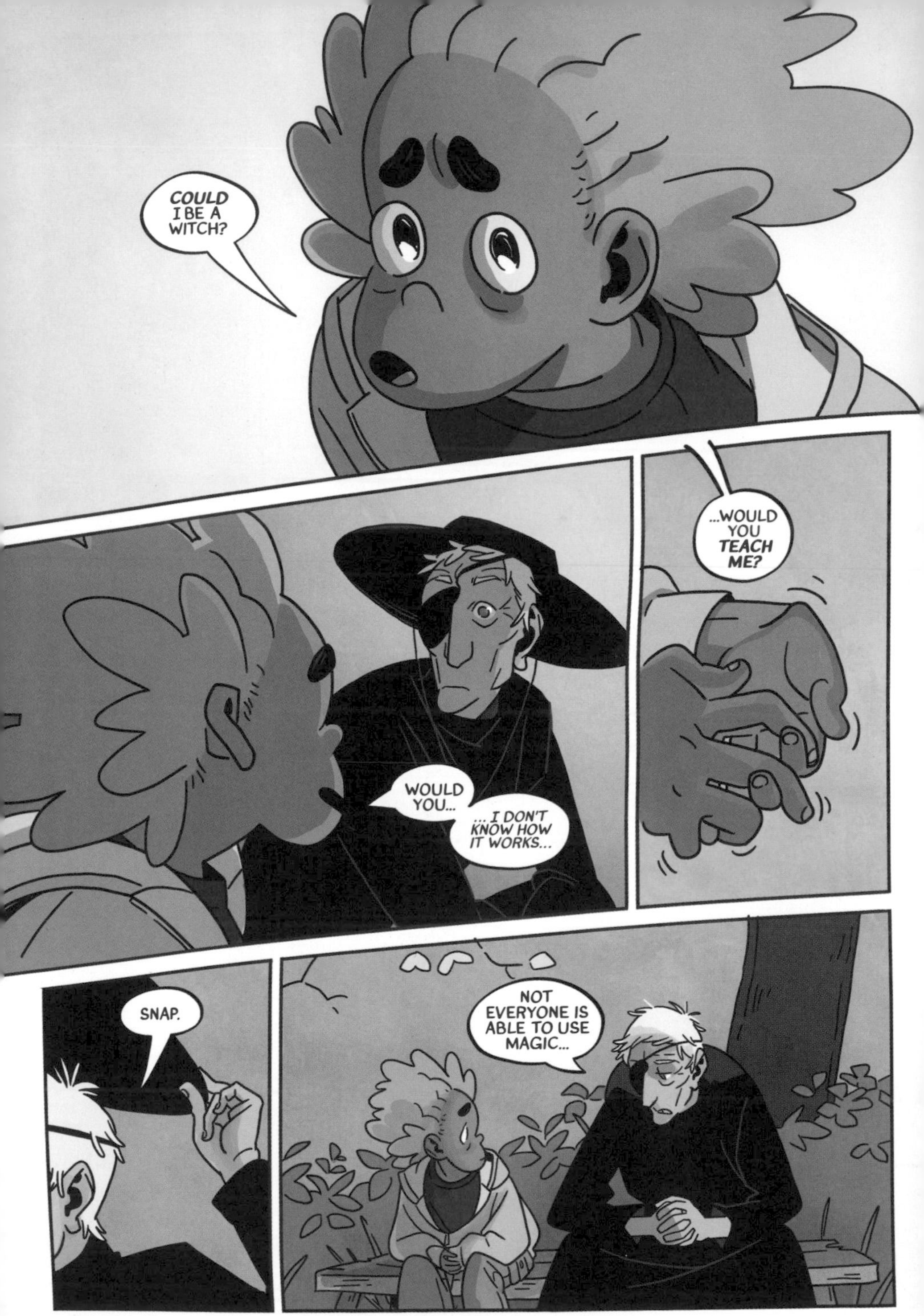
COULD I BE A WITCH?
WOULD YOU...
...I DON'T KNOW HOW IT WORKS...
...WOULD YOU TEACH ME?
SNAP.
NOT EVERYONE IS ABLE TO USE MAGIC...

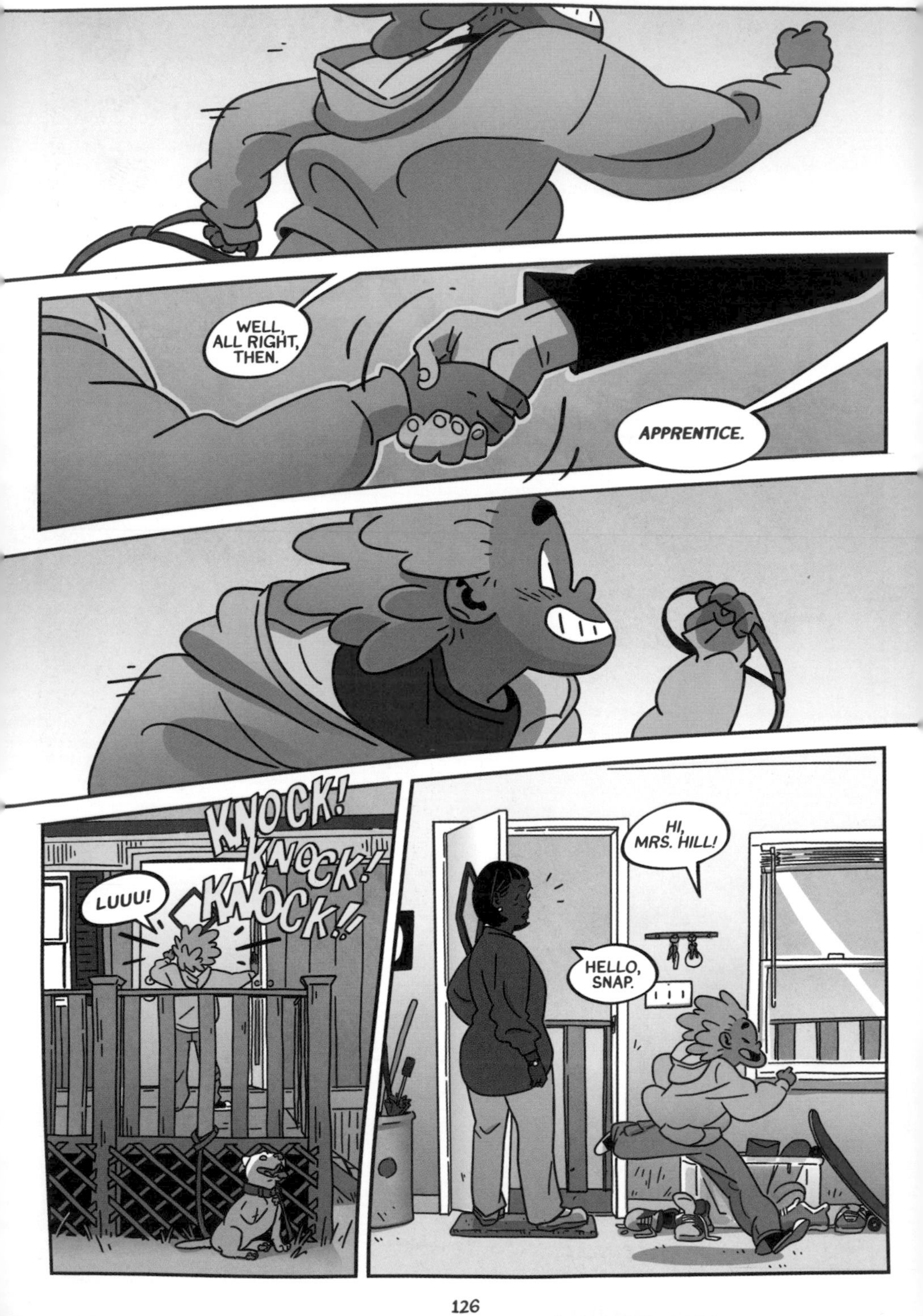
WELL, ALL RIGHT, THEN.
APPRENTICE.
KNOCK! KNOCK! KNOCK!!
LUUU!
HI, MRS. HILL!
HELLO, SNAP.

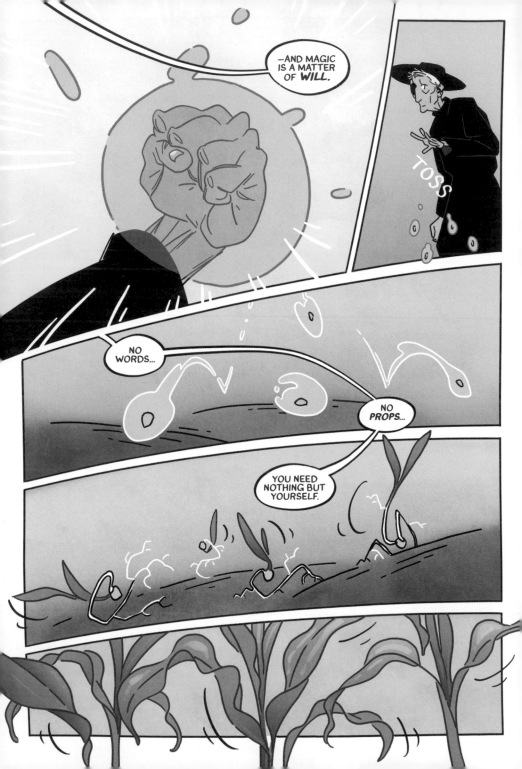

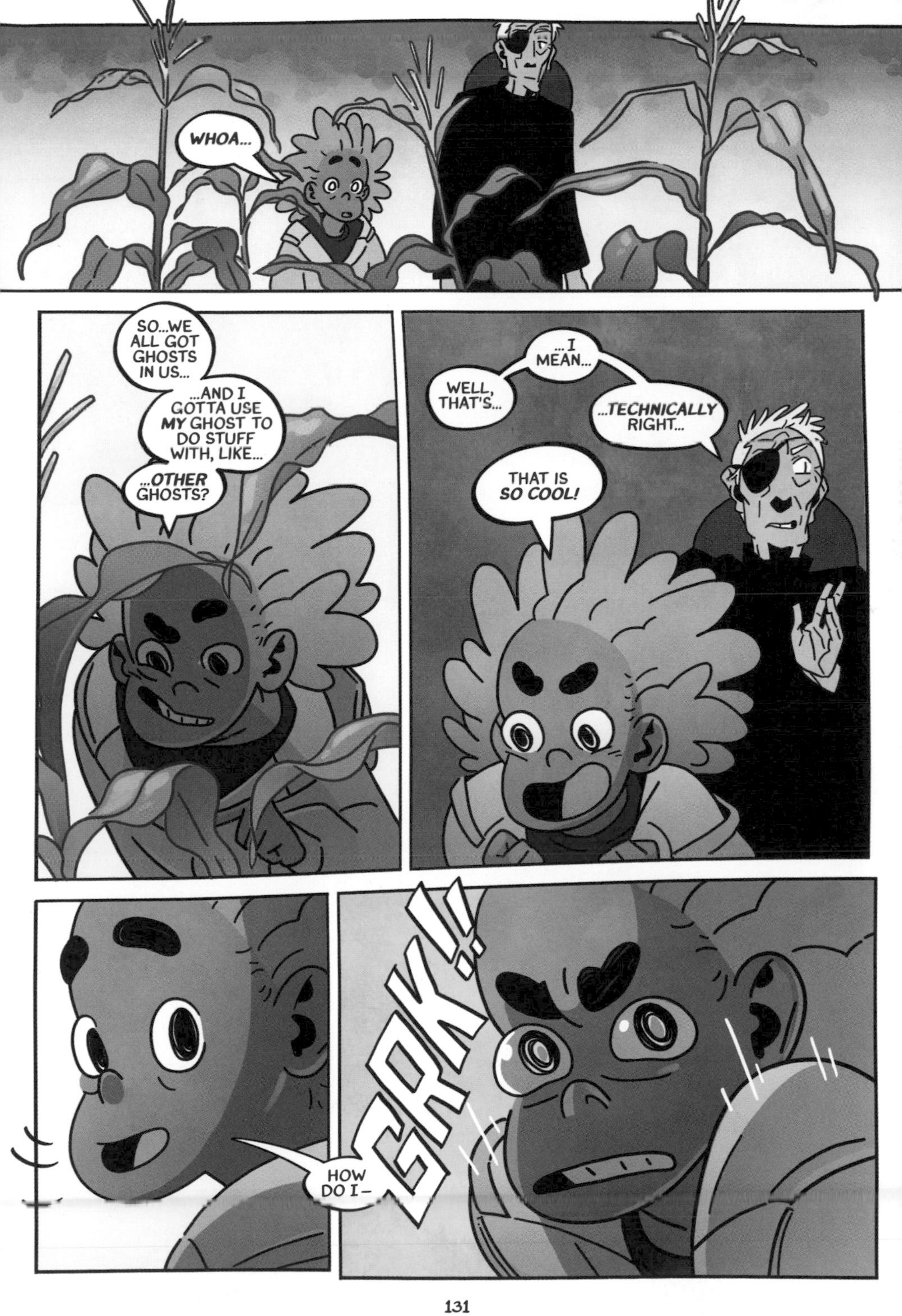
WHOA...
SO...WE ALL GOT GHOSTS IN US...
...AND I GOTTA USE MY GHOST TO DO STUFF WITH, LIKE...
...OTHER GHOSTS?
WELL, THAT'S...
...I MEAN...
...TECHNICALLY RIGHT...
THAT IS SO COOL!
HOW DO I—
GRK!!

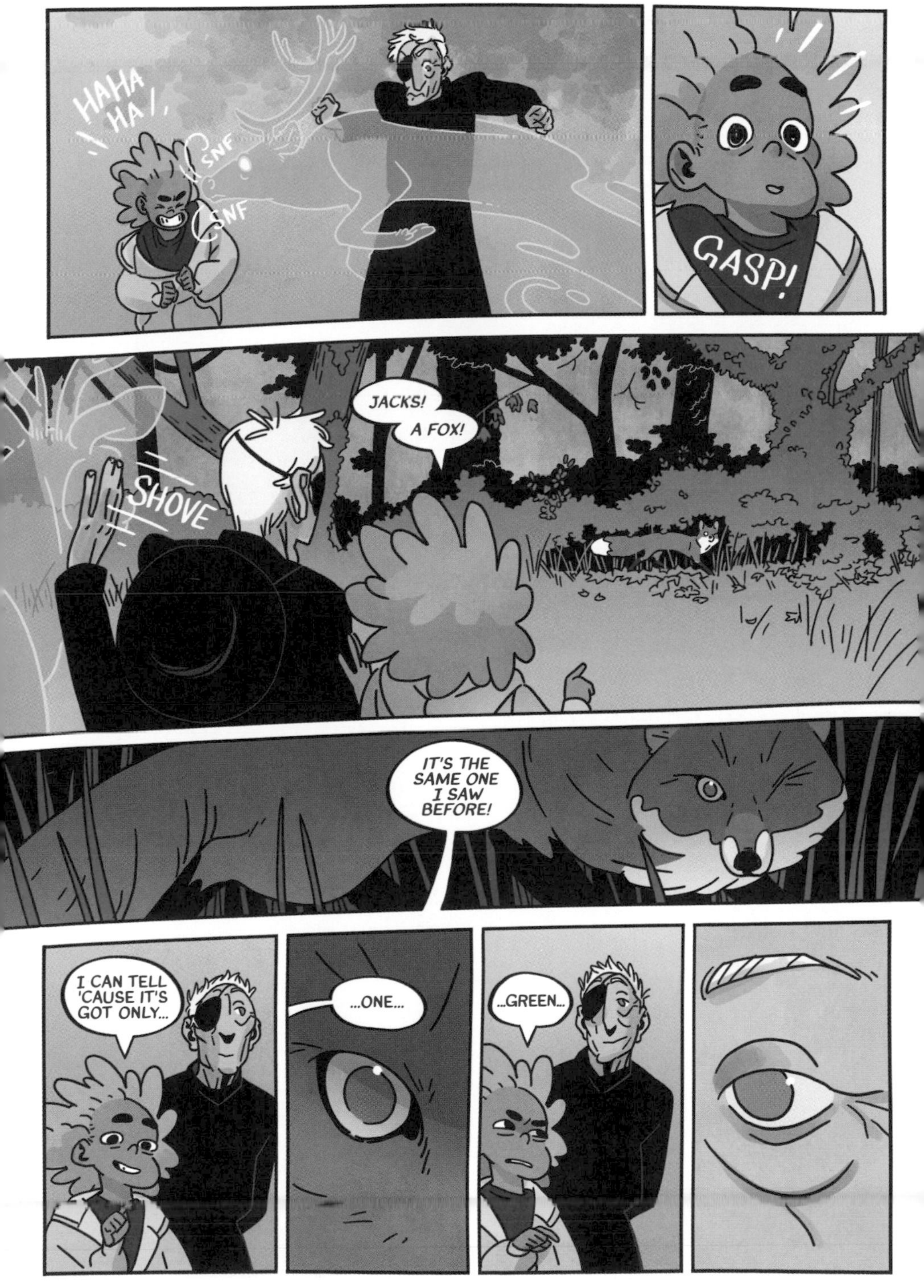
HAHA HA!
SNF
SNF
GASP!
SHOVE
JACKS!
A FOX!
IT'S THE SAME ONE I SAW BEFORE!
I CAN TELL 'CAUSE IT'S GOT ONLY...
...ONE...
...GREEN...

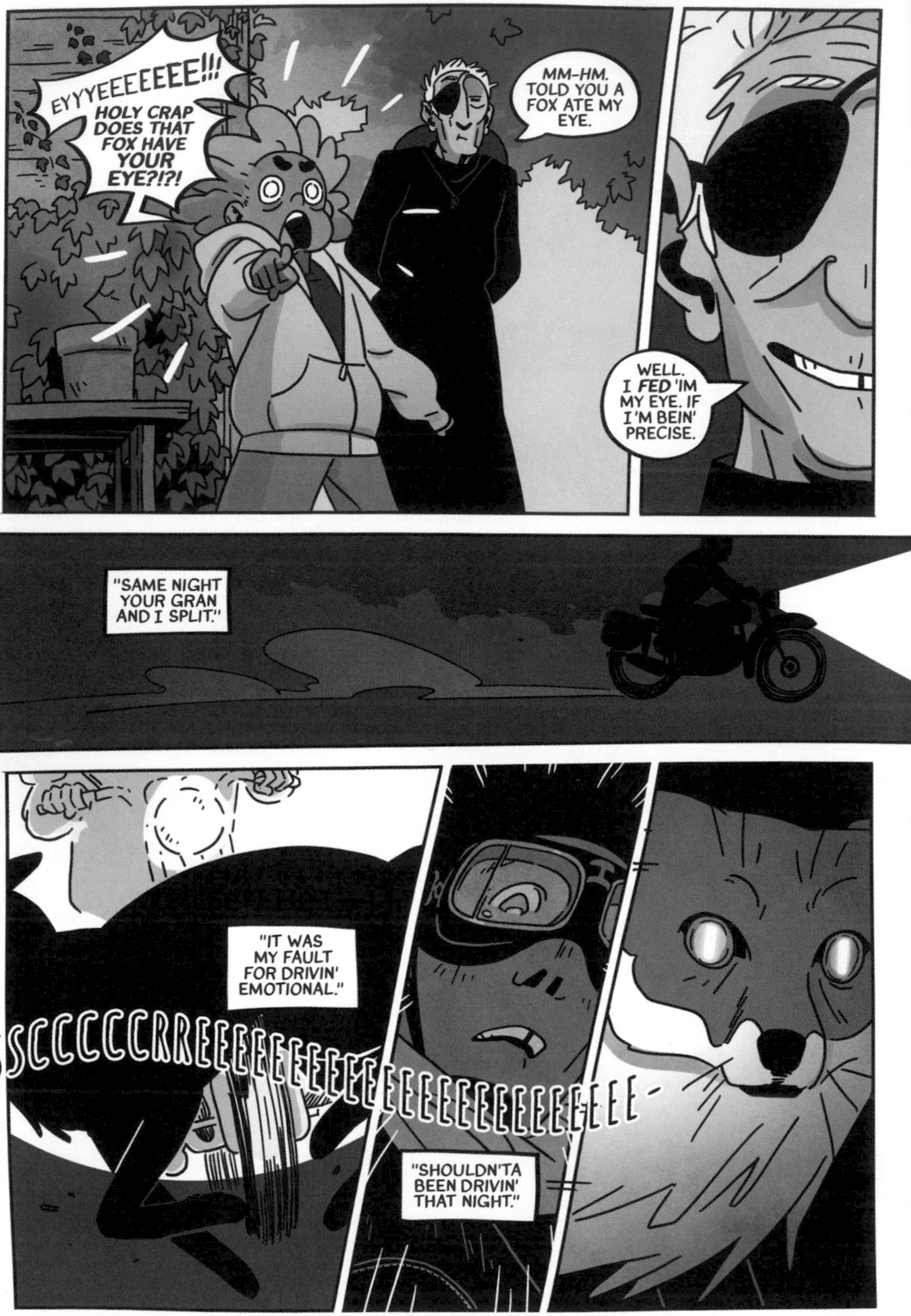
EYYYEEEEEEE!!!
HOLY CRAP DOES THAT FOX HAVE *YOUR* EYE?!?!
MM-HM. TOLD YOU A FOX ATE MY EYE.
WELL. I *FED* 'IM MY EYE. IF I'M BEIN' PRECISE.
"SAME NIGHT YOUR GRAN AND I SPLIT."
"IT WAS MY FAULT FOR DRIVIN' EMOTIONAL."
SSCCCCCCRREEEEEEEEEEEEEEEEEEEEEEEEEEEE-
"SHOULDN'TA BEEN DRIVIN' THAT NIGHT."

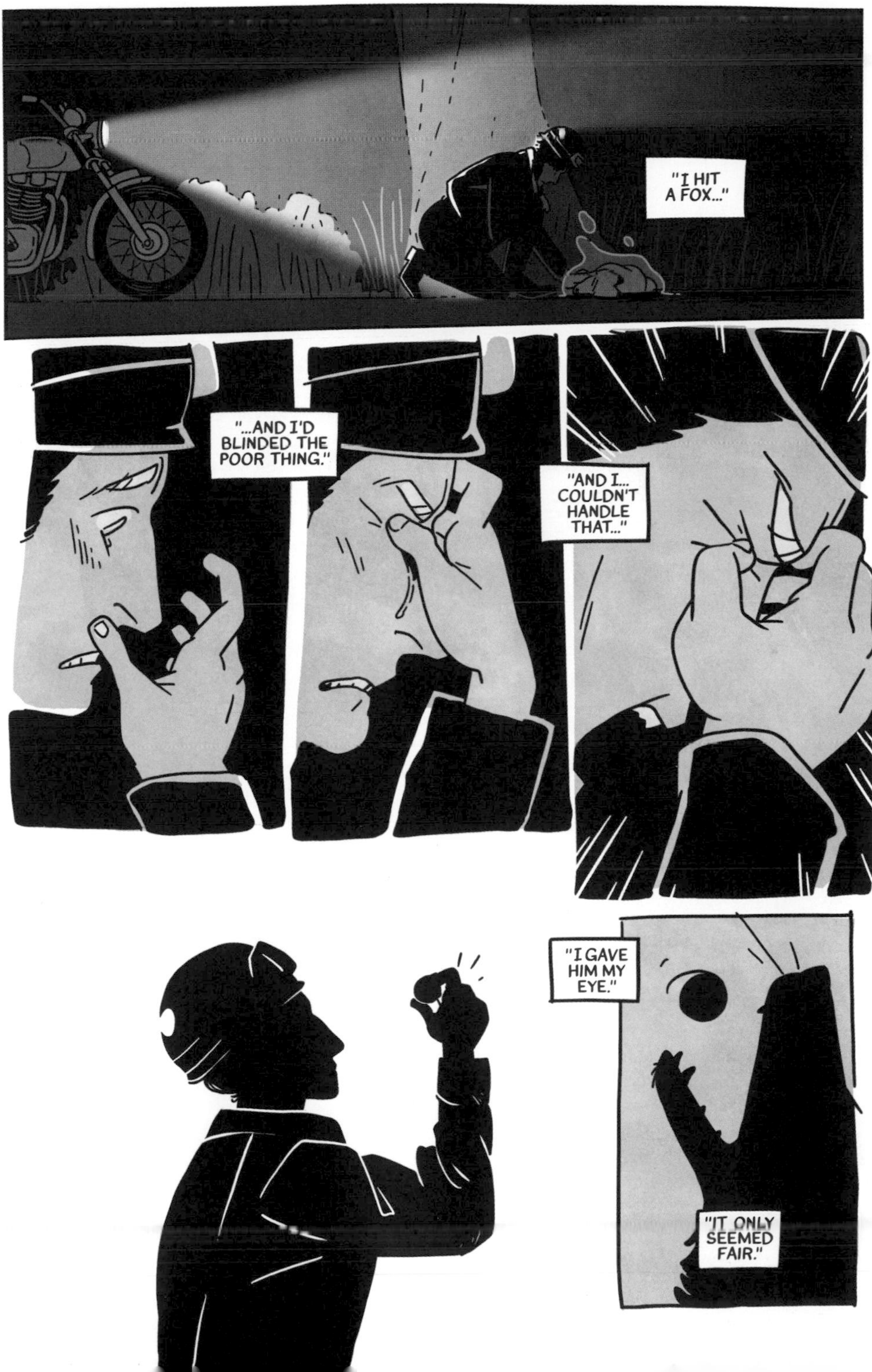
"I HIT A FOX..."
"...AND I'D BLINDED THE POOR THING."
"AND I... COULDN'T HANDLE THAT..."
"I GAVE HIM MY EYE."
"IT ONLY SEEMED FAIR."

"AND IT WORKED!"

"BUT IT WAS A SPUR OF THE MOMENT SPELL, AND WELL..."

...I MAY HAVE... *CURSED* HIM.

BY MISTAKE.

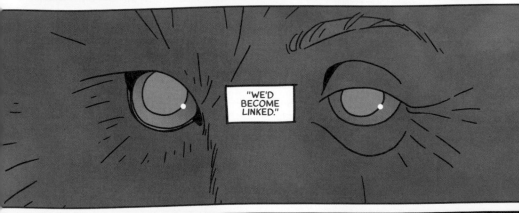

"WE'D BECOME LINKED."

IN FACT, HE'D EVEN CHECK IN ON JESSAMINE ONCE IN A WHILE

WHOA WHOA WHOA.

HOLD IT.

WHOA WHOA WHOA.

HOLD IT.

STOP.

ARE YO[U] TELLING [ME] A ONE-EY[ED]

ARE YOU TELLING ME—

ONE-EYED TOM IS A *REAL,* DECADES-OLD FOX—

—AND THE OLD LADY YOU PUT SKELETONS TOGETHER WITH *SHARES AN EYE WITH HIM?!*

YEAH.

TURNS OUT TOM WASN'T HAUNTING US, AFTER ALL.

JUST WATCHING OVER US.

"...LIKE BY KEEPIN' MY GRAN FROM DRIVING ONTO A COLLAPSED BRIDGE ON A FOGGY NIGHT..."

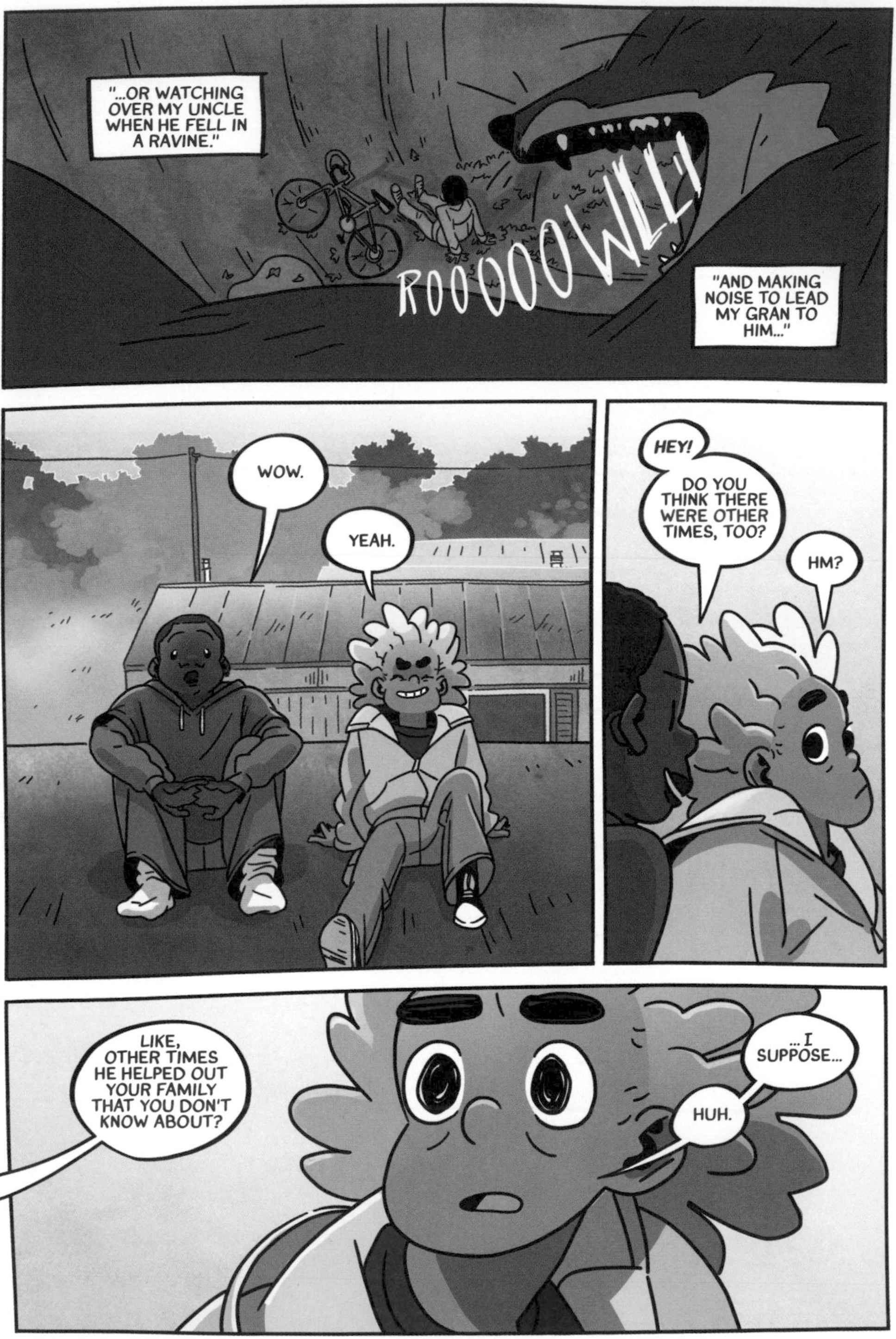
"...OR WATCHING OVER MY UNCLE WHEN HE FELL IN A RAVINE."
ROOOOOOWLL!
"AND MAKING NOISE TO LEAD MY GRAN TO HIM..."
WOW.
YEAH.
HEY!
DO YOU THINK THERE WERE OTHER TIMES, TOO?
HM?
LIKE, OTHER TIMES HE HELPED OUT YOUR FAMILY THAT YOU DON'T KNOW ABOUT?
HUH.
... I SUPPOSE...

A FEW MONTHS AGO...

"I WOULDN'T KNOW, WOULD I?"

...WHAT... THINK you're... WHAT... LEAVE...

...What do MEAN by...

—HOW MANY TIMES DO YOU NEED TO HEAR IT?!

WE'RE THROUGH, CHUCK!

NOW GET OUT OF HERE!

140

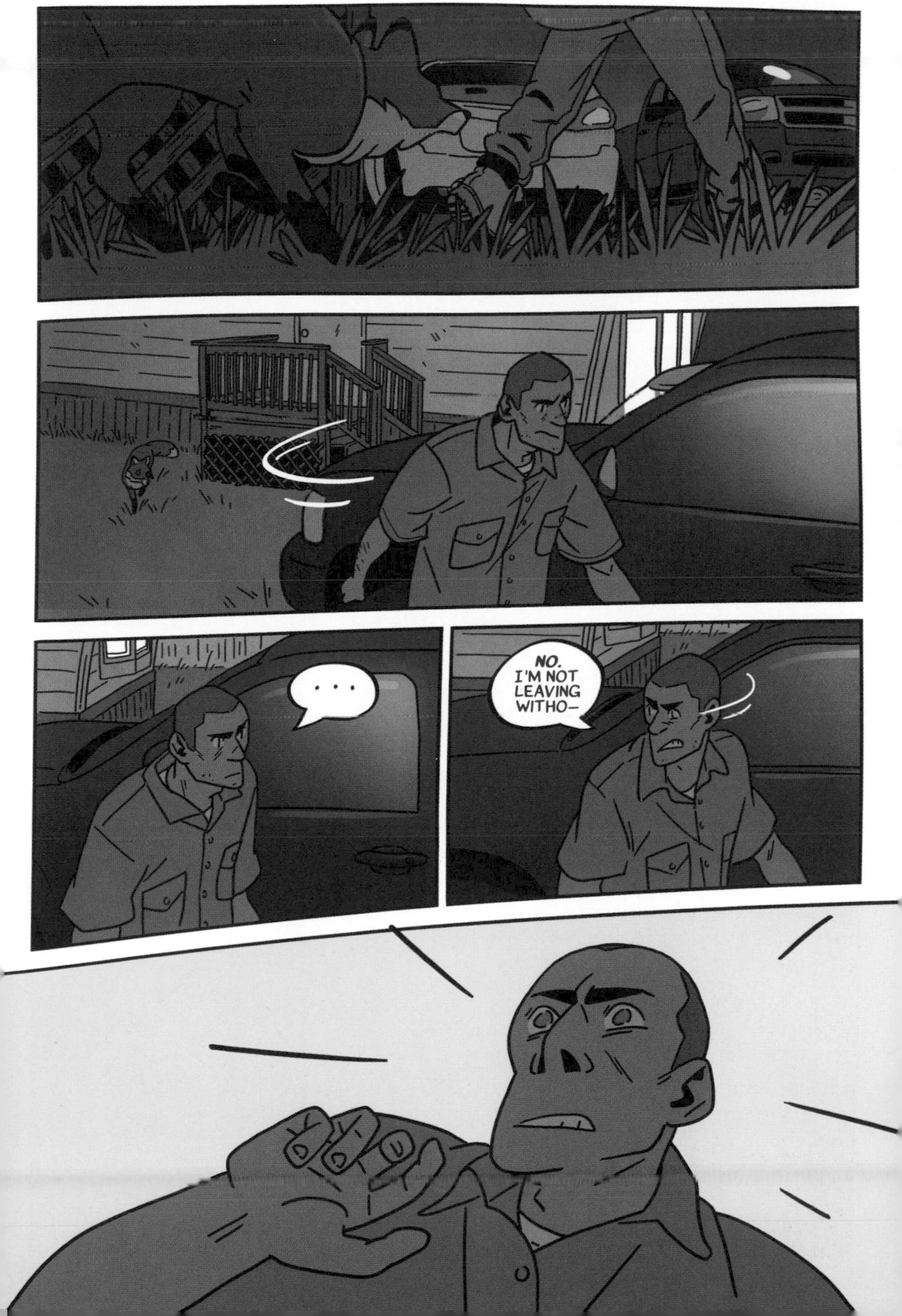
. . .
NO. I'M NOT LEAVING WITHO–

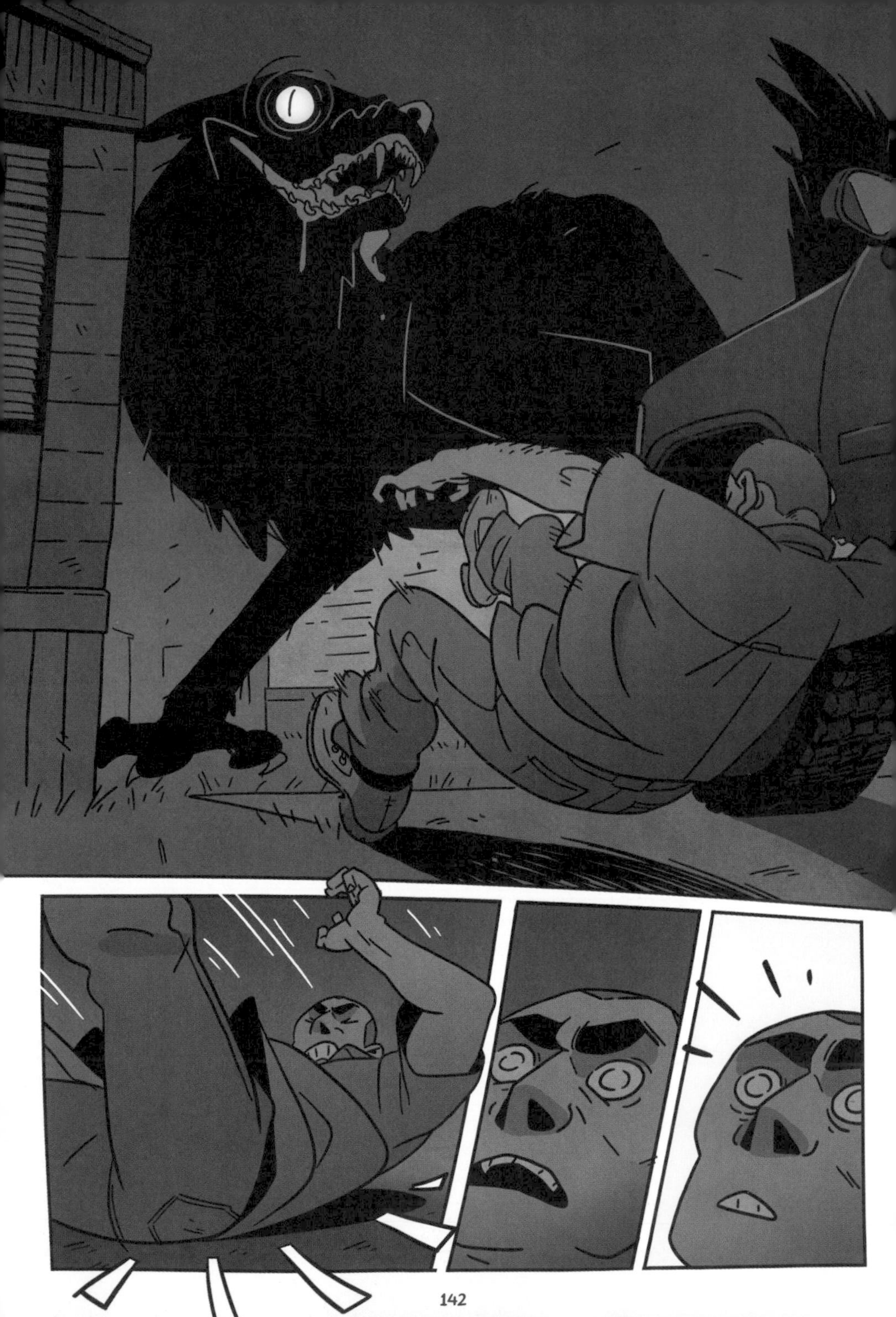

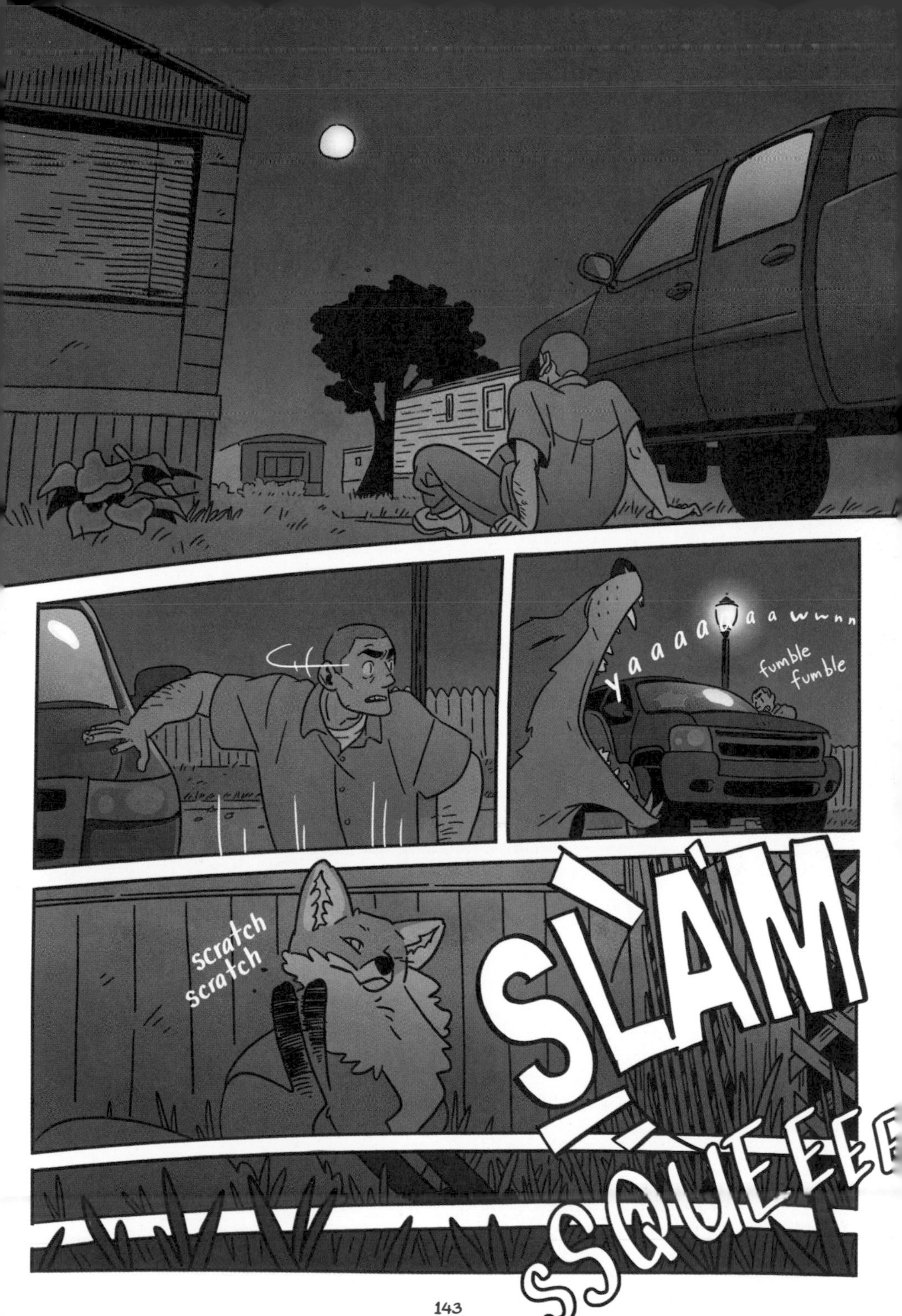
yaaaaaaawwnn
fumble fumble
scratch scratch
SLAM
SSQUEEEE

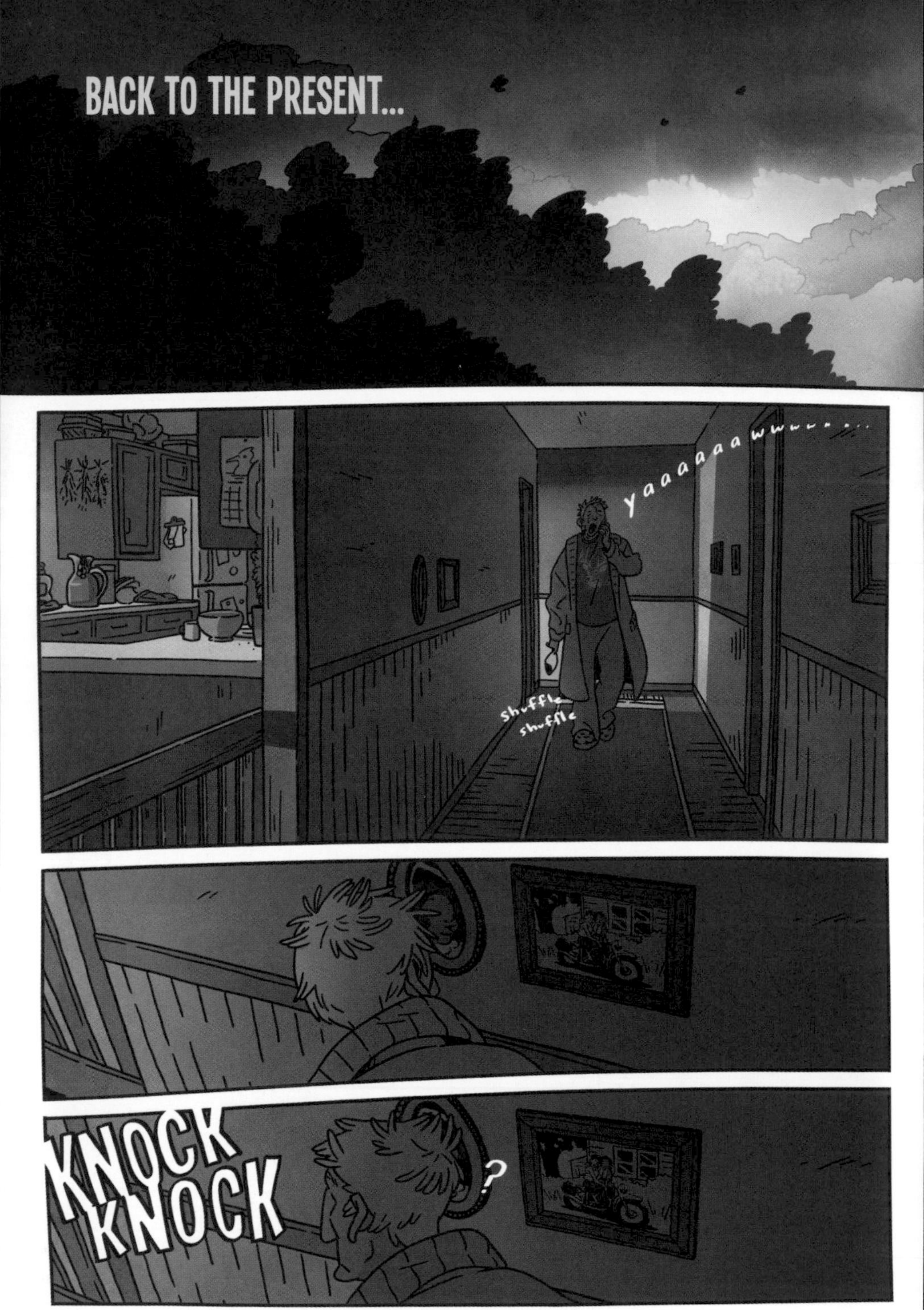
BACK TO THE PRESENT...
yaaaaaawwwn...
shuffle shuffle
KNOCK KNOCK
?

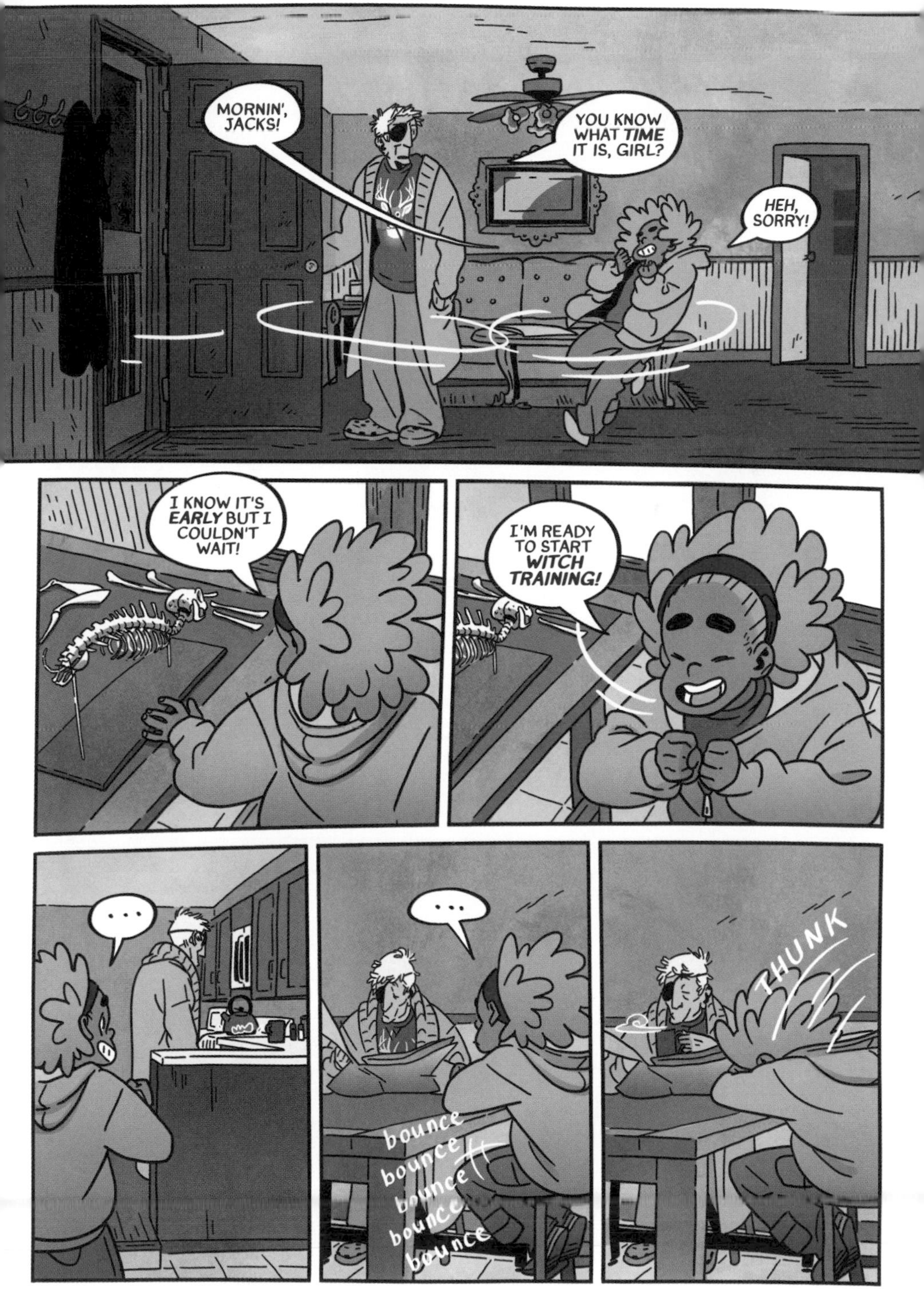
MORNIN', JACKS!
YOU KNOW WHAT TIME IT IS, GIRL?
HEH, SORRY!
I KNOW IT'S EARLY BUT I COULDN'T WAIT!
I'M READY TO START WITCH TRAINING!
...
...
bounce
bounce
bounce
bounce
bounce
bounce
THUNK

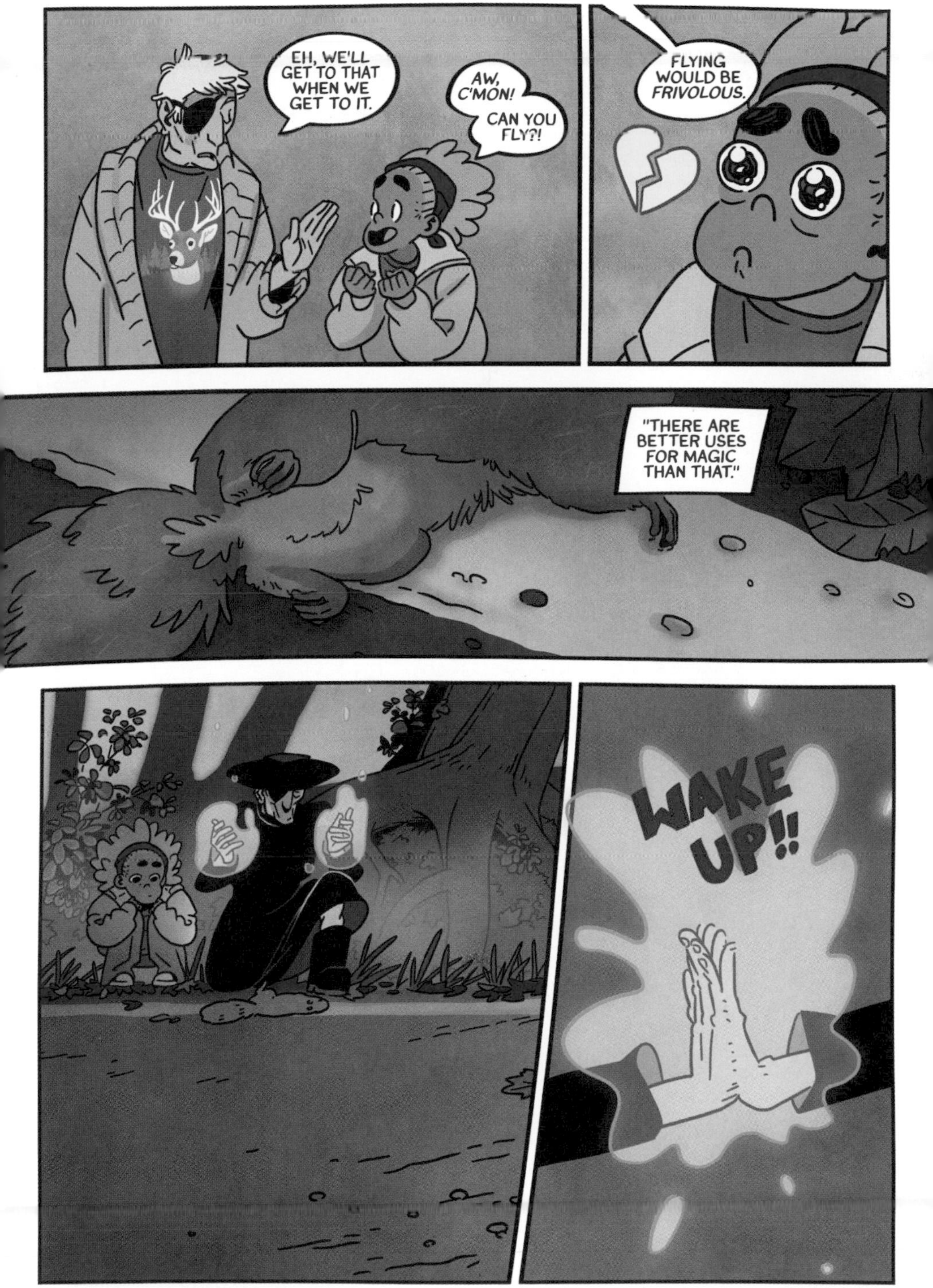
EH, WE'LL GET TO THAT WHEN WE GET TO IT.
AW, C'MON!
CAN YOU FLY?!
FLYING WOULD BE FRIVOLOUS.
"THERE ARE BETTER USES FOR MAGIC THAN THAT."
WAKE UP!!

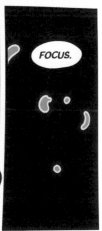

NOW TRY...

...IT DIDN'T WORK...

DON'T FRET.

IT DON'T ALWAYS CLICK RIGHT AWAY.

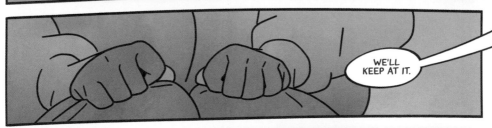

WE'LL KEEP AT IT.

OKAY...

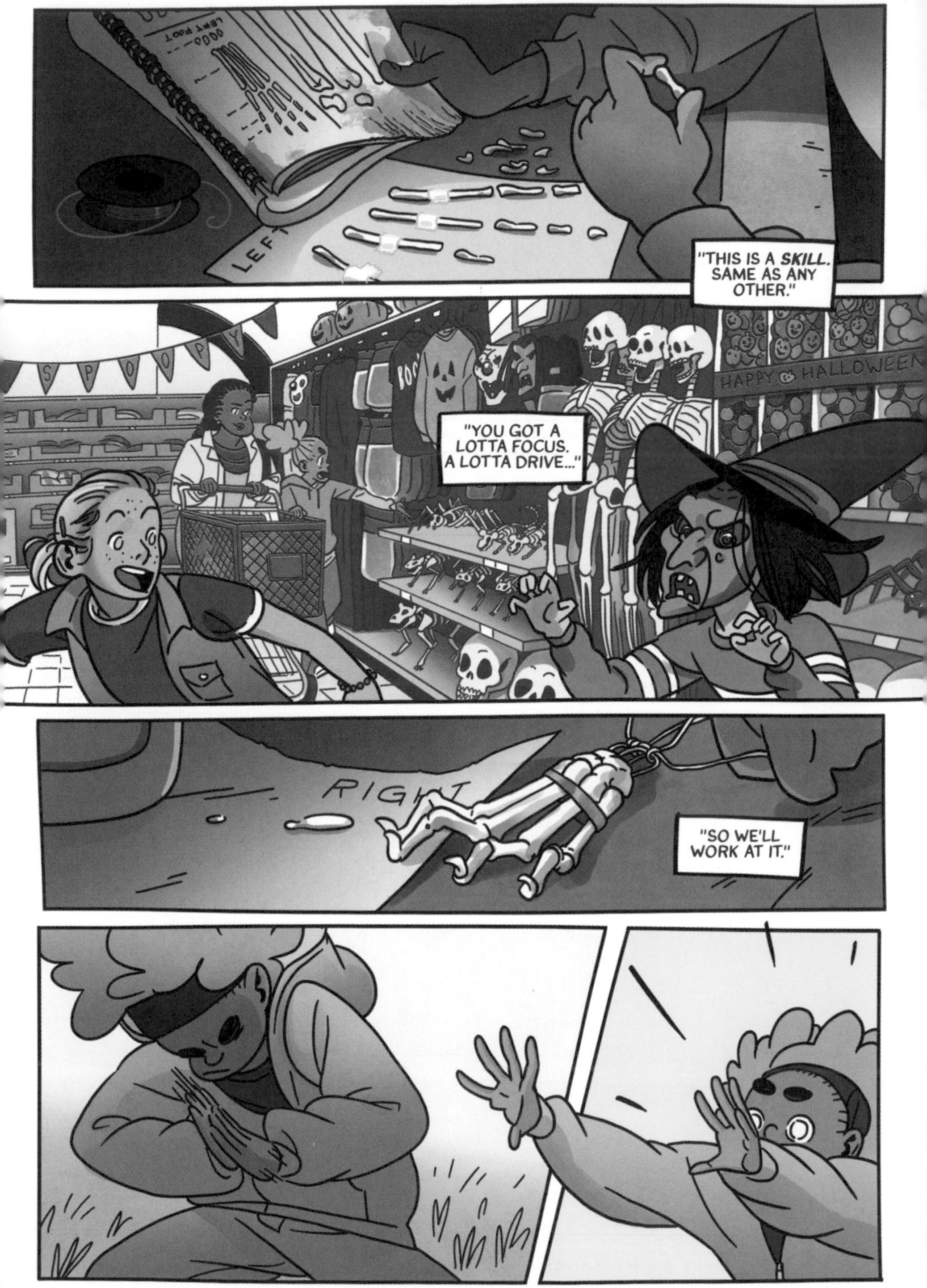
LEFT FOOT
LEFT
"THIS IS A SKILL. SAME AS ANY OTHER."
SPOOPY
BOO
HAPPY HALLOWEEN
"YOU GOT A LOTTA FOCUS. A LOTTA DRIVE..."
RIGHT
"SO WE'LL WORK AT IT."

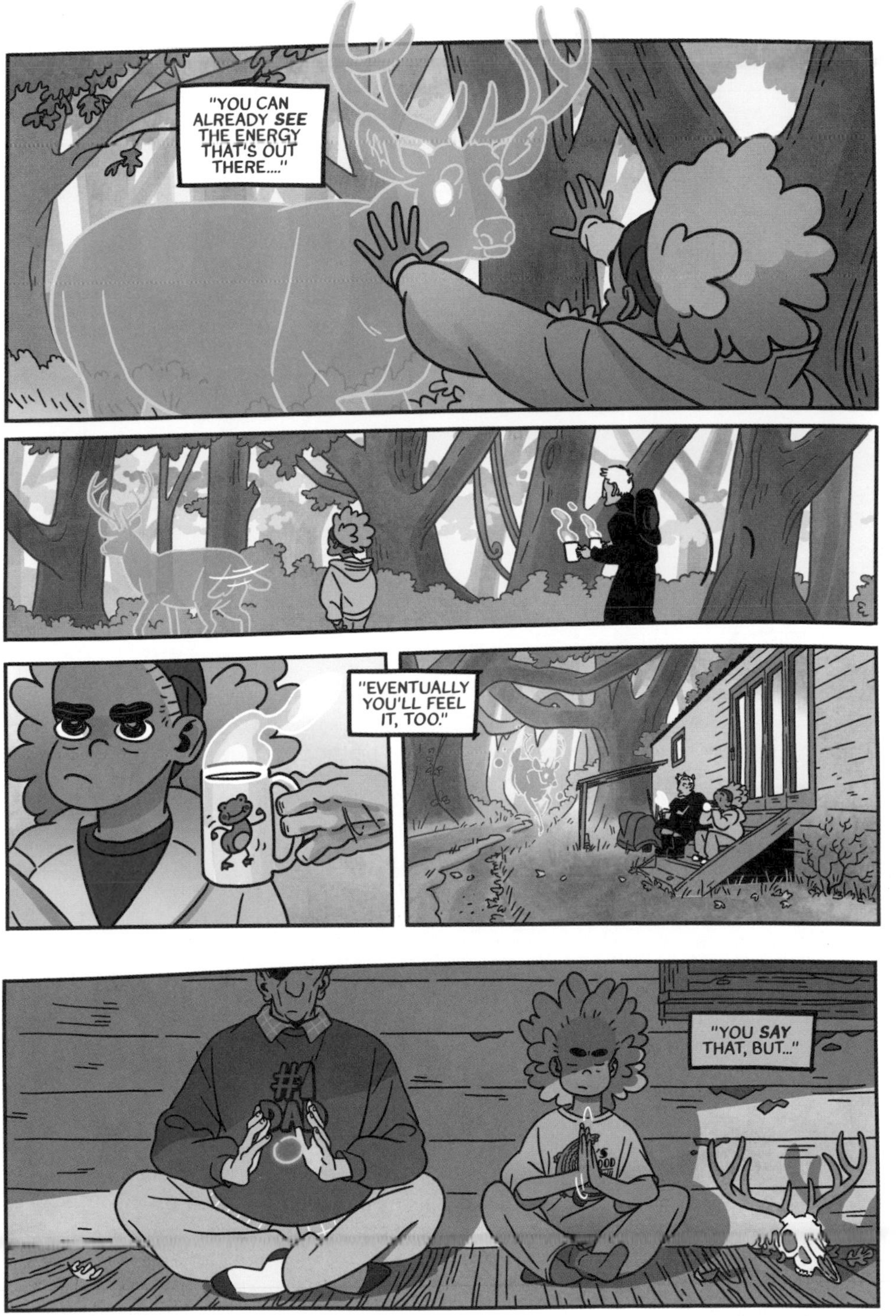
"YOU CAN ALREADY SEE THE ENERGY THAT'S OUT THERE...."
"EVENTUALLY YOU'LL FEEL IT, TOO."
"YOU SAY THAT, BUT..."

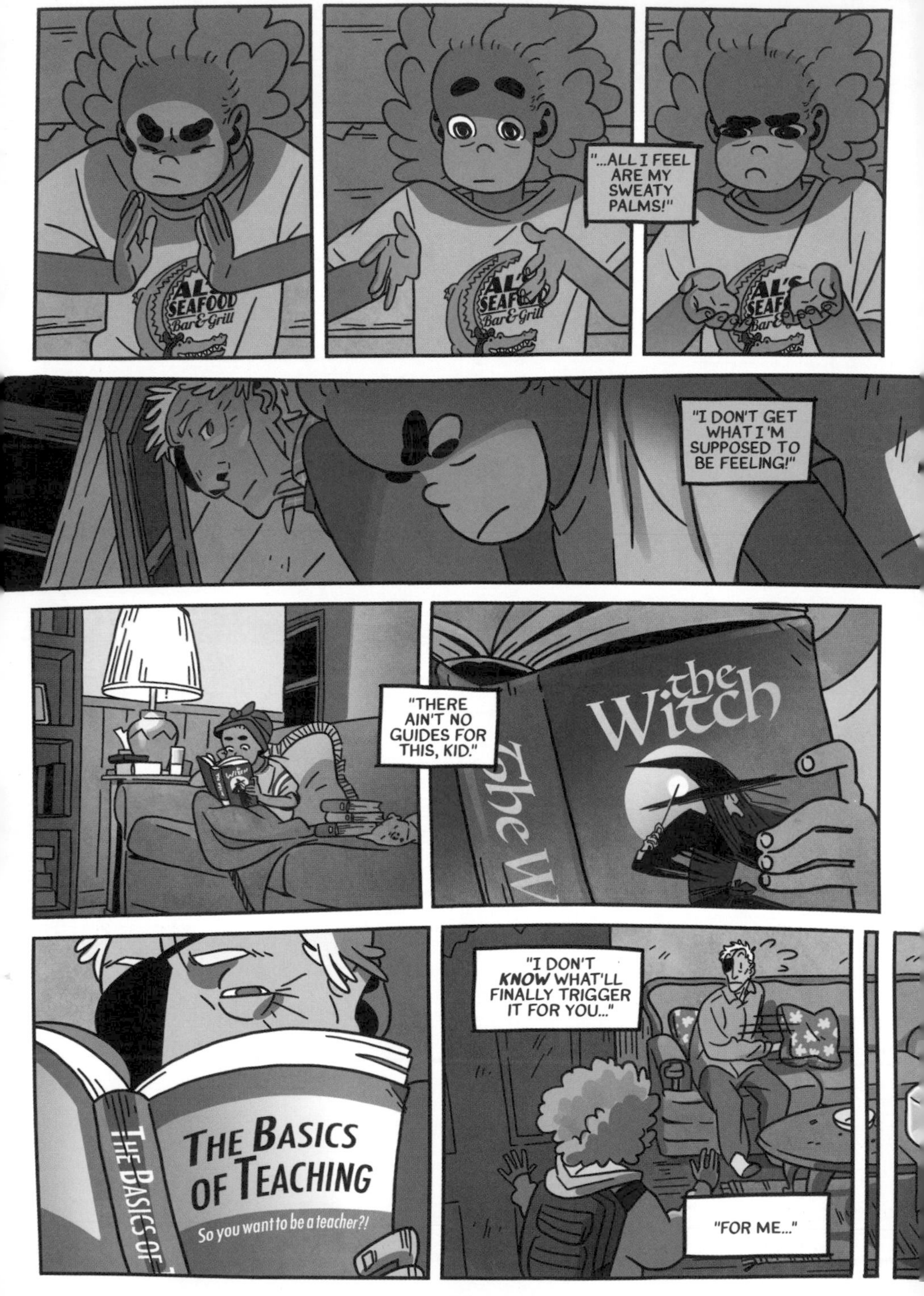
AL'S SEAFOOD Bar & Grill
"...ALL I FEEL ARE MY SWEATY PALMS!"
"I DON'T GET WHAT I'M SUPPOSED TO BE FEELING!"
"THERE AIN'T NO GUIDES FOR THIS, KID."
the Witch
"I DON'T KNOW WHAT'LL FINALLY TRIGGER IT FOR YOU..."
THE BASICS OF TEACHING
So you want to be a teacher?!
"FOR ME..."

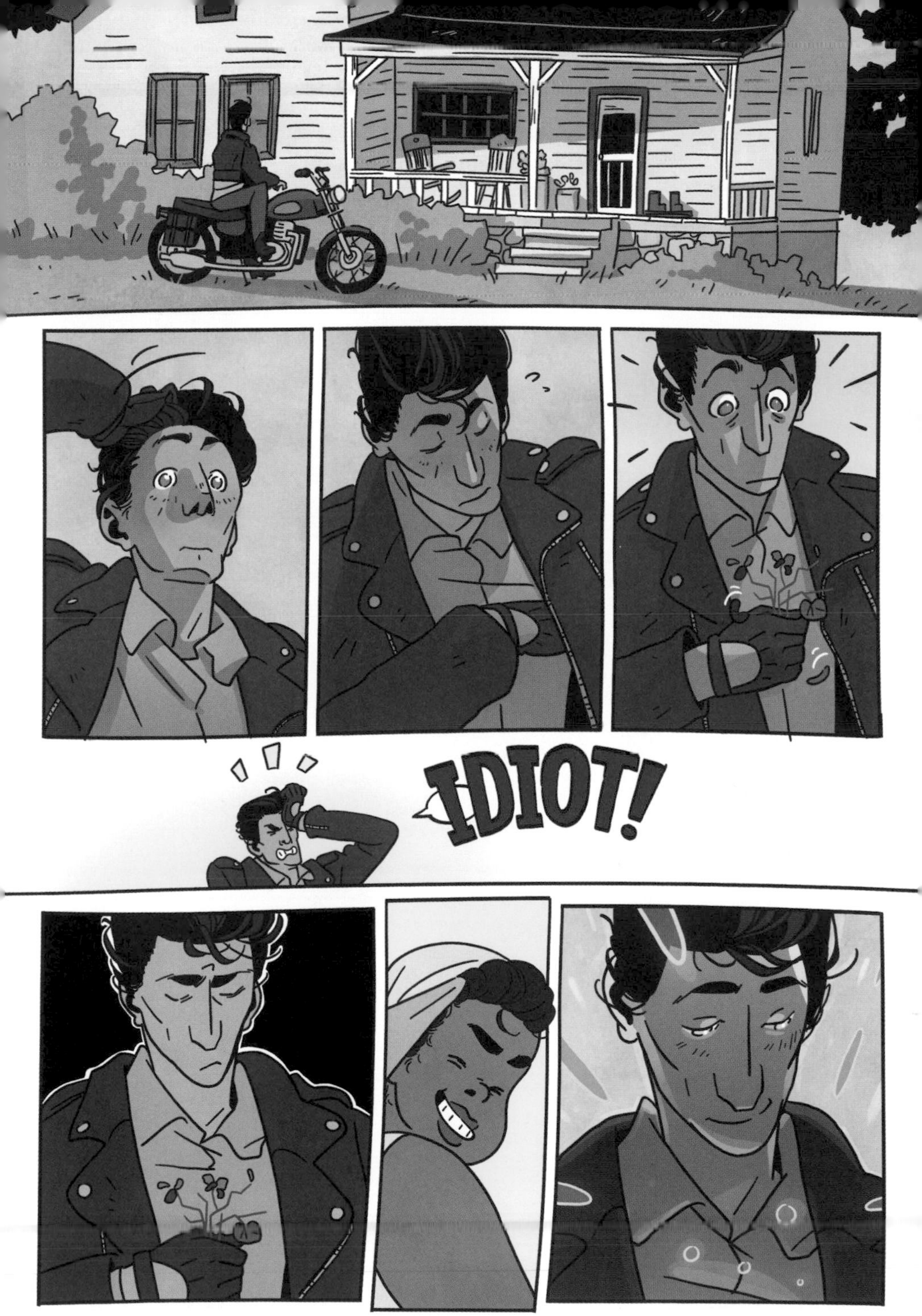
IDIOT!

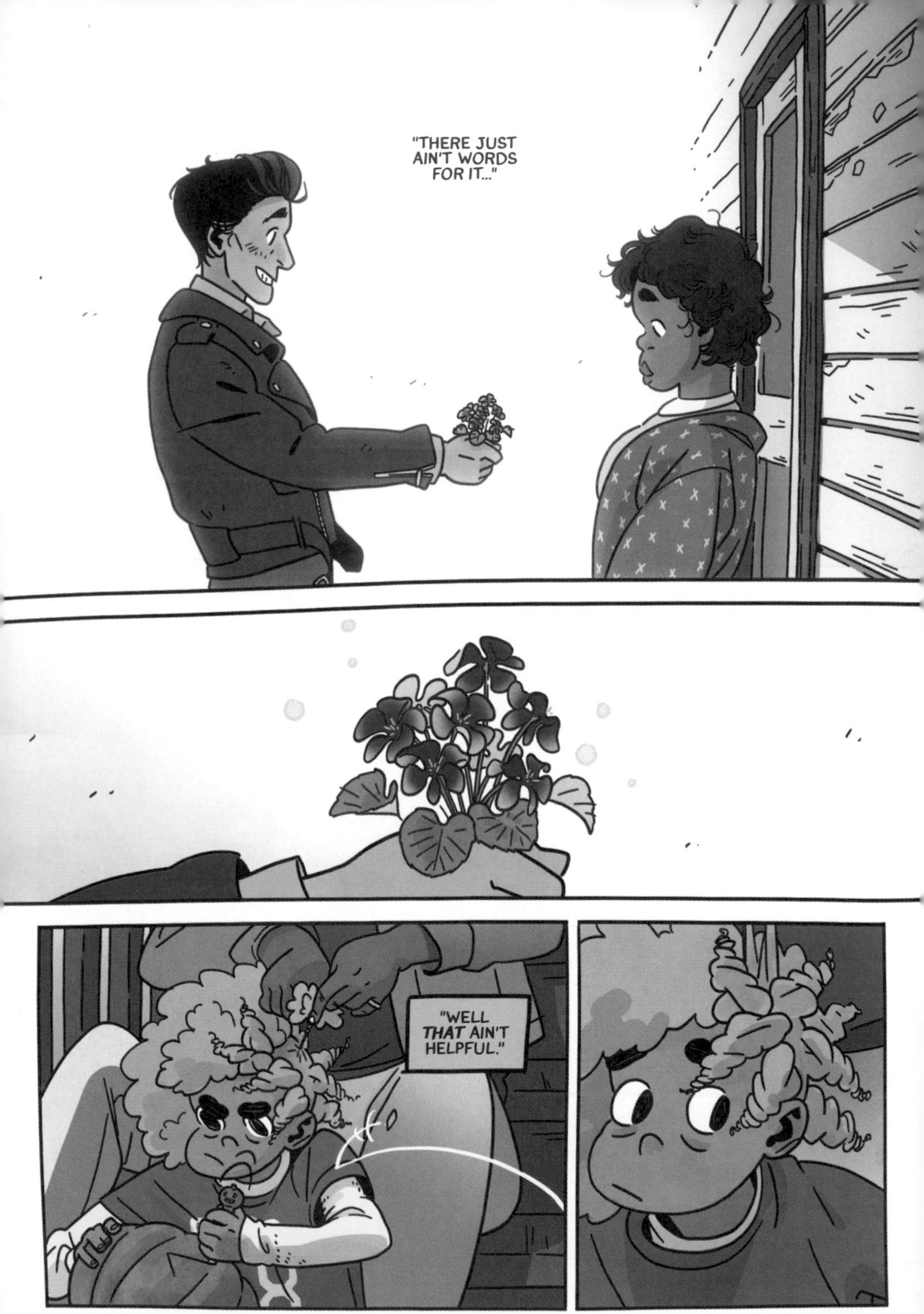
"THERE JUST AIN'T WORDS FOR IT..."
"WELL *THAT* AIN'T HELPFUL."

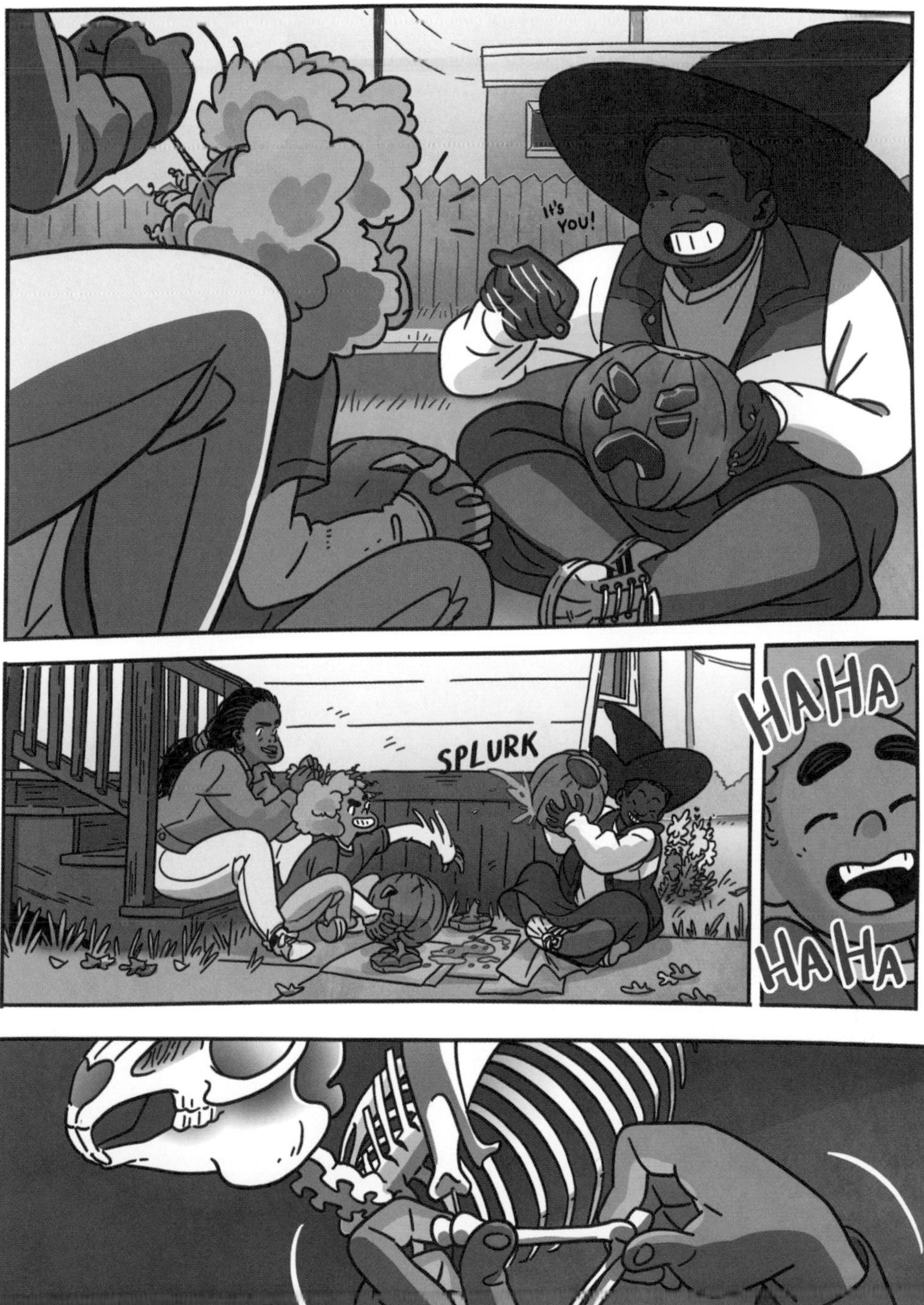
IT'S YOU!
SPLURK
HAHA
HAHA

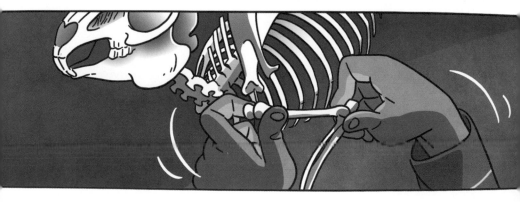

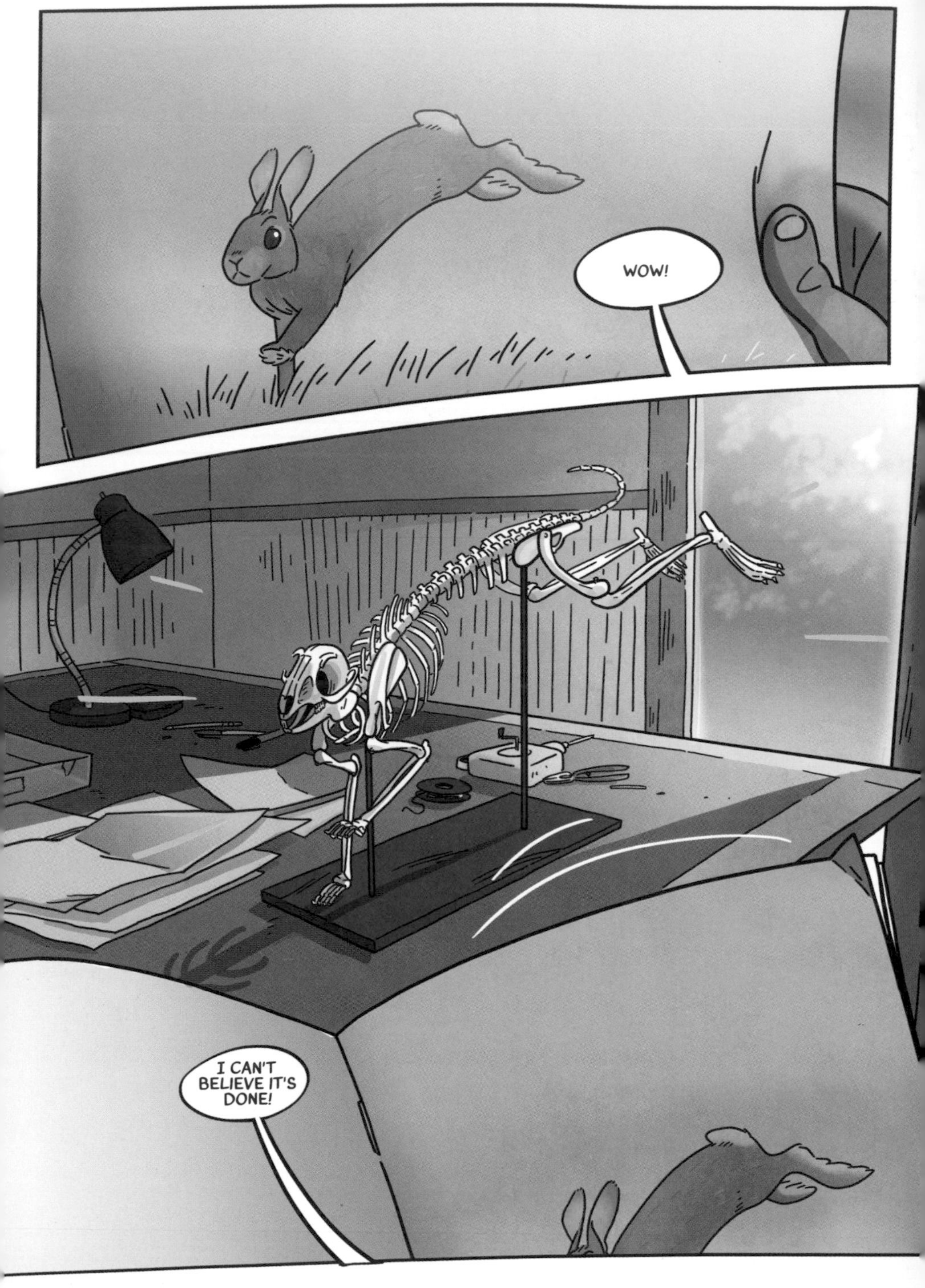
WOW!
I CAN'T BELIEVE IT'S DONE!

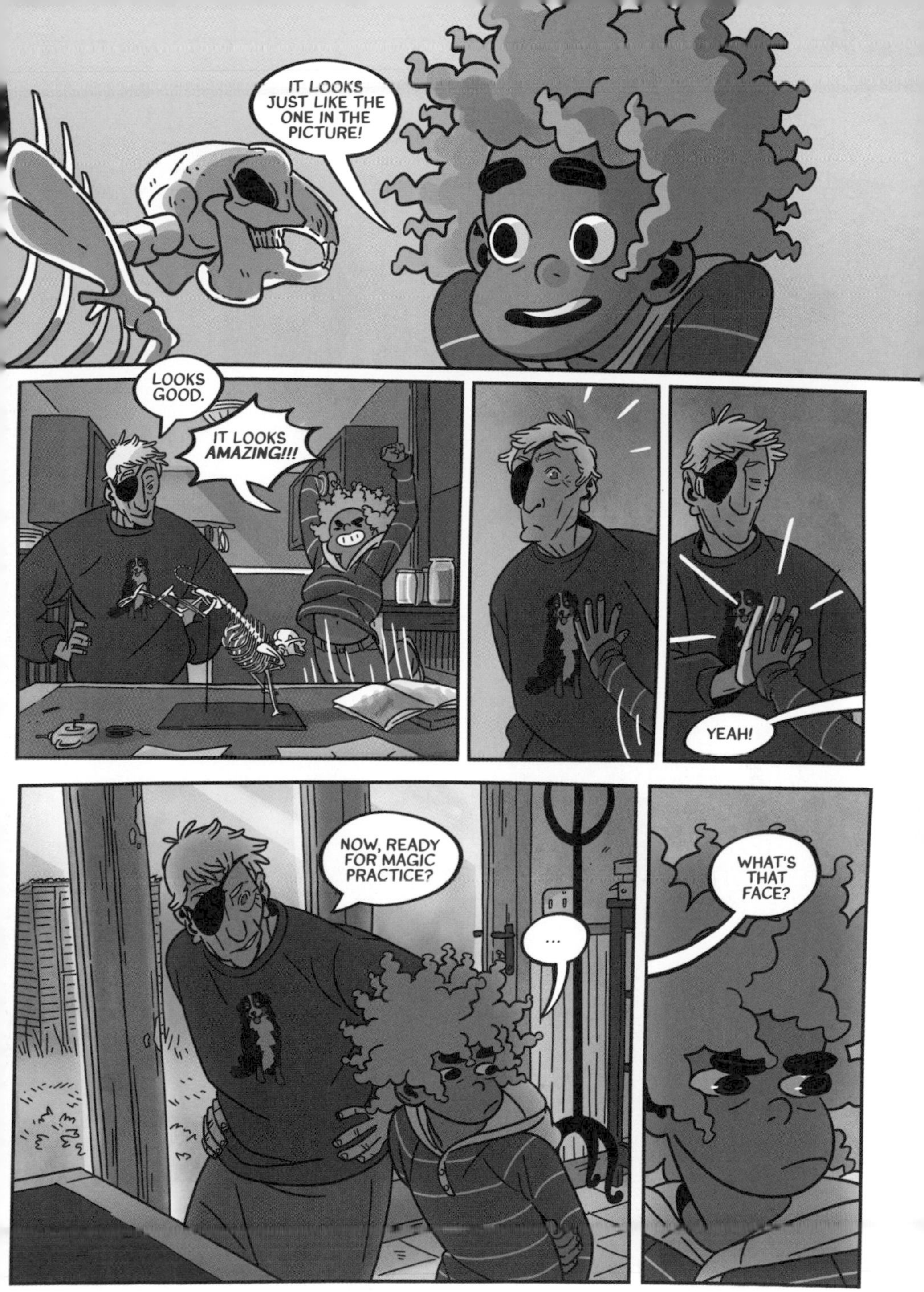
IT LOOKS JUST LIKE THE ONE IN THE PICTURE!
LOOKS GOOD.
IT LOOKS **AMAZING!!!**
YEAH!
NOW, READY FOR MAGIC PRACTICE?
...
WHAT'S THAT FACE?

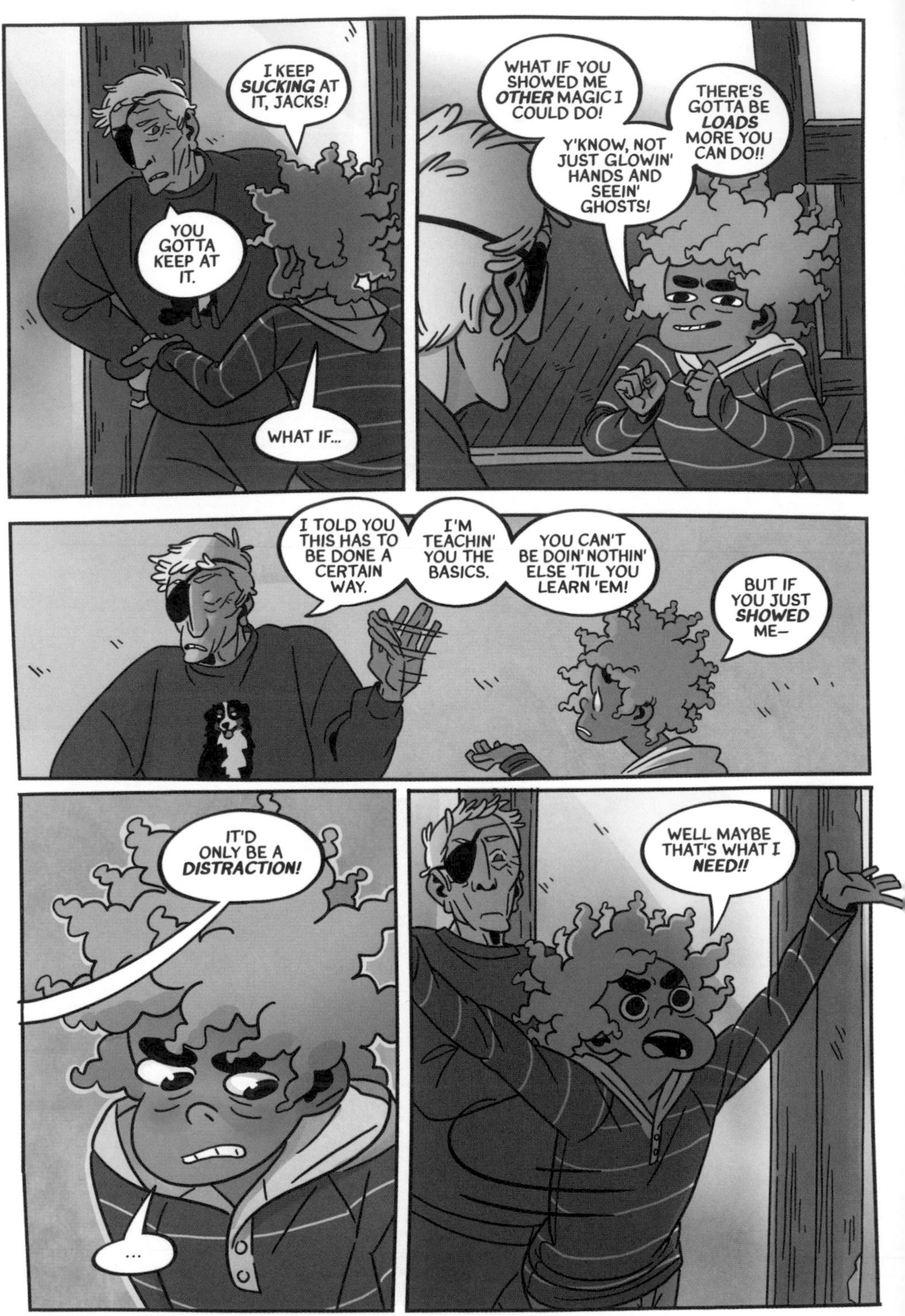
I KEEP **SUCKING** AT IT, JACKS!
YOU GOTTA KEEP AT IT.
WHAT IF...
WHAT IF YOU SHOWED ME **OTHER** MAGIC I COULD DO!
Y'KNOW, NOT JUST GLOWIN' HANDS AND SEEIN' GHOSTS!
THERE'S GOTTA BE **LOADS** MORE YOU CAN DO!!
I TOLD YOU THIS HAS TO BE DONE A CERTAIN WAY.
I'M TEACHIN' YOU THE BASICS.
YOU CAN'T BE DOIN' NOTHIN' ELSE 'TIL YOU LEARN 'EM!
BUT IF YOU JUST **SHOWED** ME–
IT'D ONLY BE A **DISTRACTION!**
...
WELL MAYBE THAT'S WHAT I **NEED!!**

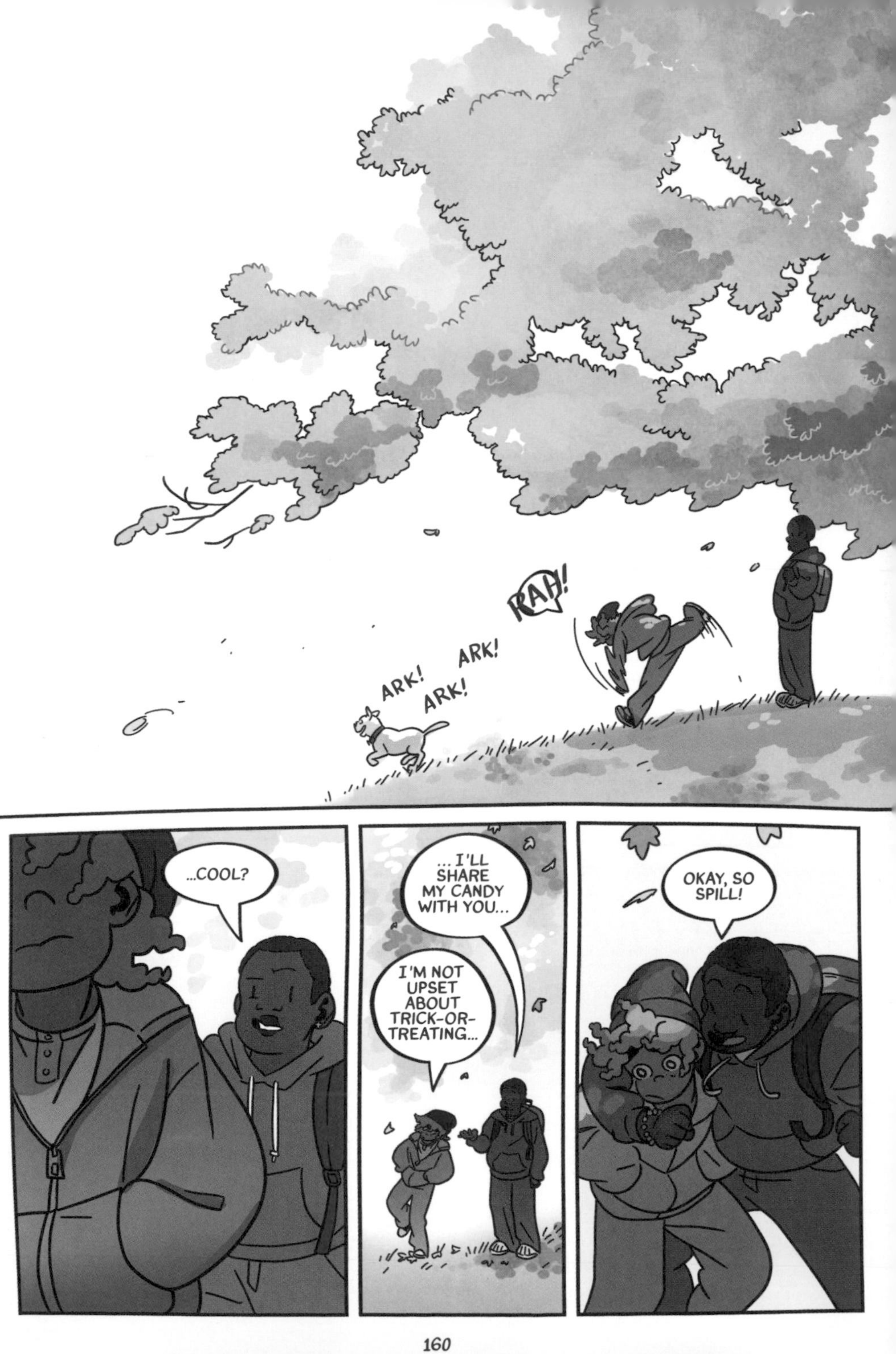
RAH!
ARK!
ARK!
ARK!
...COOL?
...I'LL SHARE MY CANDY WITH YOU...
I'M NOT UPSET ABOUT TRICK-OR-TREATING...
OKAY, SO SPILL!

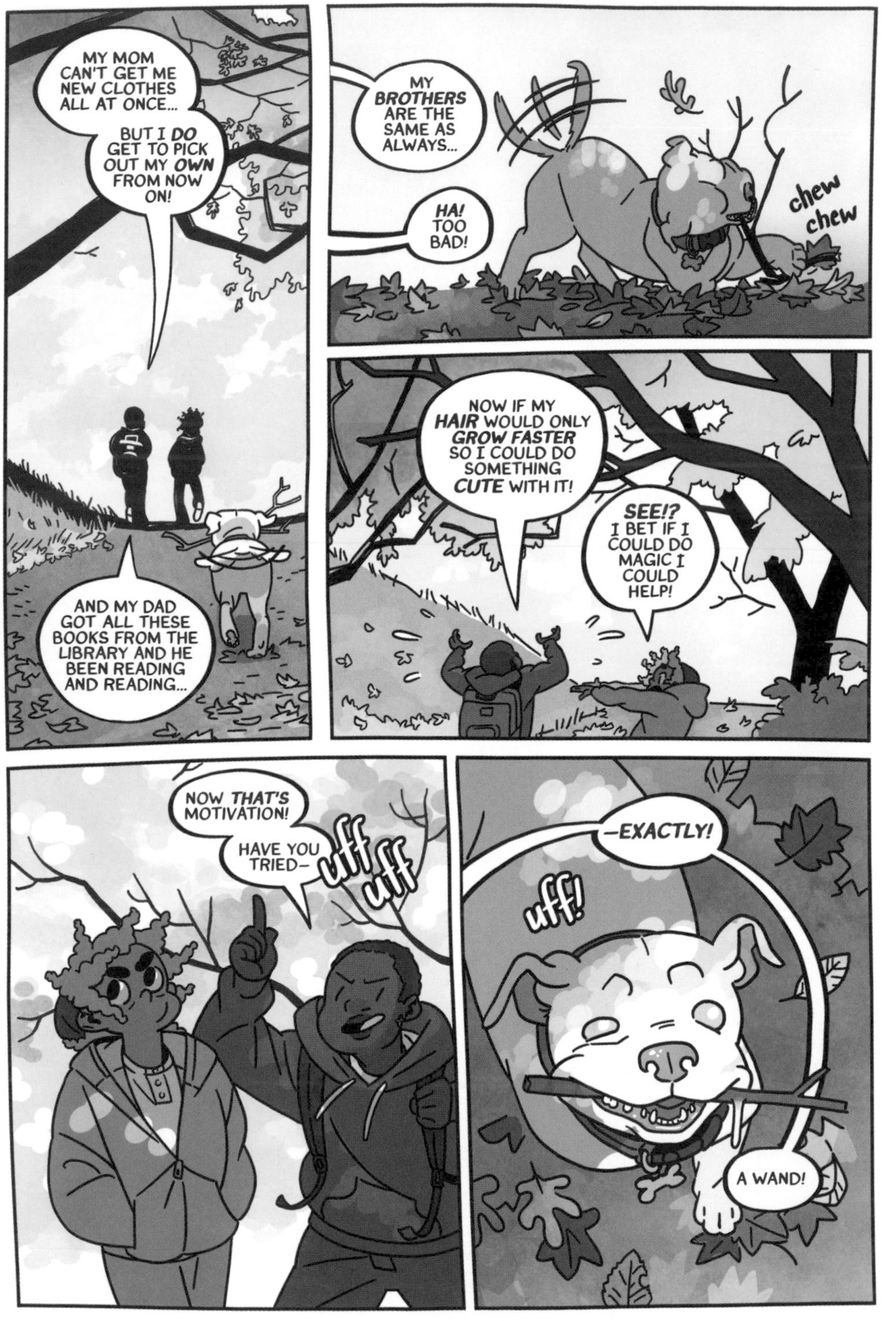

MY MOM CAN'T GET ME NEW CLOTHES ALL AT ONCE...
BUT I *DO* GET TO PICK OUT MY *OWN* FROM NOW ON!
AND MY DAD GOT ALL THESE BOOKS FROM THE LIBRARY AND HE BEEN READING AND READING...
MY *BROTHERS* ARE THE SAME AS ALWAYS...
HA! TOO BAD!
chew chew
NOW IF MY *HAIR* WOULD ONLY *GROW FASTER* SO I COULD DO SOMETHING *CUTE* WITH IT!
SEE!? I BET IF I COULD DO MAGIC I COULD HELP!
NOW *THAT'S* MOTIVATION!
HAVE YOU TRIED–
uff uff
–*EXACTLY!*
uff!
A WAND!

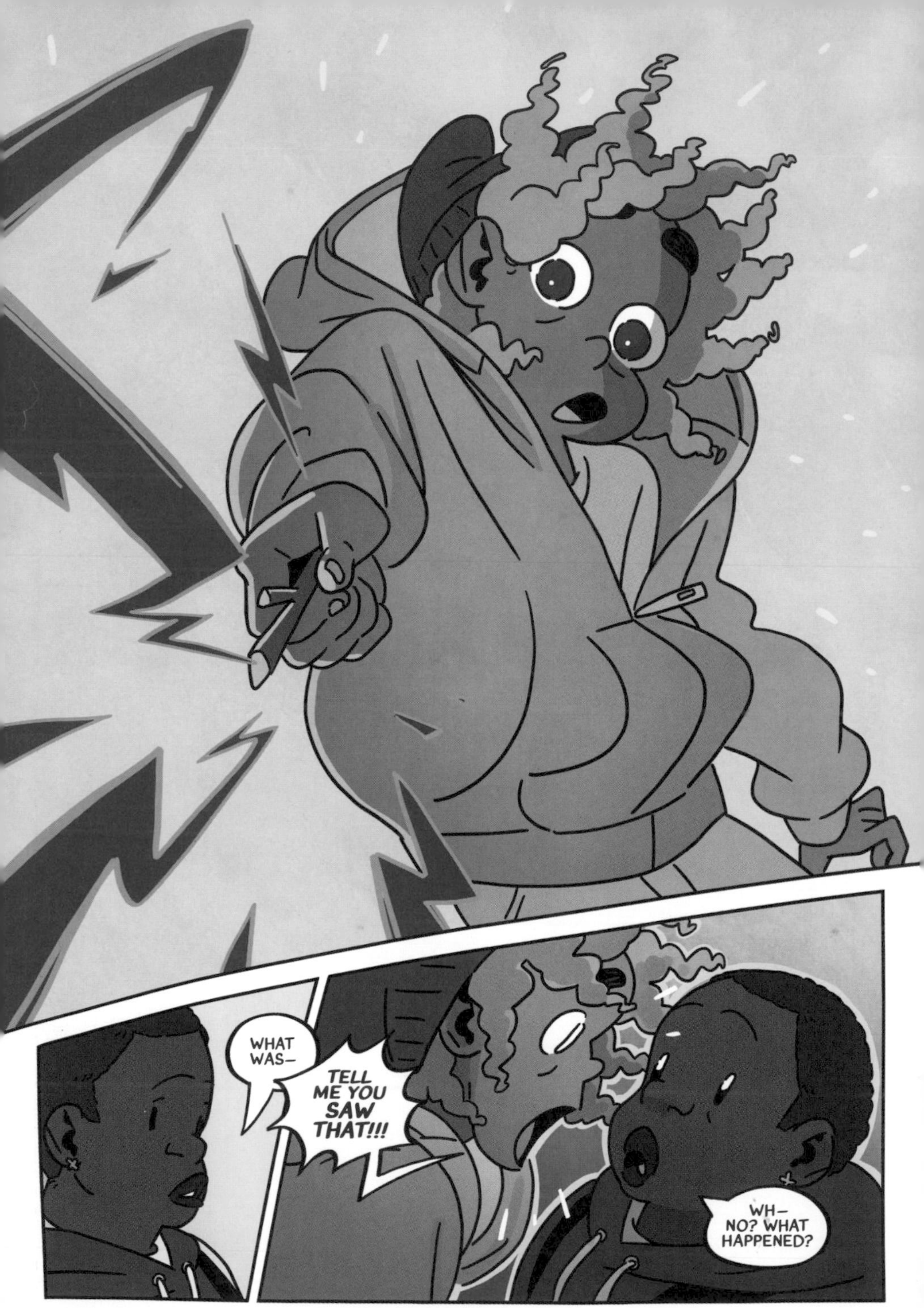
WHAT WAS—
TELL ME YOU SAW THAT!!!
WH— NO? WHAT HAPPENED?

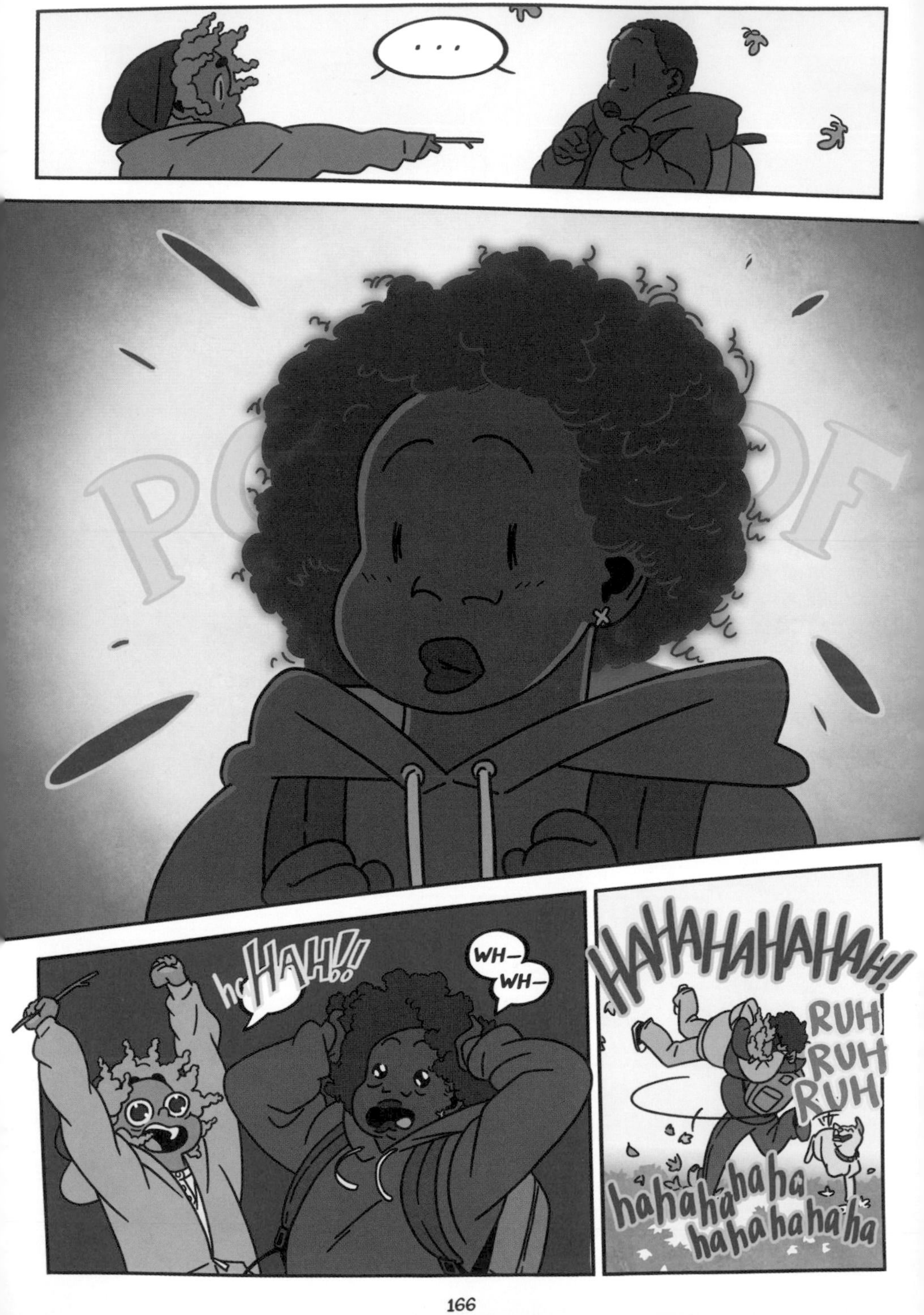
...
POOF
haHAH!!
WH—
WH—
HAHAHAHAHAHAH!!
RUH
RUH
RUH
hahahahaha
hahahahahaha

HALLOWEEN NIGHT

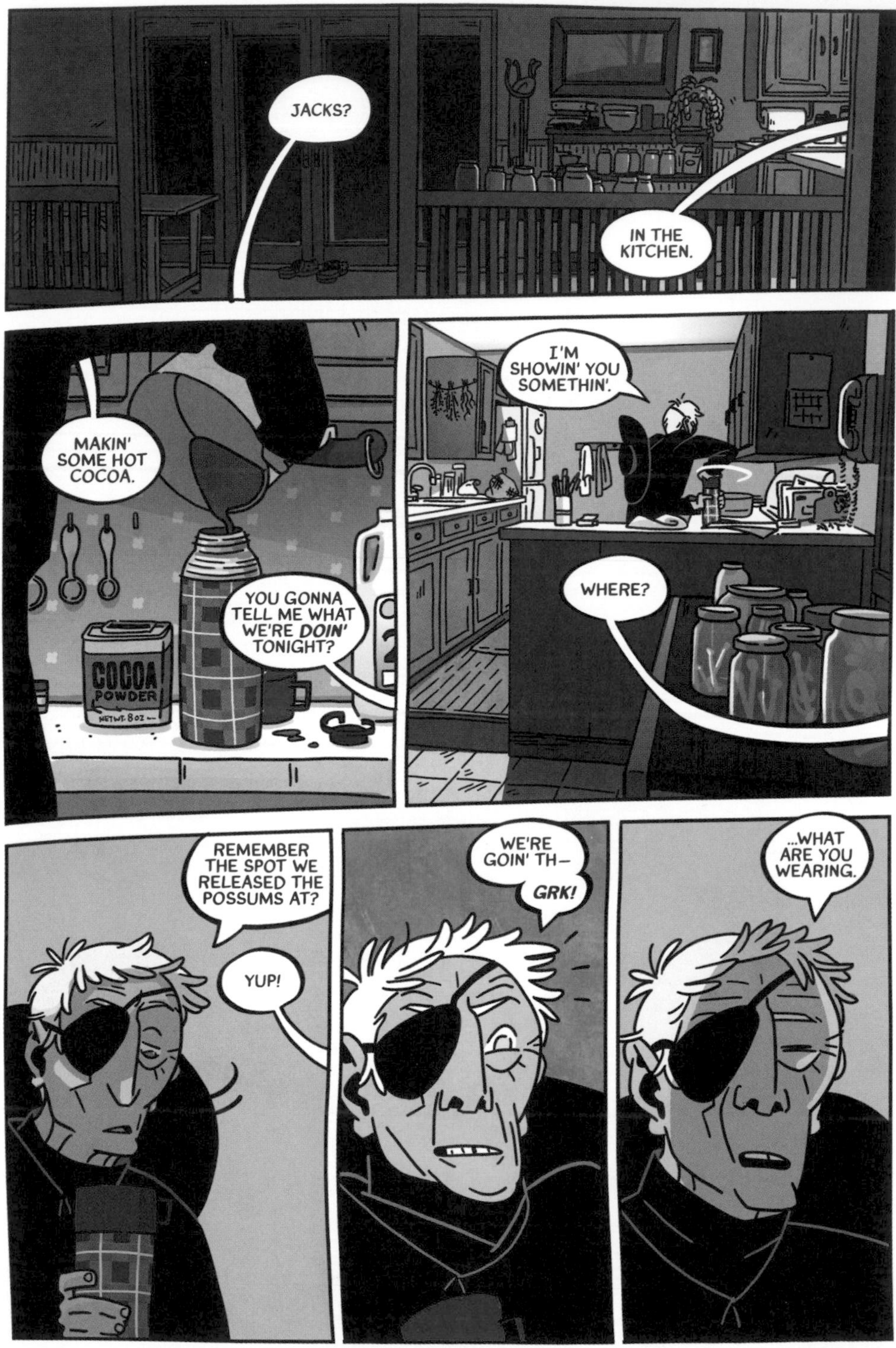
JACKS?
IN THE KITCHEN.
MAKIN' SOME HOT COCOA.
COCOA POWDER
YOU GONNA TELL ME WHAT WE'RE *DOIN'* TONIGHT?
I'M SHOWIN' YOU SOMETHIN'.
WHERE?
REMEMBER THE SPOT WE RELEASED THE POSSUMS AT?
YUP!
WE'RE GOIN' TH—
GRK!
...WHAT ARE YOU WEARING.

169

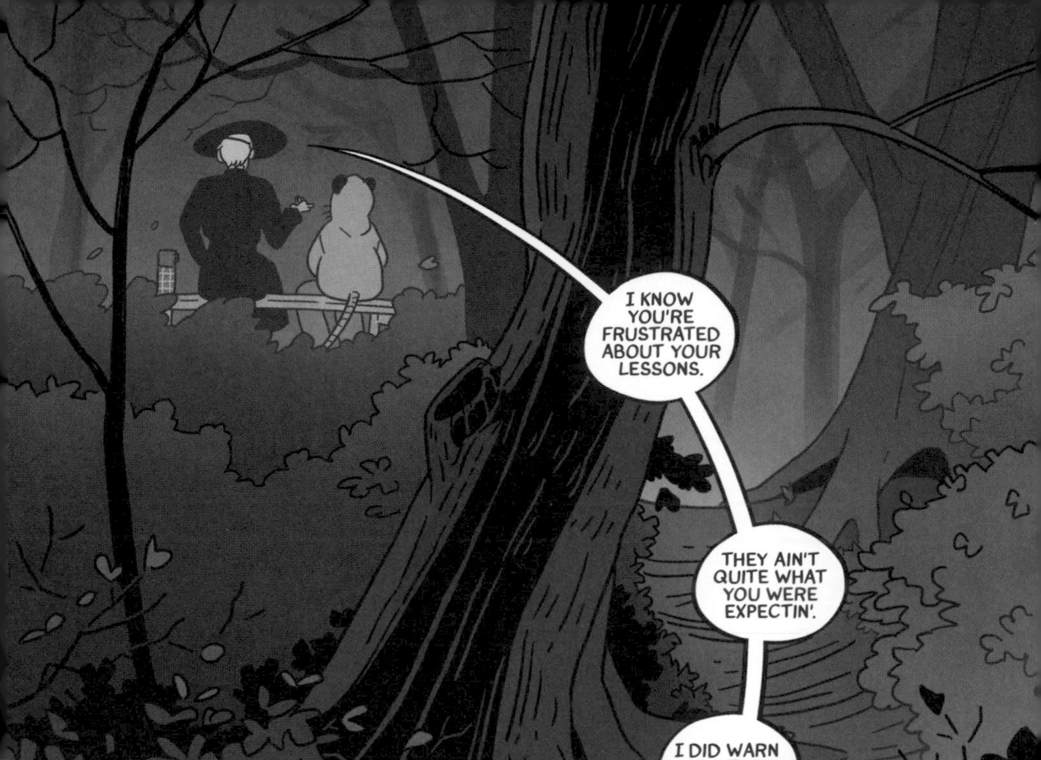
I KNOW YOU'RE FRUSTRATED ABOUT YOUR LESSONS.
THEY AIN'T QUITE WHAT YOU WERE EXPECTIN'.
I DID WARN YOU THEY WOULDN'T BE.

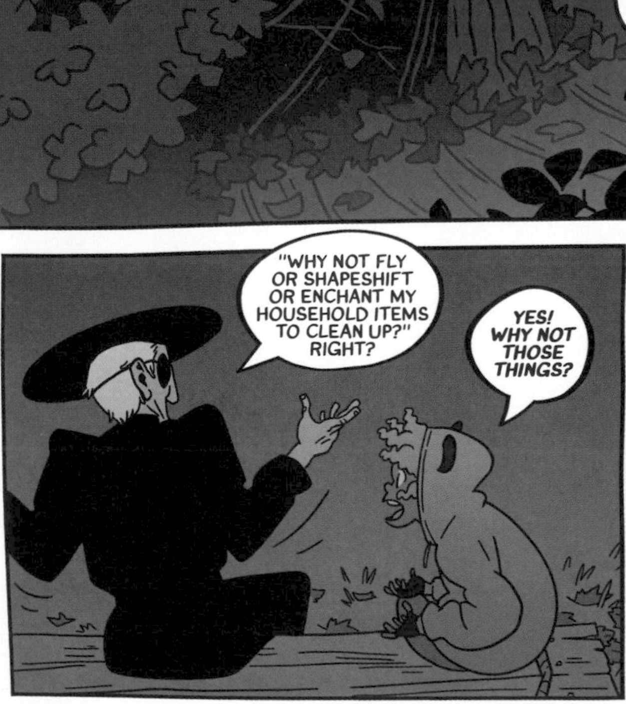
"WHY NOT FLY OR SHAPESHIFT OR ENCHANT MY HOUSEHOLD ITEMS TO CLEAN UP?" RIGHT?
YES! WHY NOT THOSE THINGS?

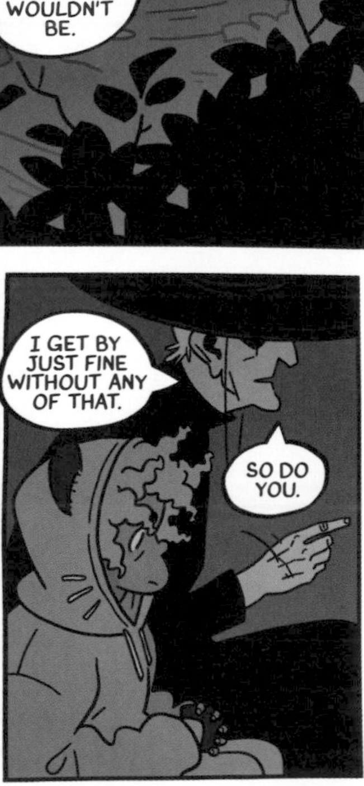
I GET BY JUST FINE WITHOUT ANY OF THAT.
SO DO YOU.

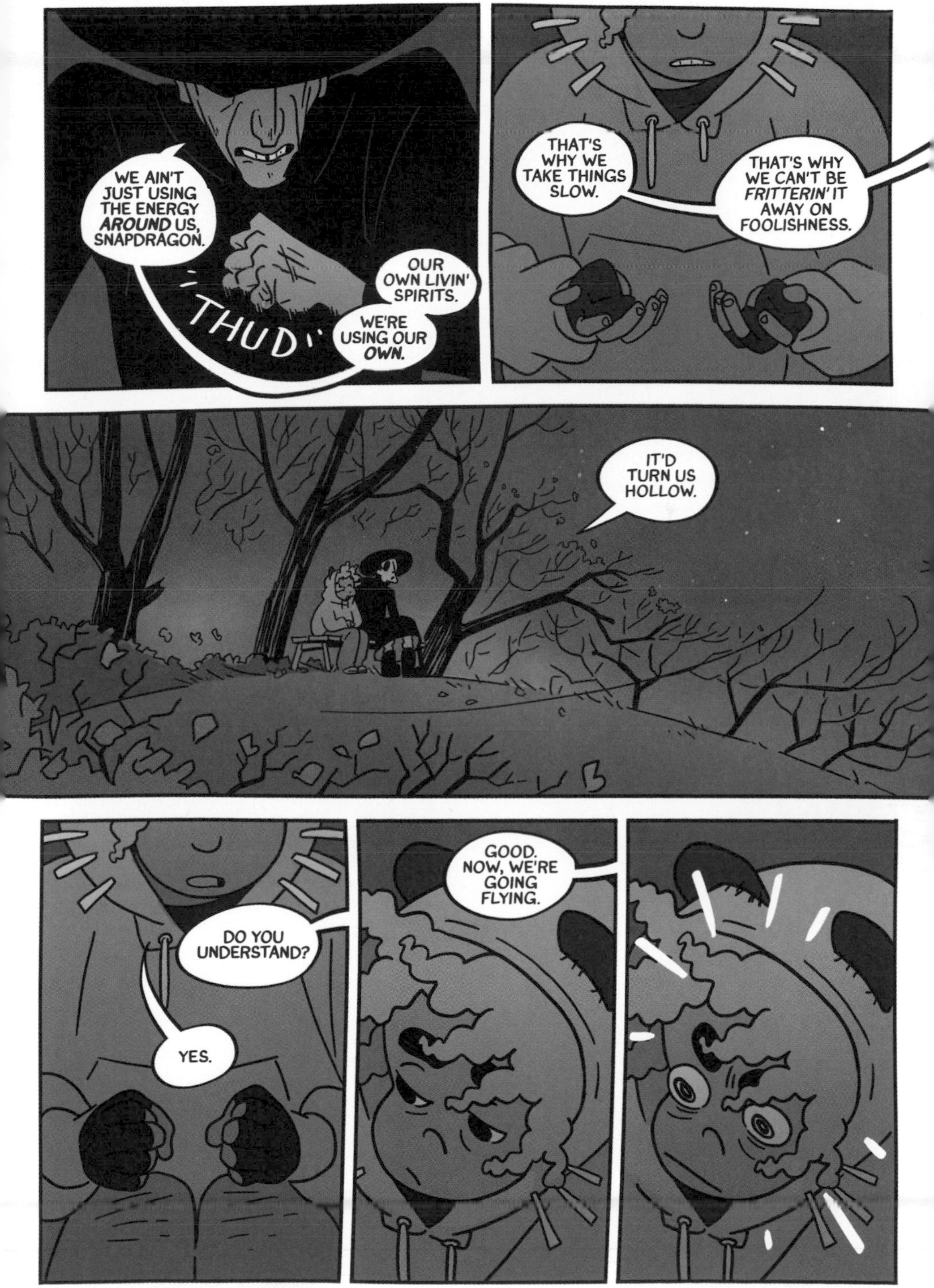
WE AIN'T JUST USING THE ENERGY **AROUND** US, SNAPDRAGON.
OUR OWN LIVIN' SPIRITS.
THUD
WE'RE USING OUR **OWN.**
THAT'S WHY WE TAKE THINGS SLOW.
THAT'S WHY WE CAN'T BE *FRITTERIN'* IT AWAY ON FOOLISHNESS.
IT'D TURN US HOLLOW.
DO YOU UNDERSTAND?
YES.
GOOD. NOW, WE'RE GOING FLYING.

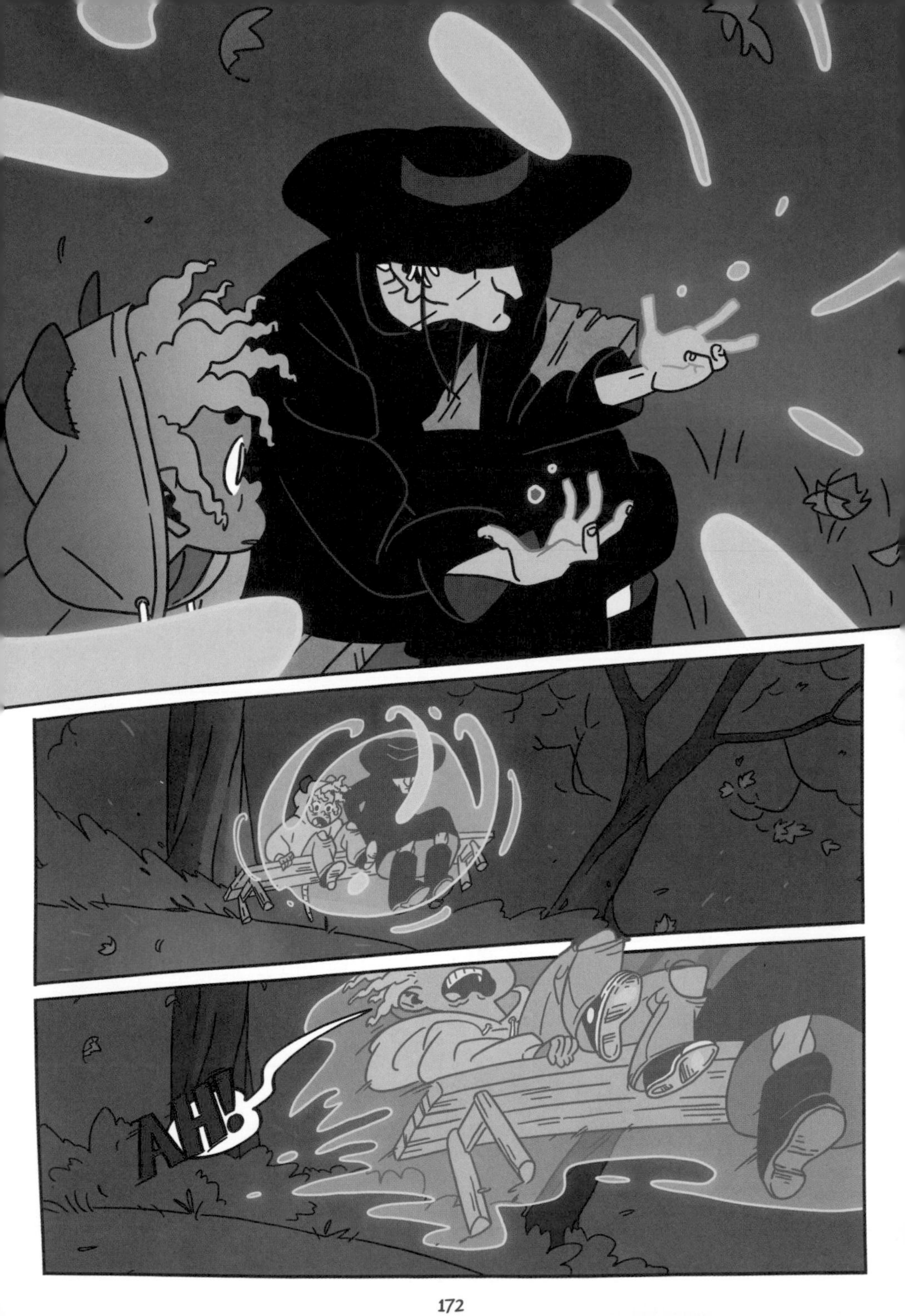
AH!

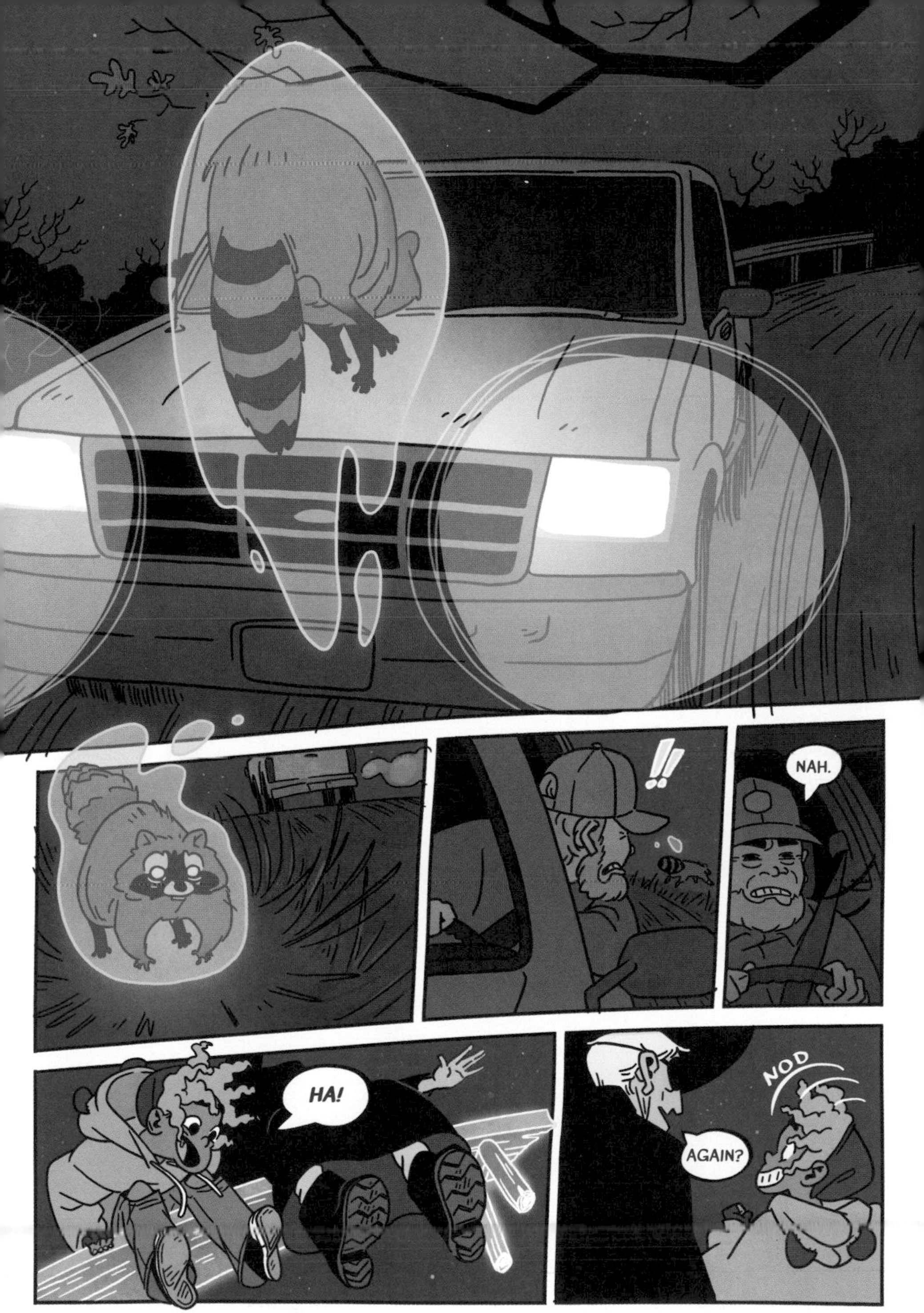
!!
NAH.
HA!
AGAIN?
NOD

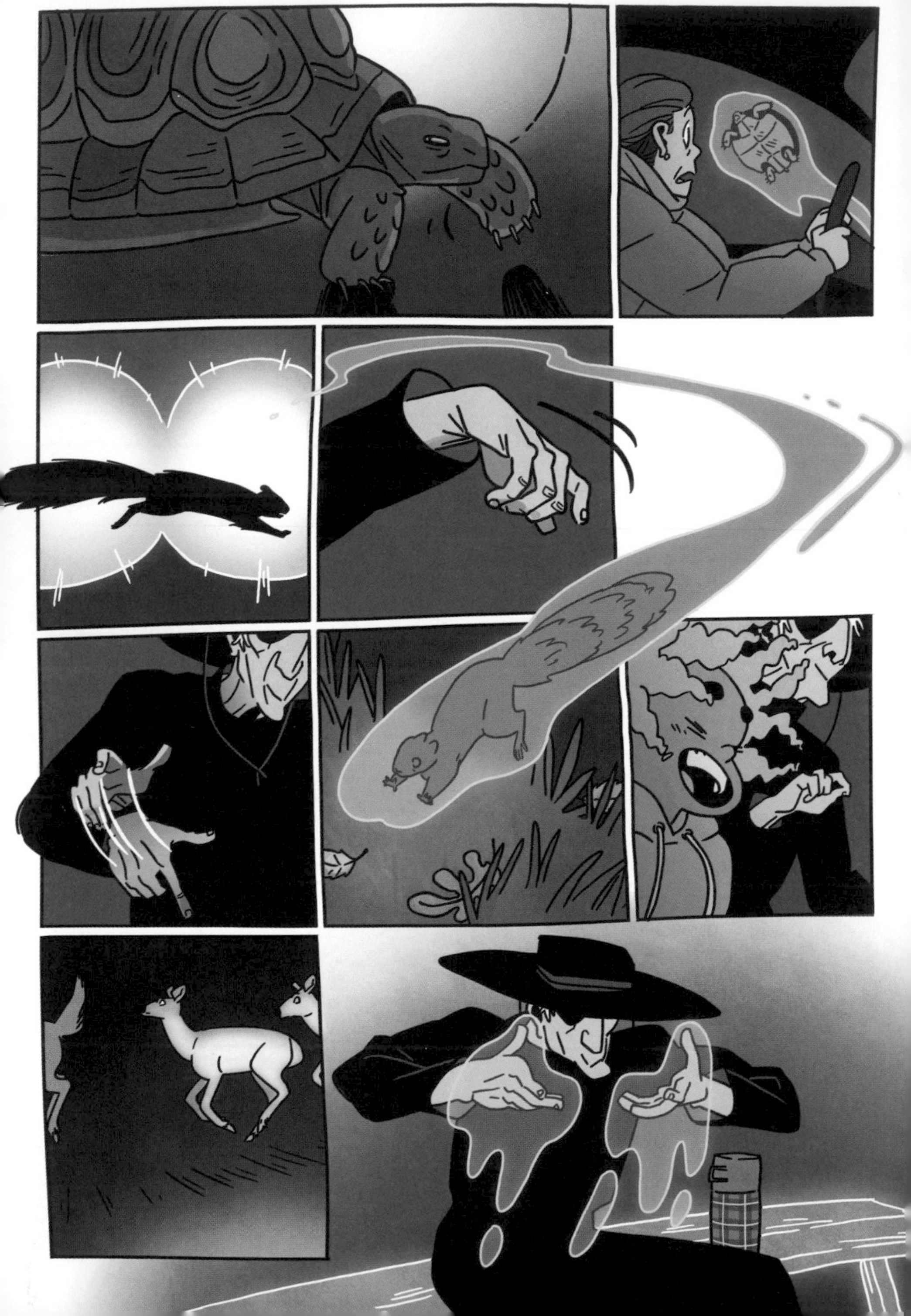

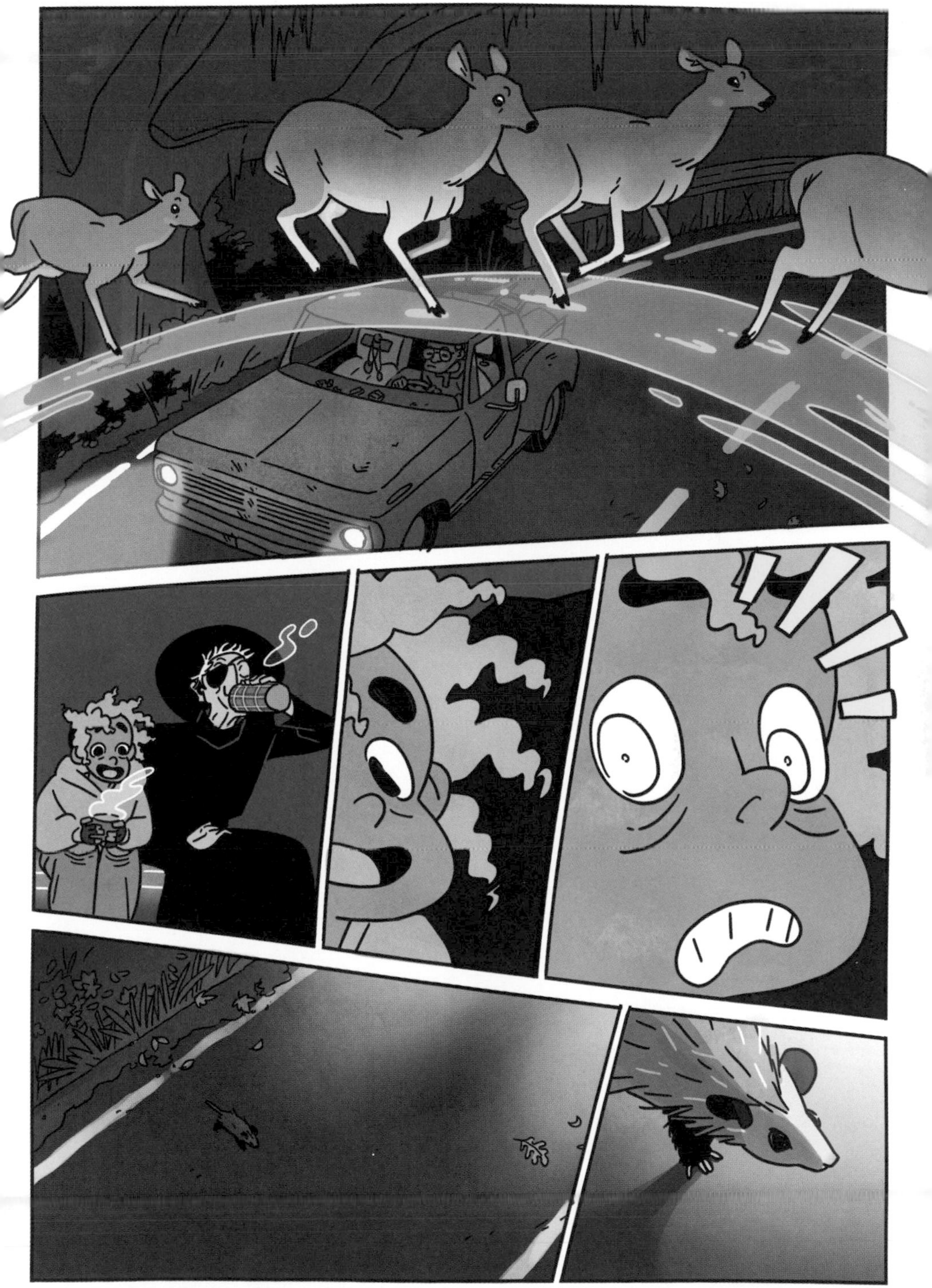

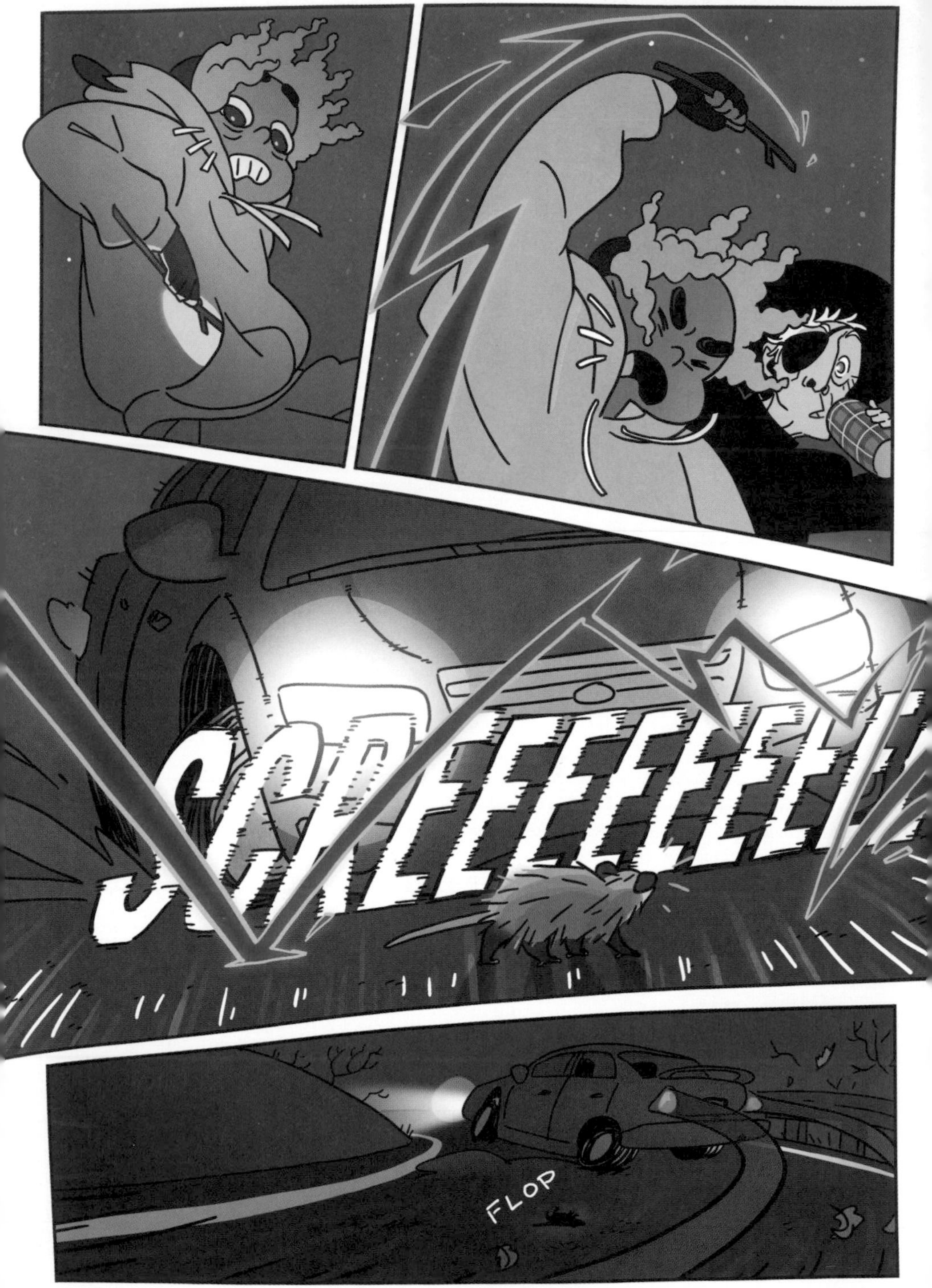
SCREEEEEEEE
FLOP

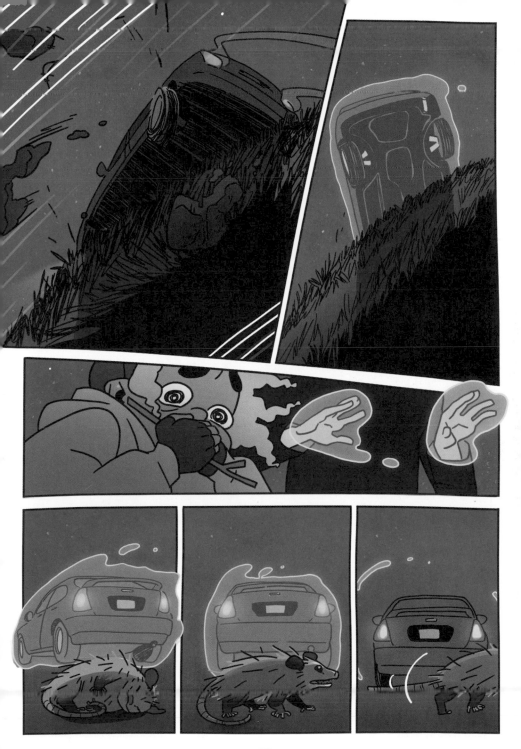

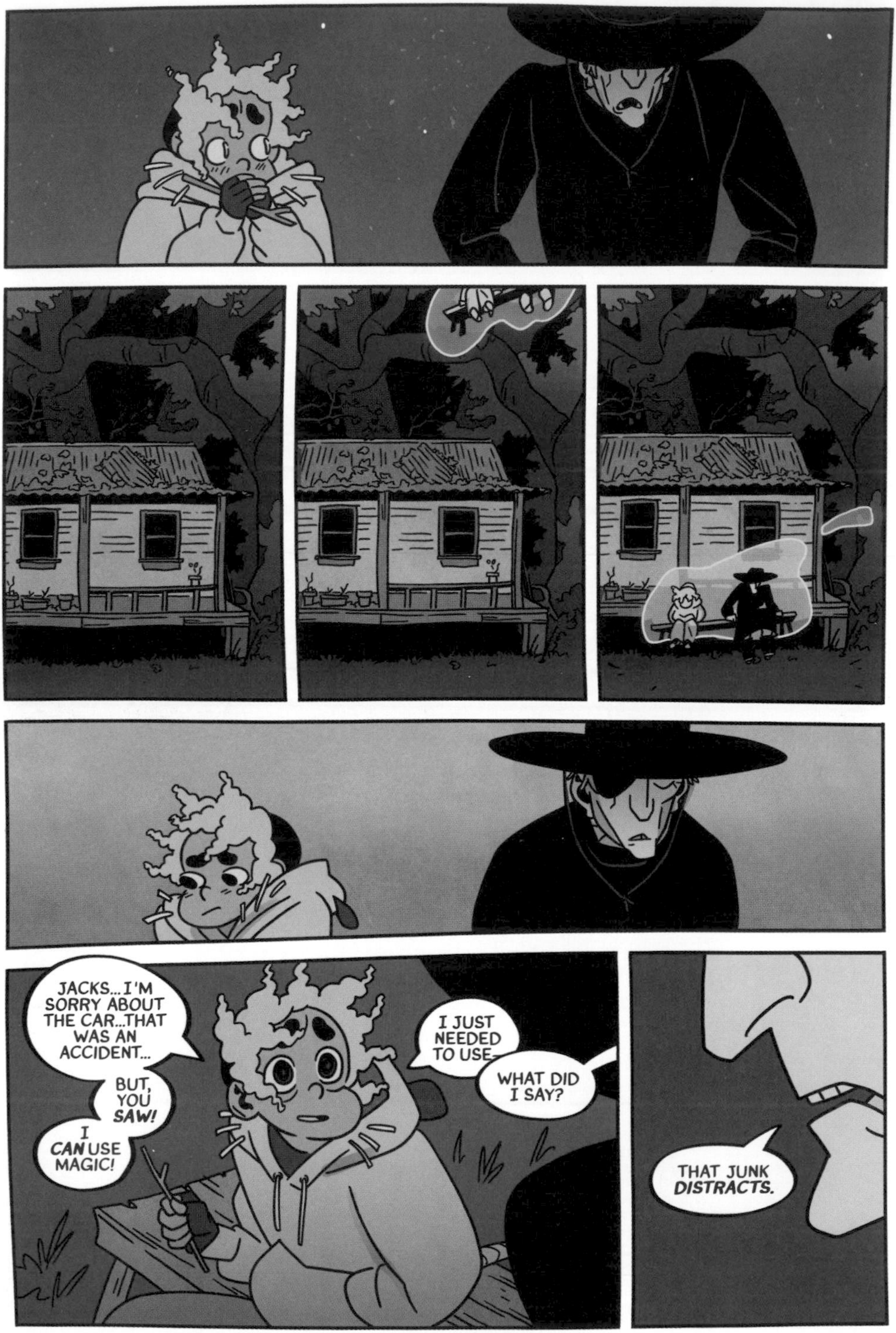
JACKS... I'M SORRY ABOUT THE CAR... THAT WAS AN ACCIDENT...
BUT, YOU *SAW!*
I *CAN* USE MAGIC!
I JUST NEEDED TO USE-
WHAT DID I SAY?
THAT JUNK *DISTRACTS.*

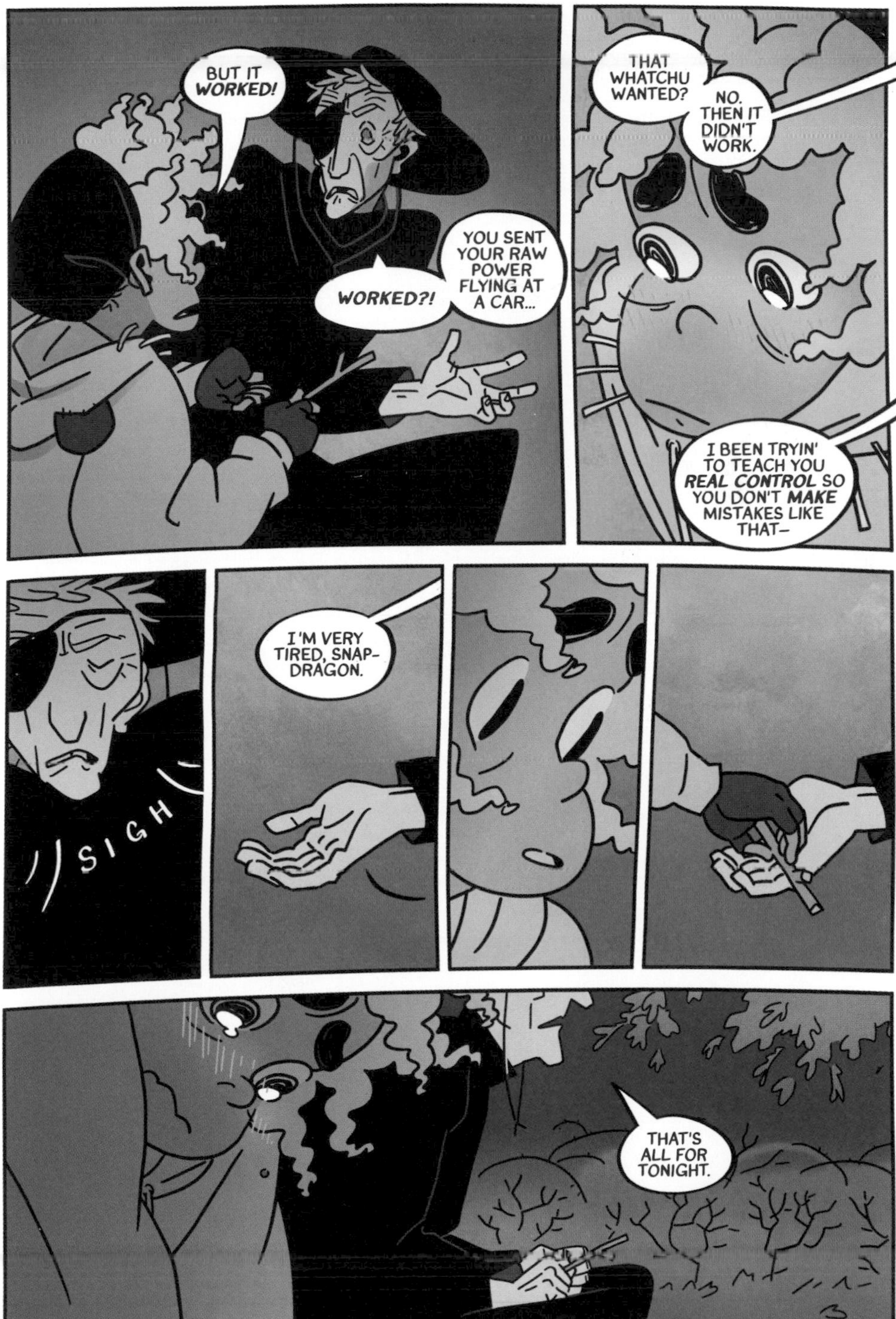
BUT IT *WORKED!*
WORKED?!
YOU SENT YOUR RAW POWER FLYING AT A CAR...
THAT WHATCHU WANTED?
NO. THEN IT DIDN'T WORK.
I BEEN TRYIN' TO TEACH YOU ***REAL CONTROL*** SO YOU DON'T ***MAKE*** MISTAKES LIKE THAT–
SIGH
I'M VERY TIRED, SNAP-DRAGON.
THAT'S ALL FOR TONIGHT.

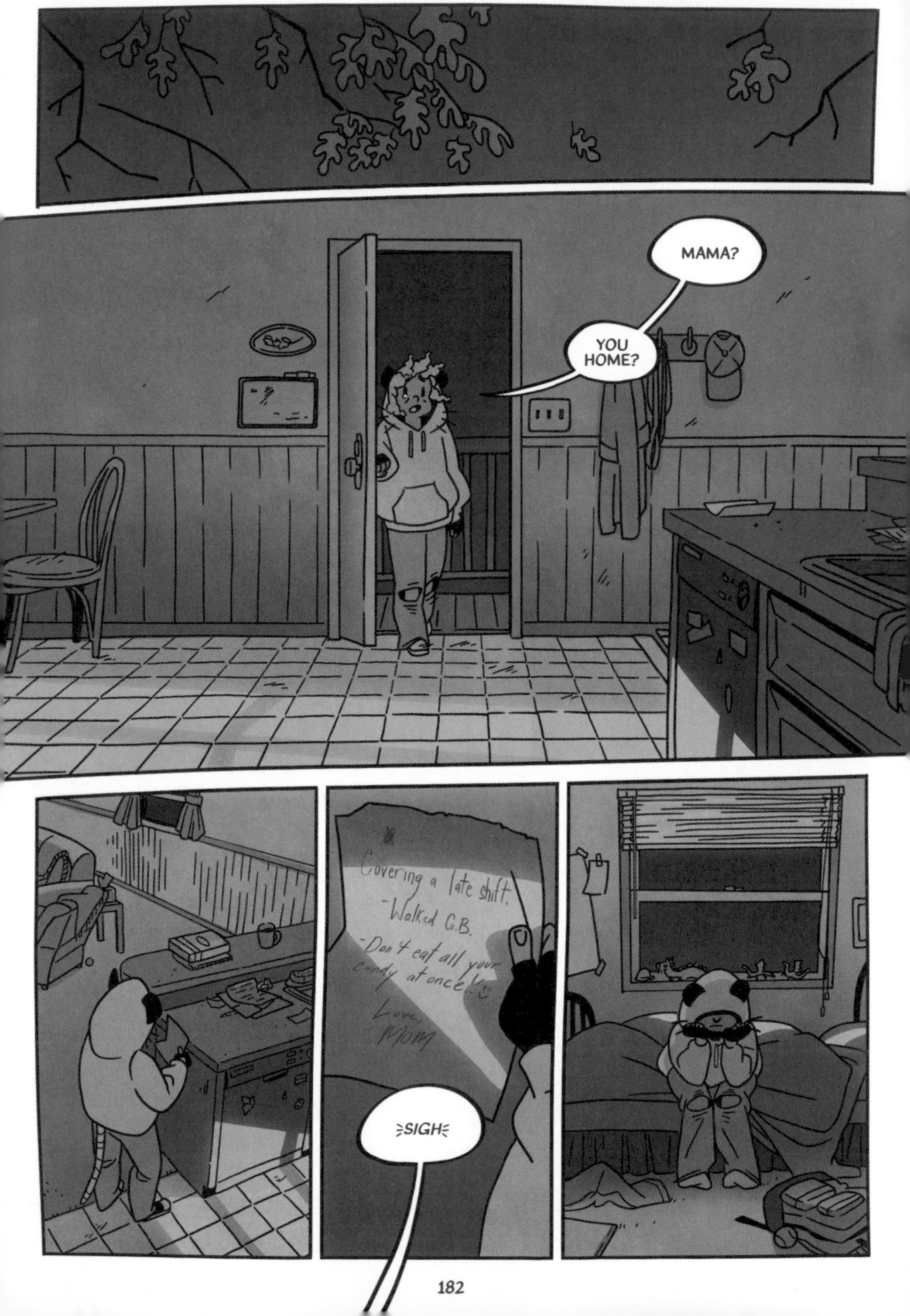
MAMA?
YOU HOME?
Covering a late shift.
-Walked G.B.
-Don't eat all your candy at once!!
Love,
MOM
SIGH

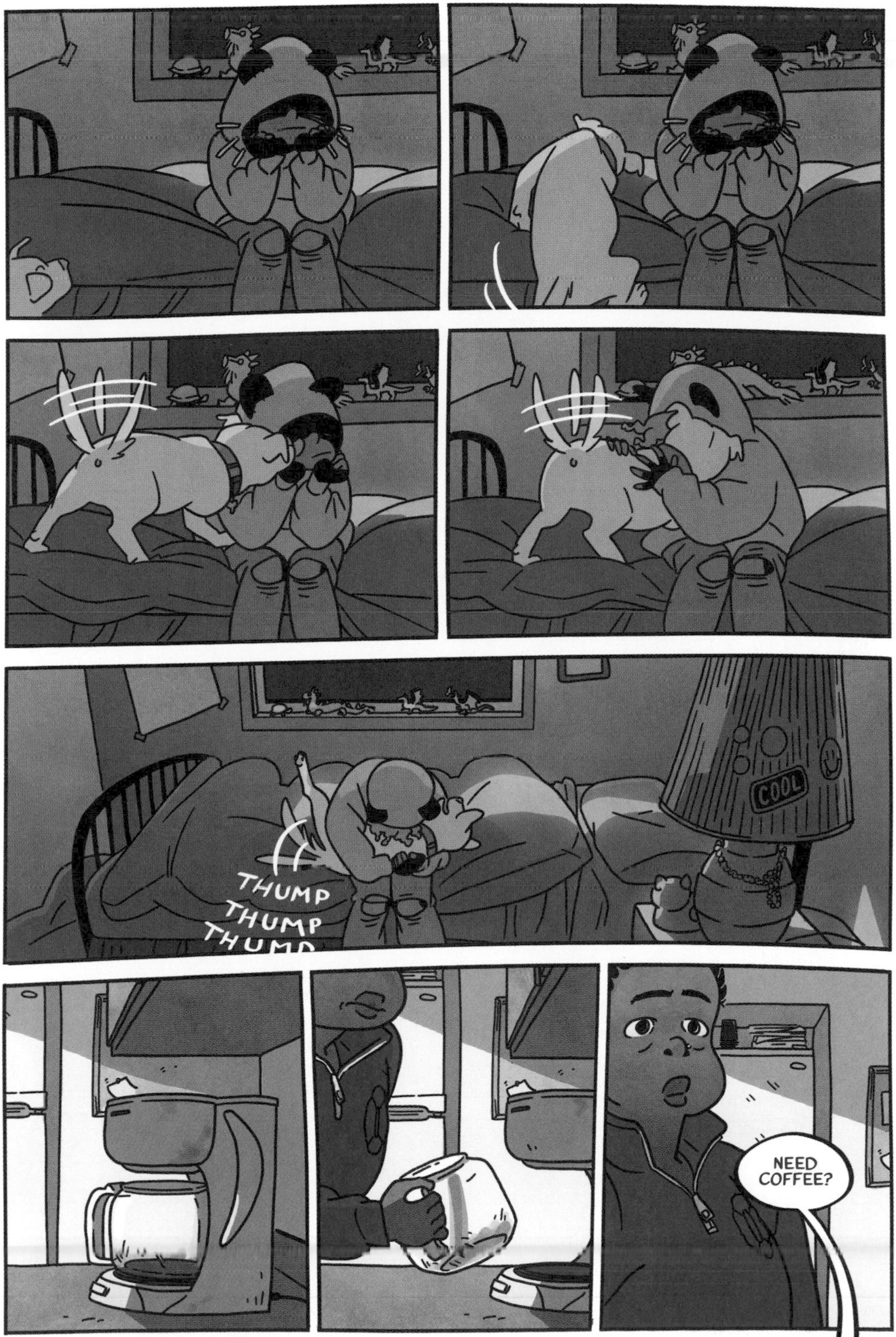
THUMP
THUMP
THUMP
COOL
NEED COFFEE?

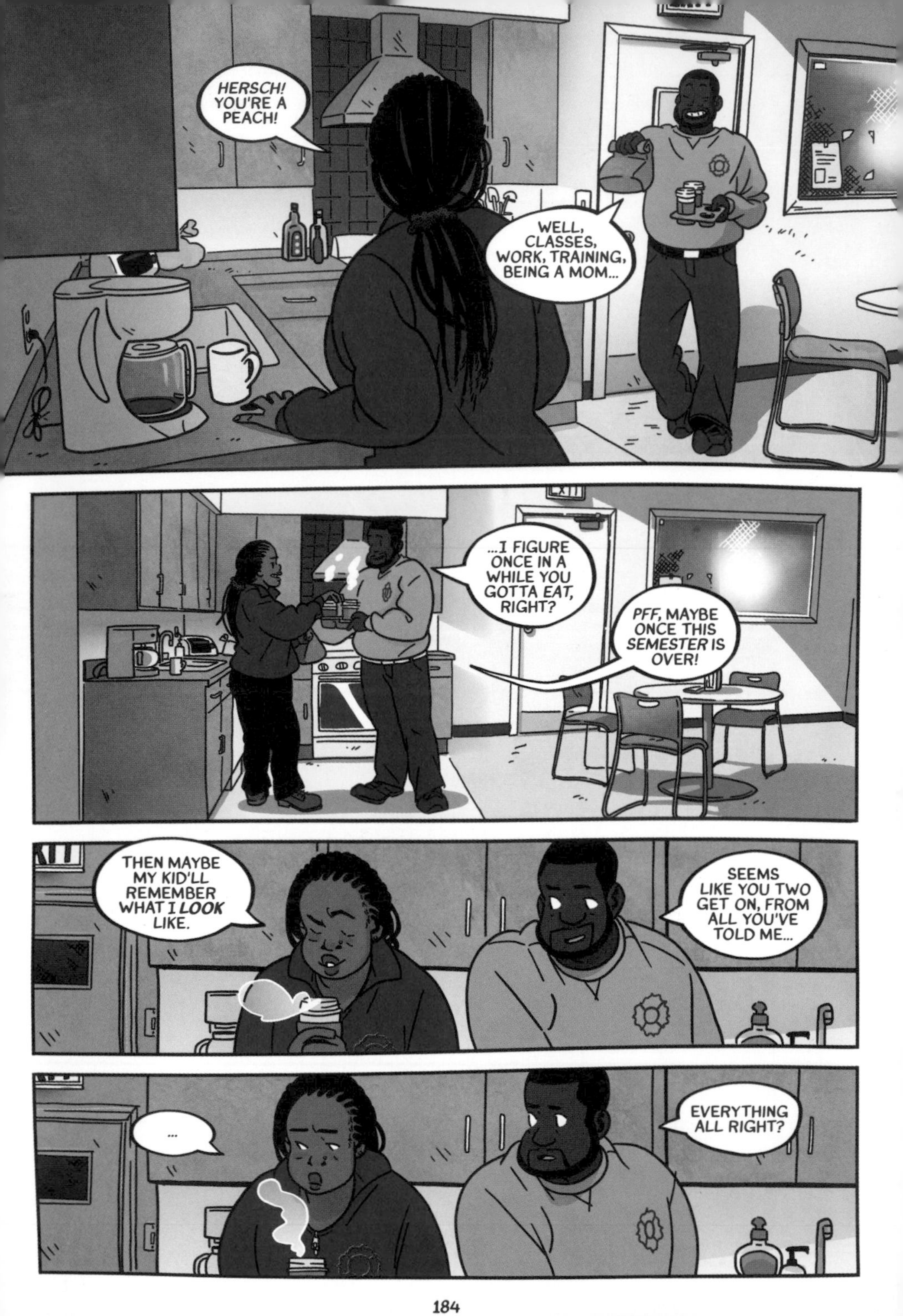
HERSCH! YOU'RE A PEACH!
WELL, CLASSES, WORK, TRAINING, BEING A MOM...
...I FIGURE ONCE IN A WHILE YOU GOTTA EAT, RIGHT?
PFF, MAYBE ONCE THIS SEMESTER IS OVER!
THEN MAYBE MY KID'LL REMEMBER WHAT I LOOK LIKE.
SEEMS LIKE YOU TWO GET ON, FROM ALL YOU'VE TOLD ME...
...
EVERYTHING ALL RIGHT?

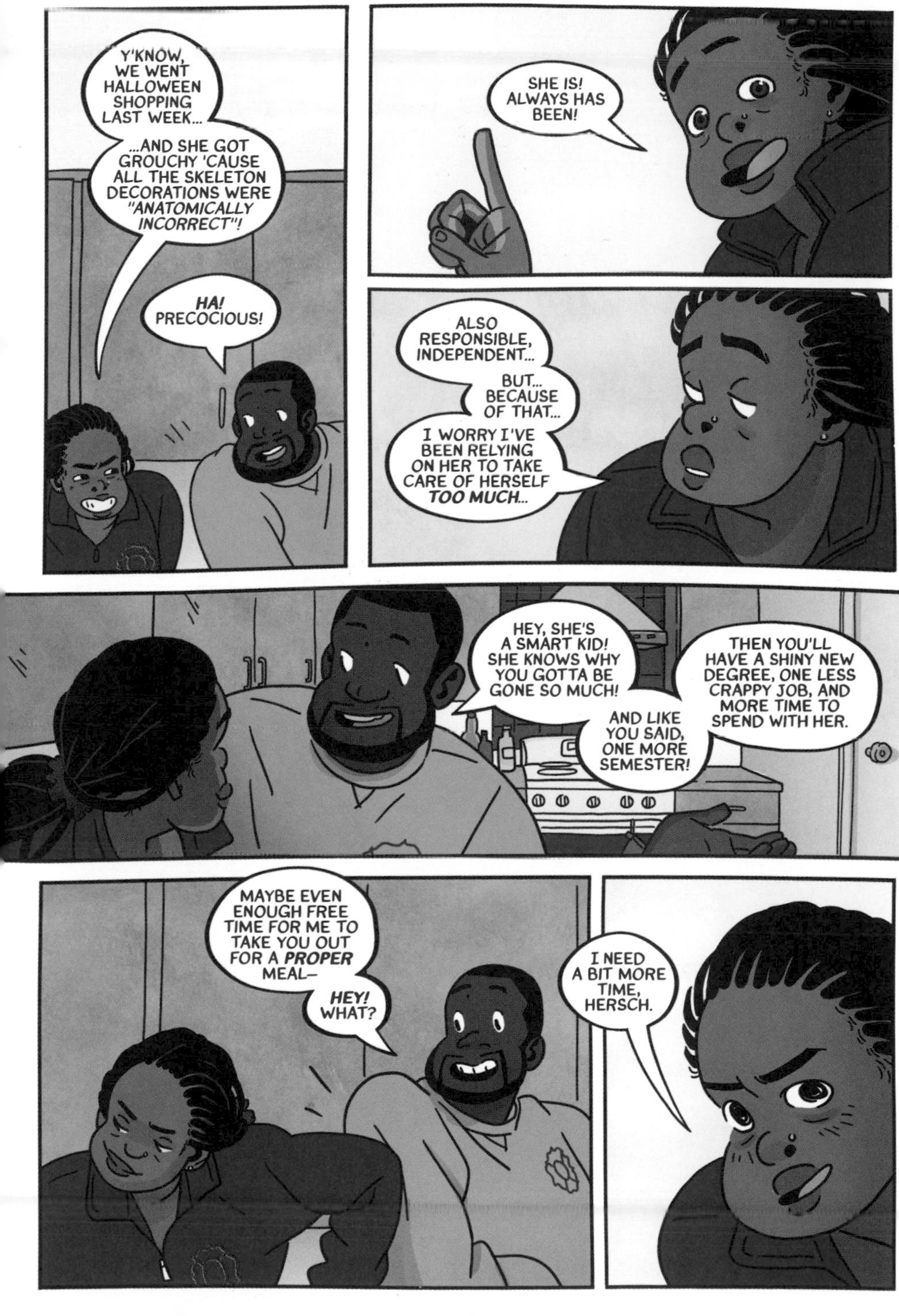
Y'KNOW, WE WENT HALLOWEEN SHOPPING LAST WEEK...
...AND SHE GOT GROUCHY 'CAUSE ALL THE SKELETON DECORATIONS WERE "*ANATOMICALLY INCORRECT*"!
HA! PRECOCIOUS!
SHE IS! ALWAYS HAS BEEN!
ALSO RESPONSIBLE, INDEPENDENT...
BUT... BECAUSE OF THAT...
I WORRY I'VE BEEN RELYING ON HER TO TAKE CARE OF HERSELF ***TOO MUCH...***
HEY, SHE'S A SMART KID! SHE KNOWS WHY YOU GOTTA BE GONE SO MUCH!
AND LIKE YOU SAID, ONE MORE SEMESTER!
THEN YOU'LL HAVE A SHINY NEW DEGREE, ONE LESS CRAPPY JOB, AND MORE TIME TO SPEND WITH HER.
MAYBE EVEN ENOUGH FREE TIME FOR ME TO TAKE YOU OUT FOR A ***PROPER*** MEAL—
HEY! WHAT?
I NEED A BIT MORE TIME, HERSCH.

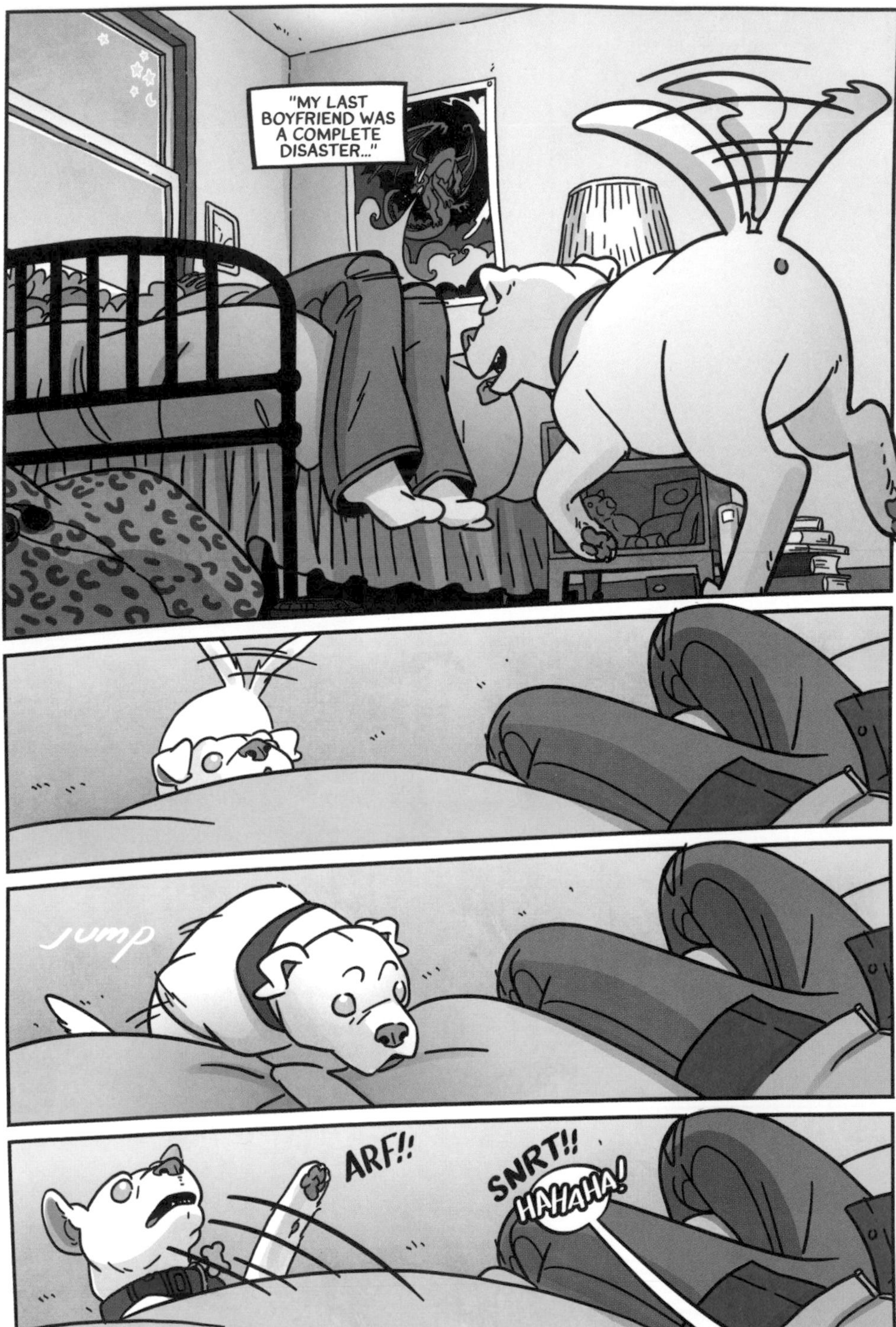
"MY LAST BOYFRIEND WAS A COMPLETE DISASTER..."
jump
ARF!!
SNRT!!
HAHAHA!

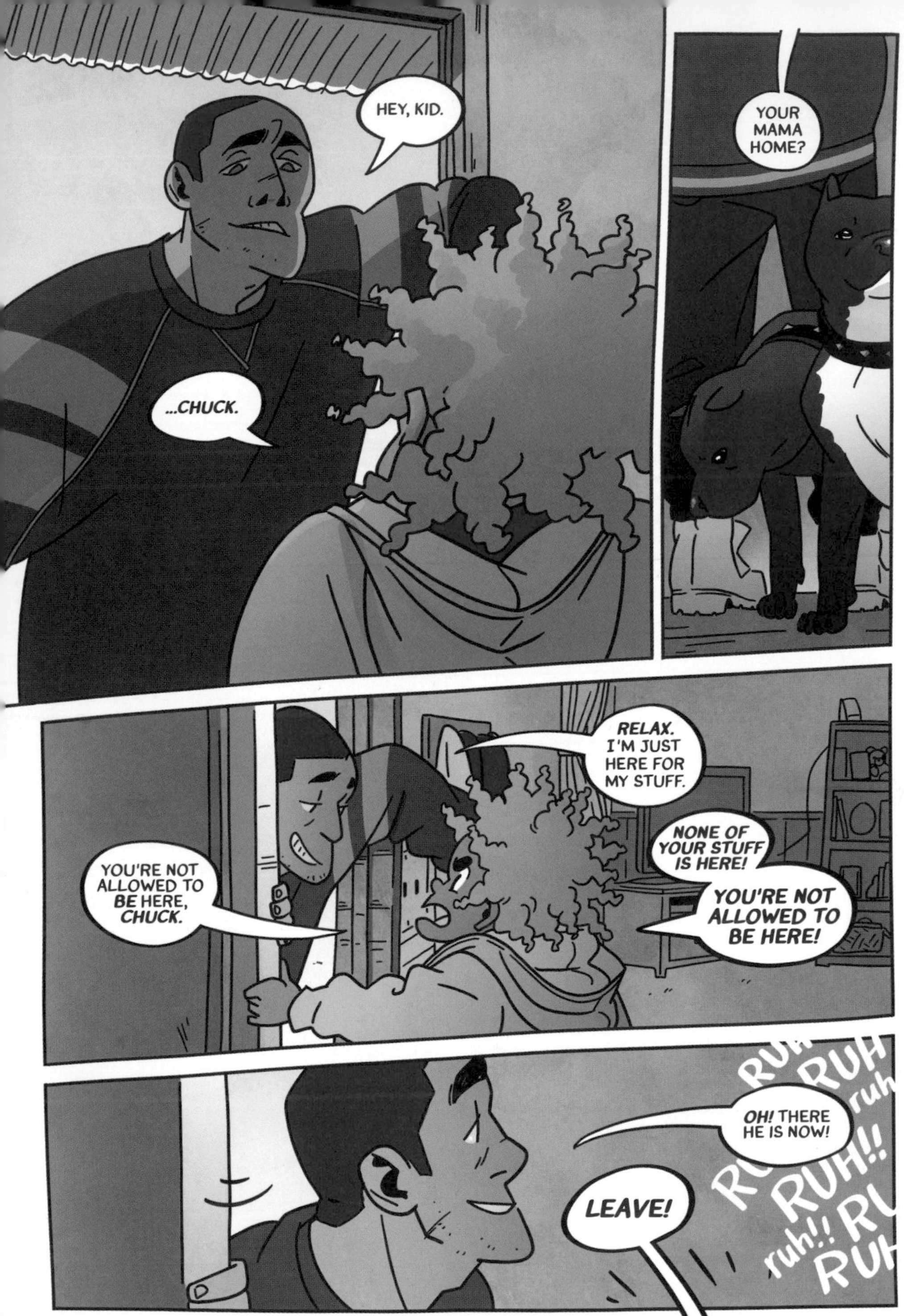

HEY, KID.
...CHUCK.
YOUR MAMA HOME?
RELAX. I'M JUST HERE FOR MY STUFF.
YOU'RE NOT ALLOWED TO BE HERE, CHUCK.
NONE OF YOUR STUFF IS HERE!
YOU'RE NOT ALLOWED TO BE HERE!
RUH RUH ruh RUH!! RUH!! ruh!! RU RUH
OH! THERE HE IS NOW!
LEAVE!

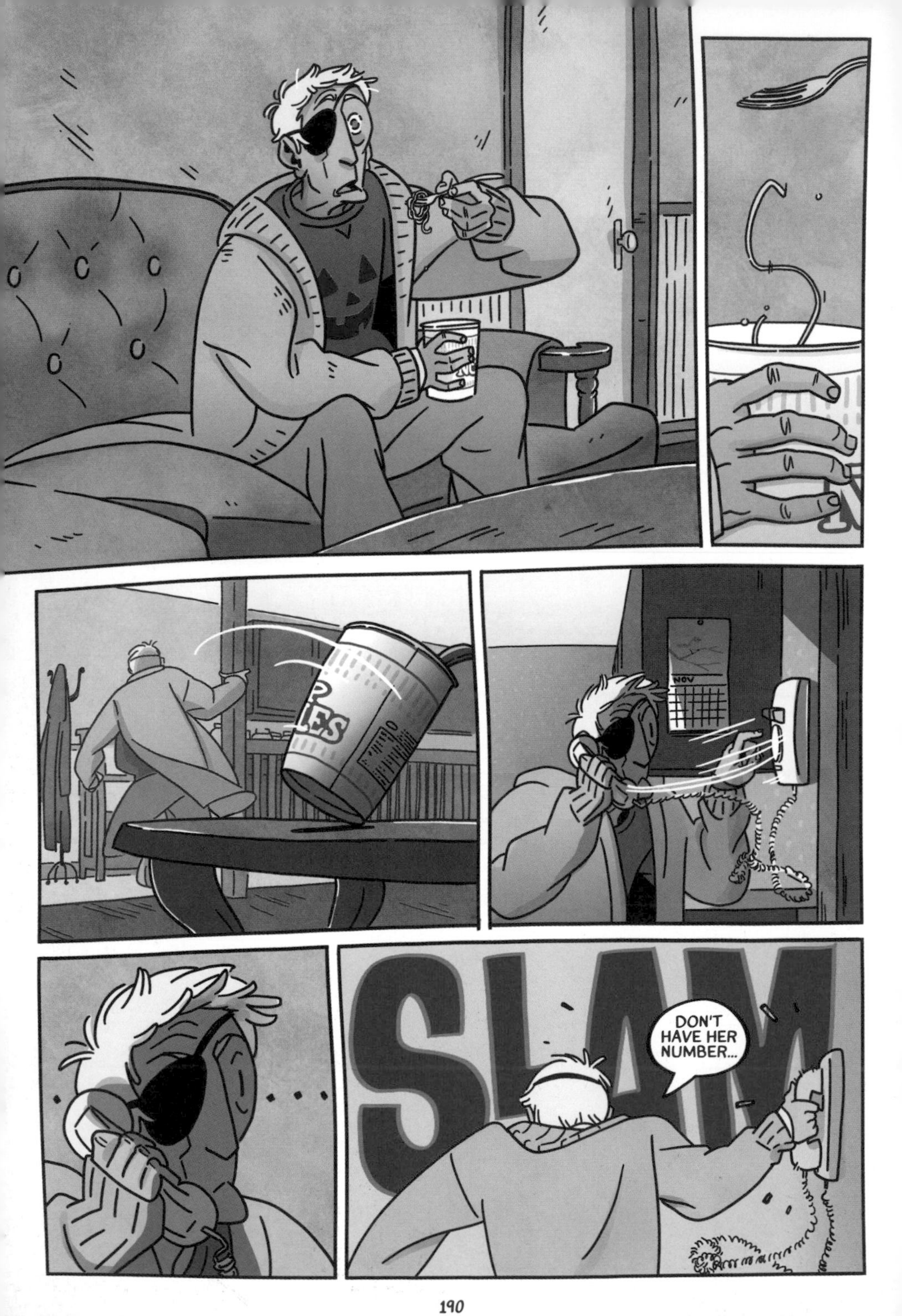
NOV
SLAM
DON'T HAVE HER NUMBER...

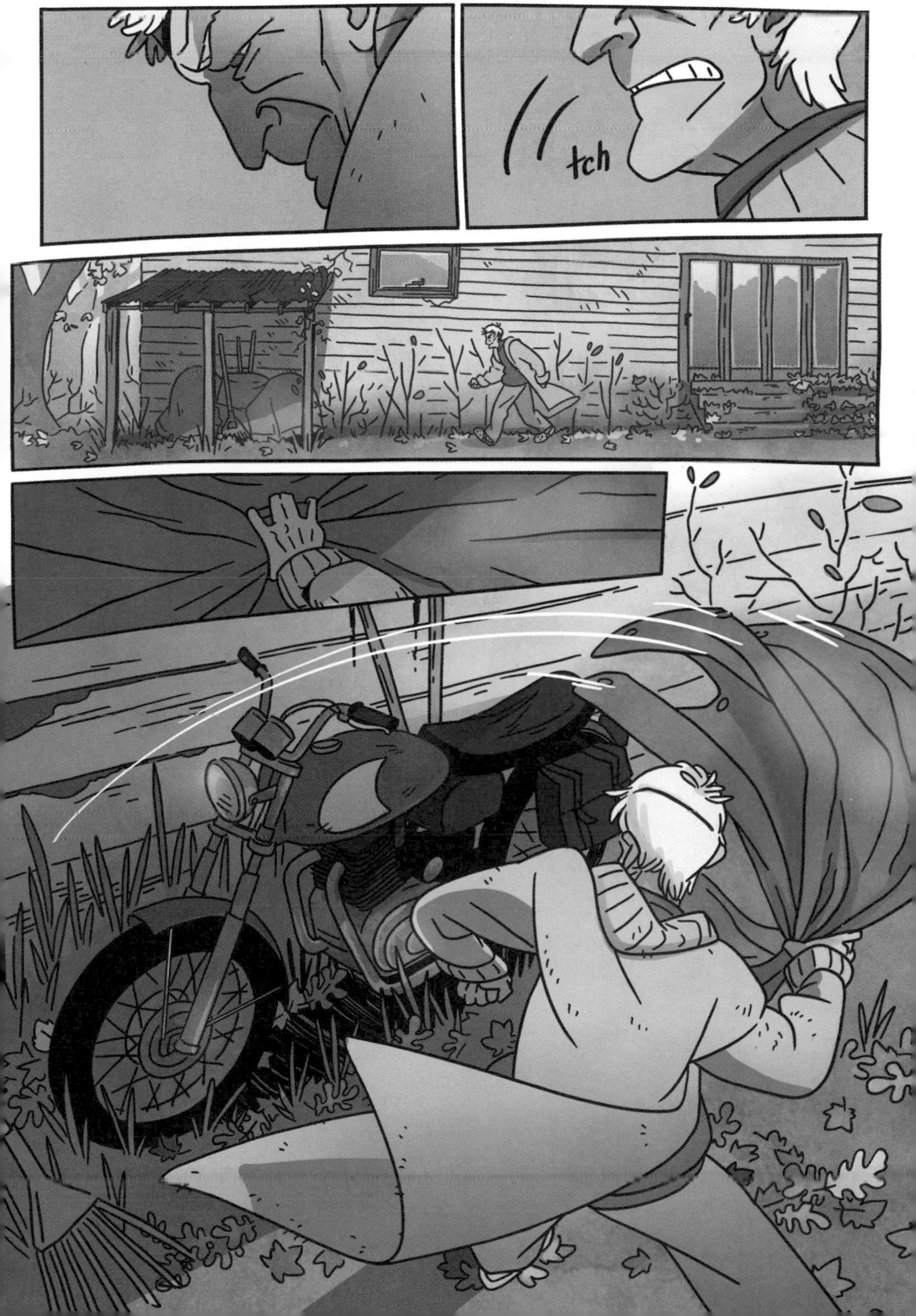
tch

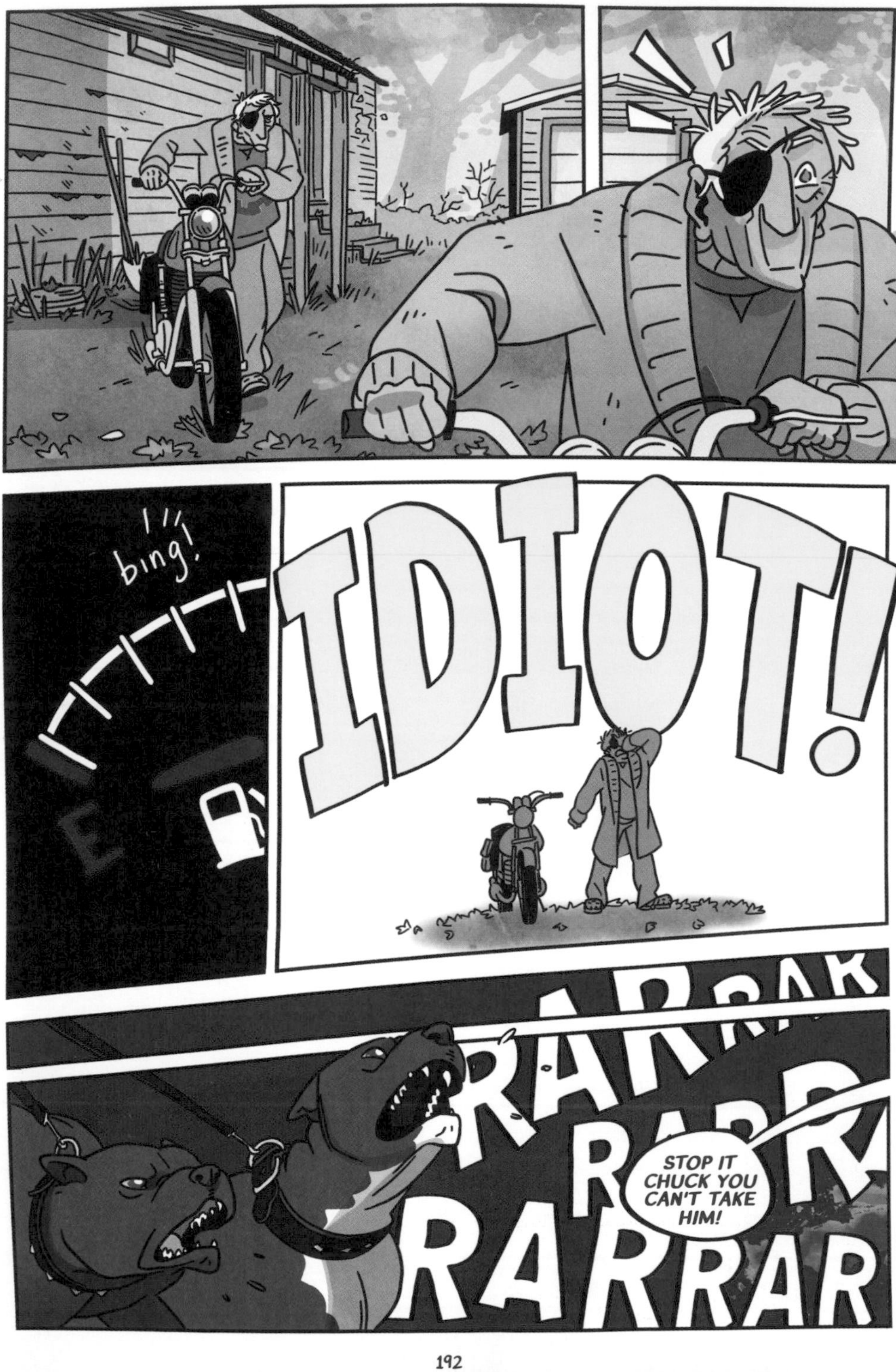
bing!
E
IDIOT!
RARRAR
RARRAR
RARRAR
RARRAR
STOP IT CHUCK YOU CAN'T TAKE HIM!
RARRAR

193

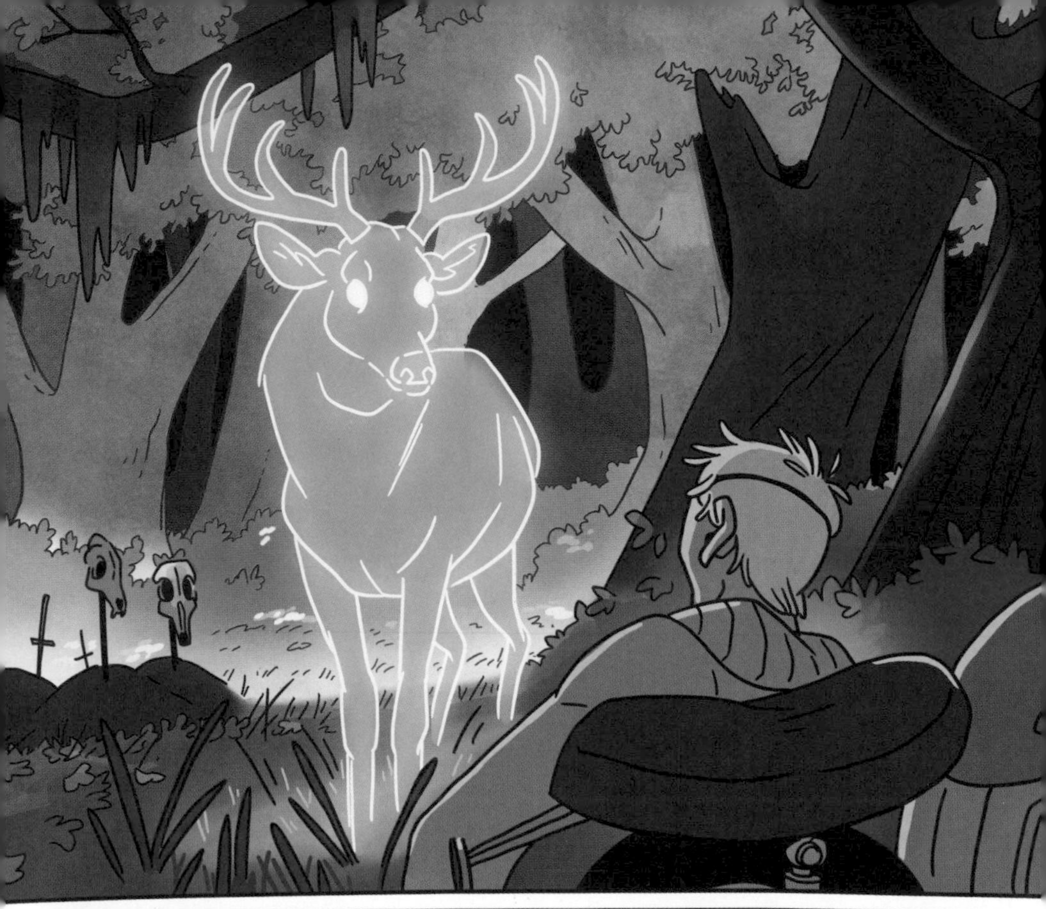

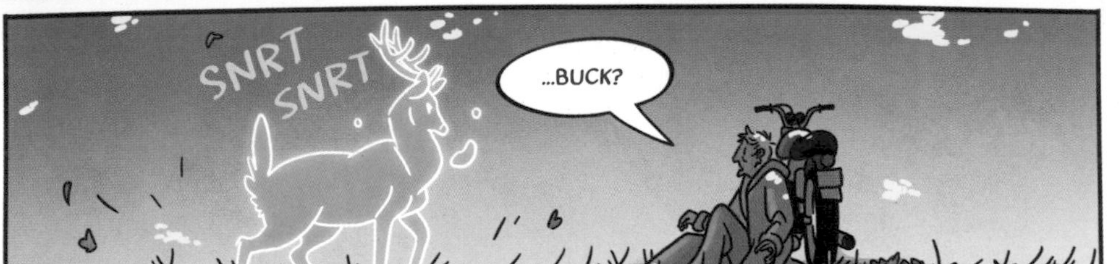
SNRT
SNRT
...BUCK?

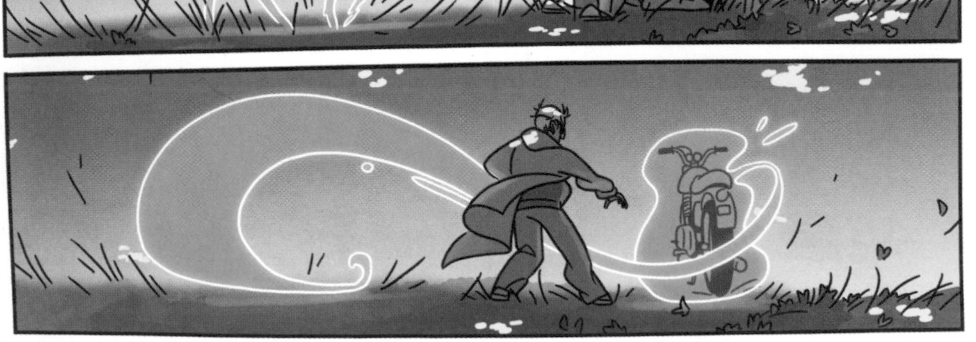

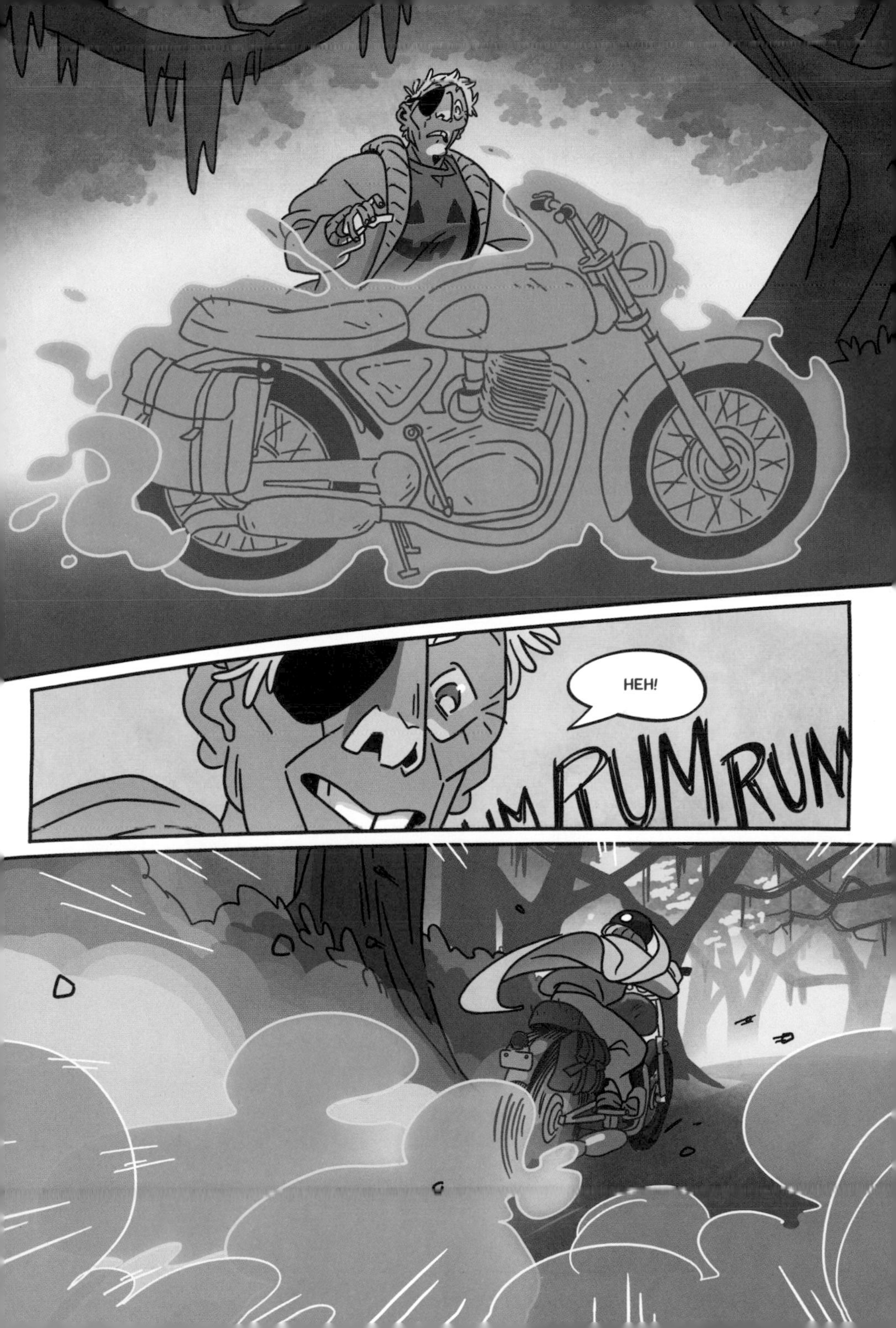
HEH!
RUMRUMRUM

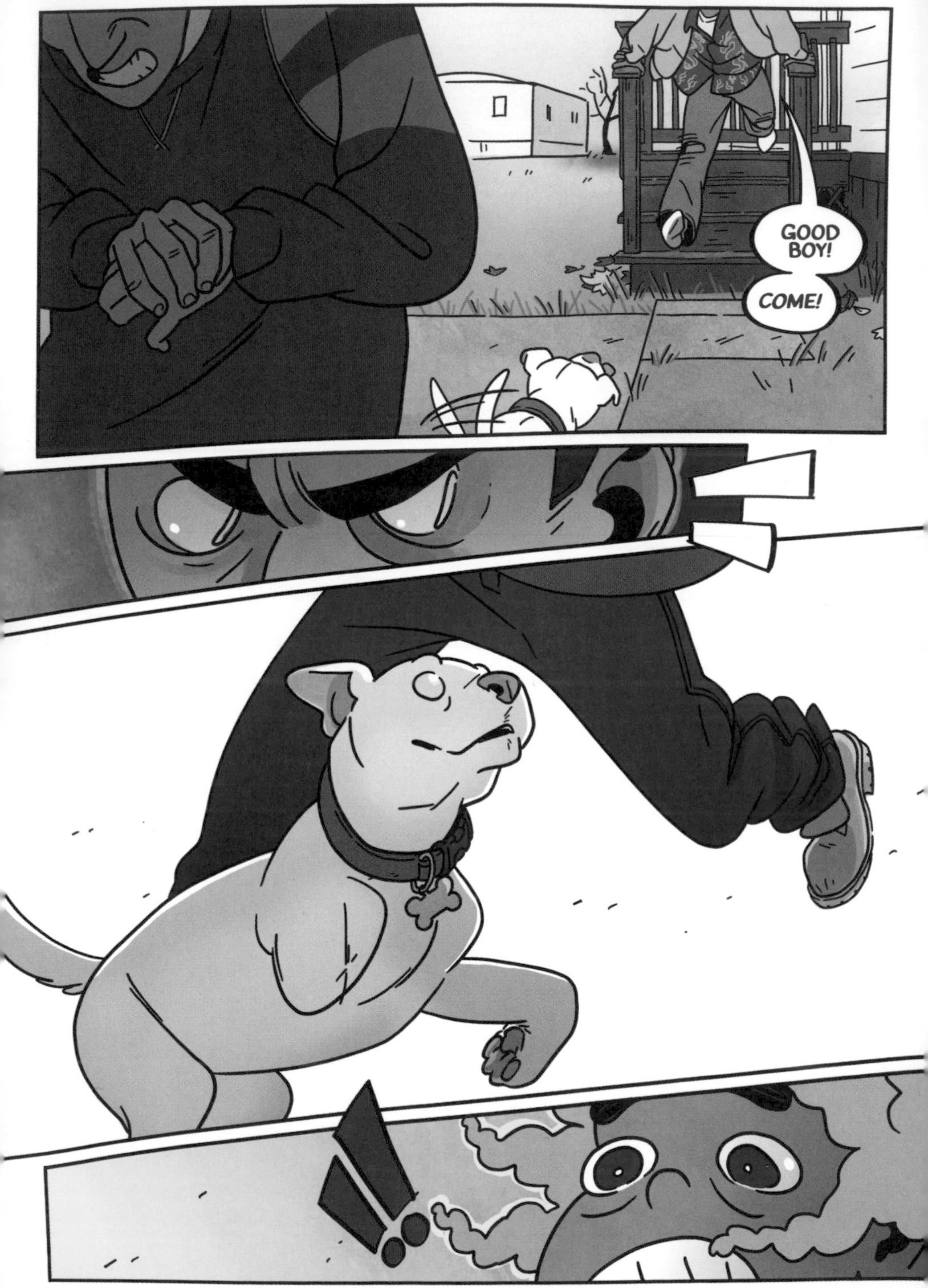
GOOD BOY!
COME!

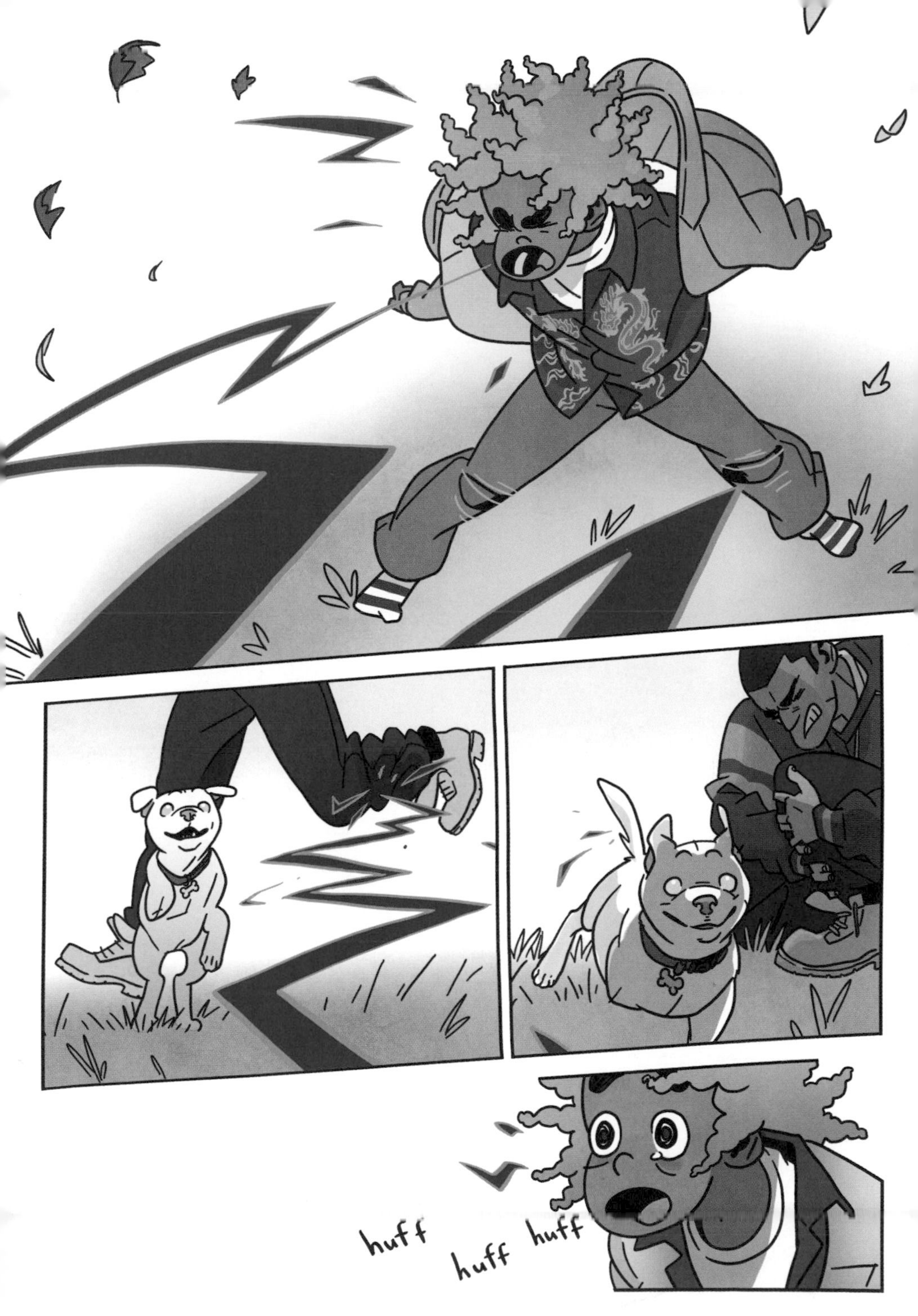
huff
huff huff
huff

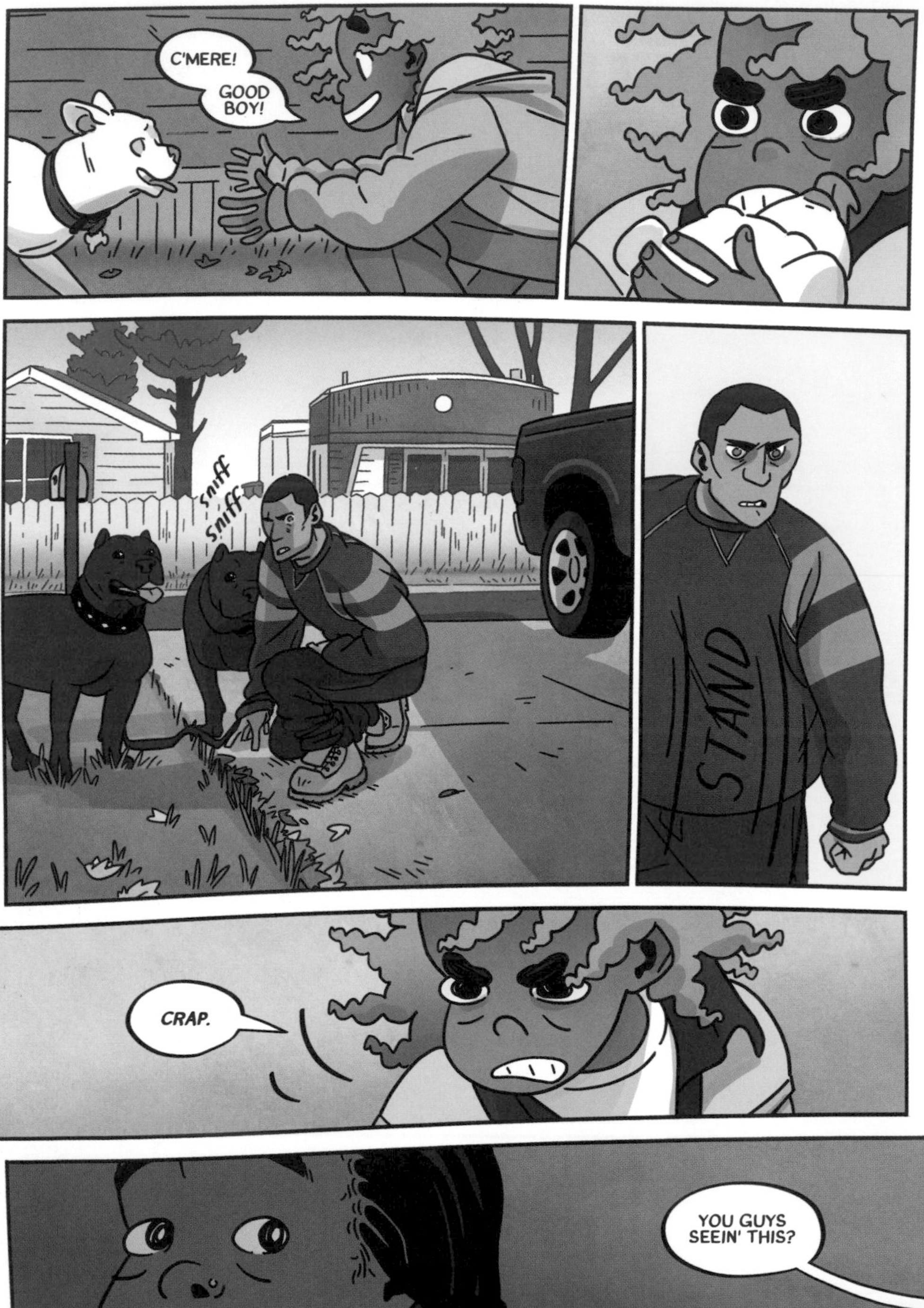
C'MERE!
GOOD BOY!
SNIFF SNIFF
STAND
CRAP.
YOU GUYS SEEIN' THIS?

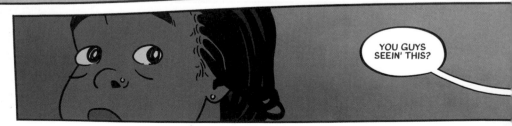

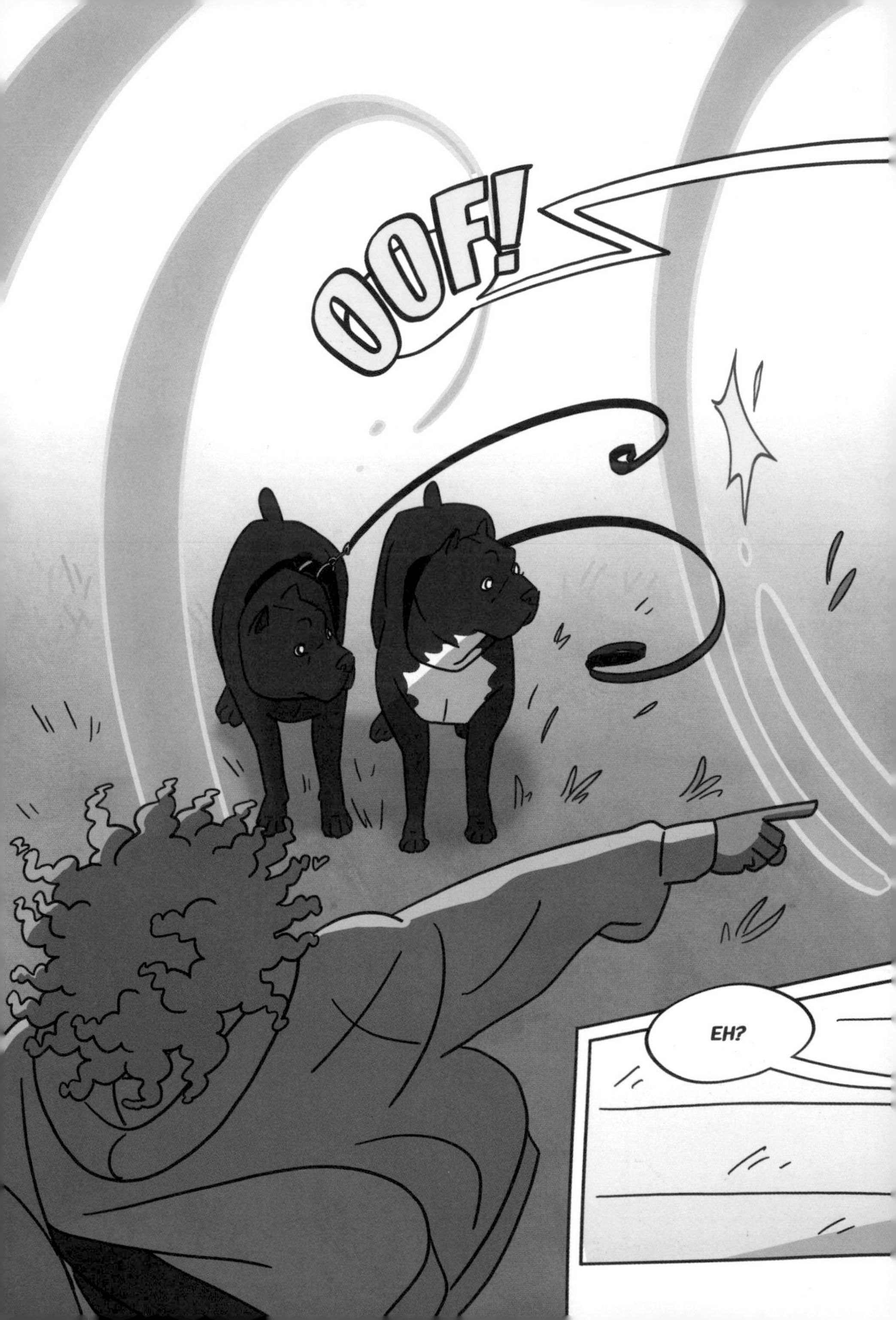
OOF!
EH?

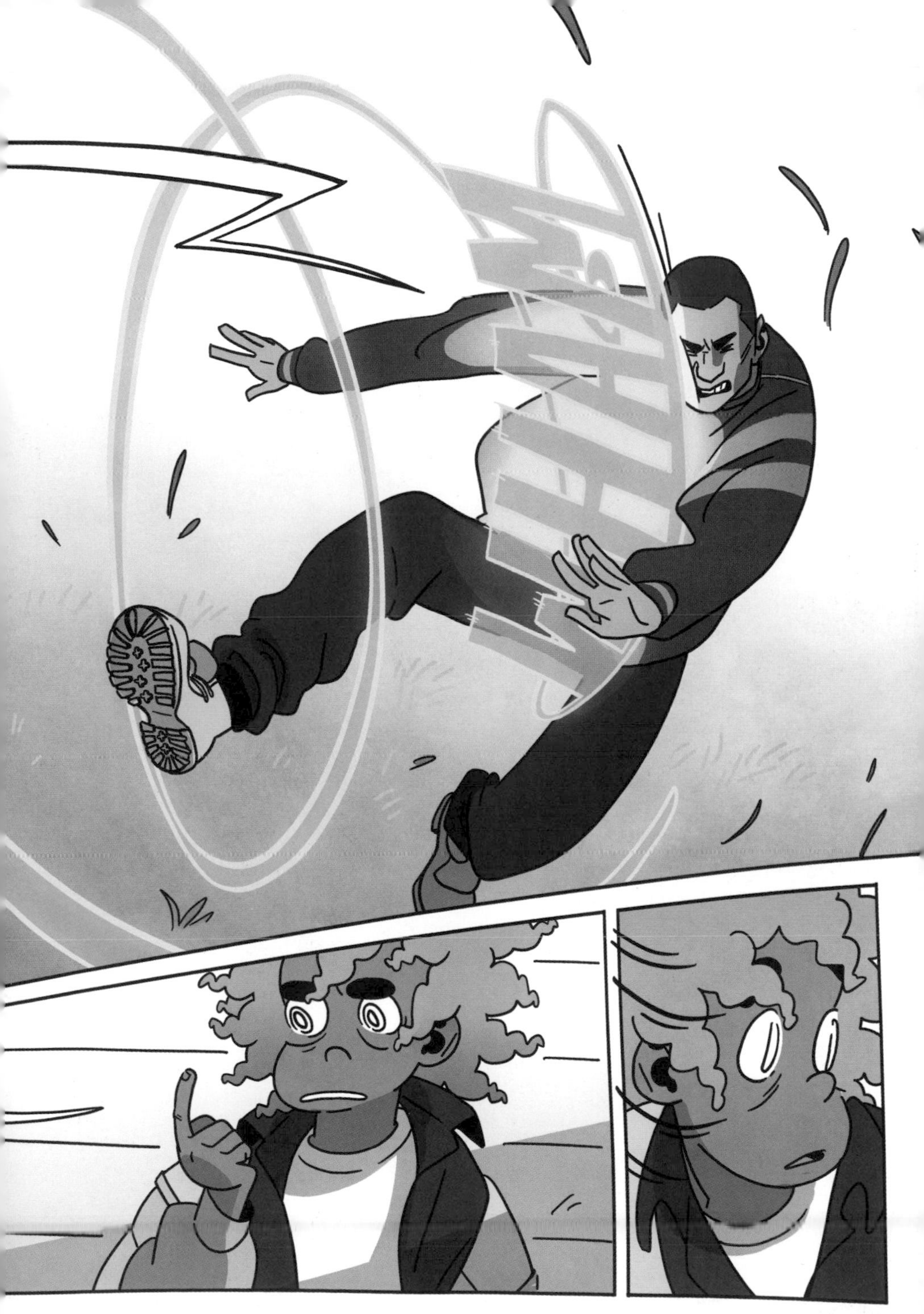

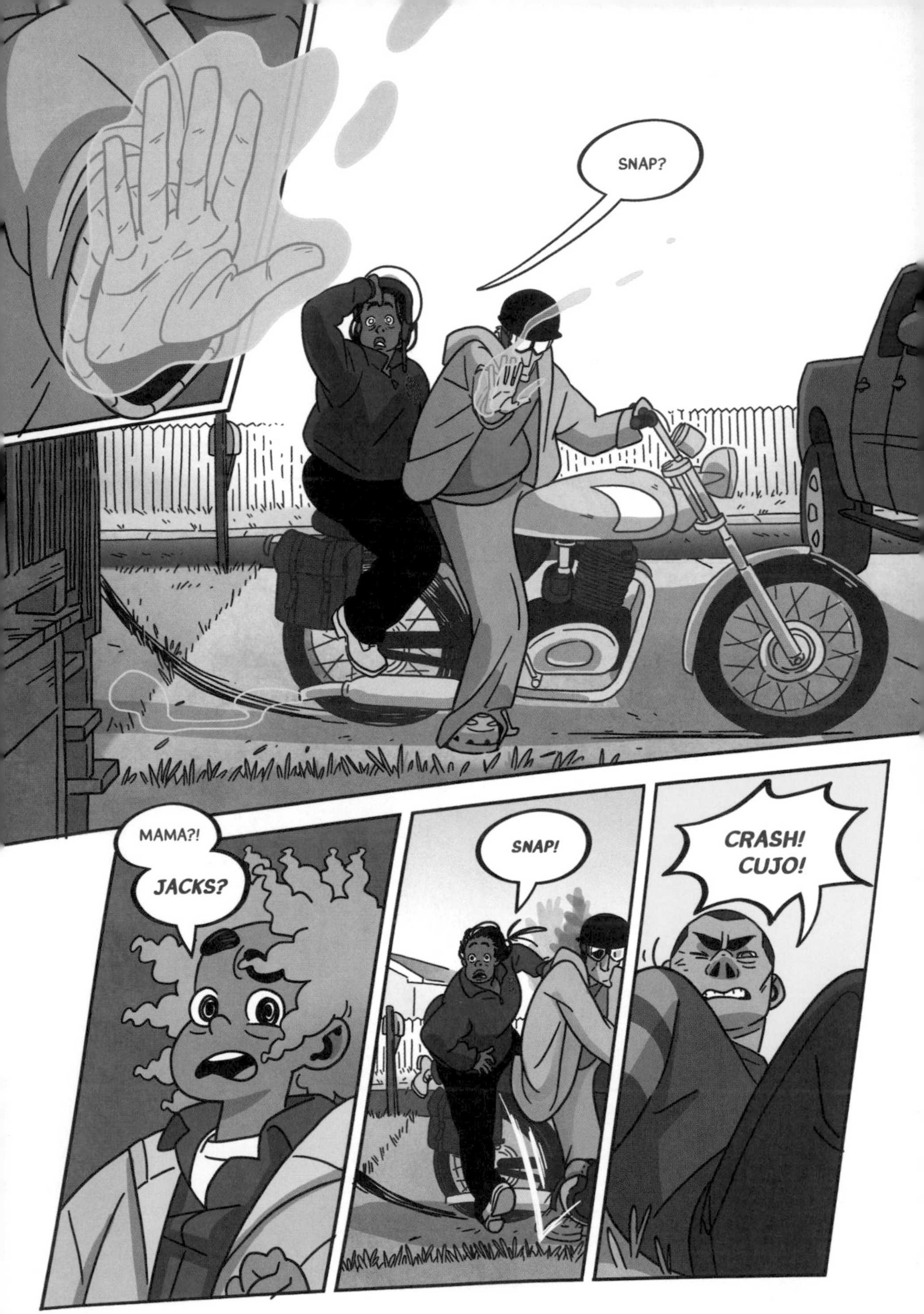
SNAP?
MAMA?!
JACKS?
SNAP!
CRASH!
CUJO!

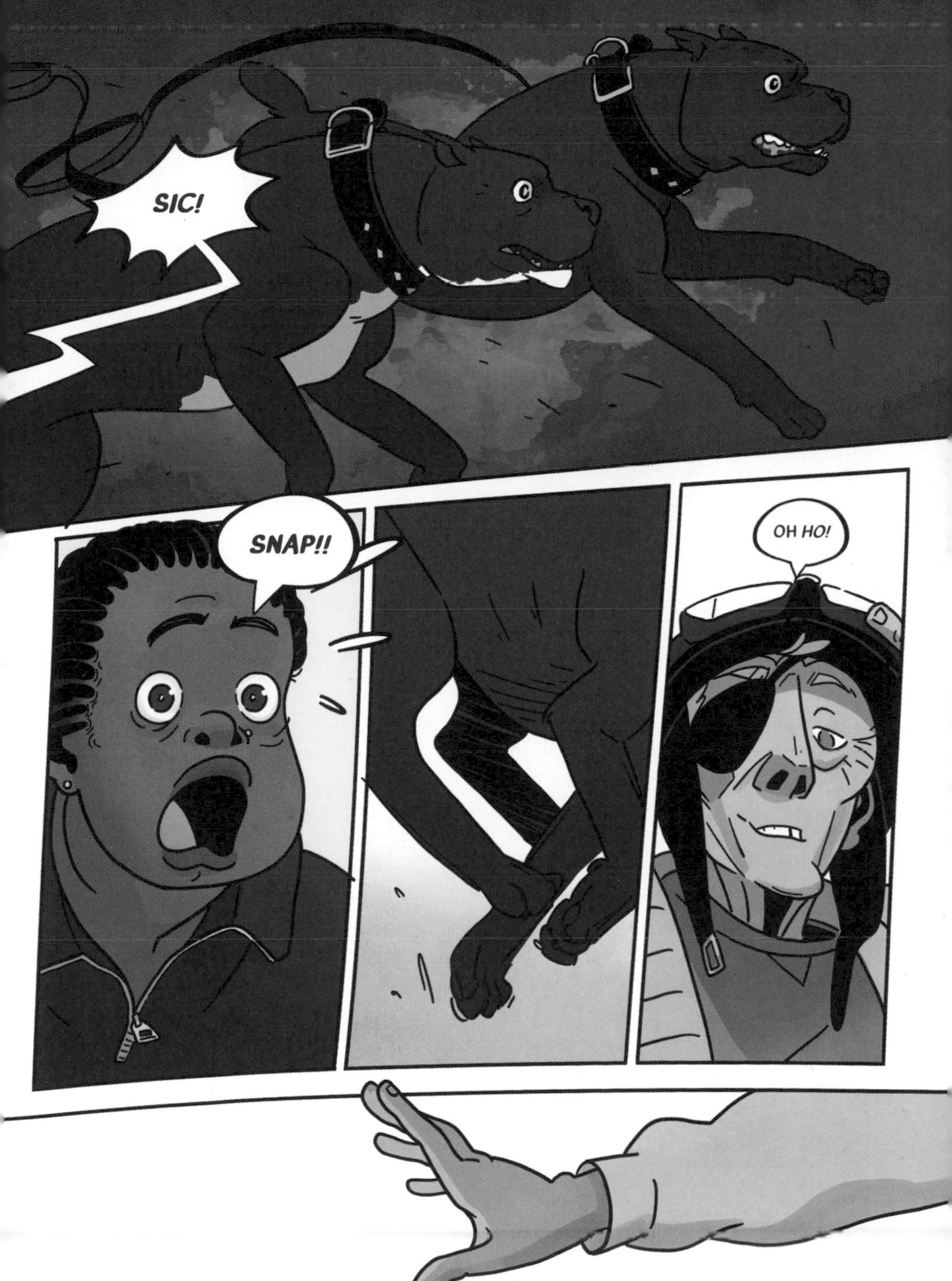
SIC!
SNAP!!
OH HO!

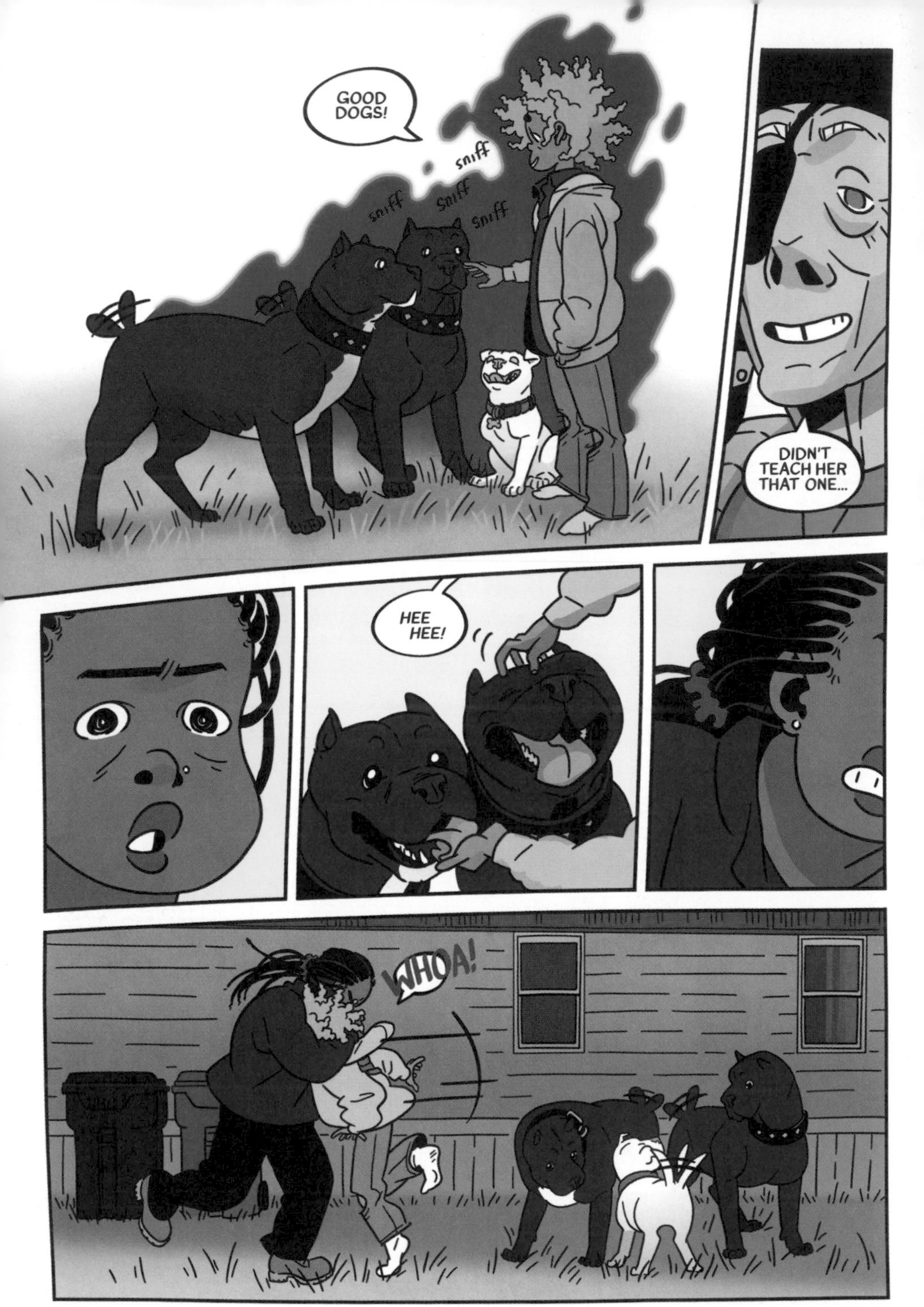

GOOD DOGS!
sniff
sniff
sniff
sniff
DIDN'T TEACH HER THAT ONE...
HEE HEE!
WHOA!

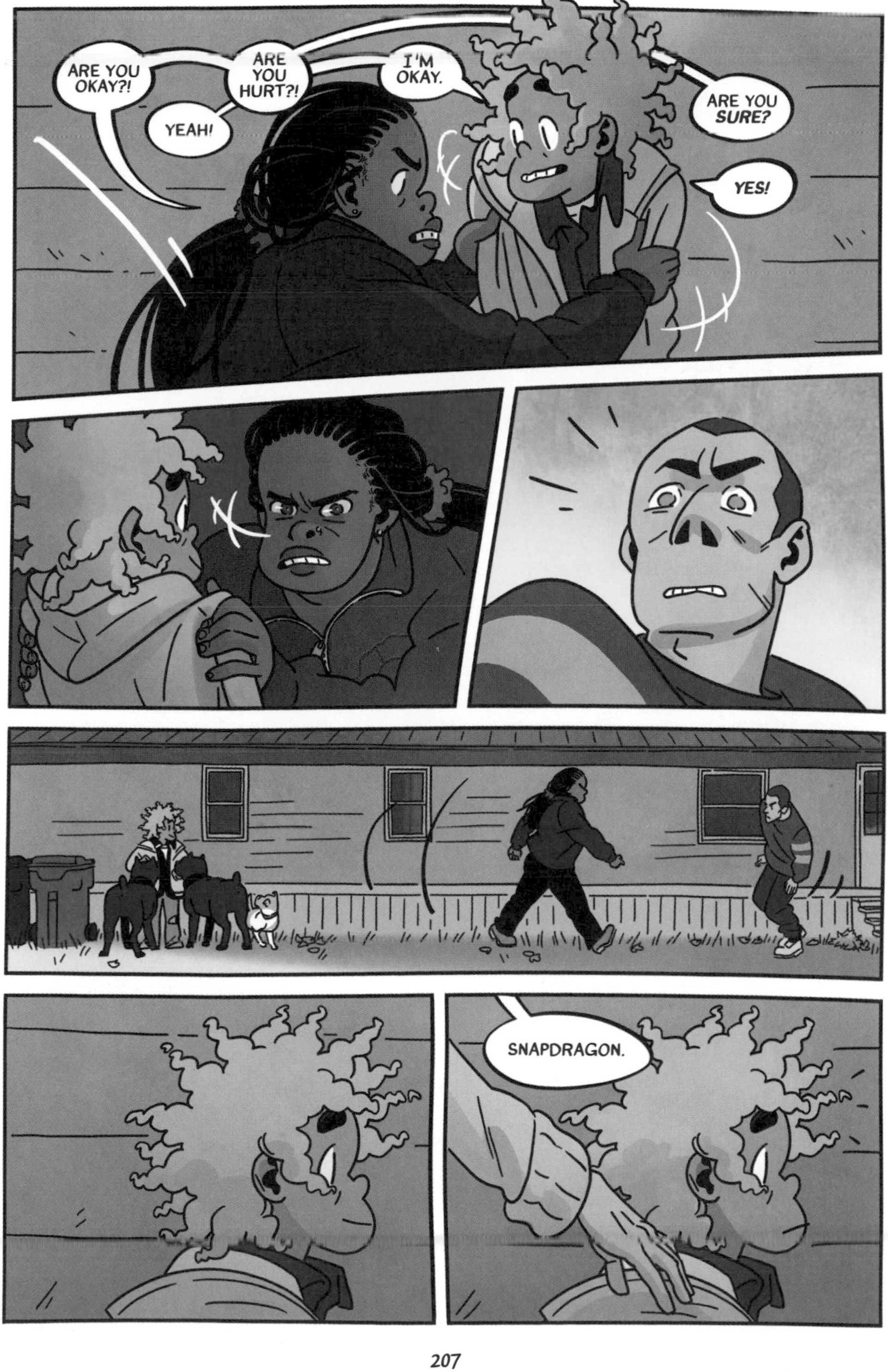
ARE YOU OKAY?!
YEAH!
ARE YOU HURT?!
I'M OKAY.
ARE YOU SURE?
YES!
SNAPDRAGON.

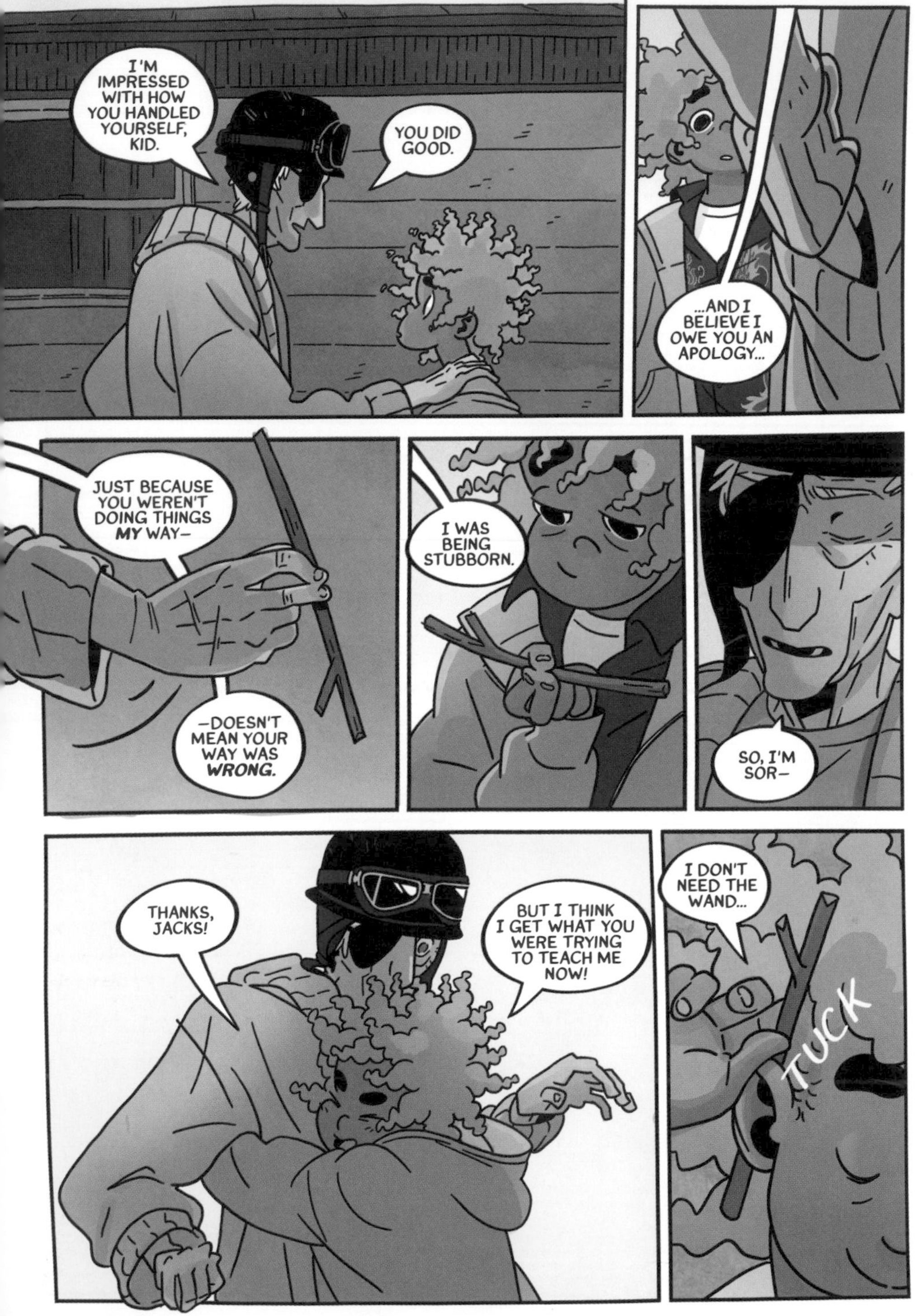

I'M IMPRESSED WITH HOW YOU HANDLED YOURSELF, KID.
YOU DID GOOD.
...AND I BELIEVE I OWE YOU AN APOLOGY...
JUST BECAUSE YOU WEREN'T DOING THINGS **MY** WAY—
—DOESN'T MEAN YOUR WAY WAS ***WRONG.***
I WAS BEING STUBBORN.
SO, I'M SOR—
THANKS, JACKS!
BUT I THINK I GET WHAT YOU WERE TRYING TO TEACH ME NOW!
I DON'T NEED THE WAND...
TUCK

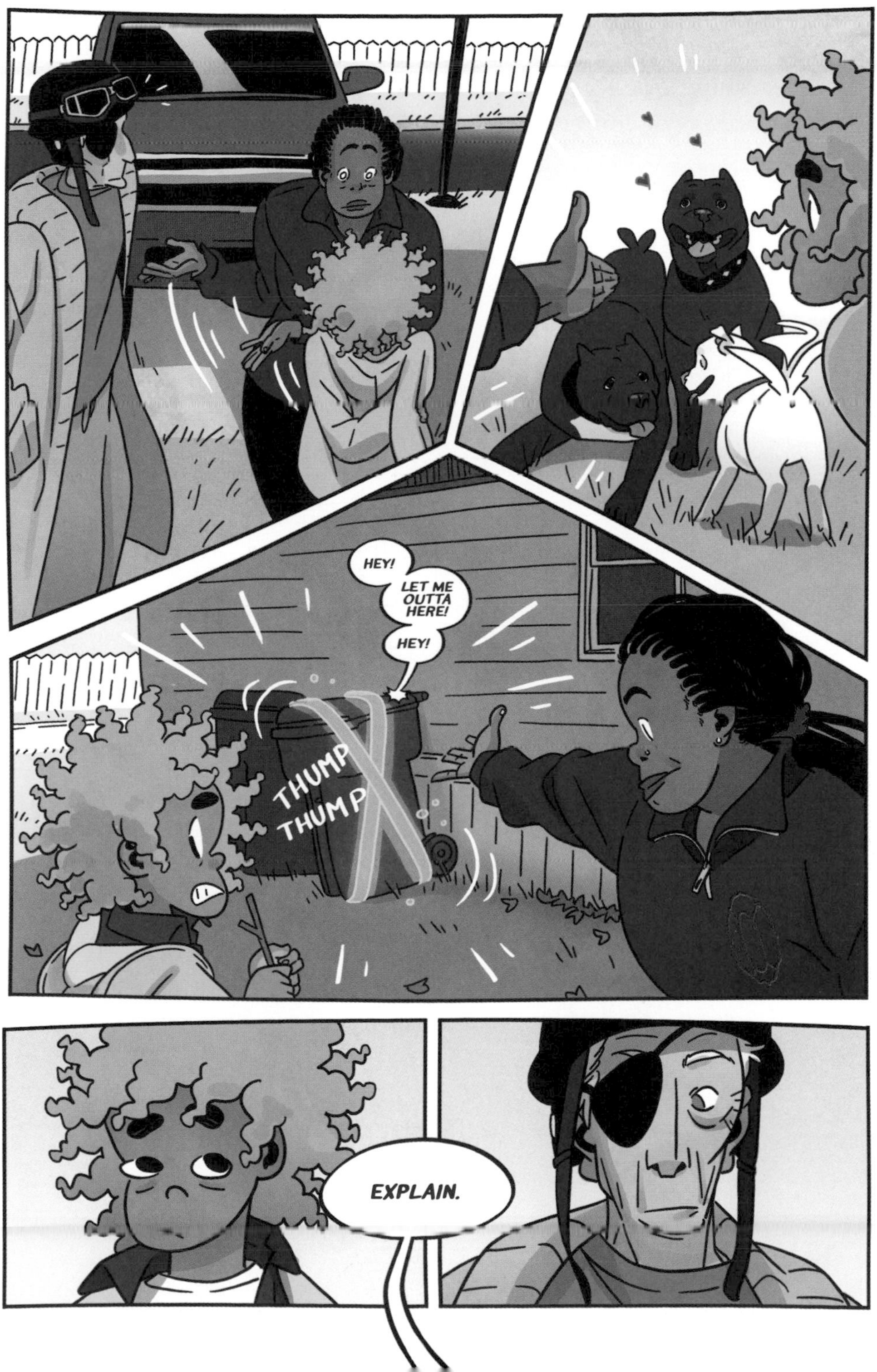
HEY!
LET ME OUTTA HERE!
HEY!
THUMP THUMP
EXPLAIN.

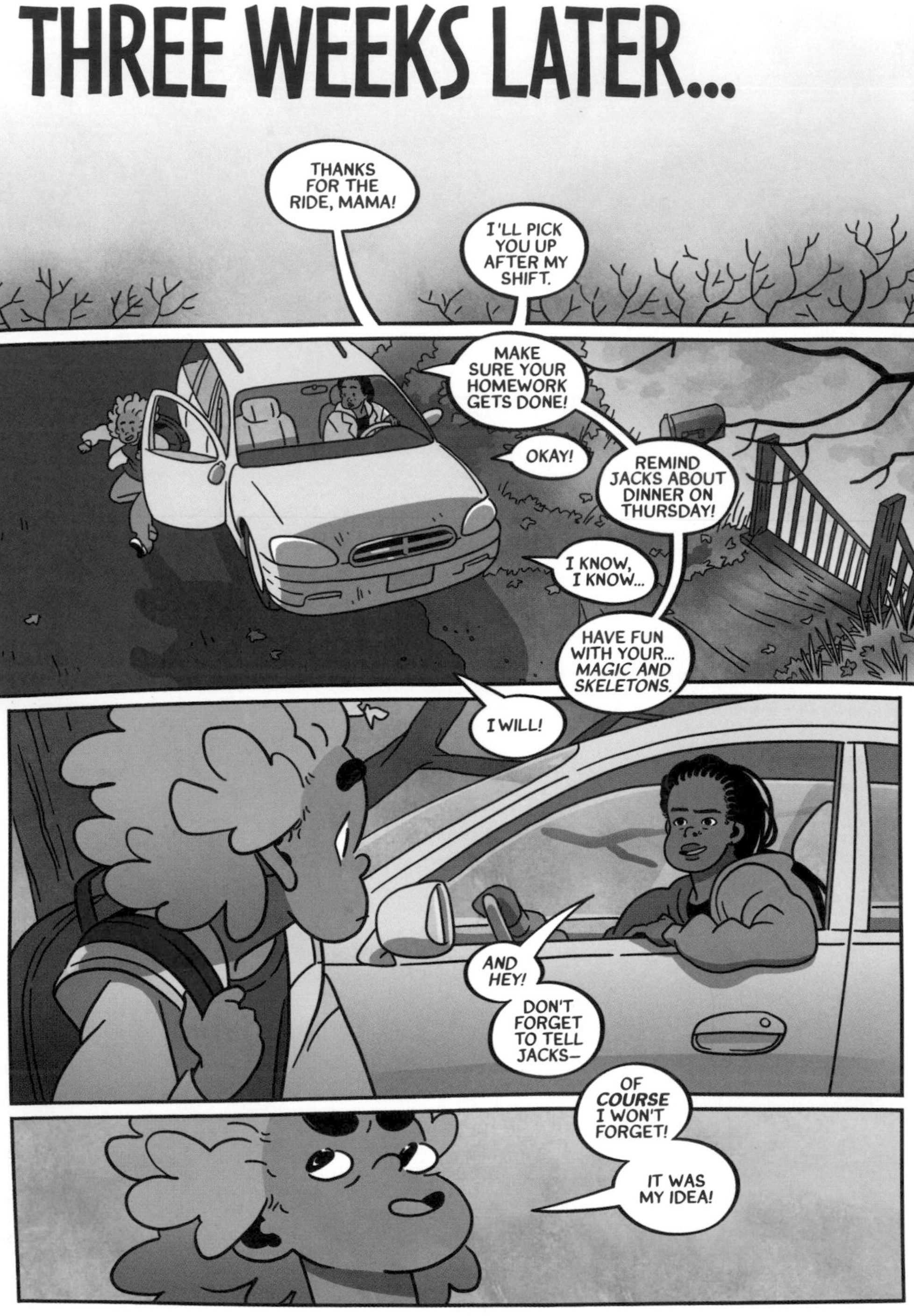
THREE WEEKS LATER...
THANKS FOR THE RIDE, MAMA!
I'LL PICK YOU UP AFTER MY SHIFT.
MAKE SURE YOUR HOMEWORK GETS DONE!
OKAY!
REMIND JACKS ABOUT DINNER ON THURSDAY!
I KNOW, I KNOW...
HAVE FUN WITH YOUR... *MAGIC AND SKELETONS.*
I WILL!
AND HEY!
DON'T FORGET TO TELL JACKS—
OF *COURSE* I WON'T FORGET!
IT WAS MY IDEA!

"SHE'S GONNA *FREAK!*"

HEY, JACKS!

OOOH! IS THAT THE RACCOON?

MM-HM. IT'S ALL CLEANED UP.

HAHA HA!!

GOOD DOGS!

CRASH! CUJO!

GO LAY DOWN!

YOU CAN START SORTING THE TOE BONES.

'KAY!

SOOO, MY MAMA AND I WERE TALKING...

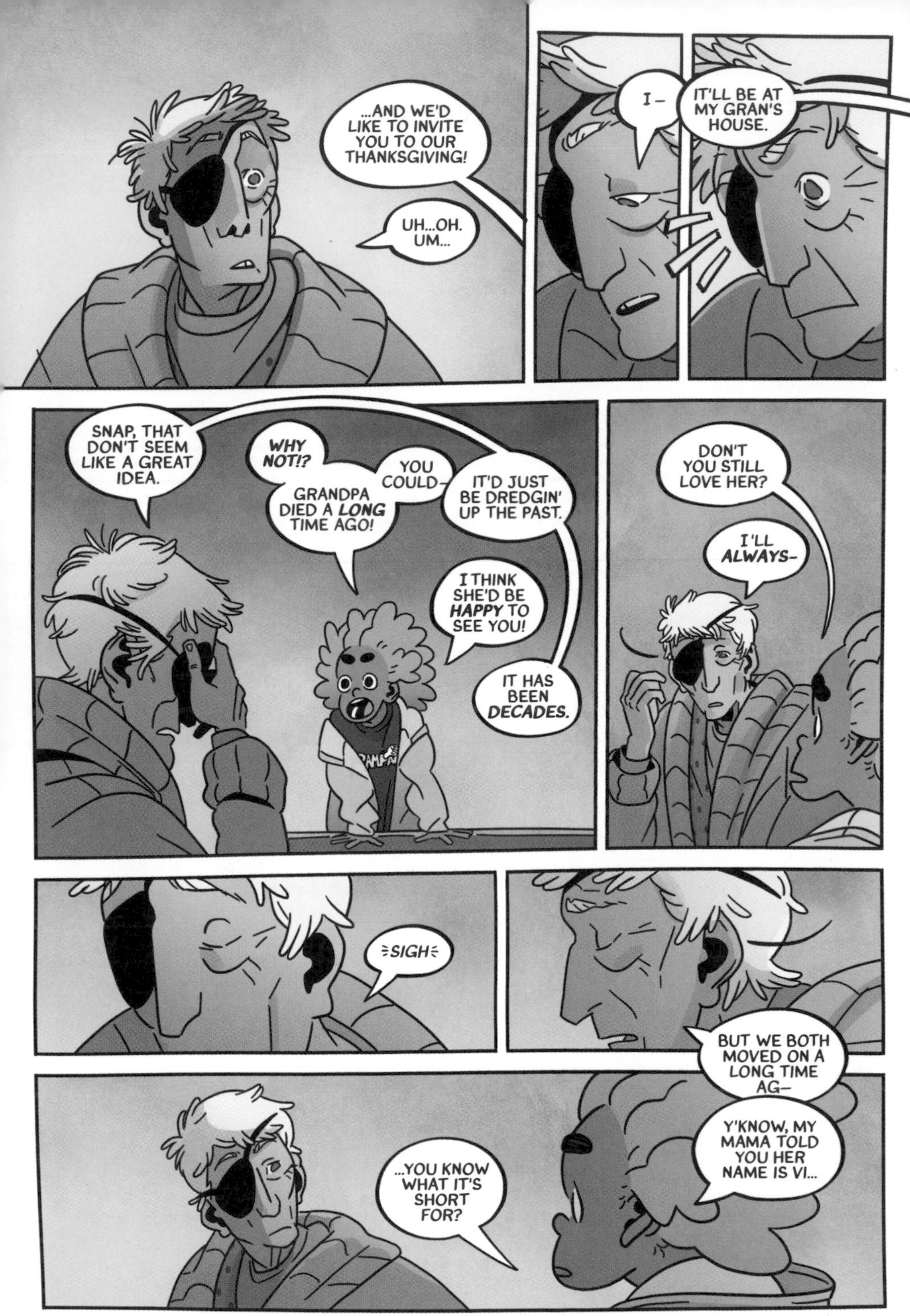
...AND WE'D LIKE TO INVITE YOU TO OUR THANKSGIVING!
UH...OH. UM...
I–
IT'LL BE AT MY GRAN'S HOUSE.
SNAP, THAT DON'T SEEM LIKE A GREAT IDEA.
WHY NOT!?
YOU COULD–
GRANDPA DIED A LONG TIME AGO!
IT'D JUST BE DREDGIN' UP THE PAST.
I THINK SHE'D BE HAPPY TO SEE YOU!
IT HAS BEEN DECADES.
DON'T YOU STILL LOVE HER?
I'LL ALWAYS–
SIGH
BUT WE BOTH MOVED ON A LONG TIME AG–
Y'KNOW, MY MAMA TOLD YOU HER NAME IS VI...
...YOU KNOW WHAT IT'S SHORT FOR?

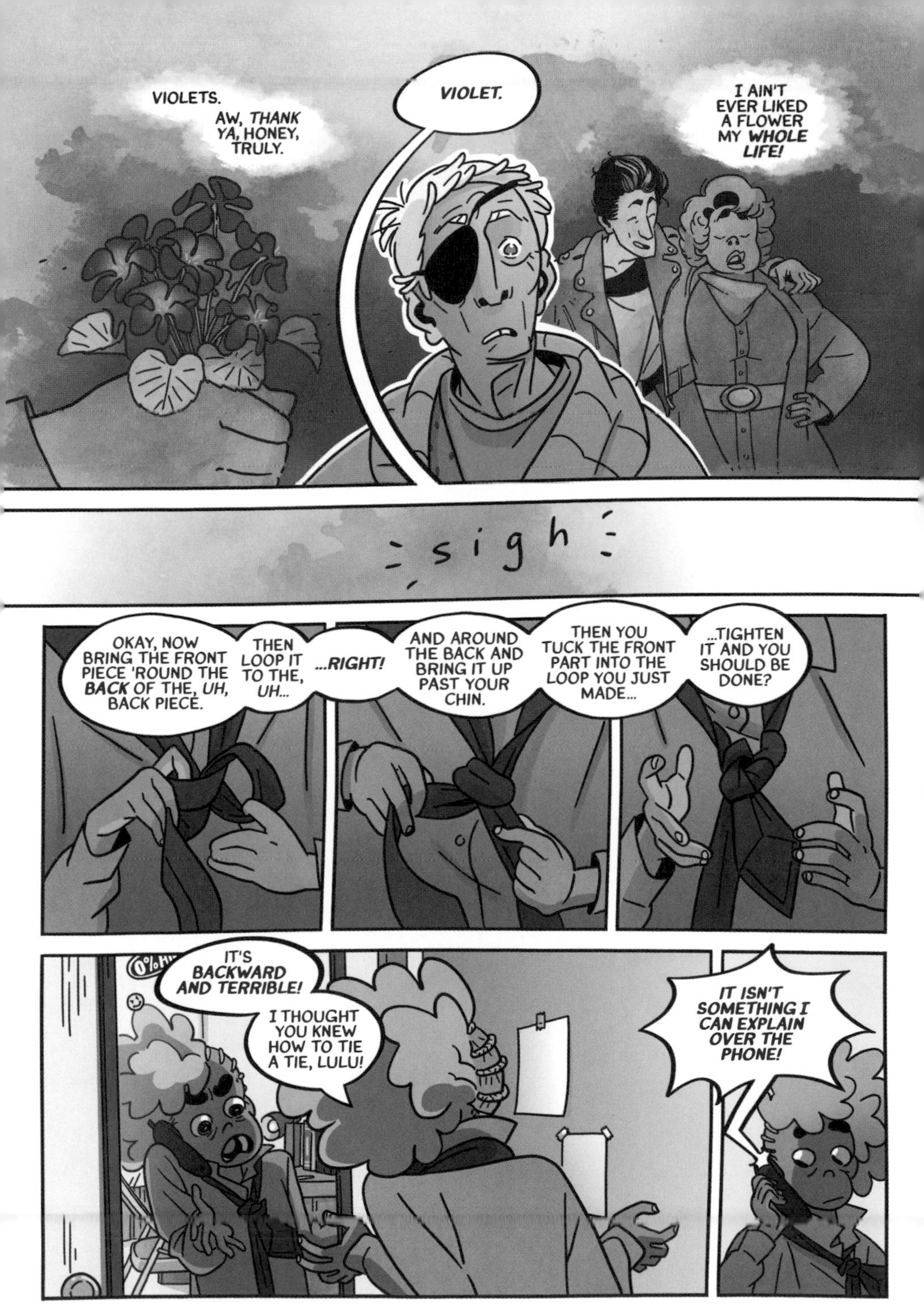
VIOLETS.
AW, THANK YA, HONEY, TRULY.
VIOLET.
I AIN'T EVER LIKED A FLOWER MY WHOLE LIFE!
sigh
OKAY, NOW BRING THE FRONT PIECE 'ROUND THE BACK OF THE, UH, BACK PIECE.
THEN LOOP IT TO THE, UH...
...RIGHT!
AND AROUND THE BACK AND BRING IT UP PAST YOUR CHIN.
THEN YOU TUCK THE FRONT PART INTO THE LOOP YOU JUST MADE...
...TIGHTEN IT AND YOU SHOULD BE DONE?
IT'S BACKWARD AND TERRIBLE!
I THOUGHT YOU KNEW HOW TO TIE A TIE, LULU!
IT ISN'T SOMETHING I CAN EXPLAIN OVER THE PHONE!

216

217

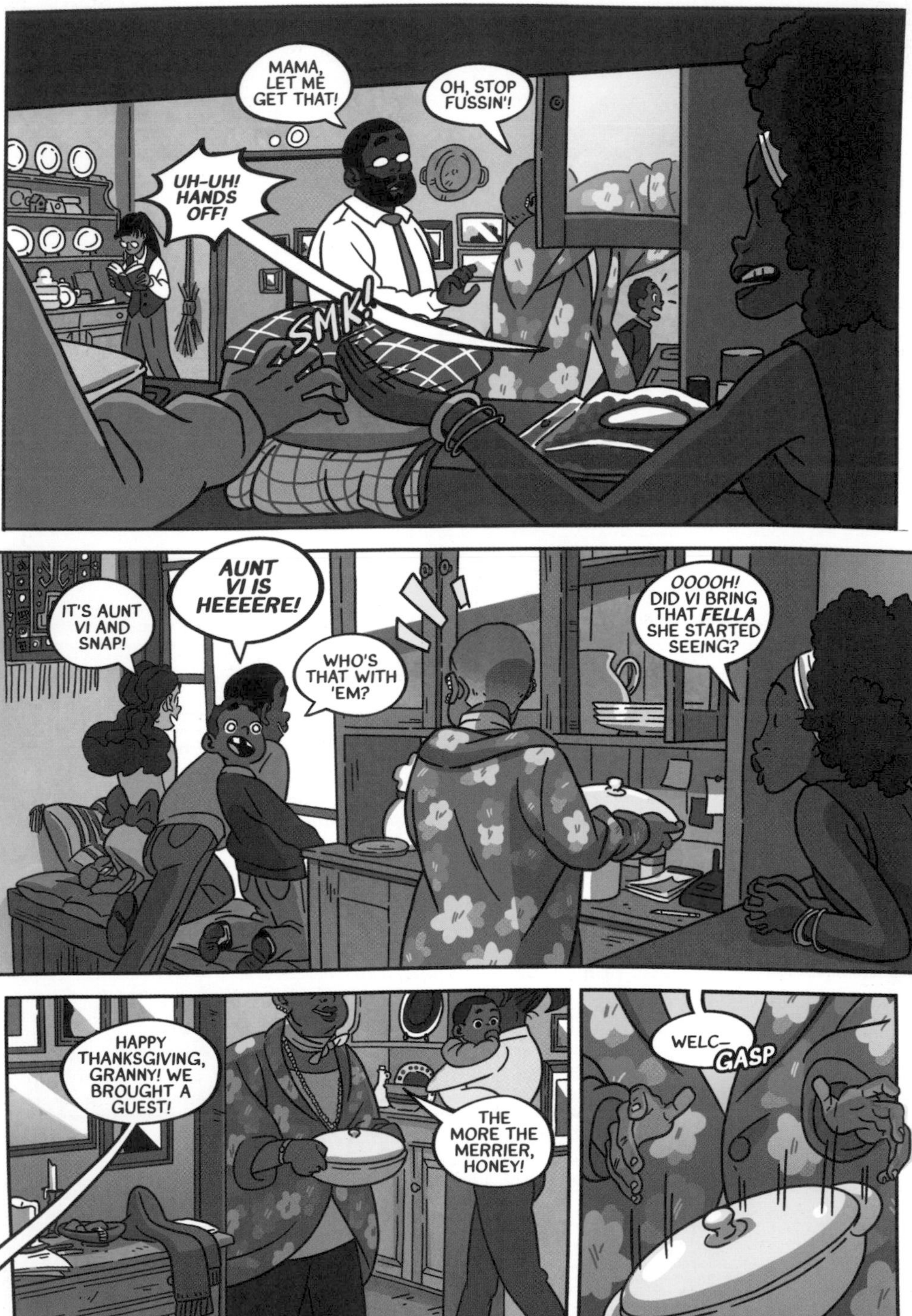
MAMA, LET ME GET THAT!
OH, STOP FUSSIN'!
UH-UH! HANDS OFF!
SMK!
IT'S AUNT VI AND SNAP!
AUNT VI IS HEEEERE!
WHO'S THAT WITH 'EM?
OOOOH! DID VI BRING THAT *FELLA* SHE STARTED SEEING?
HAPPY THANKSGIVING, GRANNY! WE BROUGHT A GUEST!
THE MORE THE MERRIER, HONEY!
WELC—
GASP

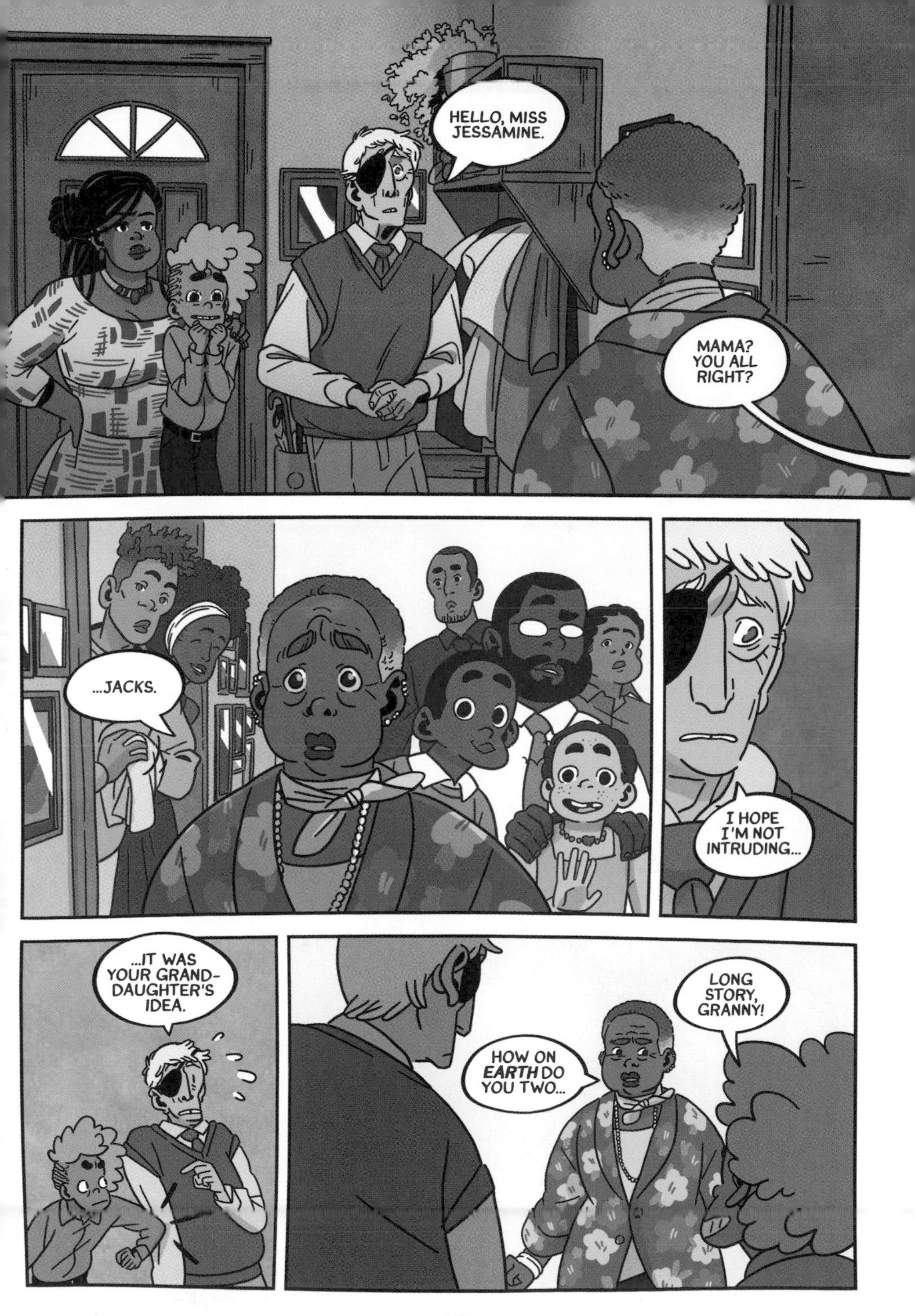
HELLO, MISS JESSAMINE.
MAMA? YOU ALL RIGHT?
...JACKS.
I HOPE I'M NOT INTRUDING...
...IT WAS YOUR GRAND-DAUGHTER'S IDEA.
HOW ON *EARTH* DO YOU TWO...
LONG STORY, GRANNY!

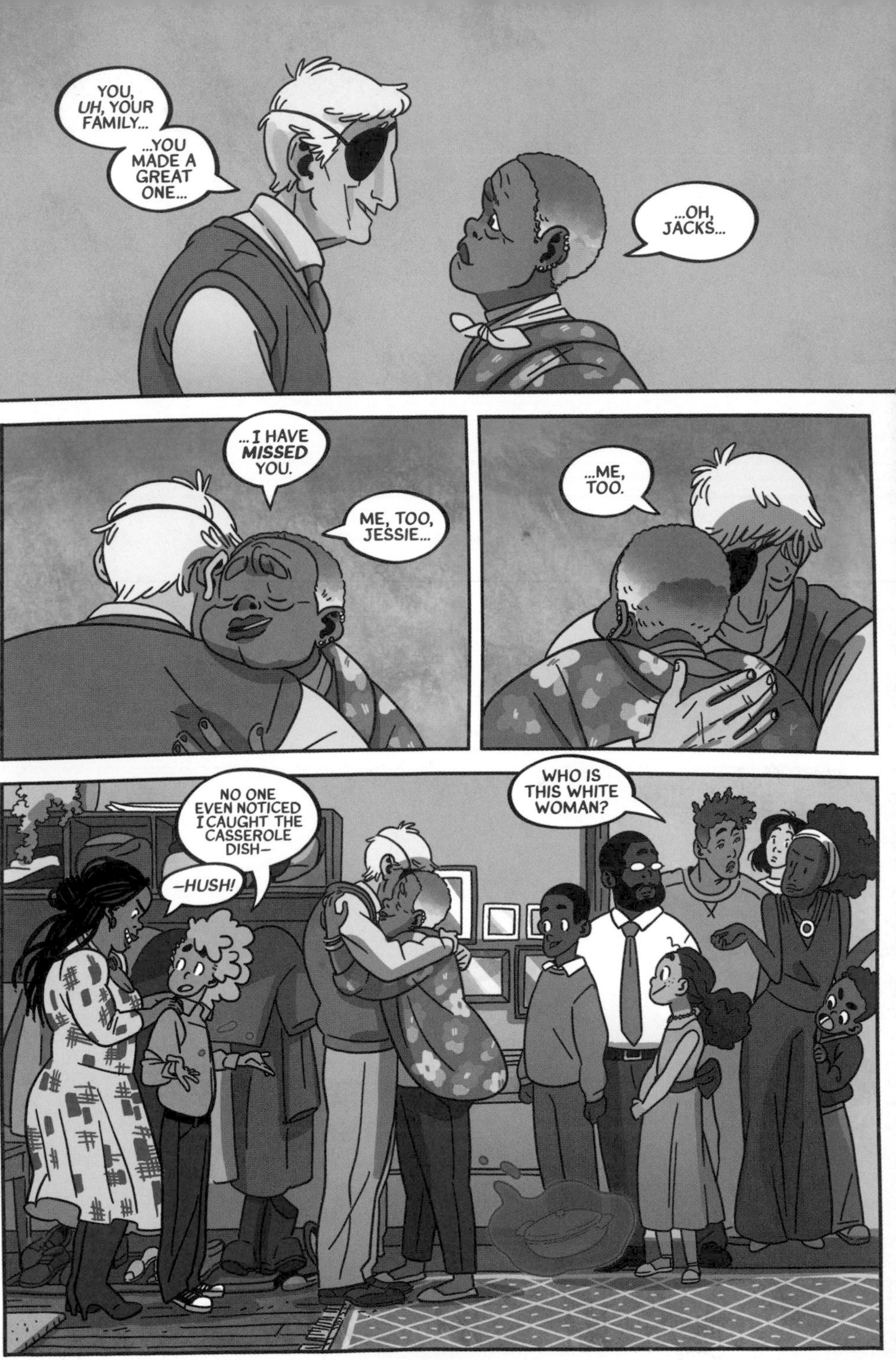
YOU, *UH*, YOUR FAMILY...
...YOU MADE A GREAT ONE...
...OH, JACKS...
...I HAVE ***MISSED*** YOU.
ME, TOO, JESSIE...
...ME, TOO.
NO ONE EVEN NOTICED I CAUGHT THE CASSEROLE DISH—
—HUSH!
WHO IS THIS WHITE WOMAN?

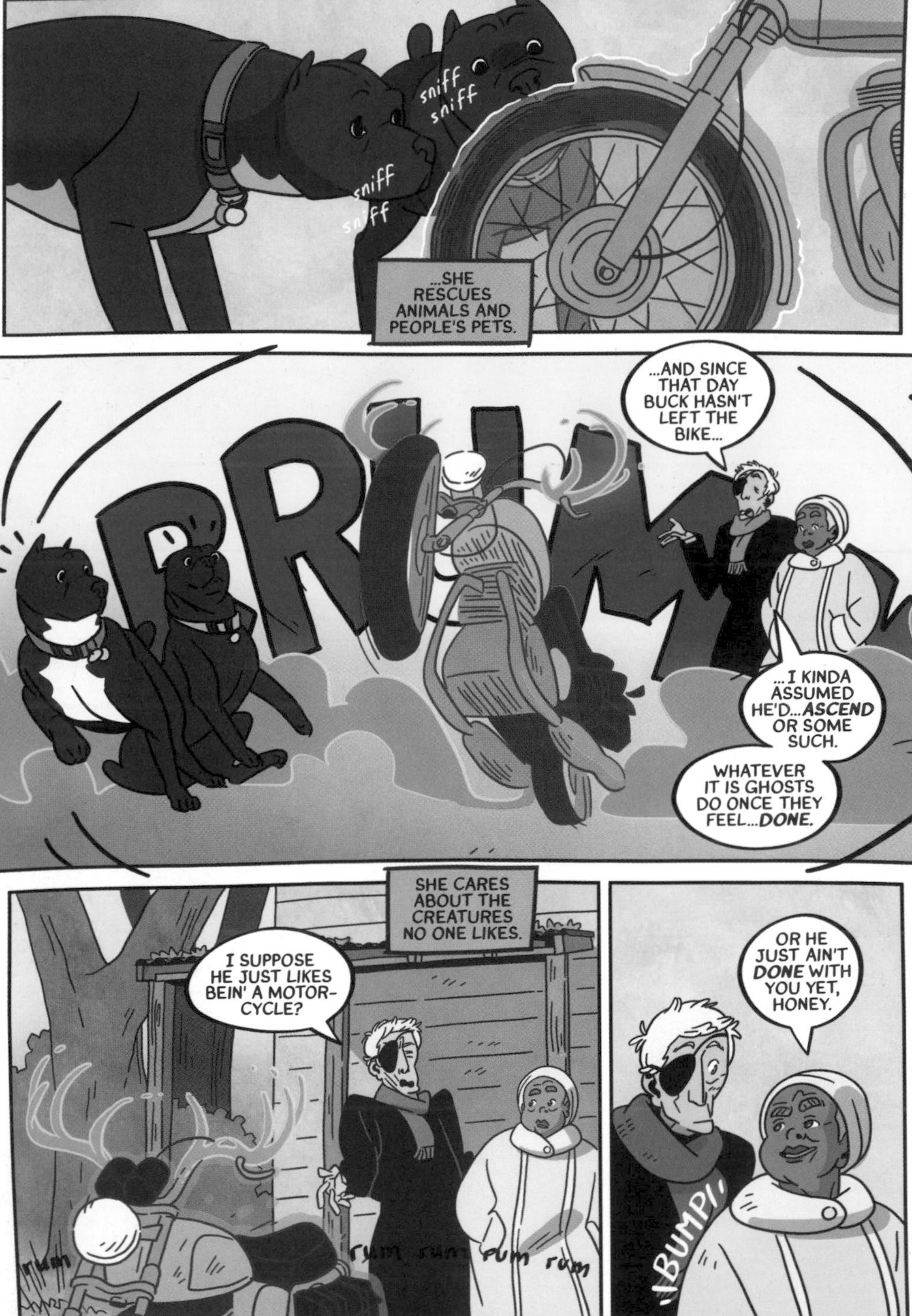
sniff
sniff
sniff
sniff
...SHE RESCUES ANIMALS AND PEOPLE'S PETS.
...AND SINCE THAT DAY BUCK HASN'T LEFT THE BIKE...
...I KINDA ASSUMED HE'D...***ASCEND*** OR SOME SUCH.
WHATEVER IT IS GHOSTS DO ONCE THEY FEEL...***DONE.***
SHE CARES ABOUT THE CREATURES NO ONE LIKES.
I SUPPOSE HE JUST LIKES BEIN' A MOTOR-CYCLE?
rum rum rum rum
OR HE JUST AIN'T ***DONE*** WITH YOU YET, HONEY.
!BUMP!

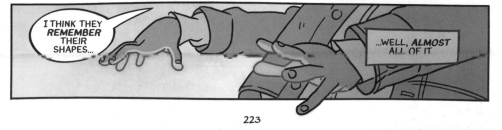

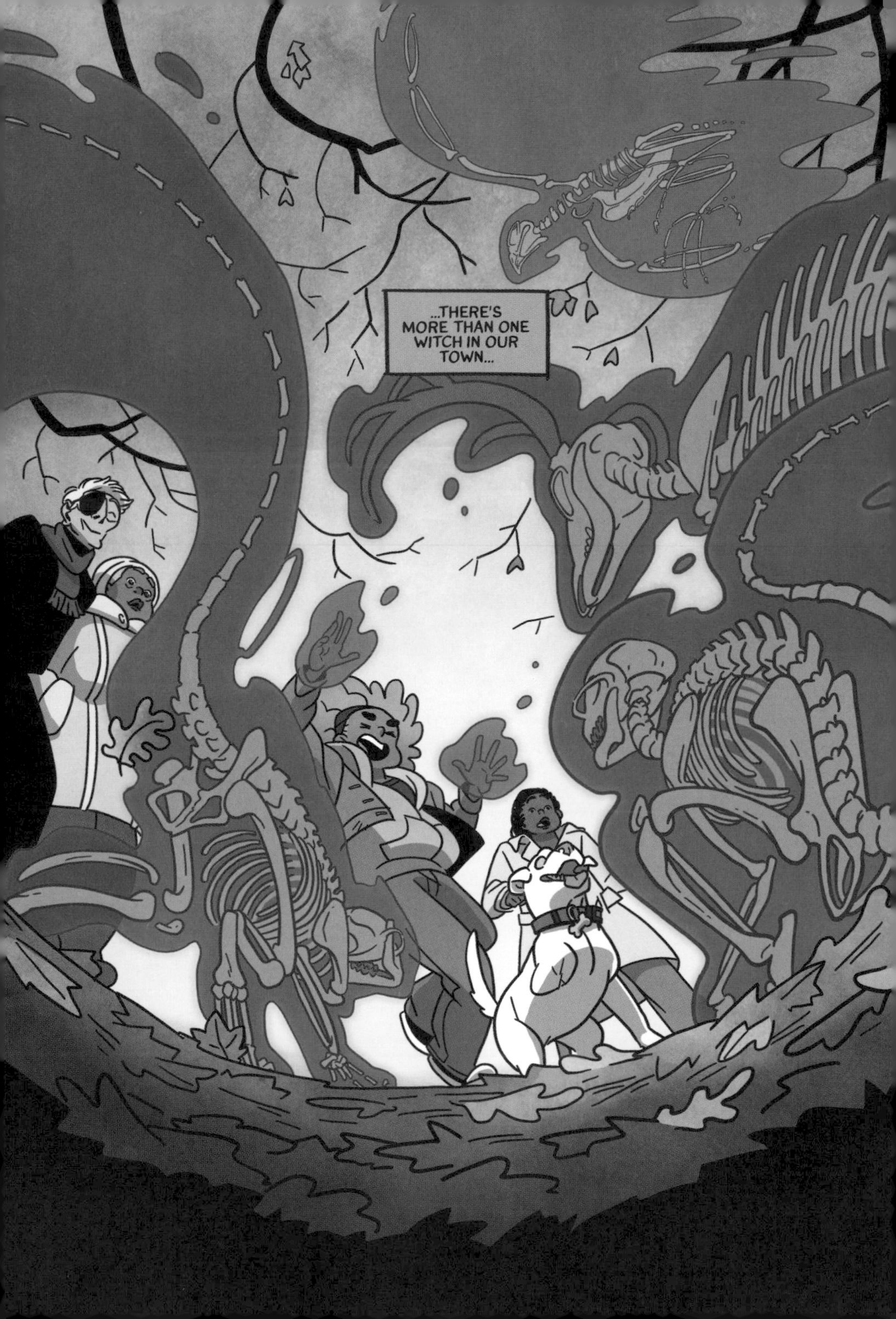
...THERE'S MORE THAN ONE WITCH IN OUR TOWN...

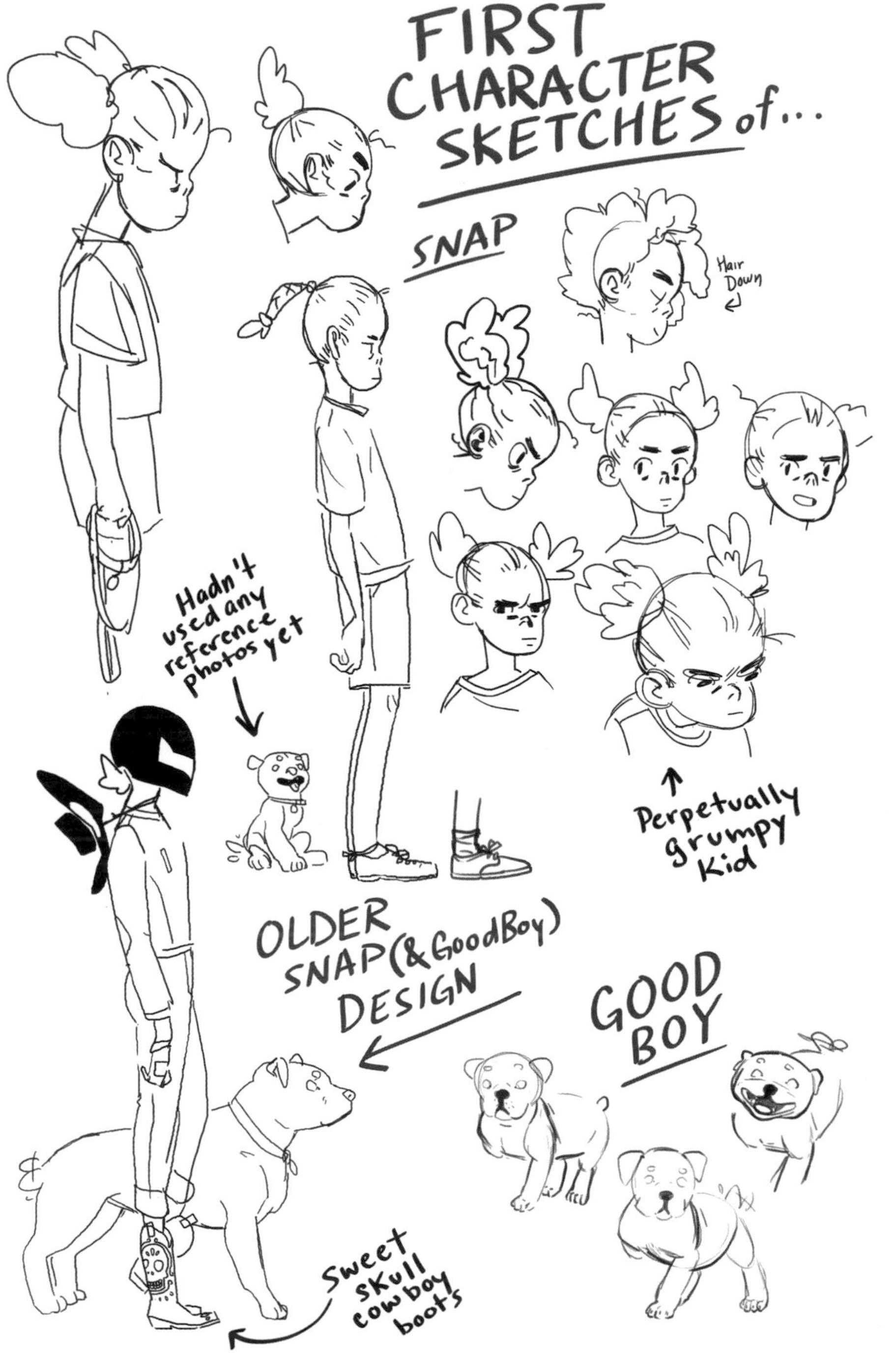
FIRST CHARACTER SKETCHES of...
SNAP
Hair Down
Hadn't used any reference photos yet
Perpetually grumpy Kid
OLDER SNAP (& GoodBoy) DESIGN
GOOD BOY
Sweet skull cowboy boots

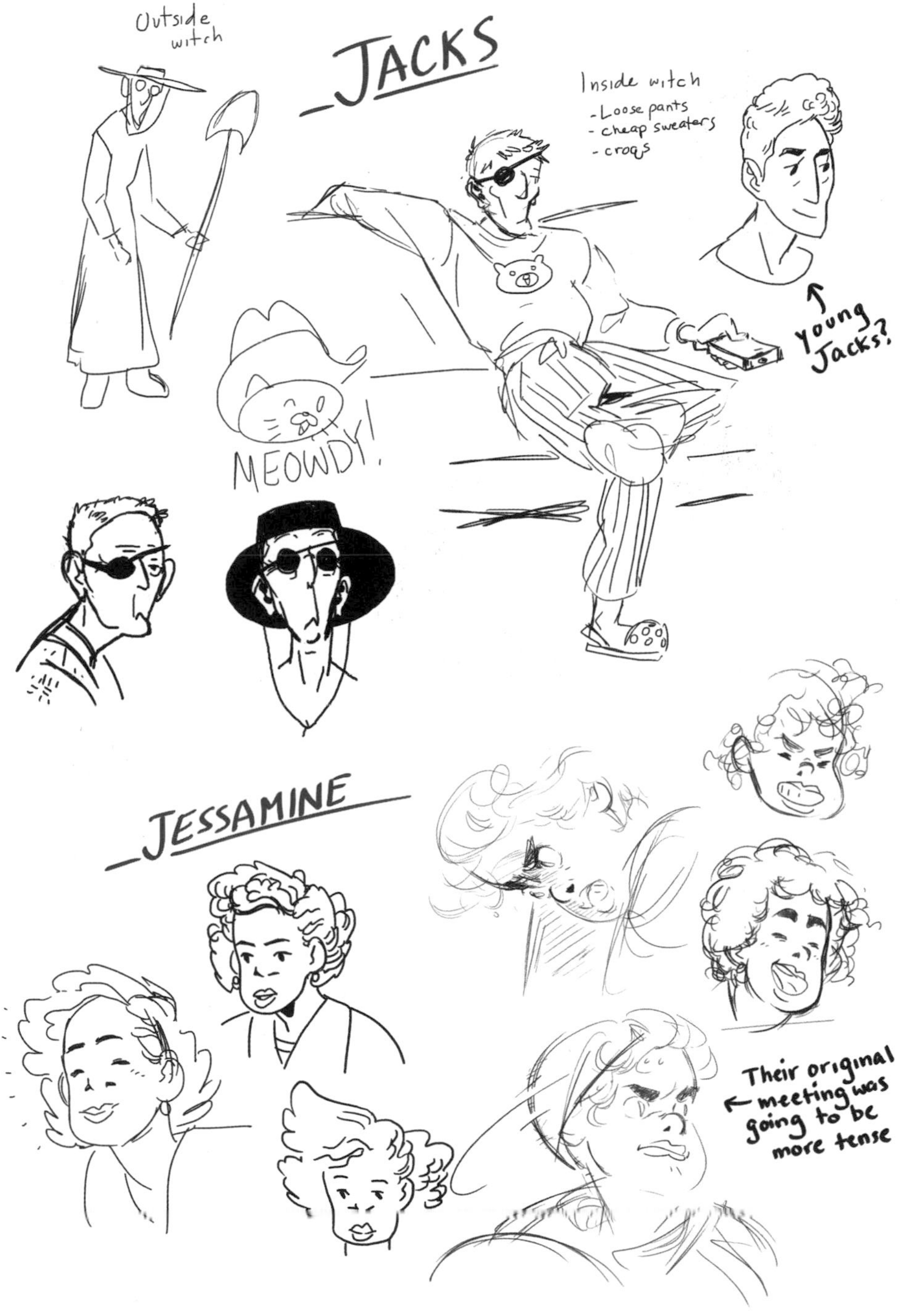
Outside witch
JACKS
Inside witch
- Loose pants
- cheap sweaters
- crocs
young Jacks?
MEOWDY!
JESSAMINE
Their original meeting was going to be more tense

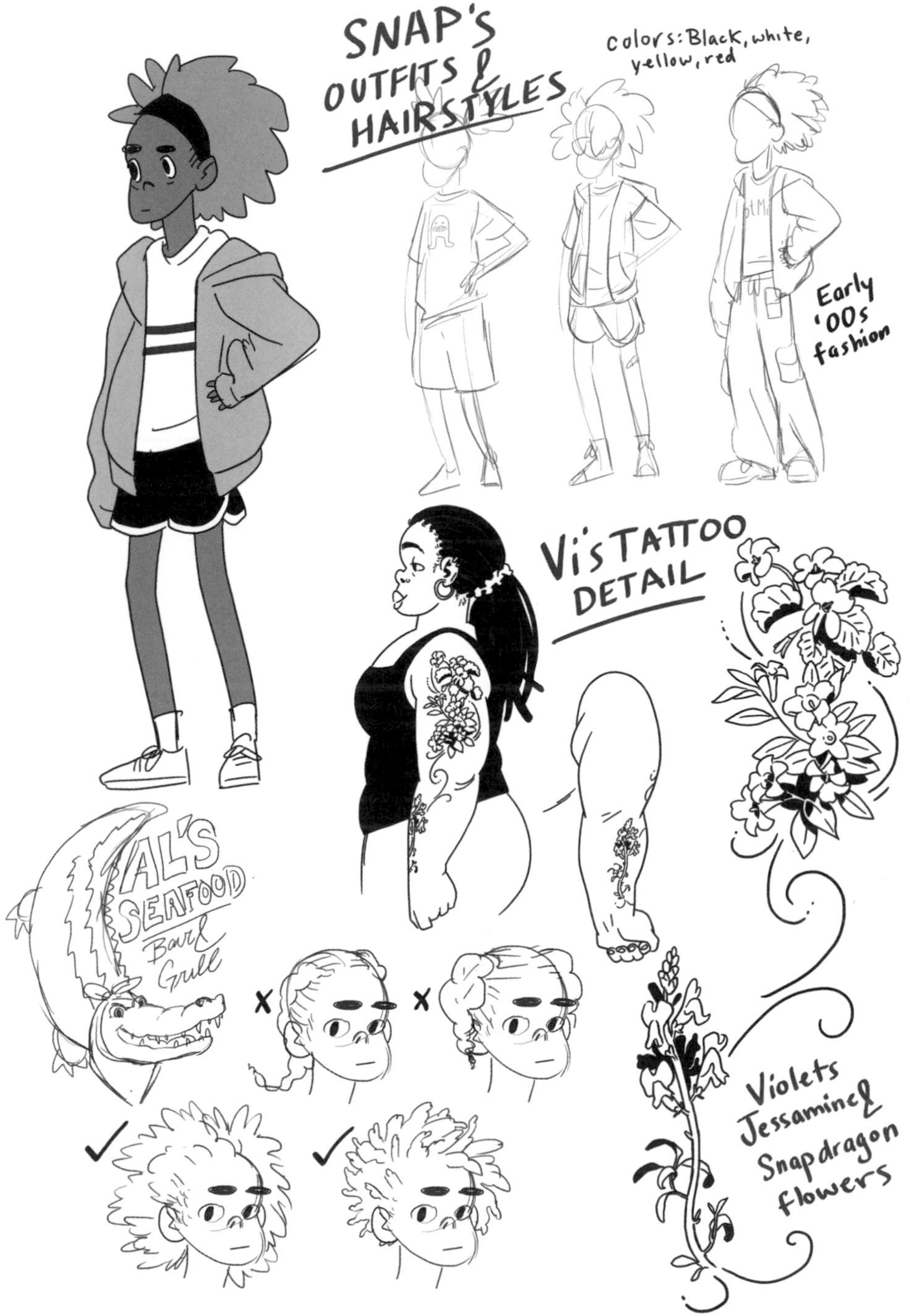
SNAP'S OUTFITS & HAIRSTYLES
Colors: Black, white, yellow, red
Early '00s fashion
Vi's TATTOO DETAIL
AL'S SEAFOOD
Bar & Grill
Violets Jessamine & Snapdragon flowers

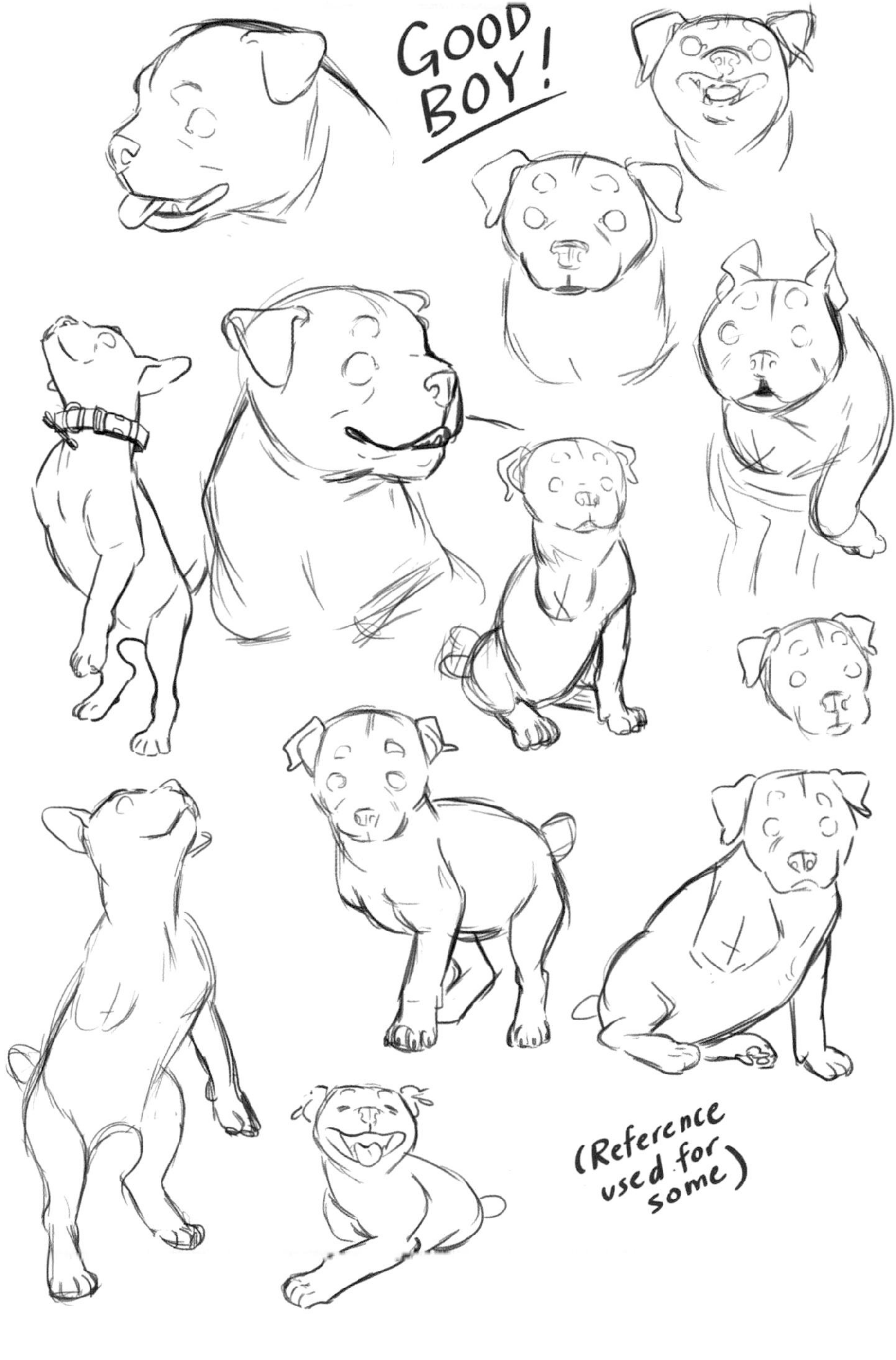
GOOD BOY!
(Reference used for some)

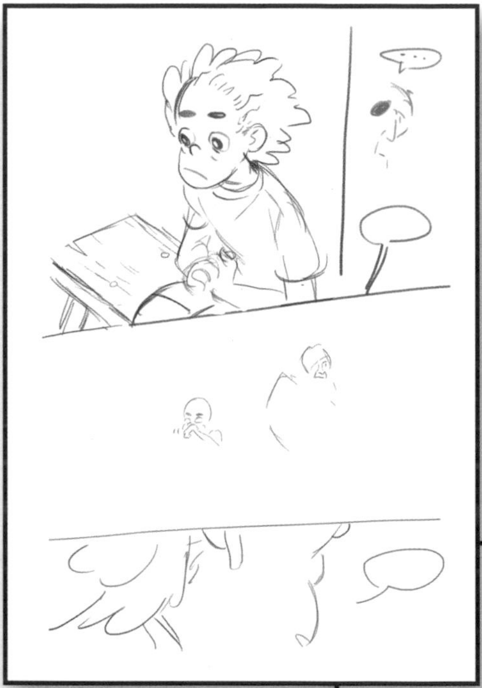

PROCESS OF PAGE 123

STEP 1: SKETCH

THIS STEP IS PRACTICALLY PART OF THE WRITING PROCESS AS I FIGURE OUT PACING, EXPRESSIONS, ANGLES...EVERYTHING!

OFTEN PANELS NEED TO BE REFINED, BUT OTHERS I TRY TO KEEP AS CLOSE TO THE ORIGINAL SKETCH AS I CAN.

STEP 2: LINES

AFTER REFINING THE ORIGINAL ROUGH SKETCH, IT'S TIME TO TRACE.

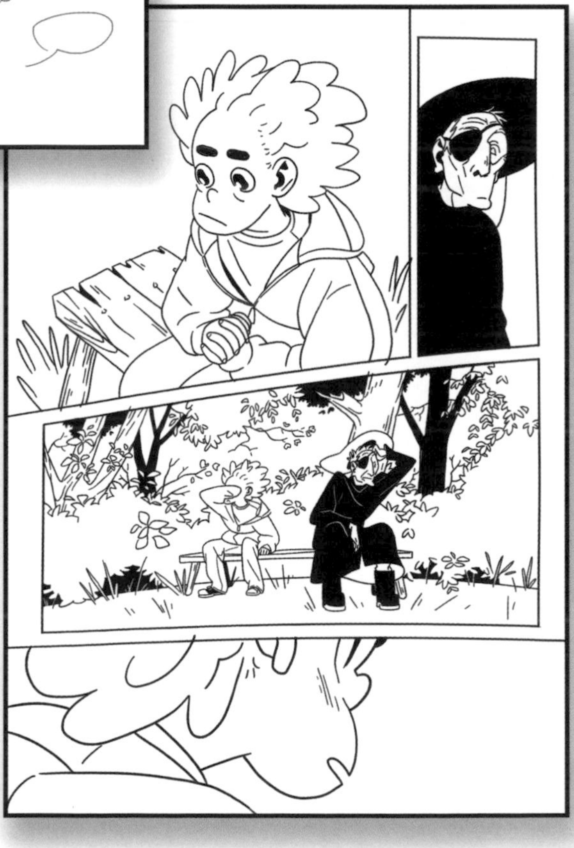

STEP 3: FLAT COLORS

JUST LIKE IN ELEMENTARY SCHOOL, I COLOR IN THE LINES BEFORE I DECIDE ON THINGS LIKE TIME OF DAY, LIGHTING, TONES, AND HUES.

(THIS STEP IS ONE OF MY FAVORITES AND CAN BE VERY RELAXING.)

STEP 4: FINALIZE

NOW IS WHEN I MAKE ALL THE CHOICES I IGNORED IN STEP 3.

I DECIDE ON THE DIRECTION AND COLOR OF THE LIGHT AND ALL THE OTHER LITTLE DETAILS THAT COMPLETE THE ART AND TELL THE STORY.

COVER GALLERY

COVER DESIGNS WITH ORIGINAL TITLE:

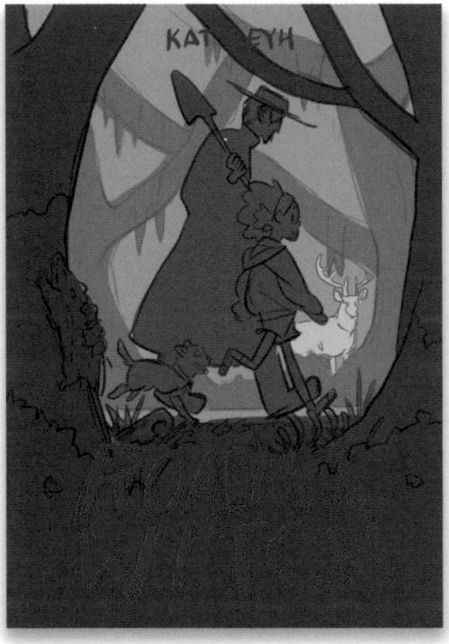

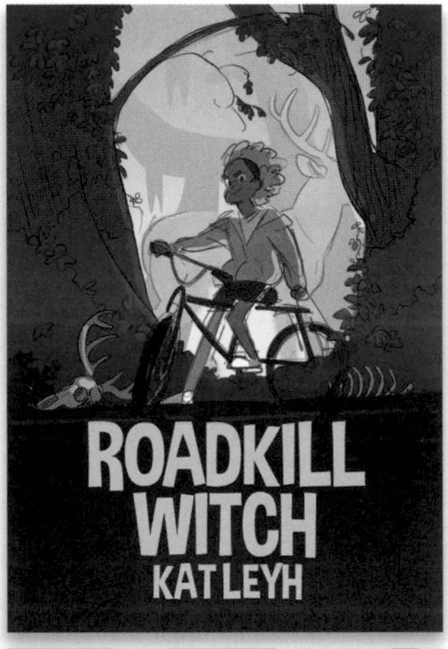
ROADKILL
WITCH
KAT LEYH

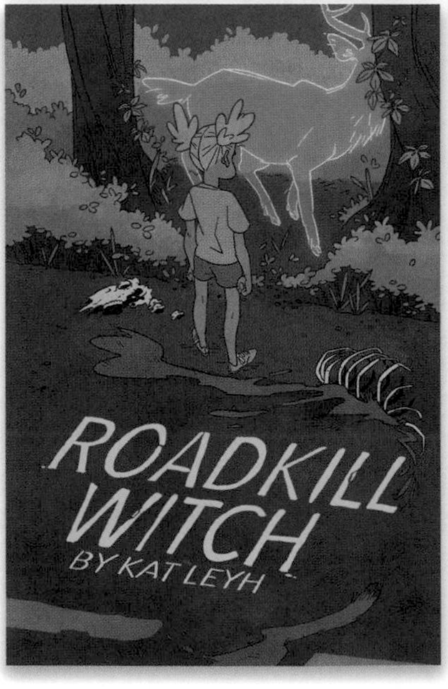
ROADKILL
WITCH
BY KAT LEYH

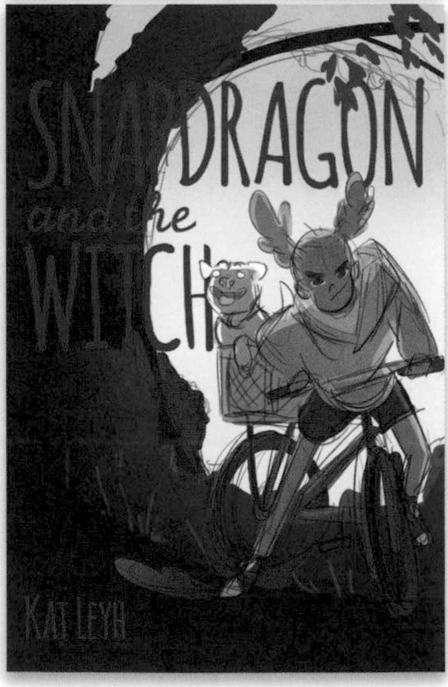
KAT LEYH

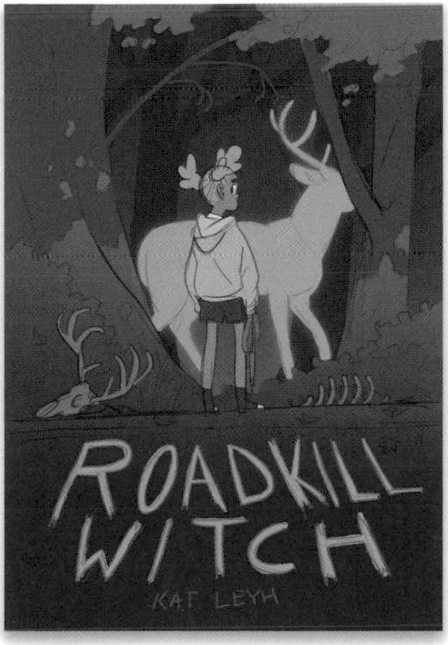
ROADKILL
WITCH
KAT LEYH

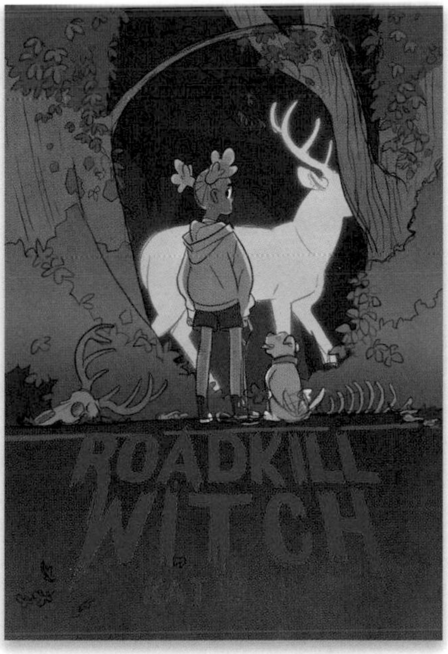
ROADKILL
WITCH

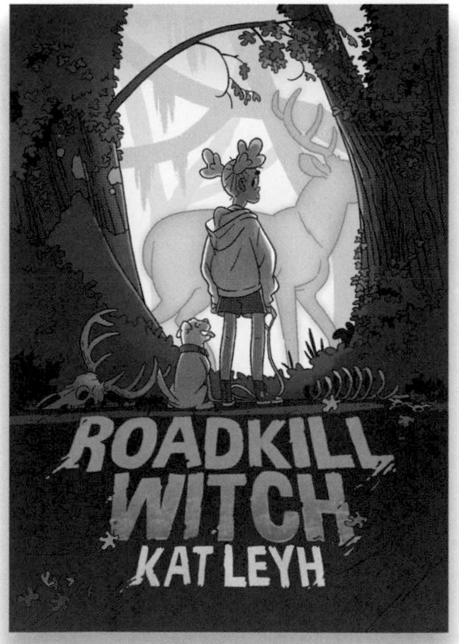
ROADKILL
WITCH
KAT LEYH

FIRST CRACK AT
A COVER BEFORE
TITLE CHANGE.

(TOO SERIOUS
AND SPOOKY
LOOKING.)

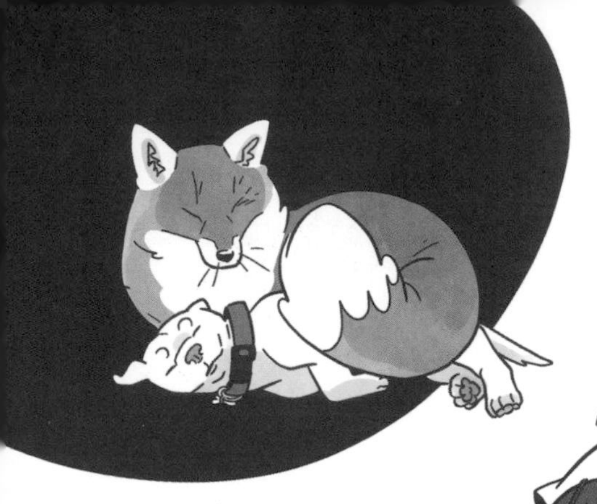

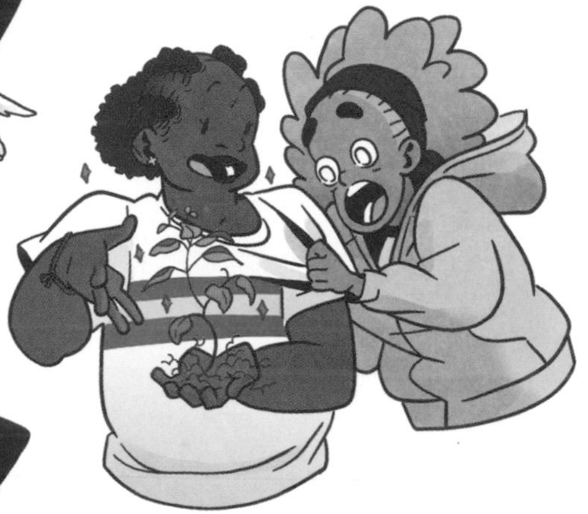

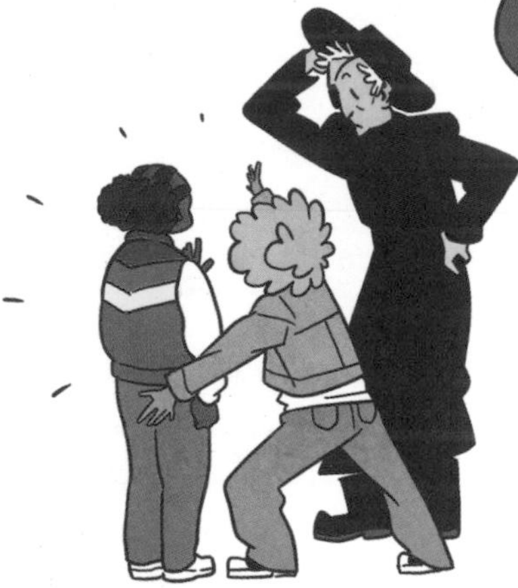

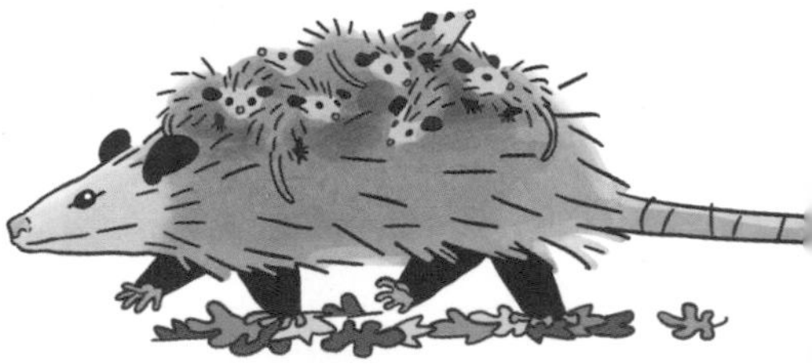

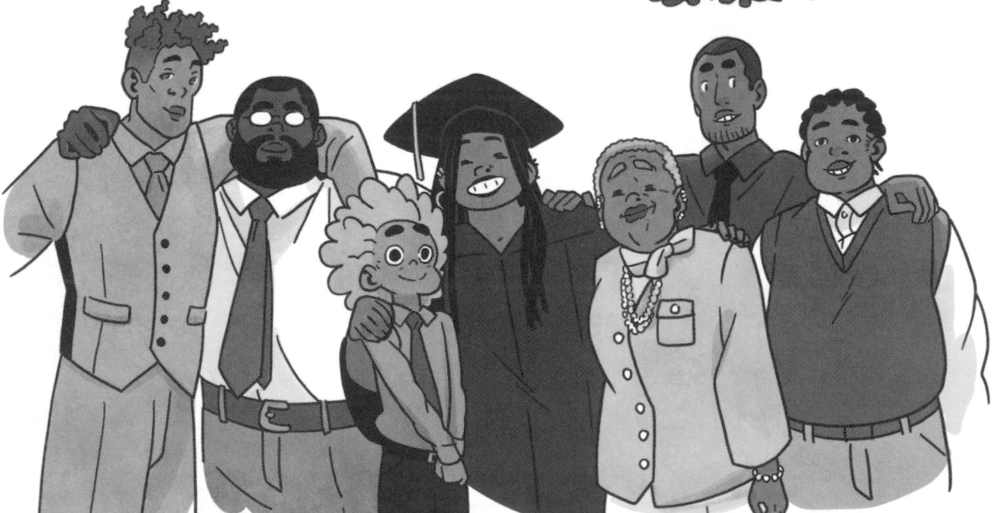

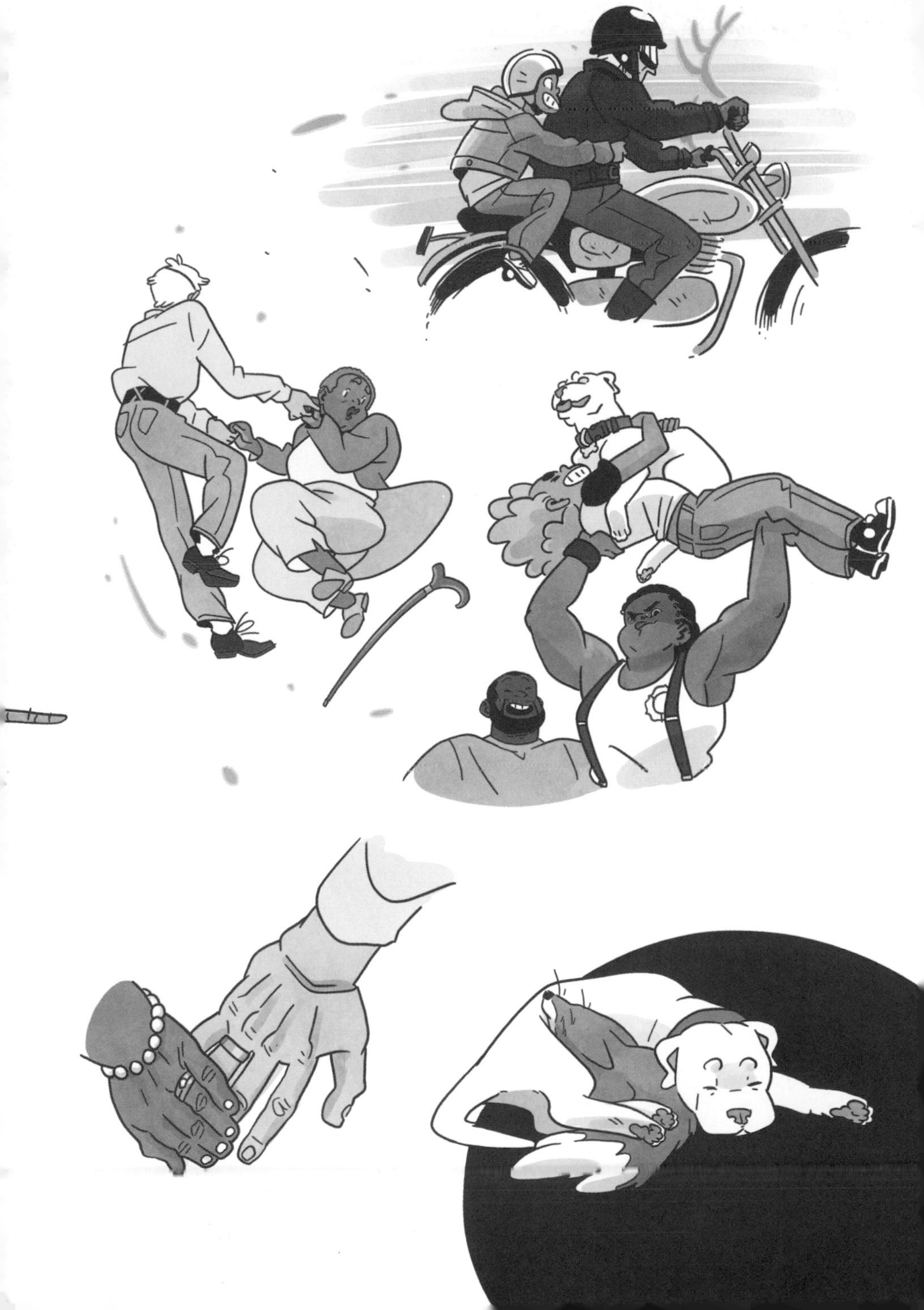

First Second

Copyright © 2020 by Kat Leyh

Published by First Second
First Second is an imprint of Roaring Brook Press,
a division of Holtzbrinck Publishing Holdings Limited Partnership
120 Broadway, New York, NY 10271

Don't miss your next favorite book from First Second!
For the latest updates go to firstsecondnewsletter.com and sign up for our enewsletter.

All rights reserved.

Library of Congress Control Number: 2018953665
Paperback ISBN: 978-1-250-17111-5
Hardcover ISBN: 978-1-250-17112-2

Our books may be purchased in bulk for promotional, educational, or business use. Please
contact your local bookseller or the Macmillan Corporate and Premium Sales Department
at (800) 221-7945 ext. 5442 or by email at MacmillanSpecialMarkets@macmillan.com.

First edition, 2020
Edited by Calista Brill and Kiara Valdez
Book design by Molly Johanson
Printed in China by 1010 Printing International Limited, North Point, Hong Kong

Drawn, colored, and lettered in Photoshop with a Cintiq.

Paperback: 10 9 8 7 6 5 4 3 2 1
Hardcover: 10 9 8 7 6 5 4 3 2 1